About the Authors

Helen Lacey grew up reading *Black Beauty, Anne of Green Gables* and *Little House on The Prairie*. These childhood classics inspired her to write her first book when she was seven years old, a story about a girl and her horse. She continued to write with the dream of one day being a published author and writing for Mills & Boon is the realisation of that dream. She loves creating stories about cowboys and horses and heroines who get their happily ever after.

By day, **Joy Avery** works as a customer service assistant. By night, the North Carolina native travels to imaginary worlds – creating characters whose romantic journeys invariably end happily ever after. Even as a young girl growing up in Garner, Joy knew she wanted to write. Stumbling onto romance novels, she discovered her passion. Instantly she knew that these were the types of stories she wanted to pen. Joy is married with one child and a spoiled dog.

Christy Jeffries graduated from the University of California, Irvine and received her Juris Doctor from California Western School of Law. But drafting court documents and working in law enforcement was merely an apprenticeship for her current career in the relentless field of motherhood and romance writing. She lives in Southern California with her patient husband, two energetic sons, and one sassy grandmother. Follow her on Facebook or visit her website at www.christyjeffries.com

D1322417

Affairs of the Heart

Affairs of the Heart:
Second Chance at Forever

HELEN LACEY

JOY AVERY

CHRISTY JEFFRIES

MILLS & BOON

First Published in Great Britain 2021
By Mills & Boon, an imprint of HarperCollins*Publishers*, Ltd
1 London Bridge Street, London, SE1 9GF

www.harpercollins.co.uk

HarperCollins*Publishers*
1st Floor, Watermarque Building,
Ringsend Road, Dublin 4, Ireland

AFFAIRS OF THE HEART: SECOND CHANCE AT FOREVER
© 2021 Harlequin Books S.A.

A Kiss, a Dance & a Diamond © 2018 Helen Lacey
Soaring on Love © 2018 Joy Avery
A Proposal for the Officer © 2018 Christy Jeffries

ISBN: 978-0-263-29963-2

A KISS, A DANCE & A DIAMOND

HELEN LACEY

For Gareth & Stephen
Because big brothers are the best.

Chapter One

Kieran O'Sullivan was home.

For good.

He rubbed the back of his neck, stretched out his spine and figured he should down another cup of coffee since he had three hours to go before the end of his double shift. It had been a busier-than-usual afternoon in the ER at the Cedar River Community Hospital, but nothing like he'd been used to when he'd lived and worked in Sioux Falls. Still, he'd treated two minor burns, a dislocated shoulder, a baby with a bad case of croup and a teenager who'd fractured her arm after falling off a horse.

He was five days into his new job at the hospital.

Five days of unpacking boxes and settling into the apartment he'd rented.

Five days pretending life was sweet.

And five days that he'd managed to avoid running into Nicola Radici.

He ignored the twinge in his gut and the way the word *coward* mashed its way into his thoughts. Because it wasn't as though he hadn't seen Nicola or spoken to her in the past twelve months. He had. Several times.

But this was different. He was now back in Cedar River for good. Back in the town where he'd been born and raised—a town of a few thousand that sat in the shadow of the Black Hills, South Dakota.

Yeah, back home for good with no way of avoiding her.

High school sweethearts.

The damned phrase still made him cringe.

It had been fifteen years since they'd spectacularly broken up after graduation. Since then he'd married and divorced, and he knew Nicola had a broken engagement in her past…so there was no logical reason he should have any feelings about her one way or another.

But he did.

He had guilt.

By the bucket load.

For over a decade and a half, he'd regularly returned to Cedar River to visit his family. But he'd usually managed to avoid running into her. She'd moved to San Francisco, gone to college, gotten a life that didn't include him…just as he'd told her to do. While he'd gone to college and med school, ending up at the largest hospital in Sioux Falls. That was where he met Tori, who soon became his wife and the mother of his son. Everything had worked out as he'd imagined it would.

Until it blew up in his face.

Kieran shook the memory off, hating that after nearly two years he still had the same aching loss seeping into his bones. Nothing eased it. And he suspected nothing ever would. But he had to pretend he was over the whole awful mess. He had a job, parents, siblings, friends… too many things and people eclipsing his grief to behave as broken inside as he felt. It was better to simply make out he was okay.

And he was, most of the time. But since he'd made the decision to move back to Cedar River a few months back and secured a permanent position at the hospital, a peculiar uneasiness had simmered in his gut. And he suspected it had nothing to do with returning home for good, nothing to do with the fact that his parents were divorcing or that months earlier he'd discovered he had a secret half brother who lived in Portland, a product of his father's thirty-year-old infidelity.

No, it wasn't anything to do with that. It had everything to do with Nicola Radici.

Because Nicola, with her long brown hair and dark eyes, was as sensational now as she'd been in high school.

And because she still clearly hated the sight of him.

Every time they'd spoken in the past twelve months, like at his brother Liam's wedding a few months back, she'd tilted her chin, pushed back her shoulders and offered a cursory response when he'd said hello and asked how she was. Even when he'd offered his condolences to her and her family over the loss of her brother, Gino, who'd been tragically killed in a boating accident eighteen months ago. He knew how she felt, since he'd lost his sister Liz three years earlier.

Kieran recognized the lingering resentment in her expression.

She hadn't forgiven him for humiliating her so many years ago.

Not that he blamed her. He had broken up with her on graduation day, just outside her locker, right in front of the whole school. He hadn't meant to do it that way, but it had happened regardless.

Kieran shook off the memory and headed for the doctor's lounge to grab a much-needed cup of coffee.

Just as he was taking a sip, one of the nurses poked her head around the door.

"Dr. O'Sullivan," she said and waved an admission folder. "There's a patient in triage, bed three. A young boy with a fish hook in his hand."

Kieran spilled the rest of the coffee down the sink and rinsed out the mug. "Okay, I'll be right there."

The nurse hovered by the doorway and gave a kind of uneasy shrug. "Um…it's one of the Radici boys."

His stomach plummeted. Particularly when he saw the nurse's expression. His old relationship with Nicola wasn't exactly a secret, and many of the nurses, including the fiftysomething woman in front of him, had lived in Cedar River all their lives. And since his family was the wealthiest and most high profile in town, gossip came with the territory. But damn, the last thing he wanted was to see Nicola, especially when he'd just been thinking about her.

"He's a patient, so it's not a problem," he said anyway, heading toward triage.

He spotted Nicola immediately, standing beside one of the beds, the privacy curtain half-pulled around. Dressed in jeans, a bright red shirt, ankle boots and with a blue sweater wrapped around her waist, she was effortlessly attractive. Her hair was loose—her wild, curly dark brown hair that hung down her back and had always driven him crazy—and he was suddenly overcome by the memory of the two of them in the back of his Wrangler, going all the way when they were sixteen and losing their virginity together.

Then, he quickly pushed the memory away and kept walking.

There was a dark-haired boy standing at her side, his arms crossed, and another, younger child sitting on the edge of the bed. Her nephews. It was common knowledge that she'd inherited custody of her brother's two kids upon his death. Kieran took a breath, put on his best physician's face and walked towards them.

"Nicola," he said quietly. "Hello."

She turned her head and met his gaze. The resentment was still there, burning bright in her lush brown eyes. He saw the pulse in her throat beating wildly as she spoke. "Dr. O'Sullivan."

Nothing else. There was no welcome in her voice. Nothing other than cool resentment. And the way she called him *doctor* made that resentment abundantly clear.

He plastered a smile on his face. "It's good to see you, Nic."

Big mistake. She clearly didn't want to be reminded of the way he used to call her *Nic* because she glared at him, pressing her lips together. Kieran watched as she swallowed hard, with her arms crossed so tightly they might snap.

One of her steeply arched eyebrows rose a fraction. "I thought Dr. Wright was on duty tonight?"

Of course. She wouldn't have come to the ER if she suspected Kieran would be there. And she obviously knew he'd started working at the hospital. News traveled fast in Cedar River. Kieran half shrugged. "She'll be here later," he explained and moved around the bed. "I'm on a double shift because we're down a doctor this week. I finish up in three hours." He felt her scrutiny down to his bones. "So...let's see what's going on with your nephew's hand," he said, getting the conversation back on track.

"I hooked myself," the child on the bed muttered,

holding up his clumsily bandaged hand, his eyes downcast. "See?"

"He was messing around," the older boy said and looked toward his aunt. "I told him to stop."

"I was not!" his brother said hotly and waved his hand and then yelped in pain. "You said I couldn't cast my line and you kept laughing."

"You were casting like a girl," the older Radici brother said. "And into a bucket in the backyard. That's not even real casting. You can't do anything."

"I can so!"

"You're such a baby," the older boy said.

Kieran looked at Nicola and saw that she was frowning.

"Johnny," she scolded. "Please don't make things worse."

The older boy had a scowl so deep it creased his forehead. He shrugged. "I'm gonna sit over there."

Kieran smiled to himself. It would be exactly the same conversation he might once have had with his own brothers when they were kids. He watched as Johnny shuffled sulkily across the triage zone and plunked into a chair, then took a gaming console out of his small backpack, shoved plugs into his ears and ignored all of them.

Kieran looked at the younger child. "You know, when we were kids, my brother Liam always said I couldn't fish as well as he could. I was younger, and my arms weren't as long as his. But you know what? I grew up taller than him."

The boy looked at him for the first time and his eyes widened. "You did?"

"Yep," Kieran replied and grinned. "And now I'm a way better fisherman than he is."

"Really?" he asked, looking pensive.

"Really," Kieran assured him.

The boy shrugged. "It's not really fishing. It's just a bucket and some plastic toys."

"Well," Kieran said as he moved around the bed and dropped the clipboard onto it. "Maybe you'll get so good you can do it for real sometime."

Kieran saw a kind of wary panic cross the child's face, and he looked quickly toward Nicola. She glanced sideways, and he saw her shake her head slightly. He sensed something was wrong but didn't comment further. Instead, he washed his hands in the sink, pulled on a pair of gloves and then gently placed the boy's wrapped hand on a small rolling table. "Okay, let's see what you've done. First, though, you better tell me your name."

"Marco," he muttered, his lip wobbling.

"Okay, Marco," Kieran said and began to unwrap the makeshift bandage. "Let's do this."

The boy whimpered a little, calming when Nicola moved forward and grasped his other hand. Kieran tried not to think about how it was the closest he'd been to her in fifteen years. Or about how he could pick up the scent of her vanilla shampoo over the antiseptic that usually lingered in the air. The scent was suddenly so familiar it made him glance sideways.

She wasn't looking at him, though. Her attention was focused solely on her nephew.

He could see how she was slightly biting her bottom lip and remembered how she used to do that when she was deep in thought, like when they'd been studying together back in high school. Of course, studying usually turned into making out, which often led to more. Back then he'd been crazy for her, mad for her beautiful hair, sexy curves and warm brown eyes. A typical horny teenage boy who couldn't get enough of his first real girlfriend. Back then, in the three years they'd dated, Kieran was sure he and Nicola would go the distance, that they'd go to college, travel the world, get married one day, have a family. But that was a kid's dream. Because the moment Nicola had suggested they get engaged before they headed off to college, he'd freaked out. He'd felt trapped and afraid that settling down so young would derail his career. And he'd never quite forgiven himself for hurting her the way he had.

And, clearly, she hadn't, either.

There were tears in Marco's eyes, and Kieran focused his attention on the child. He was a quiet sort of kid, clearly in pain, but trying to be brave. "You know, if you want to say *ouchywowah*, you can."

The child's eyes widened. "Ouchy, what?"

"Ouchywowah," Kieran said and finished unwrapping the bandage. "Saying it three times helps make the pain go away. But you have to say it quietly," he explained, not daring to look at Nicola. "Like, in a whisper…or it doesn't work."

"Really?"

"Really," Kieran assured him and smiled to himself as the boy began chanting the word over and over. Silly as it was, it seemed to help Marco concentrate on something other than his injury and, ten minutes later, Kieran had removed the fishing hook impaled between Marco's fingers, cleaned and stitched the injury and ordered some pain medication. He left the nurse to dress the young boy's hand, while he did something he didn't want to do: speak to Nicola—alone.

"I've arranged for a scrip for some painkillers you can fill at the hospital pharmacy, and I'd like to see him again in a few days, to make sure he's free from infection," he explained as they walked through triage, away from the two boys and through to the waiting room outside.

Other than her nephews, the nurse on duty in triage and a couple of nurses in the reception area, the place was empty, and Kieran experienced a sudden and acute sense of discomfort. They were, in a sense, alone for the first time in fifteen years.

And he could tell by the look in her brown eyes that he was about to get the telling off he figured was a decade and a half in the making...

Don't do it...

Nicola chanted the words to herself over and over. She didn't want to make a scene. She didn't want to spend any more time in Kieran O'Sullivan's presence. But damn, it was hard. He was still too gorgeous for words...six foot two and a half, broad shoulders, brownish-blond hair that still flopped over his forehead when he tilted his head, glittering blue eyes and dark lashes. And the whiskery shadow across his jaw was too attractive for words. Not exactly a beard, but enough to give him a kind of rugged sexiness. She wished he'd grown up to be bald and pudgy. She wished he hadn't decided to permanently return to Cedar River. She wished he hadn't been so kind and considerate with Marco and that her nephew hadn't actually responded to him—which was way more than he did with most people. She wished a whole lot of things. And in that moment she wished she could turn on her heels and leave the hospital as quickly as she could.

But she couldn't.

She had Johnny and Marco to think about.

A deep surge of grief coursed through her entire body when she thought about her older brother, Gino, and sister-in-law, Miranda. She loved her nephews but worried she wasn't measuring up in the parent department. And along with running the restaurant and her father's swiftly declining health, she had enough on her plate without adding an old boyfriend into the mix.

But…she was mad.

Seething.

Kieran O'Sullivan had no right coming back to town! He'd set the rules on graduation day. He wanted a life and a career away from Cedar River. He didn't want any ties. He didn't want a girlfriend. He didn't want to get engaged. He wanted to be able to screw around in college. He wanted his freedom.

She should have seen it coming. In the weeks before graduation, he'd been distant and closed off and had avoided her like the plague. Ever since she'd suggested they make a real commitment to one another before heading off to separate colleges. And then, on graduation day, he'd dumped her, saying he didn't want to be tied down…by her or Cedar River.

But now he was back.

And suddenly, all her pent-up rage, despair and resentment was pointing in one direction. And even though she knew that being angry was illogical after so many years, she couldn't help it.

"You're a real jerk," she said and waved her hands. "You know that? Why did you have to come back? *Egoista, bastardo di cuore freddo!*" she cursed in Italian, feeling her skin heat more with each passing second and fighting the urge to take a swipe at his handsome face. *"Ti odio!"*

I hate you…

They were strong words, and she knew he understood them. But he didn't flinch. Didn't speak. Didn't do anything other than take her ranting at him as though he'd been expecting it. And that amplified her anger tenfold. She didn't want him to be compliant and agreeable and ready for her insults. She wanted him to respond so she could go in for another round. And another. Until she was spent and done with all the pain she still harbored from her broken, seventeen-year-old-girl's heart.

"I know," he said quietly. "I'm sorry."

Nicola tilted her chin. "Your apology is about fifteen years too late."

"I know that, too."

Nicola drew in a sharp breath. Typical of Kieran to be so damned agreeable! "I'll take Marco to our usual doctor," she said flatly. "That way I won't have to see you again."

"If that's what you'd prefer."

God, he was so compliant. "I think we both know what I'd prefer, *Doctor*."

"That I'd stayed away?"

"Exactly."

"It's my hometown, Nicola…just as much as it is yours. And I'm pretty sure it's big enough for both of us."

Nicola glanced around, arms crossed, temper surging. "It doesn't feel like it right now." She sucked in a long and steadying breath. "However, I do appreciate you looking after him tonight."

She wasn't about to tell him that it was the first time she'd seen Marco really respond to someone new since his parents had been killed. And of course she wasn't surprised that Kieran had a great bedside manner. He'd always been too damned charming for his own good!

"We don't have to be friends, Nicola," he said evenly. "But we don't have to be enemies, either."

"I don't want us to be *anything*," she shot back. "Except strangers."

"You're my sister-in-law's friend," he reminded her. "This is a small town, and we're bound to run into one another occasionally. I prefer we weren't at war when we did."

He was right. Her longtime friend Kayla had married Kieran's brother, and they'd just had their first child. They would definitely cross paths.

But she resented that he was so cool, so logical…so incredibly infuriating about the whole situation.

A typical O'Sullivan trait. They were the wealthiest family in town. And the most entitled. They owned commercial and investment property and several businesses, including the hugely successful O'Sullivan's Hotel. The eldest brother, Liam, ran the hotel and most of the other holdings, while the younger brother Sean was a movie and music producer in LA. Their sister, Liz, had passed away a few years earlier from some kind of heart thing, leaving behind three young daughters. And there was another brother, too, called Jonah, who they'd just discovered existed and was the reason his parents were now in the middle of a divorce.

And then there was Kieran—the brother who'd left to pursue his dream of a medical career. And he'd got exactly what he wanted. He was smart and charming and too good-looking for words. He'd once been her closest friend, her lover, her future. Now, all she felt was hurt and rage when she thought of him. Nicola tried to wrap up her temper and put it away where it belonged. But it was so *hard*.

Pull yourself together. He's not worth it.

"Can we go now?"

Johnny's voice. Jerking her back into the land of good sense and logic.

Nicola crossed her arms and moved quickly toward him. "Of course," she said to her nephew. She glanced briefly toward Kieran. "Thank you for your help."

She didn't look at him again as she walked back into triage, quickly ushering both boys back through the corridor. And did her best to ignore Kieran. But he watched her. She could feel his gaze burning through her as she left. She made a quick stop at the pharmacy to fill the painkiller prescription and then headed home, her thoughts consumed by the last person she wanted to think about.

She was embarrassed that she'd lost her temper. But, hell and damnation, he pushed her buttons! He always had. In high school she'd been desperately in love with him.

After graduation day, she'd hated him.

That rage and anger had kept her going, made her stronger, gave her the strength to leave town and pursue her dreams. She'd headed to California and attended college in San Francisco, studied hard and graduated with a degree and a burning desire to climb the corporate ladder. Six years later, she was head of human resources at an organic food company. That was where she'd met Carl. He was the managing director of the East Coast division. He was smart and good-looking and recently divorced. They'd had a whirlwind romance. Despite her friends warning her she was his rebound relationship, within a year they'd bought a house, an engagement ring and made plans for the future. But three months later he left, claiming he still had feelings for his ex-wife. The house was sold and she quickly returned the ring.

Broken and hurt, Nicola had learned a valuable lesson—she was never going to be anyone's rebound girl again.

"Aunt Nicola," Marco said as they drove back through town, "can we have gelato when we get home?"

She glanced at the clock on the dash. It was seven o'clock, a little late for her nephew's favorite treat. "Tomorrow," she promised. "I'll get *Nonno* to make your favorite strawberry flavor, okay?"

Despite his declining health, her father still insisted on making the gelato that JoJo's was famous for. The pizzeria had been in her family for over forty years, since her grandfather had started the place a decade after he'd arrived in Cedar River. Back then, he'd planned on making a fortune mining silver, but instead Guido and Josephine Radici had turned their hands to doing what they did best—cooking the most authentic Italian cuisine this side of the Black Hills. And it was a family business in the truest sense of the word. Her father, Salvatore, had learned the business from his father and continued on alone after her mother's death a few years earlier. Her late brother Gino had learned from their dad. Although she missed her mother, Nicola was glad her mom hadn't had to endure Gino's passing. It was bad enough watching her father slowly deteriorate through his grief at the loss of his beloved son, along with a series of minor strokes. And since her older brother Vince had moved to San Francisco years ago, now there was just her…trying to cobble together some sense of normalcy for Gino's two sons.

But it wasn't easy. With Marco's emotional withdrawal and Johnny's penchant for getting into trouble, she had her hands full. Both boys grieved in their own way, but it was Marco who really concerned her. He suffered from night terrors and had developed a severe fear of water. Although neither of the boys were with their parents at the time of the accident, the fact they were killed while sailing had profoundly affected Marco, and now he refused to go near water except for a quick shower at bath time. He'd always loved fishing but now resorted to hooking plastic toys from a bucket in the backyard.

Once they were back home, Nicola parked the car, grabbed her tote and ushered the boys from the back seat. The house was where the boys had always lived—Gino and Miranda's home, which they'd bought when they got married. It was a few minutes out of town, on a wide, tree-lined street, with a swing set in the backyard and a porch out front. After her brother's death, Nicola had quickly packed up her life in San Francisco and moved in, trying to keep the boys' normal routine as smooth as possible—soccer on Saturdays, joining a couple of other parents in a carpool for school pick-up twice a week, family night on a Friday with a movie and popcorn in the rooms behind the restaurant. She even did her best to pack the same kind of lunches that their mother had each morning.

Her friend Annie Jamison was a nanny to three children, and she'd counselled Nicola to maintain as much of their old routine as possible to encourage emotional stability in the wake of their grief and loss. So she did. Normality was the key.

Even though, some days, she felt as though every moment was an uphill battle.

And tonight, she discovered about an hour later, was becoming one of those battles.

Johnny wanted to stay up late to play a computer game, and Marco refused to go to bed and was holed up in his room, hiding in the corner of his closet, rejecting her requests to come out even when she relented and offered him the gelato he'd asked for earlier.

"Please come out," she pleaded, standing by the closet door, knowing she could wrestle him out of the small space, but she didn't want to upset him any more than he already was.

Yeah…an uphill battle just about covered it.

"No," he wailed. "You don't care what happens to me."

Nicola hung on to patience and remained by the door. "Of course I do. Please, Marco…it's nearly bedtime. You have to get up for school in the morning."

"I'm not going back to that stupid school!"

She sucked in a long breath. "Marco, please—"

"Everyone's hates me. And my hand hurts," he wailed. "No one is nice to me. Not you. Not Johnny. No one except that doctor."

Except that doctor.

Nicola's breath stilled in her chest. *Kieran.* She tried to ignore the way her pulse started to beat wildly. "Well, he's not here. He's at the hospital, and you don't need to be there now. But I'm here, and I'd really like to talk to you. So, can you come out, and we'll have some gelato and spend some time together…okay?"

Silence. The deafening kind. She heard movement and thought she'd made progress when he spoke again. "You could call him. Doctors come to people's houses, too."

Nicola hung on to her patience and took a deep breath. "I can't do that."

She heard him huff. "You never do *anything* I want. Only what Johnny wants."

The pain in his voice was unmistakable. The boys had once been close, but over the past few months she'd seen the divide between them become wider.

The guilt landed squarely on her shoulders. She was a lousy parent. And she clearly needed help.

Nicola left the room and headed downstairs. She got to the living room and discovered the overhead light bulb had blown. *Great...that's all I need.* She loathed heights and had no intention of bothering her neighbor for a ladder, even though she was sure the elderly man would help if she asked. Besides, her independent streak made her resist asking anyone for assistance. But as she got to the kitchen, filled the kettle and sat down at the table, Nicola admitted that she did need help. Right now.

A minute later she was calling the hospital, feeling foolish through to her bones. He'd probably left for the night, and she hoped he had. She didn't want to talk to him. She didn't want to ask for his help. But within seconds she was connected to the ER, and a moment later she heard his deep voice.

"O'Sullivan," he said as a greeting.

She clenched the phone and sucked in a sharp breath. "Kieran..."

Silence stretched like brittle elastic, and then he spoke again. "Nicola? Is that you?"

She was shocked that he'd recognized her voice. "I... I..."

"Is everything okay?"

Her belly did a foolish loop-the-loop at the concern in his voice, and then words just blurted out. "Kieran... I need you."

Chapter Two

Twenty minutes later Kieran was pulling up outside a two-story home on Grove Street.

I need you...

It had been fifteen years since he'd heard Nicola say anything so provocative.

He glanced at the address scribbled on a crumpled note on the passenger seat and saw that he had the right place. It was ironic that she lived only a couple of streets from the apartment he'd rented. The large Victorian he'd moved into five days earlier had been divided into several apartments, and his was on the second floor. His sister-in-law, Kayla, had been the previous tenant so it had been an easy sublet, taking over the payments and dealing with the landlord. And he liked the place well enough. There was one bedroom, a combined kitchen and dining room, and a spacious living room—plenty of room for the few boxes and sparse assortment of furniture he'd brought with him from Sioux Falls.

He got out, locked the Jeep and headed for the house. The porch light flicked on the moment he closed the white picket gate, and within seconds the front door opened. Once he was up the three steps and on the porch, Nicola was there, holding the screen door open and inviting him inside.

"Thank you for coming," she said quickly as he crossed the threshold and she closed the door. "I know it's late and you've been working and I shouldn't have called but he was asking for you and I didn't—"

"Nicola," he said, cutting her off as he followed her down the hall. "Slow down, you're rambling."

She stopped and turned to face him. God, she was beautiful. His blood suddenly rumbled in his veins, and an old attraction spectacularly resurfaced, knocking him out. And in that moment he realized nothing had changed. He was still as attracted to Nicola as he'd always been.

But he would never let her know it. There was no point. They were ancient history, and he was in no condition to get involved with anyone. Particularly a woman who clearly hated the sight of him.

"Rambling?" she echoed, glaring at him.

He nodded, biting back a grin. "Yeah...rambling. Take a breath and calm down."

"I am calm," she shot back. "I've just had a crappy day. We'll have to go to the kitchen as the light bulb in the living room has blown."

He glanced into the darkened room as they passed. "Want me to fix it?"

"No," she said and kept walking.

"So, what seems to be the problem?"

"I can't get Marco out of the closet," she said and then quickly explained how the boy liked to hide there. "And when he asked to see you, I just... I couldn't think of anything else to do except call. He doesn't generally take to strangers...which is good, I suppose. But he seemed to connect with you at the hospital, and all I could do was what he asked. Right now, I simply want him to come out of the closet and get some sleep. Plus, he said his hand hurts."

"He's got a few stitches, so that's not unusual," Kieran said, realizing she was clearly frazzled and holding on by a thread. "I'll talk to him in a minute, but perhaps you should fill me in on what's been going on with him lately."

She nodded. "Sure."

Kieran followed her up the hall. "Where's your other nephew?"

"Bed. Johnny fights to stay up and play video games and then ends up flaked out on the floor in his room," she said as they entered the kitchen. "He's willful and defiant and doesn't do anything I say. Unlike Marco, who is usually a people pleaser and hates getting into trouble. But tonight… I think he's simply overwhelmed by his injury and after what happened at school…" She sighed and her voice trailed off. "It's been one of those days."

"What happened at school?" he asked, standing on the other side of the island. watching as she began pouring coffee into two mugs.

"He got bullied today," she explained quietly. "And then he got upset, and some of his classmates saw, and then he withdrew like he sometimes does and wouldn't talk to his teacher. It's happened before. I left the restaurant, picked him up early and brought him home. But he still wouldn't talk to me. I didn't even know he'd hurt himself on the fishing hook until I called him in for dinner. He'd wrapped a T-shirt around his hand so I wouldn't know."

Kieran considered her words. "Have you thought about getting him to talk with a professional?" he asked quietly. "He's obviously having trouble coping with the death of his parents, and naturally so, but I could make a few inquiries and find someone who works specifically with children if you would like a referral."

She nodded fractionally. "It may come to that. But for now, I'd just like to get him out of the closet."

"Sure," he said and noticed that her hands were shaking a little. "Does he have nightmares?"

"Yes," she replied and pushed the mug across the counter. "I have cream and sugar."

"This is fine," he said and took the mug. One brow rose. "Your tastes have changed."

He met her gaze. "Some," he said and tried to ignore the way his heart beat faster than usual. "So, about his nightmares…does he talk to you about them?"

"Sometimes. He has a fear of water," she said and sipped her coffee. "That's why he fishes out of a bucket."

Kieran recalled that her brother and sister-in-law lost their lives in a boating accident and how Marco had responded at the hospital when he'd mentioned he might want to try fishing for real. "Because of his parents' accident?"

"Yes," she replied softly. "The boys weren't with them that day. It was just pure luck, really. They'd both had head colds and my sister-in-law Miranda didn't want to risk them getting worse," she explained.

"Gino and Miranda were good people," Kieran said. "I used to stop by JoJo's sometimes, when I'd come home to visit my folks. As I recall, they were dedicated sailors."

She nodded. "They competed in all the major events. They were in San Francisco for the regatta, which they did every year. I loved it because it meant Vince and I could see them, and we could catch up as a family."

Kieran knew Vince had moved to San Francisco straight out of high school. It was one of the reasons Nicola had chosen to go to college there, to be close to her older brother.

"Vince has a big apartment in the city," she explained quietly. "And they always stayed with him when they were there. I was at my brother's apartment watching the kids because Gino and Miranda had gone for a sail outside the bay before the races started the next day. They say the storm came out of nowhere." She sighed and shrugged. "I don't know… Gino was always so careful about the dangers of doing what he loved. But on that day, he miscalculated. It was days before their bodies were found…but by then we knew something terrible had happened. Vince identified them, and then we had to tell the boys. It was the hardest thing I have ever done."

Kieran watched as her eyes glittered with tears and she blinked a couple of times. There was something incredibly vulnerable about her in that moment, and he fought the sudden urge to reach across and touch her. Comforting Nicola was out of the question. He had to remember that. She wasn't a patient or a friend. She was the girl he'd loved in high school. She was his past. End of story.

"You know," he said and met her gaze, "I've seen fear manifest from loss before…it's not uncommon, particularly in a child. In time, and with patience and maybe therapy, he'll probably overcome his fears."

"I hope so," she said quietly. "Until then, I have to work out how to make him feel safe. Unfortunately, I feel as though I'm failing at every turn."

It was quite an admission, and one he was sure she hadn't intended divulging. Hours ago, she'd made her feelings toward him abundantly clear—she still hated him. And yet now he was standing in her kitchen, listening to her earnest words, drinking coffee and acting as though it was all absurdly normal.

"I'm sure you're not," he assured her. "Parenting is a challenge even in the best of circumstances."

"You'd know more about that than me."

A familiar ache hit him directly in the center of his chest, and he quickly averted his gaze. He didn't want to see her eyes, didn't want to speculate as to how much she knew about him and his life before he'd returned to Cedar River. But people talked. He knew that. But with everything else that was going on with his family—with his parents' impending divorce, the discovery of his half brother, and then his other brother Liam secretly marrying the daughter of their father's sworn enemy, he hoped that his own smashed-up personal life might not rate a mention on the radar. But when he did finally glance at her again, he figured that she knew enough. Maybe not everything, particularly how broken up inside he felt most of the time, but she certainly had some idea of what he'd been through.

"Later," he said and shrugged. "You can ask me later."

She shrugged loosely. "I shouldn't have said that. Your private life is none of my business."

He nodded. "Anyway, for now, we should probably go and talk with Marco."

She placed her mug on the counter. "He's upstairs."

He followed her from the kitchen and up the stairway, trying not to notice how her hips swayed as she walked. Or the way her perfume assailed his senses. Other than in a professional capacity, it had been a long time since he'd been so close to a woman. He hadn't been intimate with anyone since he'd separated from Tori. Casual sex had never been his thing, and he wasn't interested in a committed relationship, so the best thing was to avoid women altogether until he worked through his demons. But he hadn't figured on his old attraction for Nicola making a comeback.

Get a grip, O'Sullivan...

Ten minutes later, he still hadn't managed to coax Marco from his hiding spot in the closet, but the child was at least answering him. To his credit, he'd made the tiny space into a fort, complete with walls and windows, out of several old cardboard boxes and several towels pegged together. Looking at how he'd used his imagination allayed some of his concerns for the boy's emotional well-being. This was clearly Marco's safe place, his go-to spot when he felt cornered or unhappy or despairing. Kieran wasn't an expert in child psychology, but he was relieved to discover that Marco wasn't simply hiding in a confined space staring at the wall.

"You've built a really cool fort," Kieran said quietly.

Marco was silent, then grunted. "Johnny says it's lame."

"Well, I'm something of an expert at fort building," he said, flicking his gaze toward Nicola, who stood in the doorway. He caught a tiny smile at the edges of her mouth and ignored the way it made his gut churn. "When my brothers and I were young, we turned our treehouse into a fort. It had a moat, too."

He heard a shuffling sound, like sneakers shifting across carpet, and then spotted Marco peering around the door frame.

"A moat?" the boy asked. "Really?"

"Yeah," Kieran replied. "It had water in it, too. I fell into it once and dislocated my collarbone."

Marco's eyes widened, and he stepped out of the closet. "That must have hurt a lot."

"It did," he said and nodded. "So, your aunt said your hand was hurting."

"Yeah," the boy said, his voice cracking.

"On a scale of one to ten, how much does it hurt?" Kieran asked.

"Ten," Marco replied quickly.

Kieran glanced at Nicola, saw the concern on her face and offered a reassuring nod. "Ten," he mused. "Really? That's a lot. Are you sure?"

Marco's bottom lip wobbled. "Well…maybe a five."

"Five… I see. Then, that's not so bad, right? Remember the word I said you need to say over and over?"

The boy nodded. "I remember."

"Good," Kieran said and smiled. "Keep saying it, over and over, every time your hand hurts. Now, your aunt also says it's way past your bedtime, so how about you get settled into bed."

"Do I have to have more stitches?"

"No, not a single one."

Marco looked pensive. "More medicine?"

Kieran checked his watch. "Not yet. Maybe tomorrow."

"Do I have to go to school tomorrow?"

Kieran looked at Nicola and she nodded. "How about you see how you feel in the morning and then talk to your aunt about it, okay?"

The boy looked thoughtful for a moment and then nodded. "Okay."

"And keep saying the special word," Kieran said and smiled. "I promise your hand won't hurt as much."

Marco grinned a little. "Okay. Thanks, Doctor."

"And you can call me Kieran, okay? Because your aunt is a friend of mine."

"Sure thing."

Kieran turned toward Nicola. "I'll leave you to get him settled."

She stepped into the room and nodded. "Thank you for this… I don't know what I would have done otherwise…" Her words trailed off for a moment. "If you give me ten minutes, we can finish that coffee."

"Sure," he said before giving Marco the thumbs-up sign. With the promise that he'd see him soon, he headed back downstairs.

He lingered in the kitchen, ditched his jacket and hung it over the back of one of the chairs and sat at the table, looking around. Like the rest of the house, it was a modern, spacious room, with granite countertops and top-of-the-line appliances. He'd noticed an array of family pictures on the wall in the hallway when he'd arrived and quickly deduced that this was once Gino Radici's home. He'd always liked Gino. They'd played football together in high school and, as Nicola's boyfriend, they all used to hang out at JoJo's pizza parlor most afternoons. Life had been easy back when he was in high school…his parents were happy, his family was a tight unit, Liz was still alive and he'd had Nicola.

Until he blew her off.

At the time, he'd believed he was doing the right thing. Maintaining a long-distance relationship from separate colleges was never going to work. She had her ambitions, and so did he. Then, the week before graduation, when she'd brought up the idea of getting engaged he'd freaked out, suspicious that she might do something they'd regret—like deliberately get pregnant. And Kieran had no intention of being a father at eighteen. So days later, he'd ended it. Badly. He'd said he wanted to see other people. Other girls. He told her to get a life that didn't include him. Remembering how stupidly he'd behaved only amplified his guilt by a million. She'd deserved better.

When she returned to the kitchen ten minutes later, she looked tired but relieved. "He's settled…finally. And I managed to get Johnny back into bed and the video game out of his hands. Thank you," she added and sighed as she moved around the countertop. "I owe you a fresh cup of coffee."

"You don't owe me anything."

It was a pointed remark…one they both knew had little to do with the situation at hand. Their history circled in the air between them. Air that needed to be cleared once and for all.

"Kieran, I—"

"I never meant to hurt you, you know," he said quietly. "I mean, I know I did…but I was too young and too self-absorbed to fully realize what I was doing. When I did have the maturity to work out that I'd been a complete jerk, we were long gone from one another's life. But I am genuinely sorry for hurting you, Nicola."

She was still as a statue. She didn't look impressed or accepting of his apology. "Sure…whatever."

"I can leave if you—"

"I promised you more coffee," she said and turned toward the pantry. "I'll make a fresh pot. Are you hungry?"

His stomach growled and he remembered he hadn't eaten since lunch. "Yeah."

A tiny smiled lifted her mouth at the edges for a moment. "Cannoli?"

He grinned. "I still have a sweet tooth."

"I figured," she said and moved around the kitchen, making coffee and preparing the dessert on a plate.

Kieran remained where he was, watching her at her task. "How are you enjoying working at the restaurant again?"

She shrugged lightly. "It's okay. Managing the place isn't exactly my dream job...but my father needs the help, and it's kind of ingrained in my DNA to work there. I've been waiting tables at JoJo's since I was ten years old. Thankfully the place is still busy and turning a profit. I have a tourist party booked for tomorrow...twenty-four hungry mouths to feed. Friday fun, I like to call it."

"Sounds like a lot of work."

She shrugged. "Necessary. My dad has slowed down a lot in the past year."

"He had a stroke, didn't he?"

"Yes," she replied. "A few months after Gino died."

He knew she'd loved her brother. He also knew what it was like to lose a sibling. And he felt her hurt right down to his bones. But he didn't press the subject. "So, did you have your dream job in San Francisco?"

"I thought so at the time," she said. "I worked for an organic food company and managed the human resources department."

"Is that where you met your fiancé?"

Her expression narrowed, and she glanced at him. "You know about that?"

"Liam told me," he replied. "I figured Kayla told him. Why did you break up?"

She came around the counter with the coffees and the plate of cannoli, placed them on the table and sat down. "He broke it off when he realized he was still in love with his ex-wife."

He grimaced. "Ouch."

"Yes," she said and pushed the plate toward him. "It sucked. Although, probably not as much as what happened to you."

Kieran grabbed the cannoli, took a bite and then remembered how much he'd always liked Nicola's cooking. Even in high school, she'd had a flair in the kitchen. "I guess you want to know the whole story?"

She shrugged and sipped her coffee. "Like I said before, it's none of my business."

He finished the cannoli in three bites. "Okay, I won't tell you."

"Suit yourself."

He lifted up the mug, took a sip and then watched her over the rim. Her eyes had darkened, and he knew the defiant lift of her chin was a facade. She had matured into an incredibly beautiful woman, and suddenly he wasn't in any kind of hurry to finish his coffee and leave. Her eyes, the delicately arched brows, her full, pink mouth, all a riveting combination of color and lovely angles. His gaze lingered on her mouth, and he experienced a sudden tightening in his groin. He knew it was stupid, knew that thinking about Nicola as anything other than an old flame was pointless. She hadn't forgiven him. And he didn't want to get involved with anyone. But still, he wasn't quite ready to get up and end the evening.

And for the first time in forever, he actually wanted to talk.

"She left me for my best friend," he said quietly.

Her gaze met his, and she held it and tilted her head a fraction. For a second, he saw compassion in her expression, a fleeting understanding that she clearly didn't want to feel because she obviously still hated him.

"I'm sorry."

He shrugged. "Thanks."

"And the other thing?"

Discomfort pierced his chest. It was always that way. Nearly two years on, and he still felt the pain of loss and betrayal as though it were yesterday. One day, he hoped the pain would lessen, that he wouldn't wake up each morning with a hole in his heart so wide he couldn't imagine it being filled with anything or anyone. He grappled with how much to tell her and then figured there was little point in being coy or secretive about the situation. "You mean my son?"

"Yes."

He let out a long breath. "Christian. Who, it turns out, wasn't *my* son but was actually fathered by my best friend."

The sympathy in her expression returned. "How awful! You really don't have to talk about it if you don't want to."

"You can hear it from me," he said and shrugged. "Or via one of the local gossip channels."

"Okay," she said, quieter than he expected. "You can tell me about him."

Kieran's chest tightened further, and the band of pressure at his temple returned. Fatigue spread through his limbs, and he sat back in the chair. "I believed he was my son for eighteen months before my now-ex-wife admitted the truth."

Memories of that awful day bombarded his thoughts. Catching Tori and Phil together And then finding out the son he treasured was not really his child. He remembered Tori crying. Tori pleading. Tori telling him she should never have married him, that she loved someone else. Tori saying she wanted to be free of him and their marriage so she could raise Christian with the man she loved...the man who was his son's real father.

"You never suspected anything?"

He shook his head. "Phil was my colleague and best friend. Tori was my wife. I guess I trusted the wrong people."

"I'm so sorry," she said.

"Yeah," he said, aching all over. "Me, too."

Nicola's heart felt heavy in her chest. She didn't like the feeling. Didn't want to imagine that she had any feelings toward Kieran other than dislike and resentment. But...his story saddened her deeply. She'd heard it anecdotally...from Kayla and her friend Connie who worked at his family's hotel and knew everything about the O'Sullivans. So yes, she knew about his marriage ending and discovering his son was fathered by someone else. And of course she thought it was cruel and despicable. But she always managed to shrug her shoulders and wave off any feelings of sympathy or compassion for the man who had callously dumped her in front of the entire twelfth grade on the biggest day of their high school lives.

But hearing it from Kieran was different. And as much as she wanted to hang on to her resentment and rage at him in that moment, she couldn't. Particularly as he'd gone out his way to help her with Marco. Thanks to his kindness and understanding, her nephew was now safely asleep in his bed.

"So...you divorced her?"

He shrugged lightly. "We divorced each other."

"And Christian?" she asked, saying the child's name almost as a whisper.

She watched as Kieran took a sharp breath and then

sipped his coffee. "I didn't want to confuse him, you know, or make things difficult…so I had to step away."

She saw his eyes darken and experienced an odd discomfort in her chest. "That must have been hard."

"The most difficult thing I have ever done in my life."

"So, you don't have any contact now?"

"No," he replied. "I made a decision that was best for him. He needed to bond with his…with his father," he said, swallowing hard. "And Tori didn't want me interfering in her new life."

Nicola tried desperately to ignore how her heart rate increased. She didn't want to feel sympathy for him. She didn't want to feel *anything* when it came to Kieran O'Sullivan. And she didn't want to listen to his apologies, either. But she couldn't help being drawn into their conversation. She'd always been a good listener—her career in human resources had demanded it.

"So this way, only one person got hurt…is that what you're saying?"

He shrugged lightly again and picked up another cannoli. "Exactly. Everyone needed a do-over. Me included."

"And that's why you came back to Cedar River?"

"Sure," he said and took a bite. "It was time I came home anyway…with everything that was imploding here."

Nicola sipped her coffee and then looked at him over the rim of her mug. It was true, he certainly had a lot going on with his family. "Do you get along with your new brother?"

His mouth curled up at the edges. "You know me, Nic… I get along with everyone."

He was right. Kieran had a reputation for being easy-going and likable. Perfect attributes for a physician. But she wasn't fooled. "Cut the crap."

He chuckled. "Have you met Jonah?"

"A couple of times, like at Liam and Kayla's wedding. He seems very…intense."

Kieran laughed. "That's a good way to describe him. He *is* intense. And moody. And kind of unpleasant most of the time. But to be fair, he's mellowed a little over the past few months. Not that I can blame him for putting up a few walls, considering he's known about us all his life, but we didn't know about him. He still lives in Portland but visits his mother, Kathleen, regularly."

"She moved back to Cedar River," Nicola remarked and then laughed humorlessly. "We're heading back in droves."

"She wanted to spend more time with her mother and brother—you know, Kayla's grandmother and father." He shrugged. "It's become something of a confusing family tree."

She nodded a little. "And your parents are really getting a divorce?"

"So they say," he replied and sipped his coffee. "Mom can't forgive him for the infidelity, even though Dad ended his affair with Kathleen before Jonah was born."

"She's a lot younger than him, isn't she?"

"Yeah," he said and sighed heavily. "She was eighteen and in love with an older man. To be honest, I don't think my parents' marriage was ever a love match. And Dad still appears to care for Kathleen." He shrugged. "Who knows? I'm not exactly an expert on the subject of what constitutes a successful relationship."

Nicola saw weariness in his expression, and her insides took a foolish plunge. "Me neither," she admitted and managed a small smile, annoyed at herself for being so easily swayed by him, but suddenly unable to fight the feeling. "You might get married again."

"Maybe," he said quickly and drained his mug. "But I have zero interest on that score for the foreseeable future."

"Not all marriages end badly," she said and shrugged. "My parents had a happy marriage. As did Gino and his wife. And your brother and Kayla seem really happy together."

"I didn't say it wasn't possible," he remarked. "Just that I wasn't interested in the idea."

"So, you've become a cynic?"

"Exactly. Haven't you?"

Nicola shrugged again. "I'm hopeful. But next time I intend *not* falling for a man who's still in love with someone else."

"So, you want assurances?" he laughed humorlessly. "Good luck with that."

She felt her tension return. "Believing in people doesn't make me naive, Kieran. I can be as cynical as the next person. Let's face it, I've been dumped more than once and have had plenty of experience at being humiliated."

He rested his elbows on the table and stared at her. "So, I guess about now is where you swear at me in Italian?"

She got to her feet and pushed the chair back. "No, it's where I say good night."

He stood immediately and, without another word, he grabbed his jacket and made his way to the door. Nicola hurried after him and almost plowed into his back when he came to a halt outside the living room.

"Do you have a spare bulb?" he inquired and gestured into the room.

"There's no need to—"

"Just find the bulb, Nic," he said and walked into the room. "And stop being a pain in the ass."

Nicola remained in the doorway and watched as he walked across the room and flicked on a small lamp by the fireplace. "I don't have a ladder."

"No need for one," he said and pointed to the wooden chair by the window. "I'll use that."

Of course, he was nearly a foot taller than she was and would reach the ceiling easily enough. She just had to get the spare bulb from the laundry room. "Be back in a minute."

Except that her *minute* turned into about ten. There were no new bulbs in the laundry room, and she had to venture to the workshop out back and rummage through a few boxes of Gino's tools and equipment to find what she needed. She headed back inside, locking the back door and swiftly making her way through the kitchen and down the hallway. When she got to the living room, she stopped dead in her tracks.

Kieran was lying on the sofa, legs stretched out, one arm over his forehead, clearly comfortable, and obviously fast asleep.

She pulled up alongside the sofa and looked down at him. His hair was a little long, like he'd forgotten to get it cut. And the whisker growth *was* too sexy for words. His feet were crossed at the ankles, and his other hand lay across his chest. She looked at his left hand, to where his wedding band would have been, and she couldn't help wondering how long it had been since he'd taken it off. The skin was paler. So, not long, by the look of things. He must still love his ex-wife, despite what she had done to him. Love often had a way of hanging around…she'd discovered that herself in the years it took her to erase Kieran's memory from her heart.

Nicola went to tap his shoulder but then snatched her hand back. She remembered how he'd said he'd pulled a double shift at the hospital…and then he'd driven straight over to help her out with Marco. A double shift, combined with his recent move from Sioux Falls, meant he was obviously exhausted. Guilt pressed inside her chest and, instead of waking him up, she grabbed a soft chenille blanket from the love seat by the window and gently draped it over him. He didn't stir, didn't move, didn't do anything other than take a deep breath and then sigh.

As she left the room and headed upstairs, Nicola mused that, if someone had told her earlier that day that Kieran O'Sullivan would be sleeping in her house, she would have told them they were out of their mind and to go straight to hell. And she didn't want to think about how she was trying to cling onto anger and resentment because hating him made things easier. Hating him made her forget how much she had once loved him.

And hating him made her immune to falling in love with him ever again.

Chapter Three

Kieran awoke with a crick in his neck, an aching back, and two sets of curious eyes staring at him.

Marco and Johnny were both sitting on the opposite sofa clearly waiting for him to wake up. He grimaced when he spotted a ridiculously pink blanket draped over his legs and quickly swung his feet to the floor. He ran a weary hand through his hair and glanced at the clock on the wall. Seven fifty. He'd been asleep for over nine hours. And on Nicola's couch, no less!

"Did you sleep over?" Marco asked, eyes wide.

"Looks like it," he replied and stretched out his back.

"To make sure I was okay?"

"Of course," he fibbed and rubbed a hand over his face. "How are you feeling, champ?"

Marco nodded. "Okay, I guess. Aunt Nicola said I don't have to go to school today. She said I could go to JoJo's with her. But Johnny has to go to school."

The older boy scowled. "At least I've got friends at school."

"Didn't I specifically tell you boys *not* to disturb Kieran this morning?"

They all looked toward the door. Nicola stood at the

threshold, dressed in a knee-length black skirt, tucked-in white blouse and black heels. Her hair was pulled back, and she wore gold loop earrings. She held a mug in one hand, and the other hand was perched on her hip. She looked smoking hot and, as awareness curdled in his blood, Kieran tried not to stare at her—but failed.

"Breakfast is on the table," she said to the boys. "Scoot. And make sure you put the dishes in the sink when you are done."

The kids took off as though their heels were on fire, and Nicola ruffled their hair as they passed. Then, she walked into the living room and passed Kieran the mug she carried.

"Thanks," he said and inhaled the heady coffee aroma and tried not to stare at her legs. "And sorry I crashed."

She shrugged one shoulder. "Sorry I made you come here last night after pulling a double shift. I think I was a little crazy with worry and didn't think about anything else."

"Once I sat down on this cushy couch last night the fatigue hit me." He drank some coffee and grinned slightly. "Well, at least you have a comfy couch. Better than the ones that are usually in the doctors' lounges at hospitals."

Her lips curved. "Would you like breakfast? I have oatmeal on the stove."

Kieran grimaced. "No thanks."

She laughed softly. "Toast, then?"

Kieran got to his feet and straightened his jacket, figuring he must look a mess in his crumpled clothes and with five-day whisker growth. "I'm good. I need to head home to shower and change. And the patient seems chipper this morning," he said, drinking the rest of the coffee and then placing the mug on one of the lamp tables. "He said you're letting him stay home today, which is probably a good idea."

She nodded. "He can hang out at the restaurant with me."

"Didn't you say you have a large tourist group coming in today that you have to cater for? Won't he be in the way?"

Her jaw tightened. "It's too late to call a sitter. There's a lady down the street who regularly watches the boys for me, but she's not available today."

Kieran nodded, thinking it wasn't any of his business, pulled his keys from his pocket and looked at her. "Okay…well, thanks for the couch and the coffee."

"Thank you for coming over last night and helping me with Marco."

He walked past her, picking up the fragrance of her perfume, and the scent quickly hitched up his awareness a notch or two. He stopped when he reached the door and turned back to face her. Her eyes looked huge in her face, and he was overwhelmed with the sudden need to stare at her some more. She was biting her bottom lip, which she also did when she was nervous, and he wondered if she'd picked up on the weird energy that was now in the room. She was close, barely a foot away from him. Desire snaked up his spine and simmered in his blood, and he swallowed hard, thinking that he hadn't felt anything so intense for a long time.

He cleared his throat and spoke. "You know, Marco could hang out with me today. I have the next couple of days off, and I was planning on heading to the hotel this morning…my mom will be there with Liz's youngest daughter," he said, then explained how his mother looked after Tina for several hours once a week as a way to spend time with her granddaughter. "My mom loves kids. And I could drop him back at JoJo's this afternoon, once you've finished with the tourists."

She frowned. "I couldn't possibly impose on you."

"You wouldn't be," he assured her. "Marco is a great kid. Give me half an hour to get home and change, and then I'll come back."

He had no idea why, but he wanted to help her out. But she didn't look convinced. She looked like it was the last thing she wanted or needed. "I can look after my nephews by myself."

"I wasn't implying that you—"

"He'll come to work with me. Goodbye, Kieran. Thanks again."

He was being dismissed. So he left and headed home. He checked his cell on the way out, finding a message from his brother, reminding him that he'd promised to stop by the hotel on his way home from work the night before—a fact Kieran had quickly forgotten once he'd received Nicola's call for help. When he got back to his apartment, he showered, changed into jeans, a polo shirt and jacket and then drove into town. Ten minutes later, he was swinging into one the reserved spaces in the hotel parking lot.

O'Sullivan's Hotel was the best in the county. Thirty rooms, two restaurants, conference rooms and a ballroom for large functions, it had a reputation for its style, ambience and service. And his brother ran the place better than their father ever had. Liam was a hard-nosed and judgmental ass, but Kieran loved his brother dearly. As he did Sean. He was even mellowing toward Jonah the more time he spent with the man. It was hard at first, knowing his father had cheated on his mom and had a secret family in another state for nearly thirty years. But it couldn't be easy for his newfound sibling either, and he didn't plan on making things more difficult by refusing to acknowledge that he did actually have another brother.

The foyer was already busy with guests and several staff milling around the reception area assisting them, their green corporate jackets giving them a professional and upscale look. He spotted his brother by the concierge desk and headed for him. Liam looked up and waved.

"Where were you last night?" Liam asked, one eyebrow cocked. "I thought you were coming here on your way home from work. We need to talk about Mom's birthday thing."

He shrugged. "I was tied up with a favor for a friend."

Liam's eyebrows further cocked with humor. "Making *friends* already? Good for you."

His brother knew he wasn't in any kind of emotional shape to get involved with anyone…but he wasn't averse to making fun if he had the chance. Kieran shrugged indifferently, ignoring his brother's tone. "No comment."

Liam grinned. "It's a small town. You know I'll find out."

Kieran managed a wry smile. "Yes, *Godfather*," he said and shook his head. "But if you must know, I stopped by Nicola's after work," he said and then quickly explained about Marco's injury and how he had attended to him at the hospital but then glossed over Nicola's frantic phone call and didn't mention how he'd ended up sleeping on her couch.

"So," Liam mused, "you and Nicola, eh?"

"Don't be ridiculous. I need breakfast, are you coming?"

"Sure," Liam said and hooked a thumb in the direction of the restaurant. "Mom's already here, by the way. With Tina and Kayla and the baby."

Liam and Kayla's son, Jack, was three weeks old and the light of their lives. "Okay."

"Don't let Mom know you were hanging out with Nicola Radici. If you do, you know you'll get the third degree. And then Mom will start sending out wedding invitations."

Kieran spluttered. "Can't I help out an old…a former…someone I used to…"

"Keep digging," Liam mocked. "If the hole gets any bigger, you'll end up in Montana."

"Sometimes I wish I was an only child."

"Where's the fun in that?" Liam teased. "And I think it's great. It's time you came back into the land of the living. I'm tired of watching you pretend to be happy. Your fake smile makes my jaw ache."

"You know what else would make your jaw ache? My fist."

Liam laughed. "Actually, come to think of it, this is all great timing. You should join the Big Brothers program at the hospital. I've been the patron of the program for a couple of years, but I think I need to pass the baton to you. I was only talking to Nicola about it a couple of weeks back. She's been having a few problems with the younger boy… I suggested Big Brothers might be exactly what both of those kids need. And since you work at the hospital…"

Kieran's gut churned. The last thing he wanted to do was be responsible for troubled kids looking for a brother or father figure. Particularly kids linked to Nicola. Liam should have known better than to suggest such an idea to him. He wasn't anyone's father. Not now. Probably not ever again.

"I need food and coffee," he said.

Liam laughed. "Okay, let's go."

When they entered the restaurant, Kieran saw his mother and sister-in-law immediately. Kayla was stunningly beautiful, but she was also kind and clearly loved his brother dearly. And Kieran had never seen Liam happier.

His mother, Gwen, was clearly delighted to see him, and her happy expression made him smile. She liked having her chicks close by and was thrilled that Kieran had returned. He knew she worried about his brother Sean's rumored wild lifestyle in LA and would be over the moon if her youngest child decided to give up his success, money and women and return home, where she believed he belonged. But Kieran wasn't so sure of that. Sean had never been small-town. He'd always craved the action of a bigger city and had certainly carved out a successful life for himself as a music and movie producer. Kieran was different. And, for him, returning to Cedar River had been an easy decision. Staying in Sioux Falls, where everything reminded him of all he had lost, was never going to be an option.

Gwen O'Sullivan was tall and statuesque, with a silvery bob and a creaseless face that defied her sixty years. She'd been a model long ago and still carried herself as though she could grace the catwalk.

"You were missed last night," his mother said when he reached their table. "We decided you are going to be in charge of sending out the invitations."

His mother's sixtieth birthday party was going to be a big bash, with out-of-state relatives already committed to the event. *"We?"* he echoed and smiled. "How come you're on the organizing committee for your own party?"

"Well, if I leave it to you and Liam, I suspect nothing will get done," she said and raised both her brows. "Thankfully, I have Kayla and Connie to help."

Liam's wife and Liam's personal assistant. Kieran suddenly felt like apologizing for the fact that he was divorced and single and had inadvertently robbed his parent of her daughter-in-law and the grandchild she'd loved. Logically, he knew that there was no malice in his mother's words. Gwen knew what he'd been through, knew how broken he was at losing his son and his marriage. But he still experienced an acute sense of failure. From his broken relationship with Nicola to his busted marriage, he clearly sucked at commitment. He glanced toward Kayla, and his sister-in-law gave him a quick, reassuring wink, as though she knew exactly what was going on in his head.

Nothing is going on...

Watching his family, Kieran couldn't help but reflect on all he had lost. He'd loved being a father and missed Christian so much he ached inside. And he missed being a husband. And then, as always, the ache was replaced by a feeling of betrayal and rage so intense he had to take a couple of long breaths to stop the sensation taking hold.

"Everything all right?"

Liam's voice. His brother knew him better than anyone. "Yeah, fine."

"You look tired."

"I did a double shift at the hospital," he said casually.

"And then had a date with Nicola Radici."

And just like that, his hold of the situation spectacularly fell apart because two feminine sets of startled eyes immediately zoomed in on him. Kayla's eyes were as wide as saucers. His mother looked at him with a kind of delighted shock. He had to backpedal—and fast.

"It wasn't a date."

Thankfully, a couple of orders of pancakes arrived just then, but Kieran knew he wasn't about to be let off the hook so easily.

"I've always liked Nicola," Gwen said quietly. "She's a sweet girl. She's helped out on the hospital committee a few times, you know. She's so good at organizing things. I might stop by the restaurant today and see if she'd like to help me with the latest fundraiser. And the way she's taken to caring for her nephews when her brother was killed…really, such a sweet girl."

"You said that already," he muttered, feigning interest in the food his mother placed in front of him.

Liam chuckled, and Kieran scowled in his direction. Just because his brother had found his happily-ever-after with Kayla, it didn't mean that everyone else would. Kieran had believed he'd had it once…until it blew up in his face. He wasn't about to go down that road again in a hurry.

He picked up his fork. "Stop reading anything into it. She hates me, remember?"

"That's true," Kayla said and smiled. "She does."

Liam chuckled. "It's a double-edged sword, though, don't you think?"

Kieran stared at his pancakes, feeling heat rise up his chest and throat and then hit him squarely in the face. He didn't want anyone speculating about him and Nicola. Because there was no him and Nicola. Not now. Not ever again. And, when he glanced at his mother, he saw that she was still smiling, still watching him with a

curious regard that spoke volumes. He knew that look.
It was a matchmaking face.

I'm so screwed.

Tour groups were usually Nicola's favorite. They
were generally cheerful, always finished their meals
and tipped big. But today she was too tired to handle
the exuberant crowd. Her limbs felt heavy with a kind
of odd lethargy that had everything to do with the fact
she'd barely managed to get any sleep the night before.
Really, how was she supposed to sleep when Kieran
was spread out on her couch directly below her bed? If
she'd had any sense, she would have woken him up and
sent him packing. But the kindness he'd shown toward
Marco was impossible to discount. And she wasn't a
mean-spirited person—even toward the man she hated
most in the world.

Okay…so maybe that was a stretch.

It wasn't exactly hate. It was…it was anger and resentment and a whole lot of bone-deep, heart-wrenching
hurt. The way he'd ended their relationship still stung.
The pity she'd endured from her friends and the humiliation she'd experienced had been almost impossible
to bear. In the end, escaping to college in California
had been a lifeline. And, for a while, falling in love
with Carl had been a lifeline, too. After Kieran, Nicola
wasn't sure she could have those feelings again. Sure,
she'd dated in college and had had a couple of short-
term boyfriends, but no one had really touched her heart
until she met Carl. And then, once she was in love and
believed she'd finally get her fairy-tale ending, the so-
called man of her dreams simply turned out to be another man who didn't want her.

As she stacked the dishwasher with pizza trays, she

checked the time. Two o'clock. The lunch crowd had thinned out, and there was only one couple remaining at one of the booth tables. Her father was slowly shoveling the coals in the fire pit at the other end of the kitchen, while Marco did some reading in the small office off the kitchen. Josie, one of the two waitresses working that day, came through the swing doors carrying a tray of glassware.

"There's a customer out front who wants to speak to the manager," the younger woman said. "And he's kind of cute."

Nicola grinned. "What's the problem?"

Josie grinned, flashing the stud pierced in her tongue, and shrugged. "Dunno…he just asked for you."

She nodded, wiped her hands and headed through the door, expecting to find a disgruntled customer waiting for her. Instead, Kieran was standing by the counter. Suspicion coursed through her veins.

"What are you doing here?"

He gave her a grin that made her insides do a foolish flip. "Just wanted to check on the patient."

Her suspicions subsided a little. "He's in the office doing his reading."

Nicola tried not to think about how her heart was suddenly racing. After so many years, he *still* had the ability to shake her composure. Because she was as aware of him as she'd ever been.

Damn it. I'm still attracted to him.

"Is he feeling better?"

"I think so," she replied. "He hasn't complained about his hand for most of the afternoon."

"That's good," he said and looked around. "Nothing much has changed in here, has it?"

She shrugged and glanced upward, taking in the

faded bunting, dusty Chianti bottles suspended from hooks in the ceiling, and countless tiny Italian flags stuck to the walls. "Dad likes to keep things traditional."

"Does he still drive that old Impala?"

"Not since his stroke," she replied and shrugged again. "It's for sale. Interested?"

A young couple came to the counter before he could reply. They paid their check and, once she'd processed the cash through the register, she noticed that he was still watching her, one elbow perched on the edge of the counter. The customers left, and Nicola observed that they were now alone in the restaurant.

She wished he would stop smiling. Wished he would stop looking so handsome and sexy in his jeans, polo shirt and jacket. She looked for imperfections and had to struggle to find a single one. "You need a haircut."

His eyes widened, and he offered a lopsided grin as he rubbed is jaw. "I know. And a shave."

Nicola's gaze lingered on his mouth and, for one crazy second, she remembered what his lips tasted like. And since he'd been her first kiss, her first touch, her first *everything*, the memories were suddenly acute and made her knees tremble. They'd lost their virginity together. It had been nerve-racking and a little clumsy—but it had been other things too, like gentle and emotional and achingly sweet. She'd cried afterward, and he'd held her as though she was the most precious thing in his world, muttering soft words against her neck, telling her he loved her, over and over.

"Nicola? Is everything okay?"

His voice jerked her back into the present, and she shrugged a little too casually. "I can get Marco if you want to see him."

"You look tired," he remarked.

"Gee…thanks."

He grinned again and her stomach dropped. "You're still beautiful, so don't worry."

He looked as startled by his words as she did. Heat crawled up her neck, and she knew her cheeks were going to burn. He still thought she was beautiful? Realization suddenly curdled through her blood. Whatever she was feeling, he was feeling it, too. Because, after so many years, the attraction they'd once had for one another was still there.

But he also looked like he wanted to dive into a sinkhole!

"What are you *really* doing here?" she asked.

The door opened, and its bell chimed before either of them could say anything else, and then Gwen O'Sullivan entered the restaurant, carrying a cardboard box Nicola suspected was filled with donuts from the bakery down the street. She didn't seem surprised to see her son standing by the counter. In fact, she looked… well…pleased. Alarms bells pealed inside Nicola's head, but she quickly forced them back.

"Nicola," Gwen said, smiling widely. "How lovely to see you."

"Hello, Mrs. O'Sullivan." Even after so many years she still struggled to call the other woman by her first name. When she and Kieran had dated, she had spent countless hours at the big O'Sullivan house. The ranch was the most impressive in the county. "It's good to see you, too. How can I help you?"

"I bought these for your nephew," the older woman said and smiled as she placed the box on the counter. "Kieran told me about his accident, so I thought he might like a special treat."

"That's very kind of you. Thank you."

Gwen shrugged. "Well, actually, I did have something of an ulterior motive."

Nicola stilled instantly. "You did?"

"I was hoping to persuade you to volunteer for the latest hospital fund-raiser. And I'll completely understand if you can't, since you're so busy here and with your nephews."

She met Gwen's gaze and nodded. "Of course I can. Although, I'm not sure how much help I'll be."

Gwen's eyes darted quickly toward her son, and then she smiled warmly. "Oh, I'm sure you'll become invaluable."

Marco chose that moment to skip through the doors connecting to the kitchen and was clearly delighted when he spotted his favorite doctor. And even happier when Gwen announced that the donuts were for him.

"What do you need to say to Mrs. O'Sullivan?" Nicola prompted.

Her nephew nodded enthusiastically and said thank-you several times as he took the box and held it against his chest. "Do I have to share them?" Marco asked.

Nicola bit back a grin. "If you mean with Johnny, then no, you don't *have* to…but it would be the nice thing to do, don't you think?"

Marco's mouth twisted thoughtfully. "Even though he's mean to me?"

"Even then," she said and ruffled his hair a little. "Now, why don't you go and show *Nonno* your donuts and then get back to your reading?"

He nodded, said a cheerful goodbye and then skipped out of the dining area and into the kitchen. When he was out of sight, Nicola turned back toward Gwen. "Thank you for your kindness."

"He's a delightful child," Gwen said and nodded

approvingly. "You should be very proud of all you're doing for him and his brother. Losing a parent when a child is so young—it's incredibly traumatic. I know from watching my three granddaughters cope with my daughter's passing, and they still had their father. Of course, my son-in-law has now remarried, and the girls are very attached to his wife, Marissa, which was hard to watch at first…but it really has been for the best for my granddaughters. At the end of the day, if a child feels loved, then they feel safe, and Marco obviously feels like that with you."

Nicola's throat tightened and, for a moment, she felt like rushing forward and hugging the other woman for being so supportive and understanding. With only her father and her friends to offer advice, she missed having an older woman in her life, someone with experience who could offer comfort and support and tell her that she was getting some things right. In that moment, she missed her own mother so much her chest ached.

She swallowed hard and managed a smile. "Thank you. It means a lot."

Gwen nodded thoughtfully. "If you ever need anything, you can reach out anytime."

The lump in her throat intensified, and she managed a tiny nod, trying to get her thoughts away from her grief. "Uh…can I get you something? A late lunch perhaps?"

Gwen waved a hand. "Not for me, I have to get to a charity meeting at the museum," she said and sighed. "We're trying to raise more money to fund the planned extension. I'm sure Kayla has told you all about it. But since my son barely touched his breakfast and probably skipped lunch, you might just be able to persuade him to stay," she said and raised an eyebrow in Kieran's direction. "If I remember correctly, he always did have a thing for your cooking."

Within seconds, the older woman was gone, but her provocative words lingered in the air. Nicola looked toward Kieran and realized he was staring at her.

"What?" she asked sharply.

"I just love it when my mother talks about me as though I'm not in the room."

Her mouth curved. "I've always liked your mom."

"She's always liked you, too," he said and shrugged, almost as if suddenly he couldn't stand being in his own skin. "That's the problem."

"Problem?"

"Yeah," he flipped back. "A problem."

Nicola's nerves rattled. "I don't see why. Your mother and I have always been friendly."

He made an impatient sound. "Come off it, Nic. You know what I mean. She's fishing."

"Fishing?" she echoed, heat burning her cheeks as the sound of her shortened name rolled off his tongue. "For what?"

He shrugged, but his shoulders seemed incredibly tight. "For any indication that I might be ready to...you know...get back on the horse."

She frowned, working out where he was going, and not liking it one bit. "And who's the horse in the little scenario?"

"You are."

"I am?" She planted her hands on her hips as her temper flared. "I'm the horse?"

"Well, of course you're not really a—"

"A horse that you might want to *get back on*...correct?"

"I didn't mean it like—"

"Don't flatter yourself," she said hotly, glancing around to ensure Josie, Marco or her father weren't in earshot. Thankfully, they were all still in the kitchen. "Thank you for stopping by to check on Marco, but I'd like you to leave."

"You're angry."

"Damned straight!"

He took a step closer. "So, I'm guessing you've never learned how to conquer that famous temper of yours."

The blood surged in her veins. "Since my temper only comes out around you, I haven't had to worry about it."

"Look, all I'm saying is my mother seems to have developed this crazy idea that we're… That you and I are somehow… I don't know—" he said the words on an exasperated breath and ran a hand through his floppy, gorgeous hair "—reconnected."

"But we're not," she shot back quickly. "You would be the very last man on the planet that I would want to *connect* with. Next time I see your mother, I'll make sure I tell her that."

He laughed. He laughed so hard it made Nicola madder than hell.

"You sure about that?" he asked, his blue eyes glittering so brilliantly she could barely stand to look at him.

"Am I sure I'll tell your mom?" she shrugged. "Of course."

"That's not exactly what I meant."

Nicola stilled. "Do you mean about you being the last man on the planet? Sure, I meant it. And if you're offended, that's just your supersize, overinflated O'Sullivan ego talking."

He laughed again, and the sound rumbled in his chest and made her awareness of him skyrocket like a zephyr.

It's just physical attraction. She'd get over it. All she had to do was remember what a complete jerk he was, and then any stupidly lustful feelings she had aiming in his direction would spectacularly fade.

She stormed across the room and opened the door, waving one arm in a dramatic arc. "Now, take your ego, your horse analogies and every other annoying part of yourself and get the hell out of my restaurant."

He lingered for a moment, as though he had something else to say to her. But then he did leave—slowly, quietly, deliberately…and when Nicola closed the door behind him she sagged back against it, suddenly all out of energy. Because she wasn't only angry…she was hot and bothered and, even though she was loath to acknowledge the fact, her stupid hormones were raging.

By the time she'd pulled herself together, then gathered up Marco and his backpack and donuts, the assistant manager had arrived to take over from her and work through until closing. Nicola headed straight for the local elementary school to collect Johnny, and by three thirty both boys were home and out in the backyard, with Johnny shooting hoops and squabbling over donuts with Marco. The rest of the evening zoomed by, but by eight thirty the boys were finally settled and she was in kitchen, making tea and filling a bowl with pretzels. She had some bookkeeping to do for the restaurant, like selecting the following week's produce order, but she wasn't in any mood for sitting in front of a computer. Instead, she settled herself in the living room and watched television, flicking channels for a few minutes with as much interest as she could muster.

Until she heard her doorbell chime.

From her spot on the couch she noticed the sensor light was on, so she quickly got to her feet and peered through the front window, recognizing Kieran's tall, broad-shouldered frame instantly. She was through the hall in seconds and opened the door.

"What are you doing here?" she asked and held the screen back.

He held up a light bulb. "For your living room."

She stepped back and allowed him to cross the threshold, her brows up. "A bit late for a house call. Where's your car?" she asked, peering outside.

"I live two streets away. I walked."

She remembered suddenly that Kayla had mentioned he'd sublet her old apartment. So close. Too close. "I have bulbs, so you didn't have to go to this trouble."

"It's no trouble."

She held her ground and her nerve. "You're an idiot."

"Around you," he acknowledged and walked through the hall as she shut the door. "Yeah. History would say that I am an idiot." Within half a minute he had the bulb replaced and the old one was left on the mantel of the fireplace. He flicked the light on and off a couple of times and remained by the door. "Disaster averted."

Nicola stared at him, caught up in his blisteringly intense gaze. "What are you really doing here?"

He took a couple of steps toward her. There was uneasiness in his expression. And something else. Something she wasn't quite sure she had the courage to admit. Until he spoke again.

"I wanted to find out if my mother was right."

She frowned, unmoving, even when he reached her and there were barely inches of space between them. "About what?"

"About you. About me."

Nicola swallowed hard, feeling the heat radiating from his body even through the layers of clothing. She hadn't been this close to a man for so long; she hadn't seen that almost hungry look in a man's eyes since forever. And in that moment she knew that his mother *was* right. They *had* reconnected. There was no denying it, no running from it. But she knew she had to fight it.

Without another word, his hand looped around the nape of her neck, and he pulled her closer, until suddenly there was no space between them at all. Just heat and awareness and desire and memory.

And then, as though they had been transported back fifteen years, he kissed her.

Chapter Four

Kieran hadn't planned on kissing Nicola. Not ever again. But he'd forgotten how much she could make him feel. And even though he'd imagined she might push him away…she didn't.

She kissed him back.

Her lips parted, and he gently drew her tongue into his mouth, curling it around his own in a way that was shatteringly familiar. He knew her mouth. He knew the sweet taste of her lips and the erotic slide of her tongue only too well. Time hadn't diminished the memory. Time had only tucked the memory away, sending it into the shadows until this moment, and now everything resurfaced, making the memories of her more acute than he'd believed possible. And like an old video tape set to rewind, Kieran remembered everything they had been to each other. Every recollection amplified by the next, sending his senses hurtling toward a longing he'd forgotten existed. He didn't press too close, didn't want her to feel how hotly aroused he was by her kiss.

But he wanted to haul her into his arms and kiss her like they used to kiss. Touch her like they used to touch. Possess her and feel her shudder with pleasure beneath him.

"Please," she muttered against his mouth. "Stop."

He pulled back immediately, putting space between them. Her breathing was ragged, her cheeks flushed and her lips were red. "Nic, I—"

"What do you think you're doing?" she demanded, cutting him off.

"Isn't is obvious?"

She eyes flashed angry sparks. "Well, don't do it again."

"Okay," he said and stepped back. "If that's what you want."

"It is."

Kieran took a few steps down the hallway, got to the door and then turned back to face her. "You know, Nic, it doesn't matter how much we try to deny it, we'll always have a history."

"I'd prefer to forget the past," she said and stormed past him, opening the door wide.

She might prefer it, but Kieran suspected she had as much chance of forgetting their history as he did. For three years they had been inseparable—best friends as well as young lovers. They had shared dreams and plans—and the memories were acute. Forgetting Nicola had never been an option—he'd just buried the memories deep, forging another life, blurring the lines of how much they had once meant to one another. And, yeah, now she hated him and she'd never forgiven him for the way he'd humiliated her. But there was something else, too. Kieran could feel it right through to his bones. The pull between them was still there.

"We're still attracted to one another, that much is obvious," he said bluntly and watched as her cheeks burned with color. "And it feels like unfinished business."

"We've been finished since graduation. You made that clear enough. But if you're implying that we should act on some lingering...*feelings*...well, you can forget it. I'm not interested in reconnecting, revisiting or *rewriting* history."

"Are you sure?"

Her eyes rolled. "God, you're an egotistical jerk. Yes," she insisted. "I am sure. But I do want to thank you for fixing the bulb. I appreciate your thoughtfulness."

"Just not my honesty, right?"

Her gaze sharpened. "I don't have time for...for..."

"Romance?"

She laughed. "Seriously? Is that what you think is going on?"

"I'm not really sure what's going on."

"It's sex," she said, her voice little more than a whisper, before it rose higher after she sucked in a long breath. "Obviously. And I get it...you're back in Cedar River, you're trying to readjust to being here and, despite your family living here, too, you're alone and maybe a little lonely. I understand, believe me. This town can do that to a person—you can be surrounded by people and friends and still feel alone. But now, you've discovered that *I'm* here—good old Nic—familiar and clearly struggling to work out a way to be a parent to the boys, and here *you* are—*Doctor Dreamboat*. It makes perfect sense, doesn't it?" she shot out, her face a glorious shade of pink because she was angry and passionate and clearly hating him with every fiber of her being. "We pick up where we left off, and everyone is happy—your mother, who clearly has matchmaking plans, and Marco, who thinks you hung the moon. The whole town knows how goddamned wonderful you are, I'm surprised they didn't have a ticker tape parade to celebrate your homecoming!"

There it was—her famous temper.

He'd witnessed it firsthand many times, like when he'd accidentally stuck two of her fingers together with glue while they were working on a joint display project for chemistry class, or the time he'd forgotten to notice that her braces had come off three days before junior prom. She'd been a passionate girl and had matured into an even more passionate, vibrant woman. And she knocked him senseless with her beautiful hair and pink lips. She always had.

Kieran rocked back on his heels. "Good night, Nic. Sweet dreams."

He left her without another word, striding through the doorway, heading down the steps and out the front gate. A few minutes later, he was back home.

He changed into sweats, grabbed a beer from the refrigerator and then flopped onto the sofa, flipping through channels on the remote until he landed on a nature documentary. He tried to get interested in the show about animal migration but within ten minutes he was asleep.

He awoke before midnight, cursing the uncomfortable sofa—and the dreams of Nicola that kept his body achingly aroused—poured the untouched beer down the sink and then went to bed.

It was past eight the next morning when he planted his feet again on the floorboards. He got up, inhaled a bowl of cereal, drank two cups of coffee and changed into jeans, shirt and jacket. It was after nine by the time he was outside and took twenty minutes to drive to the family ranch.

Although there were still several head of cattle and a few horses running around the place, it hadn't been a working ranch for many years, not since his grandfather had gotten out of beef and into real estate. But the wide gates, endless white fencing and perfect manicured lawns and gardens made the place look like it could be on the front page of a style magazine. When they were kids, there had been a more lived-in feel around the ranch. A bike leaning against the front steps, a skateboard on the porch, Liam's old Mustang parked in the driveway. Or Liz's dogs standing point around the yard. His sister had a way of collecting animals—a pig named Frank, a mean gold rooster she called Nobby.

A familiar ache made its way deep into his bones when he thought about the sister he'd lost. Thankfully, Liz's husband ensured that their kids still had a relationship with the family, and Kieran was grateful for that. He had always liked Grady, even though their father had never considered him good enough for the only O'Sullivan daughter. Liz's death meant change for everyone involved, and Kieran knew his parents were worried they would lose their grandchildren… like they'd lost Christian.

Stepping back from his marriage and his son was the hardest thing he'd ever done. He could have fought… he could have hired a good lawyer and insisted he get some kind of regular visitation so he could maintain a relationship with the child he'd raised as his own for eighteen months. But at the end of the day, Christian *wasn't* his child. Staying in the boy's life would only add confusion and heartache to an already impossible situation. But it hurt. It hurt so much he knew he never wanted to feel that kind of despair again.

Kieran walked up through the garden and headed for the front door. His mother pulled back the screen the moment he tapped and, although she was smiling, he sensed something else was going on.

"Everything okay, Mom?" he asked as he crossed the threshold.

She nodded and ushered him down the hall. "Of course," she said, her back rigid. "So, I've got everything ready in the dining room. You might have to make two trips."

Two trips to remove all of his father's personal belongings out of the ranch house and into storage at Liam's place. With the divorce already in motion, Kieran knew there was no going back for his parents. Their marriage was over, and they were both moving on with their lives.

The dining room was littered with cardboard boxes, all taped up and labeled. His mother had been busy. Kieran glanced at her as she walked around the table, hands on hips, back straight.

"Mom, I could have packed this up. You didn't have to do it all yourself."

She half shrugged. "I needed to. Think of it as a cleansing. And it's not as though I'm attached to any of these things…they belong to your father. I simply want to start over."

Kieran understood that feeling better than most. "I get it, Mom. I just don't like the idea of you rattling around in this big house by yourself."

One silvery brow rose. "You could move in, then I wouldn't be alone."

"I'm not much company these days," he replied.

"And I want to be close to the hospital for the next few months."

She grinned. "Plus, it might ruin your reputation as Cedar River's most eligible bachelor, right?"

Heat crawled up his neck. "I don't think I—"

She laughed and touched his arm. "I'm just teasing you. Now help me with these boxes while I make some coffee. You look like you need it."

He headed down the hallway and started on several trips back to his Jeep, loading the boxes inside. On the third trip back, his mother had a mug of coffee waiting for him.

"I was talking to Liam yesterday," she remarked. "He said he'd talked to you about the Big Brothers program that is run by the hospital—as you know, I've been involved with the program for a number of years. There's a child I think would benefit from your guidance."

"Mom, I really can't commit to—"

"Nonsense," she said and waved a hand. "I know you would never turn your back on someone in need. And this child needs guidance. He lost his parents a while ago, and his—"

Kieran's suspicions soared. "Mother," he said, harder than usual. "Are you talking about one of the Radici boys?"

She shrugged. "Well, yes."

"Forget it," Kieran said quickly and grabbed another box. "I know what you're doing. You're matchmaking."

"Of course I am," she admitted.

"Well, it's got to stop."

She waved a hand. "I'm not going to stop being concerned about you. I'm not going to stop wanting to see you happy. It's been nearly two years and—"

"Twenty-one months," he corrected. "And I am happy. I'm happy to be back home."

"I know how it feels to lose a child," she said, cutting him to the core. "It feels like someone has ripped your heart out. But we have to move on. It's hard but necessary."

Kieran ignored her and swallowed the heat burning his throat, and then began walking down the hall. "I can fit a few more boxes in the Jeep."

"I'm serious about young Marco needing guidance," she said. "You've met him, so you know how troubled he is. And I think it would be good for you, too," she added. "You know, to think about someone other than yourself."

Kieran stopped midstride. He loved his mother. But sometimes she was out of line. "If you're implying that I am wallowing in self-pity these days, then you are way off base. I'm fine," he insisted. "And Marco needs his family, not some stranger who—"

"Marco needs compassion and understanding—qualities you possess by the bucketload. But," she said and waved a loose hand, "if you want to be selfish and refuse to help him, I suppose there would be someone else willing to give up their time."

Guilt hit him smack in the center of his chest. His mother should have been a shrink, he figured, since she was so good at mind games. "Okay," he said and headed off down the hall. "Sure. Whatever. I'll let you know what shifts I'm working and you can arrange something around those times. But good luck trying to get his aunt's consent. She hates me, remember."

Except she didn't kiss me back like she hated me.

Kieran shook off the memory. When he returned to the house, his mother was waiting by the door, holding out the mug again. Kieran took the cup, drank the contents quickly and passed it back to her.

"I'm sure I can get Nicola's agreement. At the end of the day, she'll want to do what's best for her nephew."

"And you think that's me?" he asked, moving back toward the dining room for another box.

"I think it will be good for you both," his mother replied.

Kieran wasn't so sure. Nicola had made her feelings abundantly clear—she wasn't interested in rekindling *anything*. And truthfully, neither was he. But his attraction to her had built momentum since that night at the hospital, and he suspected it wouldn't abate until they purged whatever was left of their connection. Which they wouldn't do. Nicola wasn't about to jump into his bed, no matter how strong their attraction. And Kieran wasn't ready for anything more.

It was a stalemate.

He knew that all he had to do was get his mother to stop interfering in his life, to get his brother to stop suggesting he get involved in the Big Brothers program, and to stay as far away from Nicola Radici as possible.

He also knew that none of that was going to happen.

It was a bad idea, Nicola thought later Wednesday afternoon. Maybe the worst of her life. Okay, not the worst. But agreeing to allow Kieran to be a Big Brother to Marco was up there with *Stupidest Choices Ever*. But Marco had been so delighted by the idea that she didn't have the heart to say no to Gwen's suggestion. Of course, she knew Kieran was talked into it by his mother. Gwen could be very persuasive.

Now she was simply waiting for him to arrive. She'd picked up Marco from school, and her nephew had quickly changed his clothes and was sitting patiently on the porch, waiting for Kieran to turn up. Johnny was upstairs doing homework, and Nicola was pacing the kitchen, thinking about how she was going to face him after her behavior the last time they'd been together.

Foolish.

Knowing how she'd willingly responded to his kiss filled her with humiliation and dread. Because she felt like such a fraud. She'd spent years avoiding any thought of him—she'd gone to college, forged a career, fallen in love, and ultimately had her heart broken—and during that time, Nicola had rarely allowed the memories of Kieran to invade her thoughts. She'd moved on. So had he. But proximity had altered everything. Now she couldn't avoid her thoughts. She couldn't avoid the way her body remembered what they had once been to one another. Because she'd never reacted to Carl the way she had to Kieran. Once upon a time, he only had to trace a fingertip along her spine and she was instantly *his*. He was her sexual Achilles' heel—the one man who could jump-start her libido with a simple look. And he'd jump-started it with a bang.

But it was just sex.

Chemistry. Alchemy. Hormones running riot.

She shook her head as if to clear it. It had been so long since she'd made love to anyone that her body was simply responding to its most basic yearnings. And being around Kieran in the past week had amplified those feelings tenfold. Sure, she *could* jump into bed with him. And she was pretty sure he wouldn't need a whole lot of encouragement. But sex without commitment had never appealed to her. Besides Kieran and Carl, she'd had one other lover, her on-again, off-again boyfriend during college. Taking random lovers wasn't in her plans, or in her nature. And she wanted to be a good role model for the boys and not confuse them by acting as though she was a single woman without responsibilities.

Sure, she liked sex as much as the next person. And she missed it. But she wasn't about to jump into the first bed that took her fancy—particularly since the other person in that bed was the one man she wanted— *needed*—to avoid.

Nicola heard Marco's excited voice and walked down the hall. Sure enough, Kieran had pulled up outside the house. He got out, locked up and moved through the front gate. In jeans, a blue sweater and a dark aviator jacket, he looked too gorgeous for words. She swallowed hard and opened the screen door, watching as Marco raced down the steps and greeted Kieran with a high five.

"You're here," her nephew said, grinning widely.

"Sure am, buddy."

When they reached the steps, Nicola spoke. "Hi."

He looked up. "Good afternoon."

The tension between them was raw and complicated and exactly what she wanted to avoid. But she plastered on her tightest smile. "It's good of you to do this."

He shrugged lightly. "No problem."

"So, we get to hang out together for a whole two hours?" Marco asked, clearly delighted by the prospect.

"We sure do," Kieran replied. "What would you like to do?"

"A video game," her nephew suggested and then held up his still-bandaged hand. "I can still press the buttons."

"Sounds good. Let's go."

Nicola opened the door and stood back as he walked

past, unwittingly inhaling the scent of his cologne, and she suppressed the sudden urge to sigh.

Get a grip, Radici. It's just cologne.

She waited until they had moved into the living room, then she closed the door, spotting Johnny standing at the top of the stairs. He looked furious, and she experienced a sharp pain in her chest. Her eldest nephew had so much anger in his heart. He wasn't as outwardly emotional or needy as his brother, but Nicola knew he was hurting. He missed Gino and Miranda so much, and most days Nicola felt like a very poor replacement for the parents he had adored. She was about to speak and offer that he join her in the kitchen, but he simply glared and then turned, heading to his room with a decisive slam of the door.

Nicola sighed, took a long breath and headed into the living room.

But she had already been usurped. They were sitting on the couch, snacking on the chips and sodas she'd placed on the coffee table, each holding a gaming console. Marco was chattering on about some game, and Kieran was listening to him with an intensity she envied. Most days, she simply covered the basics—food, clothes, school, and a reasonable bedtime. It left little time for anything else. For the most part, Nicola felt as though she was barely treading water when it came to her parenting skills.

She stood by the door and listened to the conversation, to Marco's enthusiasm and Kieran's deep voice answering his many questions. He would, she thought, make a wonderful father. Just the idea made her ache deep down in her belly. She thought about the child he'd raised as his own and then given up—it took strength and integrity to do something so selfless. Nicola wanted a child of her own and had believed she'd have her happily-ever-after with Carl, including a home and a baby. But when he had broken off their engagement, it turned her dreams to dust. Then, her brother had passed away, and she had taken guardianship of the boys, and her dreams were tucked away, forgotten alongside the life she believed she would have.

Maybe it was time she got back into circulation. She had a reliable sitter down the street, several friends in town and knew her father would watch over the boys if she needed a sitter for the evening. A night out would do her good.

Feeling suddenly better about her prospects, Nicola headed for the kitchen and began making manicotti for dinner. Once she'd popped the casserole dish into the oven, she got out her laptop and did some paperwork, including wages and ordering for the following week. She called her friend Annie and arranged to meet her and Connie for a drink and a gossip catch-up on Friday night at O'Sullivan's and then puttered around the kitchen for a while. It was nearly six o'clock when she heard Kieran's voice.

"Got a minute?"

She turned on her heels, met his gaze, wiped her hands on a tea towel and nodded. A familiar surge of awareness swept through her blood. "Sure. Video game all done?"

He lingered by the doorway. "For now. Marco's hand was aching, so he's settled on the couch reading a book."

Her heart beat faster. "Thank you for doing this. I know your mother probably pressured you into it."

"A little," he admitted and grinned. "But she's a smart woman. Tell me something, do the boys spend much time together?"

She frowned. "Not a lot. Why?"

"Marco mentioned something about Johnny blaming him for their parents' accident," he said and came into the room. "But neither boy was on the boat that day, correct?"

Nicola nodded. "That's right. They both had head colds, and Miranda didn't want them out on the water. I don't understand why Johnny would say that."

Kieran's mouth thinned. "Well, a child's perspective on things is often relative to the impact it has on their situation. In Johnny's mind, he may have blocked out the fact that he was also ill…perhaps that's why he lays the blame on his brother."

"Poor Marco," Nicola said with a heavy heart. "He's been through so much. They both have."

"That's true. But children are also surprisingly resilient. And I'm sure they both know you love them very much and will keep them safe."

Nicola's eyes suddenly burned. "I'm trying. Although sometimes I feel like a complete failure as a parent. It's not easy."

He moved around the counter. "No. And certainly not alone. I remember one time that Tori and I—"

"That's your wife?" she asked, cutting him off.

"Ex-wife," he corrected.

"Sorry," she said quickly. "I didn't mean to interrupt. I just never knew her name." Nicola met his even gaze. "Can I ask you a question?"

"Sure."

"How long ago did you take off your wedding ring?"

His eyes widened, and he glanced down at his left hand. "A few months ago."

She didn't bother to hide her surprise. "But you've been divorced for over a year, right?"

"Yes."

A heavy lump formed in her throat. "You loved her that much?"

His glittering gaze was unwavering. "No."

"I don't understand why you—"

"It was because of my..." His words trailed off for a moment. "Because of Christian. It was about staying connected. Being a part of his life even though I hadn't seen him in over twelve months. It was a way of—"

"I understand," she said quickly and came around the counter. "I mean, I get it. That's why I stayed in this house with the boys—it was a way of feeling like Gino and Miranda were still a part of things."

He shrugged loosely. "Yeah. And it also helped avoid too much unwanted...attention."

Nicola's mouth widened in a smile. "From women?"

"I wasn't ready to start anything with anyone."

Her blood heated. "And now?"

"I think you know the answer to that."

She swallowed hard, watching him, feeling the intensity between them gather momentum. And as much as her body was screaming to say *yes*, logic intervened. "Casual sex isn't the answer."

"I don't know about that," he said and shrugged lightly. "It's never been my...thing. I don't have anything by way of comparison."

It was quite the admission. "I thought you wanted to screw around in college?" she asked, remembering his words from graduation day.

Color blotched his cheeks. "I said what I had to say that day."

"You mean, so I would hate you?"

"Exactly."

"It worked," she said flatly. "I've hated you for fifteen years. Part of me still does."

"And the other part?" he asked.

Nicola shrugged. "That's the part I'm trying not to think about. I'll get over it."

"Are you sure?"

"Positive," Nicola replied. "And there's way too much history between us to start something that has no chance of going anywhere."

"On the other hand," he said and took a few steps closer, "it might be fun."

"And complicated," she added. "Who needs that?"

He laughed softly. "You're probably right. And of course, if we did anything, we'd have to stay on the down low, considering my mother is hell-bent on matchmaking at the moment."

"If," she said and rolled the word around on her tongue. "It would *just* be about sex."

He was close now, barely inches away from her. "Of course. Friends with benefits."

"Except that we're not friends," she reminded him. "We're...*frenemies*."

He chuckled. "Is that a word?"

Nicola shrugged. "I think so. It still doesn't mean I'm going to sleep with you."

"Actually, sleeping would be against the rules," he said, his voice as seductive as a caress.

"Because that sounds too much like a relationship?"

"Exactly," he replied.

Nicola turned and faced him, her hip pressed against the counter, arms crossed, her breath barely making it out of her throat. "So, this hypothetical interaction would be solely about the physical. It wouldn't be confused by...feelings?"

He nodded, looking down at her, his blue eyes glittering and intense, and desire scorched through her blood, climbing over her skin, amplifying every sense she possessed. And Nicola realized she wasn't over him. She still wanted him. And perhaps he was right. Maybe a mindless, utterly sexual encounter with him was exactly what she needed to get him out of her thoughts, once and for all. Cathartic sex. Not quite revenge, even though the lines were a little blurred. Sex to exorcise the past. Sex to banish her humiliation and heartbreak.

"Okay," she said softly.

His gaze narrowed. "'Okay'?"

She shuddered out a breath, then smiled, tugging on one side of her bottom lip with her teeth. "Let's have an affair."

Chapter Five

Kieran was still thinking about Nicola's proposal forty-eight hours later.

An affair.

Sex without strings. Sex without an emotional commitment. Sex without expectations.

It was a new concept for him. He'd had a couple of lovers during college, but met Tori just after med school and hadn't been with anyone since his divorce. But what Nicola was proposing was something else. He should have agreed immediately. It's what he wanted, to purge any lingering feelings with hot, guilt-free sex. To kiss her beautiful mouth, to lose himself in her lovely curves and feel her beneath him. Yeah...he should have agreed then and there.

Instead, he'd bailed.

And two days later he had no logical reason for his reaction.

He was back at work, tending to a busload of tourists who had all eaten bad crab cakes at a shabby diner, and trying to not think about Nicola every minute of the day.

"Dr. O'Sullivan," one of the nurses said to him as

he walked from triage toward the nurse's station, "you have a phone call. Line six."

Kieran thanked her, grabbed the telephone and pressed the button. "O'Sullivan."

"We're heading to JoJo's for dinner," Liam said without introduction. "Mom's watching Jack for a couple of hours. Six o'clock."

"Why didn't you call my cell?"

"Because you would know it was me and then wouldn't pick up."

Kieran knew his brother was right. "Can't we go to the hotel instead?"

"No," Liam replied and chuckled. "My beautiful wife wants pizza. And what she wants, she gets. We need to talk about Mom's birthday party some more. So I'll see you there."

As he ended the call, Kieran silently cursed his brother. Liam could be damned annoying at times. His brother knew him well enough to figure out he wouldn't want to spend time at JoJo's.

He spent the remainder of the afternoon in the ER and, once his shift finished at five, he headed home, showered and changed and then drove into town.

JoJo's was busy, but Kieran found his brother and family at one of the booth tables and headed directly for them. He spotted a young waitress at a table and another by the bar. The place was busy, and he looked around for Nicola as he slipped into the booth and sat down. She might be at home with the boys.

There were curly fries and bread sticks in the middle of the table and a pitcher of beer, although Kayla was drinking club soda, since she was nursing. Liam had his arm around her. Kieran watched his brother and sister-in-law together and saw the love they had for one another, the kind of love he'd once believed he had with Tori.

Now it all felt like a lie. Tori had never really loved him. She'd wanted to get married, to settle down and have a family. At the time, Kieran did, too. Looking back, he couldn't believe how blind he'd been to the truth. Because it hadn't felt like love should. It was about timing, about being a certain age and having certain expectations.

"Everything okay?" Liam asked, frowning.

Kieran shrugged. "Yeah…fine."

"It will get easier," his brother said quietly, so that only he could hear. "And one day, you will be happy again."

"Maybe," he said and drank some beer. "So, have you heard from Sean lately?"

"Not much. I know he calls Mom every couple of weeks. He's hiding so he doesn't have to deal with Mom and Dad's divorce, not to mention Jonah's existence."

Kieran grimaced. "Being angry at Jonah isn't helpful. Even if he is an obnoxious jerk most of the time."

Liam laughed. "He's growing on me, though. And, since he's my wife's cousin, he's family on both sides, so I figure I have to make more of an effort."

"Things have certainly changed a lot in the last few years," Kieran said, glancing toward Kayla and then back at his brother. "I guess change is inevitable in life."

Liam grinned. "And sometimes you just have to let life happen."

Kieran's gaze instinctively flew toward the door leading to the kitchen. And, almost as though he had conjured her up from his thoughts, Nicola appeared in the doorway, looking out-of-this-world beautiful in a long-sleeved black dress that flared over her hips and showed off her curves. Her hair was loose, and she wore bright red lipstick. And boots. Shiny black boots that reached her knees. If he hadn't been sitting down, Kieran was certain he would have dropped like a stone.

"Wowser," Liam said and whistled softly. "Looks like someone's got a hot date."

Kieran scowled at his brother, saw that Liam was grinning and then cursed the stupidity of his reaction. "She can do what she likes."

"God, you're predictable," Liam said and raised his glass in Nicola's direction.

She saw them, gestured a greeting and then met Kieran's gaze for a long and excruciating moment. He held her stare, managed to remain impervious and waited until she turned and headed through the restaurant before he took a breath.

"Why don't we order?" he suggested and grabbed a menu.

"Friday night cocktails," Kayla said and grinned. "At O'Sullivans. It's an institution. She's meeting up with friends tonight."

Liam touched her shoulder lovingly. "Do you miss being part of the single-and-mingle crew?"

"Nah," she said and smiled. "I'd much rather hang out with you guys. Besides, we promised your mother we'd be back by eight thirty. And since neither of us can bear to be away from Jack for more than a couple of hours at a time, our late nights are over for some time."

Kieran remembered that feeling. When Christian was first born, he'd never liked letting him out of his sight. And although he was genuinely happy for his brother, watching Liam with Kayla and Jack amplified his regret and feelings of loss. But with time, it would get easier. It had to.

They ordered pizza, discussed his mother's up-coming birthday party and by eight they were done. Kieran waved them off and drove down the block toward O'Sullivan's. He spotted Nicola the moment he entered the bar. She was sitting alone at the end of the bar, legs crossed, the sexy boots heightening every raunchy thought he possessed. She was staring idly into a drink that looked untouched. He walked up and sat down on the stool beside her, saying nothing. She glanced sideways, quickly recognized that it was him, and a soft smile curved her lips.

He ordered a club soda, waited for it to arrive and then spoke. "You shouldn't drink alone."

"I'm not," she said, staring ahead. "My friend Annie has just gone to the bathroom. And Connie will be here soon. Girls' night out," she said pointedly.

Kieran ignored the dismissive tone and sipped his drink. "You look incredible."

"Thank you."

He turned in the stool. "Nice boots."

"Impractical," she said and touched the top of the leather as she met his gaze. "But they were one of those things that I just *had* to have. Have you ever experienced that? You know, when there is something you simply have to have…and nothing else matters."

Yes…

Kieran stared at her, swearing she had somehow swayed toward him because she seemed close. So close that the scent she wore traveled along every sense he possessed and made his libido jump. Her red lips were tantalizing, her boots a complete turn-on, her hair so beautiful he wanted to fist a handful of it and kiss her smooth neck.

"Right now?" He smiled fractionally. "Yeah."

She met his gaze. "So, what are you doing here?"

He shrugged. "Nightcap."

Her mouth curved in a slight smile. "Liar."

Kieran didn't bother to deny it. "I thought we should talk."

"You didn't want to talk the other night," she reminded him. "You couldn't leave quick enough."

"I was in shock," he admitted.

"And now?"

"I'm wondering what you meant."

"What I meant?" she echoed. "What do you think I meant?"

"That we should sleep together."

She grinned. "I thought sleeping was out of question? Just sex, remember...no strings."

Kieran's insides did a crazy flip. Just talking to her, just being close to her scrambled his brain and sent all his good sense rushing south. But if she was offering a no-strings, no-expectations relationship, then he wasn't stupid enough to refuse. But he wasn't quite convinced she'd go through with it. The Nicola he knew wasn't a casual-sex kind of woman. "Okay."

Her eyes widened, and she sat back on the stool. "Um...great. So, when do you want to...start?"

He shrugged loosely. "You can call the shots on this one, Nic," he said and slid off the stool. He grabbed a napkin, pulled a pen from his pocket and wrote down his cell number. "Call me when you want me."

Then he left, passing her friend Annie on the way out.

I've lost my mind.

That was all Nicola could think as she stared at the bold scrawl on the paper napkin now sitting in her palm.

Her heart rate churned. *Sex without strings.* Yeah... right.

"You were right," her friend Annie said as she slid onto the stool that he'd just vacated. "He's as hot as ever."

Mortified, Nicola shook her head. "That's not what I said."

Annie's long, light brown hair swayed and she grinned. "Sure, you did...maybe not in so many words, but I'm good at reading between the lines."

Nicola took a long sip of her wine. "I'm going to sleep with him," she announced and tilted her chin. "To get him out of my system once and for all."

Annie raised a cynical eyebrow. "Do you think that will do it?"

"Yes," she replied. "It will be cathartic."

"That's not all it will be," her friend said and winked. "Just don't do something foolish like fall in love with him again."

"I won't," Nicola assured her and smiled. "I hate him too much to fall in love with him."

As the words left her mouth, Nicola tasted the lie... because she didn't hate Kieran. Sure, she'd spent the best part of fifteen rage-filled years resenting him...but she wasn't that angry, self-absorbed teenager any longer. Time had helped heal the wound. And his kindness toward Marco had made her realize that he'd changed, too. He'd always been kind...despite how cruel he'd been to her when they'd broken up.

And he was clearly a wonderful doctor and cared for his patients. He was good with kids, too. She admired those qualities. Which didn't mean she still harbored feelings for him...but it didn't mean she hated him, either.

"Have you ever had sex just for fun?" Annie asked and grinned.

"Nope," Nicola replied.

"Good luck, then. Twenty bucks says you're back in love with him within two weeks."

Nicola laughed at her friend's ridiculous suggestion. She liked Annie, but the other woman was a pure romantic.

"In love with who?" another voice said from behind them.

Connie Bedford was smiling as she greeted them. Several years younger than Nicola and Annie, Connie had worked as Liam O'Sullivan's personal assistant for five years and for J.D. prior to that and was well acquainted with all the O'Sullivans.

"One guess," Annie replied and smiled broadly.

Connie laughed and took the stool beside her. "Do you need to see a doctor?" she asked, grinning.

"No... I need to find some new friends," Nicola said and laughed.

"You'd be lost without us," Annie said and grinned. "So, when are you going to do this?"

"Do what?" Connie asked quickly.

"Sleep with you-know-who," Annie supplied and gave a wicked laugh. "Of course, we all know where that's going to lead."

"To heartbreak," Connie said, as though it was inevitable.

"Gosh," Nicola said and gave a fake grin. "You two are so good for my ego and self-confidence."

Annie tapped her arm reassuringly. "We just want to make sure you don't get hurt."

"I won't," she assured her friend. "Whatever is going

on between me and Kieran, it's complicated. I don't expect anyone to understand."

Both women nodded, and Nicola knew she was being cryptic but couldn't explain her feelings toward Kieran any other way. They were wrapped up in memory and resentment and the need to purge all her lingering humiliation. And, yes, they were clearly still attracted to one another. Perhaps because they'd had such a public breakup, their connection was inevitable. Whatever the reason, Nicola was sure the only way to rid Kieran from her thoughts once and for all was to have a whole lot of hot and wild sex with him. Then so be it. It was the price she would have to pay.

She left not long after, tired of pretending to be out having a great time. Not that she didn't enjoy the company of her friends…she did, very much so. But she wasn't in the mood to discuss her complicated love life. Not that her friends didn't have problems. Annie didn't date because she was secretly in love with her boss, and Connie didn't date because she was focused on her career. Even so, Nicola didn't want her own complicated mess to be the main topic of conversation.

Her father was watching the boys, and she picked them up at nine o'clock. Johnny was happy to leave, and Marco dozed in the back seat on the drive home. Neither of them offered any resistance when they arrived home and were sent straight to bed. Once the kids were settled, Nicola changed her clothes and tossed the boots in the closet, remembering the way Kieran had looked at her wearing the ridiculously flirtatious heels. She'd purchased the boots on a foolish whim and had never worn them before, which meant she was paying the price with some mean-looking blisters on her heels. She made green tea, placed her laptop at the kitchen table and was about to settle in for an hour of doing wages and scheduling when her cell pinged. She checked the message immediately.

I thought I'd spend some time with Marco tomorrow. And Johnny, too, if he's interested. Okay? K.

Nicola's fingers tensed around the phone. She was grateful he was committing himself to the Big Brothers idea, but she couldn't help thinking that the more time he spent with her nephews, the more it would complicate their own ridiculous relationship. *Not* that they had a relationship. They didn't have anything. Just some silly flirting and the vague intimation that they wanted to sleep together. Still, her nephew's happiness came first. And she knew Marco would flourish under Kieran's guidance. And Johnny, too, if he would agree to it. She typed a response.

Sure. They'd like that.

She waited for the familiar ping. It took a couple of minutes, and she wondered if he was having the same kind of ethical crisis that she was.

See you tomorrow. Around 10. K.

Nicola replied immediately, arranging the time before placing the phone back on the table. She spent the next hour neck-deep in scheduling and wages, but her wayward thoughts constantly strayed, thinking about seeing Kieran the following day. She turned in around midnight and woke after seven, getting little more than a few hours' sleep, since Marco had had a bad dream in the middle of the night and she had been up and down trying to console him. Once the boys were out of bed and she had made breakfast, she informed Marco that Kieran was coming over. From that moment, her excited nephew remained on the porch waiting for him. Johnny didn't seem as interested, but shrugged and said he'd think about it.

Nicola didn't do anything as obvious as hanging around on the porch but instead spent the morning busying herself with laundry and housekeeping. She was in the kitchen, making up a batch of lasagna for later, when she heard her nephew speaking excitedly, firing out questions she knew might have made anyone else run a mile. But not Kieran—he was patient and kind and listened to Marco's suggestions without so much as a frustrated sigh. And suddenly she was jealous and wishing she possessed the same quiet endurance that he did. Most days, Nicola felt as though she was hanging on by a thread, trying to figure out parenting as she went along. But Kieran was a natural, so at ease and confident. And she envied that ability.

She was wiping her hands with paper towel when she heard him speak.

"Morning, Nic."

Nicola turned and spotted him in the doorway. In jeans, a pale blue polo shirt and his aviator jacket, he looked wholly masculine. His hair was mussed, like he'd just run a hand through it, and she noticed his jaw was clean-shaven. He looked so gorgeous that her knees almost gave way when he smiled. And suddenly she was seventeen again and hopelessly in love with him. Nicola took a long breath and willed away the images that bombarded her thoughts—Kieran kissing her gently at their special spot down by the river; Kieran dancing with her behind the barn at the O'Sullivan ranch; Kieran telling her she was the love of his life after they'd made love for the first time. The memories resurfaced with a vengeance, making a mockery of every ounce of rage in her heart. Because she could handle *wanting* him. Sex was one thing. But feelings—real ones—they were harder to explain away. And she didn't want to hang on to any lingering feelings she had for Kieran—that would be plain stupid.

"Hi," she managed to say. "Where's Marco?"

"Getting a pad and pencil," he replied and moved into the kitchen. "I had an idea I wanted to run by you."

She shrugged. "Sure."

"A pond," he said and came around the counter. "Like a fishpond in the backyard. I thought it could be a good project to get Marco interested in. And help with his fear of water."

Nicola stilled. "Oh… I guess. Although I'm not sure I can afford too much—"

He waved a dismissive hand. "I'll pay for it."

"I couldn't possibly accept—"

"No point in having all the O'Sullivan money if I can't put it to good use every now and then," he said and grinned, cutting her off again. "Right?"

"I'm not a charity case," she said, her back straightening, her pride bolstering. "And I have no intention of taking—"

"Oh, for god's sake, Nic," he said impatiently, cutting her off yet again. "Stop being so damned stubborn. I want to do this. Actually, I insist," he said pointedly.

"And you always get what you want?" she shot back.

His head tilted fractionally. "Not always. Time will tell, I suppose."

Nicola wasn't even going to try to touch that one. "You're so...so..."

"I'm back!"

Marco... Nicola was grateful her nephew had bounded into the room. As he began dragging Kieran outside, her irritation turned into an inexplicable sense of gratitude. Marco was happy. And that was all that mattered. Not her old resentment, her fears or her traitorous libido. She *could* compartmentalize her feelings for Kieran and make them only about sex.

She had to.

"I think it should go right here."

Kieran raised both eyebrows and shook his head. "I don't think your aunt would appreciate a fishpond right next to the vegetable garden, do you?"

The boy's mouth twisted. "I suppose not."

Kieran looked around the yard, ignoring the twitch in his gut when he thought about Nicola. He'd been outside for about five minutes, and it still wasn't enough time to forget about the way she wound him up. She always had. Even when they'd been dating, she'd always been fiercely independent. And she hadn't shed a tear the day they broke up—instead, her notorious temper had surfaced, calling him every name she could. Not that he hadn't deserved it. He had and probably still did.

But he was suddenly tired of the animosity. He didn't want to be at war with Nicola.

He wanted her in his bed.

Kieran shook off the thought and walked around the yard. It was neat, with a swing set in one corner and a garden shed in another. And several empty garden beds that looked as though they had once thrived. The stump of an old oak tree that had been turned into a bench sat near the fence line.

"My dad made that seat for my mom," Marco said, bottom lip wobbling. "But I don't remember much about it. I miss them a lot."

"I know you do."

"But I think Johnny misses them more than me."

Kieran kept walking. "You do? Why?"

"Because he never talks about them."

The boy's logic was spot-on. It was why Kieran never spoke about Christian. Because it was too hard. Too painful. He looked up to the second story and spotted Johnny standing in the one of the windows, staring down at them and scowling before he turned away and disappeared.

"Do you think your brother might want to help out with the fishpond?"

Marco shrugged. "Dunno. He doesn't do much except play video games. He plays them even more than me."

Kieran grinned. "If it's okay with you, how about we ask him?"

Marco considered the idea, his expression suddenly serious. "I guess. As long as he's not mean to me."

"I'm sure he won't be," Kieran assured him as they reached the step by the small back porch.

Nicola was by the door, watching them, wearing a long dress that floated over her curves. Her hair was down, and her face was free of makeup. She looked young and as pretty as hell.

"So, what's the verdict?" she asked, stepping toward the edge of the porch and leaning on the balustrade. "Doable?"

"I think so," he replied. "We just have to pick the right spot."

She pointed toward an old, staggered flower bed. "Over there."

He nodded. "Sure. The ground isn't level, so it will need a bit of work, but I think it's as good a spot as any."

Her mouth curled at the edges. "Can it have a fountain?"

Kieran half smiled. "It can have anything you want."

She came down the steps. "And a sculpture?"

He expelled a breath. "Uh…sure."

The scent of her fragrance assailed his senses, and he instinctively took a step back, putting space between them. Last night, they'd talked about sex…about giving in to the desire that was clearly still between them. But today…today wasn't about that. Today was about friendship. About a connection deeper than simple sex. Not that sex was simple, either. Nothing was simple when it came to Nicola.

"And maybe it could have a light…you know, that would stay on in the evenings."

His simple fishpond idea was taking on a life of its own. "Okay… I might need to take a quick class at fishpond design school."

She laughed, and the sound hit him directly in the solar plexus. "Sorry, I'm getting carried away."

"Don't apologize," he said and passed her the notepad and pencil. "Sketch."

She shook her head. "You know I can't draw."

He did. "Just put down your ideas."

She sighed. "If you're sure…"

"Positive," he replied.

She sat down on a small garden bench by the steps and sketched for a few minutes, Marco hovering over her every stroke. They looked alike, he realized, and Kieran suddenly had a vision of Nicola with a child of her own, a girl with dancing eyes and curly dark hair. The idea hit him with the force of a freight train. Back when they'd dated, he'd been super careful about birth control, determined not to get her pregnant when they were so young. He pushed the thought away, refusing to imagine how beautiful she would look with a child growing in her belly.

His child...

"Are you okay?"

Nicola's voice, jerking him from his foolish trance. "Yes, of course."

She got up and passed him the sketch pad. "You're right," he said and grinned. "You can't draw."

Marco began to laugh, and Nicola waved her hands. "Okay, you two, stop making fun."

Kieran fought the urge to grasp her hand and pull her close because, in that moment, she was eminently kissable. His palms itched, and he quickly pushed the idea away.

"So," he said, looking at the sketch. "You want a pond, and a waterfall with a statue that looks like a tuna fish and—"

"That's a man and a woman embracing," she said indignantly and stepped closer, tracing a finger along the line of the sketch. Then she spoke softly. "See, that's the outline of the woman's..."

Kieran met her gaze, watched as her eyes widened, and her lips parted fractionally. The awareness between them ramped up a notch. And then another. He stared at her mouth, fought the overwhelming urge to kiss her. Of course, he wouldn't. Not with Marco standing close by.

"I know what it is," he said, his voice so quiet she

actually moved closer. She shivered, and he reacted instinctively, shrugging out of his jacket and draping it around her shoulders.

She protested immediately. "I couldn't possibly—"

"Keep it," he insisted, ignoring how the brisk morning air immediately etched into his bones. "So... I think I'm going to need some help with this pond."

She frowned. "What kind of help?"

He shrugged. "The professional kind."

"Meaning?"

Kieran pulled his cell from his pocket, scrolled through the saved numbers and found the one he wanted. His call was answered on the fourth ring. "Are you busy?" he asked.

"Not exactly. Why?"

"Feel like helping out your favorite brother?"

More silence. "I guess."

He rattled off Nicola's address, ended the call and then turned back to face her.

"Who was that?"

"Jonah," he supplied and saw her eyes widen. "He's in town for the weekend, visiting his mother. If you want the best job done, get the best person for the job."

She glanced toward Marco and nodded. "I think that's exactly why your mom suggested you spend time with my nephew."

"My mother is a smart woman," he said quietly. "So are you."

"With foolish inclinations," she said softly and pulled his coat tightly around her waist.

"I guess chemistry can be damned inconvenient."

"*You're* inconvenient," she said and smiled fractionally and then, when Marco wandered off for a moment, spoke again. "I've spent so long hating you...the thought of anything else is exhausting."

"The thought of us being lovers, you mean?"

He watched, fascinated, as color flooded up her neck and spotted her cheeks. Nicola was an independent, modern woman, but there were elements of her that were delightfully naive.

She shrugged a little. "I thought you'd forgotten about that."

"Forgotten?" he echoed and smiled. "We only talked about it last night. Since then it's pretty much all I can think about."

"Me, too," she admitted and sauntered off toward her nephew, hips swaying, her beautiful hair flowing in the breeze.

Suddenly he felt about seventeen years old.

And as much in love with Nicola Radici as he'd ever been.

Chapter Six

Nicola had met Jonah Rickard a few times. He was handsome and serious-looking. True, all the O'Sullivan brothers were attractive, but she'd always considered Kieran the handsomest of the group.

Love is blind...

She shuffled the thought from her head. She wasn't some giddy teenager anymore. And, sure, she suspected they were heading toward a night in bed together, but she wasn't foolish enough to think it was anything more than a kind of sexual exorcism.

Watching the brothers walk around her garden, with Marco hanging on their every word, she saw the similarities. Even though Jonah had darker hair, they shared the same walk, the same broad shoulders and many of the same mannerisms. Which was odd since they hadn't grown up together, but DNA was a strange thing. She knew Jonah was a successful architect—actually, he was an award-winning architect, one of the best in his field. She wondered what he must be thinking as his brother led him around the backyard. Nicola joined them after a while, listening as Kieran explained what she wanted.

Jonah had the sketchpad in his hand and stared at the page, turning it around a couple of times. "So, you want a statue and a waterfall?" He looked toward his brother. "In the shape of a tuna fish?"

"It's a man and a woman," Nicola said and rolled her eyes. "Embracing."

Jonah frowned. "Really?"

Kieran laughed, and she scowled instantly. "When you two have finished making fun, I'll be in the inside. I have work to do."

She left them and headed inside. She made a couple of phone calls, paid a few accounts for the restaurant and spent some time working on the menu for an upcoming event. She was closing down the laptop when there was a knock at the front door. She walked down the hall, opened up and found Connie on the other side of the screen door. She'd forgotten that her friend was dropping by with a stack of flyers promoting the upcoming rodeo. She'd promised to give them out to customers who came to JoJo's.

"Sorry I'm late," Connie said as she crossed the threshold.

"You're late?" Nicola said, checking her watch and grinning because Connie was the most organized person she knew and was never late for anything.

"I had a mishap with Mr. Jangles and the cat next door," she explained.

Mr. Jangles was one of Connie's many dogs. Her friend had a collection of strays and lived alone with them in the house that had once belonged to her grandparents. "Nothing serious I hope?"

"No," she replied and grinned. "There are a couple of cars out front. Are you having a party?"

Nicola laughed and ushered her friend through the

hall and into the kitchen. "I'm guardian to two young boys...my partying days are over. Kieran's here."

"I see," Connie said, chuckling, and she dumped the bag she was carrying on the counter. "Then I won't stay and be a third wheel."

"Fourth wheel," Nicola said and grabbed a few coffee mugs. "Jonah's here, too. The Big Brothers thing I told you about, remember?"

"I didn't realize that...that *he* was a part of that."

"*He's* not," Nicola replied, sensing that the last place Connie wanted to be was in her kitchen, since she knew her friend didn't like Jonah Rickard one iota. She didn't know much about it because Connie was an intensely private person, but it had something to do with Connie's loyalty toward the O'Sullivans and Jonah's apparent determination to hate his father, J.D. "Kieran is working on a project with Marco and needed a favor. If you're quick, you might be able to sneak away unseen."

"Good idea," she said and was just about to leave when they heard Kieran's voice.

"Hey, Connie."

When both men came through the door with Marco in their wake, the air suddenly became loaded with tension. Oh, yeah—there was so much tension between Connie and Jonah it was impossible to miss. Thankfully, it was Jonah who said he had to leave. He offered a quick goodbye to Nicola and then walked from the room. Kieran followed and, once they were out of view, Nicola hovered in the doorway, hearing their voices travel down the hallway.

"I'll talk to you later in the week," Kieran said casually.

"Sure," Jonah replied. "Oh, and next time you want a

favor, don't hide behind a story about some Big Brothers thing. Just admit that it's about a girl."

She heard the door open and close and then shuffled back behind the counter.

When Kieran returned, he was smiling. "He's such a pleasure to be around, don't you think?"

Nicola grinned. "At least he made the effort."

"He's one of those people that grows on you over time," he said, still smiling.

"Like a fungus," Connie said and then gasped. "Uh... sorry. I shouldn't have said that. I should get going. I have a load of laundry waiting for me, four pooches that need washing, and my favorite Jane Austen to read."

She was gone within a minute and, by the time Nicola returned to the kitchen after seeing her friend to the door, only Kieran remained in the room. Marco had clearly grown tired of the adult conversation and had disappeared upstairs.

"That was weird," Nicola said and took the coffee mug Kieran had poured. "Connie usually likes everyone. Your brother is obviously the exception."

"I don't think he cares whether he's liked or not. But he did agree to help out."

She nodded. "That's good of him, considering. I heard his comment, by the way. The one about why you're doing this."

"I'm doing this for Marco," he assured her. "The you-and-me thing...that's a separate issue."

"I know that. Believe me, I'm trying to compartmentalize whatever is going on here."

"How's that working out so far?" he asked and rested his rear against the counter.

She chuckled. "I'm trying to keep things real. The boys have to come first, and I don't want to get swept up in…anything that will distract me from being the best parent I can be to them. They've had enough drama in the last couple of years. And I owe that to Gino and Miranda."

"Is that why you stayed in this house?" he asked quietly.

Nicola met his gaze. "I wanted to keep things the same."

"Except that things aren't the same," he remarked.

Her back straightened, and a surge of resentment curled up her spine. "This house is filled with the memory of all they had."

"Or all they've lost."

Nicola moved around the counter and planted her hands on her hips. "Do you have an opinion about everything?"

"Pretty much."

She expelled a heavy breath. "I'm doing the best I can."

"I'm not criticizing you."

"Sure seems like it."

He reached out and cupped her cheek, trailing his thumb along her jaw. "I think you're doing an amazing job, Nic."

Her bones liquefied. Most of the time, Nicola felt like a complete failure. "Sometimes…it's so…so very…"

"I know," he said quietly, his voice suddenly like a tonic. "Being a parent can be hard work. But I think that, one day, you'll look back and realize that this will be the most important thing you have ever done."

Heat burned her eyes. "Thank you."

His gaze was blisteringly intense. "I guess you feel like you're all alone in this?"

"Mostly," she admitted and pulled away. He dropped

his hand, and she suddenly missed his warm touch. "My father's getting older, and Vince is in San Francisco... I have good friends, though, who are very supportive."

He didn't move; he simply kept their visual connection locked. "One day you'll find someone to share this with."

Nicola swallowed hard. "I'm not so sure. Taking on two kids is a big commitment for anyone. I know that Carl couldn't have done it."

His expression narrowed. "That's your ex?"

She nodded. "He wasn't ready for commitment with me, even though he'd proposed and I had said yes. The truth is, he was still hung up on his ex-wife. But we were already over by the time Gino and Miranda died. He sent me a card offering condolences, and that's the last I heard from him."

"So, he did you a favor," Kieran said quietly. "He refused to marry someone he wasn't one hundred percent in love with. Believe me, you don't want to be married to someone who isn't in love with you—no good can come of it."

"Like your ex-wife?"

He drew in a breath. "She wanted a husband...and a certain kind of life. And I made it easy for her, I guess. Tori was attractive and smart and marriage material, if that makes sense. And I was never very good at being single."

Nicola realized that they were now directly in front of one another.

"What happened to your plans for college? All that screwing around? All those girls?"

He shrugged. "Like I said before, there were fewer than you think. I only said that to—"

"To make me hate you?" she said. "Yes, I know. It worked."

"And now?" he asked.

She looked up, saw desire in his eyes and couldn't deny what they were now both thinking. Both wanting. Both needing. "Kieran… I… I want…"

"I know," he said softly, moving closer as his hand curved around her nape. "Nic," he said her name softly, almost on a whisper. "Can you find a sitter for tonight?"

"A sitter?" she whispered, mesmerized by his gentle touch, seduced by his voice because she knew exactly what he was asking. "Tonight…no. The lady down the street is away visiting her daughter in Boise until Monday. Dad goes to the home to see my grandmother every Saturday evening. And Annie is—"

"Tomorrow night?"

She could barely concentrate with the way his fingertips were caressing her skin. "Yes."

He was so close they could have easily kissed, but he didn't kiss her…he stared at her, his gaze searing, scorching her right through to her bones. She heard a noise, like footsteps on the stairs, and then quickly pulled away, putting space between them.

"I'm back!"

Marco's exuberant voice quickly defused the heat building between them, and Nicola moved back around the counter. While Kieran and her nephew sat at the table and looked over the fishpond plans, she got busy preparing an early lunch, and Marco quickly invited Kieran to join them.

"Are you sure?" Kieran asked Nicola.

She nodded vaguely. "Of course."

Nicola spent the next twenty minutes making a pile of sandwiches, pouring a pitcher of orange juice and putting on a fresh pot of coffee. When she was done, she instructed Marco to get his brother and then she set the table.

"Marco's excited about the pond," she said as she moved around the room and collected plates. "No mention of the water, either."

"No," Kieran said quietly. "He's all about the fish at the moment. I spoke to Liam about maybe taking the boys down to the jetty at his place by the river for a fishing expedition. Marco would be perfectly safe, and it might help with his fear of water. As long as you're okay with it, of course. And you'd be very welcome to come, too."

She nodded. "Yes, okay. I think that's a great idea." She sighed. "You know, you're so good with kids I almost envy you."

He smiled, and her insides tightened. "You're good with them, Nic," he assured her. "Don't ever doubt that."

The boys came into the kitchen, interrupting their conversation. Marco was beaming, but Johnny looked sullen and as though he wanted to be somewhere else. Once they were seated, she knew why.

"Can I go to my friend's house?" he asked, tearing the unwanted crust off his sandwich.

"Which friend?" she enquired.

He rattled off the name, but it was not one she recognized. "Do you have his mom's or dad's cell number?"

Johnny shook his head. "He only lives in the next street."

"No number, no visit. You know the rules."

He grunted. "Typical."

"Johnny, you know I can't allow you to visit with someone I don't know.'

There were more grunts. "I'm not hungry."

Nicola expelled an exasperated sigh, and her gaze flashed toward Kieran. He nodded slightly, as though he was agreeing with her, and it made her resolve stronger. And less alone than she'd felt in over eighteen months.

"If you can get the number, we'll discuss it. So, how about we all eat?"

"Good idea," Kieran said and grabbed a plate.

As they ate, it occurred to Nicola how absurdly normal it all seemed. Johnny grumbled his way through most of the meal, but Marco was cheerful, and Kieran entertained them with tales of his antics when he and his brothers were young. He mentioned the fishing trip idea and both boys seemed keen, though Marco was a bit more hesitant than his brother. Afterward, the kids disappeared into the yard to play, and Kieran remained to help her clean up.

"No work today?" she asked as he handed her a couple of plates.

"Back Tuesday," he explained. "Night shift until the end of the week."

She made a face. "How are you enjoying working at the hospital?"

He shrugged. "It's good. The staff are all highly competent, and the facilities are very—"

"That's not what I meant," she said and shoved him playfully, her fingertips coming into contact with rock hard forearm muscle. "I meant how are you *feeling* being there."

"Feeling?" he echoed.

"Regrets?" she asked. "Do you miss Sioux Falls? You must have had a lot of friends there and miss them."

"Like you miss San Francisco?"

"I do," she admitted and sighed. "Well, I miss some things. I miss my friends, of course. And I miss my career. And I miss Vince. I mean, he calls every week to touch base, but it's not the same as having a big brother on hand to talk things through. You've got siblings, so you know what I mean."

His mouth twitched. "Yeah, but we don't sit around talking about feelings all the time."

"But you and Liam are close?"

He nodded. "Sure. But we've had to work at it. He can be an arrogant and opinionated jerk when he wants to. Sean lives his own life in the fast lane, which is not my scene. And Jonah...well, the jury's still out on that one."

"You were close to Liz?"

She watched, fascinated as he swallowed hard. Finally, he nodded and spoke. "Yes, we were good friends as well as brother and sister."

Nicola's skin warmed with memories. "We were dating the same time she was going out with Grady. We used to say we'd be bridesmaids at each other's wedding."

He met her gaze. "But you didn't go to their wedding," he reminded her. "You were in San Francisco by then."

"We'd broken up, and the wounds were still too raw," she admitted. "But Liz understood."

"Yeah," he said and smiled. "She would. Sometimes...sometimes I miss her so much I can barely stand being in my own skin. That's the thing about loss: it never really goes away. In my job, I deal with other people's loss all the time. It's only when you get hit with it yourself that you can understand how it truly feels. Losing my sister and then my son...it gave me a different perspective. It made me want to be a better doctor," he said softly. "And a better man."

Nicola instinctively reached up and laid a hand on his shoulder. "Well, you've succeeded."

Kieran stared at her, focused solely on her upturned face and the understanding in her expression.

"Thank you," he said and covered her hand, entwining it with his own. "I don't think I've ever admitted that to anyone before. And it's probably much more than I deserve from you."

She shrugged loosely. "We all have to let go of the past at some point."

"If we want to have a future, you mean?"

"Something like that," she replied and sighed. "At the moment, I would just settle for a *now*."

"Me, too," he said and raised her hand, pressing his mouth briefly to her knuckles. He felt her shiver, noticed the way her pupils darkened, and she bit down on her lower lip. "Since the boys are right outside and it's daytime, would it be inappropriate to say that I want to make love to you?"

Just mentioning it sent his body into overdrive. But everything about her assailed him—her skin, her hair, the scent that was uniquely hers. Pure Nicola. The one woman he had never been able to forget.

"Yes," she said and smiled. "But I want that, too. I want to get you out of my system once and for all."

It was a nice idea. But not one he was sure would work. "What if it backfires?"

"It won't," she said firmly. "I've *been* in love with you. I've had my heart broken by you. And I've been out of love with you. It's not a pattern I plan on repeating."

The raw honesty in her words rocked him to the core. "So, you think that we can successfully have a no-strings relationship, even with our history?"

"Yes," she insisted. "I think we can. I think we should. Actually, I think it's inevitable."

Kieran's libido stirred again. "So, tomorrow night?" She nodded. "Yes."

"Uh…would you like to go to dinner first?"

"No," she replied. "It's not a date. We're not dating. We're having sex."

It sounded cut-and-dried. Almost like a business deal. He should have been jumping through hoops at the idea. But oddly, he wasn't. "Okay. My place. Seven o'clock?"

She nodded and pulled her hand free. "Sure. And thank you for spending time with Marco today. It's very kind of you."

He shrugged, faintly embarrassed. "No problem. I'll keep you posted on the pond plans. Once the work starts, I'll make sure it happens around your schedule at the restaurant."

"Thank you. I'll see you tomorrow."

"Do you need my address?"

She shook her head. "I know where you live. It used to be Kayla's apartment. So, see you then."

It was his cue to leave, and he did so quickly after saying a brief goodbye to the boys. Once he was in his car and down the street, Kieran headed into town, keen to shake off the memory of the past few hours. Knowing Liam would be working, he headed directly for the hotel and discovered his brother barking out orders by the concierge desk.

"Busy morning?" he asked, seeing his brother's frustration.

"Overbooked for the rodeo weekend," Liam said, flipping his cell into his pocket. They headed upstairs to his office. "Damned computer glitch. I now have four very unhappy customers."

"I'm sure you'll smooth it over."

"Of course," Liam replied. "I'd just rather not have to. Since Jack was born, I've spent more time at home than I have here…and it shows. And poor Connie is taking the brunt of my bad mood."

Kieran grinned. Whatever his brother's faults, honesty was at the top of the list. When they reached his office, Liam grabbed a couple of beers from the bar fridge. "Maybe you need to share the load a bit," Kieran suggested. "Find a manager to fill in when you're not here."

"The duty manager resigned last month, and I haven't replaced her."

"I'm not talking about a duty manager," Kieran said and slapped his shoulder. "I'm talking about a partner, a comanager, someone who can take the reins equally."

Liam's gaze narrowed. "Like who?"

Kieran shrugged. "I don't know…maybe you should give Connie a promotion. She's certainly earned it after being your PA for five years."

His brother frowned. "I'm not bad to work for. But you're right about Connie. Frankly, I don't know what I'd do without her."

"Be an even more bad-tempered boss."

Liam laughed. "Probably. But I'll think about your suggestion. So, how's the Big Brothers thing going?"

He shrugged again. "Okay, I guess. Marco's a good kid."

"And his aunt?"

"She's not part of the program."

Liam's mouth twisted. "Jonah said you were landscaping her garden. I wasn't sure if it was meant to be a metaphor…or whether you had developed a sudden interest in horticulture."

Kieran scowled. "News sure does travel fast. Since when have you and Jonah spent time sharing chitchat?"

"He's learning to share," Liam said, grinning. "Dissing his brother is a place to start. So, about Mom's birthday party next Saturday…are you bringing a date?"

"A date?"

"My wife is trying to finalize numbers for the catering."

Kieran drank some beer. "Then, no."

Liam dropped onto the sofa. "Coward."

"Is there a point to this question?"

"Nicola," Liam said flatly.

"Nicola's not interested in dating me," he said and wandered to the window, looking out down the street, which was unusually busy for a Saturday afternoon. "And frankly, I'm not ready to date anyone seriously."

"Bull," Liam interjected. "You've been divorced for over a year. That's long enough to—"

"You ever been divorced?" Kieran asked, harsher than usual as he turned back to face his brother. "Ever had your heart ripped out by the person who's supposed to love you the most?"

Liam looked instantly somber. "No. But I was only trying—"

"I know what you're trying to do," Kieran said, cutting him off. "And I appreciate your concern. But I have to do things in my own time. And with Nic…things are complicated."

Liam shrugged one shoulder. "You have a lot of history, so that's understandable. But sometimes history repeats itself."

Kieran looked at his brother and half smiled. "I think

getting married and having a baby has turned your brain to mush."

"Probably," Liam said agreeably. "I never imagined I could love another human being the way I love Kayla and my son."

"I understand."

"Sorry," Liam said quickly. "I didn't mean to remind you of—"

"It's okay," Kieran said and waved a hand. "Time makes things easier. And Christian is where he needs to be—with his parents. I'm grateful for the time I had with him but, at the end of the day, I'm not his father, and nothing will change that. If finding out about Jonah has shown me anything, it's that the truth is always best brought out in the open. Just think, if we'd known about our brother thirty years ago, our family would probably look very different now."

"Maybe," Liam agreed. "At the very least, we would have grown up knowing our brother."

"And perhaps he wouldn't hate J.D. as much as he does."

"Love and hate," Liam mused. "There's a fine line between them sometimes."

Kieran smiled. "You're getting philosophical in your old age."

"I'm just not prepared to waste time holding on to wasteful emotions. Or avoiding the hard stuff." Liam met his gaze. "Maybe you should try that yourself."

"I'm not ready."

"For what? A relationship? Commitment?"

"To…risk," he admitted, placing his beer on the desk. Kieran appreciated his brother's support, but Liam knew nothing about real loss. He had the woman he loved and a son that was his own. And nothing would change that. "I can't go there...not yet."

"One day, maybe?" Liam asked.

He shrugged again. "I don't know. The truth is, I haven't been involved with anyone since Tori left."

"Understandable," Liam said. "But you left Sioux Falls to start a new life, right?"

"Sure."

"So, there's nothing in your way. And Nicola is—"

"Nicola is no more interested in a serious relationship than I am. She has her nephews to think about, the restaurant, and her father is getting older. Whatever is still between us, it's just a...physical thing."

Liam grinned. "It's a place to start."

"With the potential to end badly," Kieran said, eyebrows raised.

Liam laughed. "Since when did you become such a defeatist?"

"Since my wife left me for my best friend and I found out that my son wasn't actually my son," he said, hating the way the words made him ache inside. "I don't want to hurt Nicola any more than I already have in the past. And I don't want her nephews getting too attached to me. And I don't want that for myself, either."

Liam nodded. "I get it, you know. I understand that you don't want to get close to the kids in case it doesn't work out between you and Nicola."

"It's not going to work out," he said firmly. "Nic and I are not together. We're not dating. We're just...skirting around the edges of one another."

Which meant one thing...like it or not, making love with her was out of the question.

So much for his date tomorrow night.

Chapter Seven

Nicola pulled clothes out of her dresser and realized one depressing fact—she owned not one piece of sexy underwear. And since it was Sunday afternoon, she had no chance of purchasing any unless she took the forty-minute drive to Rapid City and back. The one store in Cedar River that sold lingerie was closed Sundays. Even if it weren't, stocking up on sexy undergarments there would only set tongues wagging. She was well-known around town—as was her single status. And given that she was now guardian to a pair of young boys, hanging her reputation out to dry wasn't in the cards. Nicola didn't want her love life to be the topic of conversation for anyone.

Not that she was in any way, shape or form *in love* with Kieran O'Sullivan.

It was simply a sexual memory that had somehow been rekindled and needed to be sated. End of story. They'd have sex, and then it would be over. They were both adult enough to see that it stayed that way. Sex for pleasure. A roll in the hay. A one-night stand at best.

But as she showered and dressed in a knee-length blue dress and paler blue cardigan, Nicola felt some of her resolve slipping. She did her hair and makeup and by six was hustling the boys into the car and dropping them at her father's place for a sleepover, promising she'd be at the restaurant first thing in the morning to take them both to school. Marco was his usual curious self, but Johnny was even more sullen than usual, grunting a few responses when she said good-night, and she watched them flop onto the small sofa in the living room.

"I'll see you in the morning, Papa," she said and kissed her father's cheek. "Thank you for watching them."

Salvatore grinned. "They are my only grandchildren. I love to watch them. Now, go on your date and have a nice time," he said and winked.

"It's not a date," she insisted. "I'm just going to see a friend."

Her father shrugged and shooed her through the doorway. "Then go, or you'll be late."

She lingered by the door and then wasted time checking a few things in the restaurant before she finally made it to her car and headed down Main Street. She was a hundred yards from his driveway when she considered driving straight past and going home.

Coward...

You wanted this. You suggested it. You know it's the only way to be free of him.

Nicola pulled up outside the large Victorian and noticed that the place was lit up like a Christmas tree. She got out, locked the car and headed up the garden path. She'd been in the house several times when Kayla had occupied the second-floor apartment and had always admired the long, shuttered windows and wide veranda. There was a gazebo out back in a huge yard, and she followed the trail of lights that lit up the pathway, before entering around the side and heading upstairs. She reached the second floor a few moments later and was about to knock when the door opened, and Kieran stood in front of her. In jeans and a black shirt opened at the collar, he looked wholly masculine, and her heart skipped a beat. His hair was damp and he was clean-shaven, and she picked up the scent of some kind of citrusy cologne that wreaked havoc with her senses.

He was too damned sexy for his own good.

"Hey," he said and stepped aside to let her pass.

"I'm here," she announced and walked down the short hallway.

"So I see."

"I almost bailed," she admitted and turned on her heels when she reached the living area.

Kieran followed her footsteps. "So, why didn't you?"

She shrugged. "Because ignoring this thing between us won't make it go away."

"True," he said and moved into the kitchen area. "But if you have doubts…"

"I don't," she assured him, feeling her resolve waver but determined to go ahead with their plans. "Do you?"

"Absolutely."

"So, you've changed your mind? You don't want me?"

"Of course I want you," he said quickly. "I just don't want us to do something either of us will regret."

"I don't believe in regrets," she said flippantly. "At least, not for tonight."

"So, sex for pleasure and no strings?"

"Exactly. I don't want or expect anything from you or…*this*."

"Women generally think about sex differently than men," he remarked.

"Well, we're clearly thinking about it differently right now."

He made an impatient sound. "I just want to be clear about the boundaries here, Nic. It's easy to spout words like *no strings* or *casual sex*…but I don't want to mislead or put either of us at risk."

"There's no risk," she said. "So your conscience is safe. I have no intention of rekindling any old feelings I had for you. Not ever."

He took a moment to respond. "Okay."

Nicola stared at him, watching as he uncorked a wine bottle and poured two glasses. She saw a couple of pots on the stovetop and could smell something delicious in the air.

"Did you cook?"

"No," he replied and came around the counter to pass her a wineglass. "I ordered from the restaurant at the hotel. The chef prepared something, which I'm heating up."

"Abby did takeout?" she asked, making it clear that she knew the chef by her first name. Abby was Paris-trained and had been to JoJo's several times with her young son.

"Being an O'Sullivan has its perks."

"Obviously."

He grinned. "No need to feel threatened. Nothing beats your cooking."

She met his gaze, felt the intention of his words down deep into her bones. "Stop flirting," she said and moved to the window, staring out toward the street for a moment. "We weren't doing dinner, remember? This isn't a date."

He didn't move and inch. "I know it's not a date. But since it's dinnertime, we both need to eat at some point. Don't get all worked up about it."

Her back straightened. "I'm not worked up."

His eyes darkened. "Not yet, at least."

The innuendo was not missed. "I guess that depends on how much you've learned in the last fifteen years."

He laughed, and the sexy sound reverberated down her spine. "I guess time will tell."

Nicola sipped her wine. "Such modesty."

He shrugged and moved around the couch. "Tell me why *you* almost bailed?"

"Because I've never done this before," she admitted. "This?"

"You know, had a one-night… A casual…" Her words trailed off, and she lifted her shoulders. "I'm not much of a party girl. I've only had three lovers in my life…you, my college boyfriend and my fiancé. It's a low number for a dance card, I suppose, but casual sex has never interested me."

"Me, either," he said quietly. "But for the record, your dance card stays the same."

"Yes, I guess it does. So, since your divorce you haven't…" She didn't finish the sentence. She didn't have to. They both knew what she meant.

"No," he replied and drank some wine.

Nicola stared at him, consumed by the burning intensity in his gaze. "Why not?"

"Because I'm not wired that way," he said quietly. "I'm not like my brothers. Sean has a revolving door on his bedroom, and Liam wasn't much better before he met Kayla. But that kind of life has never interested me."

Even though she knew they weren't heading toward

any kind of future, Nicola was pleased to hear he hadn't been bed-hopping since his divorce. Even back in high school, when they'd been dating and completely in love with one another, the idea of being with anyone else was out of the question. And back then, girls clamored for the attention of all the O'Sullivan boys, particularly Kieran with his quiet, charming appeal. But Kieran had been hers…wholly and completely. Which was why his callous words on graduation day had cut so deep. Being lovers, being faithful to one another, had meant everything to her. It was as though they were in a kind of couple bubble, impervious to anyone or anything. But their breakup showed another side of him—one that had blatant disregard for the deep feelings and love they had shared for nearly three years. And it hurt. In her heart, it still did.

"How long do you think you'll stay here?" she asked, shifting her thoughts.

"I'm not sure," he replied. "My mother wants me to move back to the ranch. Since J.D. moved out, it's pretty quiet out there."

"Are you tempted?"

"A little. I'm happier staying close to the hospital for the moment. But it was great growing up on the ranch. There's something soothing about wide-open spaces."

"I wouldn't know," she mused. "I spent my childhood living above the restaurant and then sharing a dorm room at college before I moved into my apartment in San Francisco. But I remember spending time at the ranch when we were young. I remember the loft in the barn."

"Me, too," he said. "We had some fun times in that loft. But the ranch is too big for a just a couple of people. It needs a family in it. Liam's not interested in living there, since he and Kayla have that big house down by the river. I don't know, maybe she should sell the place and start afresh."

Nicola sighed. "She and your dad were married a long time—it would be hard to let go completely."

"For sure, but divorce changes everything. And Dad is spending time working on his relationship with Jonah—which I think he should do—but that means he's not quite as alone as my mom. The whole situation is confusing and complex."

"Like most families," she added. "Spend a day in mine. My father is sad all the time, my brother won't come back to Cedar River because he blames himself for Gino's death and I'm trying to be the glue that keeps it all together."

"You think Vince blames himself?"

She nodded. "Vince insisted Gino and Miranda go sailing, even though she wanted to stay at the apartment because both the boys weren't feeling well. He said the boys would be fine. And then Gino and Miranda died. Instant self-blame."

"That's got to be tough," Kieran said and moved into the kitchen. "I mean, it was an accident."

"I know," she replied. "But loving someone takes all the logic out of things, doesn't it?"

He half smiled. "Yeah, it sure does."

Nicola felt the edge to his words and thought about all he had lost—his wife, his son and his sister all in the space of a few short years. "Do you miss being married?"

"Yes," he replied and smiled. "I was good at it."

"I'm sure you were. Maybe you'll get married again one day."

He shrugged a little. "Maybe. But next time I'll

choose someone who is actually in love with me and doesn't prefer my best friend."

She shuddered. "I can't imagine how hard that was. I mean, Carl and I broke up because he still had feelings for his ex-wife…but he was honest about it once we'd become engaged and once he knew he still had those feelings. But the idea of lying to someone so blatantly like she did to you…it's difficult to comprehend."

"I don't think it was intentional," he said quietly. "I don't think either of them deliberately set out to fall in love and have an affair. Phil was living with someone… Tori and I were married…and we were all friends. Nothing seemed off-kilter until the day I caught them in bed together."

Nicola gasped. "You found them together. Wow, how awful."

He laughed humorlessly. "It was certainly a shock."

"Did she admit to the other thing straightaway?"

"You mean that my son wasn't actually my son?" he queried and pulled a couple of plates from the cupboard. "Not long after. I think by then she was relieved that it was out in the open. So I moved out, and she moved on."

Nicola walked toward the counter and placed her glass down, meeting his gaze steadily. "How do you…" She stopped, her words trailing off.

"How do I what?" he queried.

She took a steadying breath. "How do you trust anyone again after that?"

He shook his head. "Honestly, I have no idea. A part of me wonders, if I ever do get seriously involved with someone again, how I won't question everything. But I don't want to be that person, Nic. I don't want to be suspicious and paranoid and uncertain because that's no way to live a life. The truth is, I'm not sure if I'll ever have the courage to get married again or have kids. I don't know if I'll always be thinking *Is she being faithful?* or *Is this child really mine?* It's too early, I guess. Too raw."

Nicola swallowed the tightness in her throat. "I'm sorry that happened to you."

"Yeah, me, too."

In that moment, her earlier reservations slipped away. Because there were just the two of them in the room, two slightly broken people who had somehow found a way back to one another, even if it was simply for a few hours.

She met his gaze head on and stepped back. "Can we skip dinner?"

He stilled. "If that's what you want."

Nicola nodded and moved back, heading around the sofa. She took a breath, let the air fill her lungs and flow through her veins and then spoke. "Come here."

He moved around the kitchen counter and stood in front of her, looking all serious and gorgeous. "Okay, I'm here."

She raised one eyebrow. "Sit down."

He did as she requested, settling onto the sofa, arms draped across the back. "Okay, I'm sitting."

Nicola moved in front of him, her legs in front of his knees. She took a breath, galvanized her back bone and then smiled. He returned the gesture, his eyes darkening, his gaze unwavering. She moved toward the sofa and straddled his lap, holding on to his shoulders, feeling the muscles bunch and tense beneath her palm and fingertips. There was something intensely erotic about the moment, as though they were the only two people on the planet. And to his credit, he didn't move. He didn't make an instant and gratuitous grab for her. That wasn't his style. He simply stared deep into her eyes, maintaining a visual contact that was so intense it burned her right through to her bones. She pressed closer, feeling him harden against her, feeling his body in a way she hadn't for fifteen years. He'd changed some, filled out, gotten broader in the shoulders and added muscle to his bones. He was no longer a boy. She was no longer a girl. He was a man; she was a woman. And they were both experienced in life and love and loss.

Nicola traced her hands along his shoulders and reached his neck, gently threading her fingers through his hair. Long ago, his hair had been longer, but it was still silky and sexy between her fingers. She touched his jaw with the back of her hand and realized how labored his breathing was, as though every ounce of air was a battle.

"Are you okay?" she asked.

He smiled fractionally. "I'm fine."

"I'm just getting reacquainted."

His mouth twisted sexily. "I know exactly what you're doing, Nic."

Heat pitched in her belly, and she pressed closer, waiting for his arms to come around her and for his hands to latch on to her hips. But they didn't. He hadn't moved. Except for the hard length of him pressing directly against her through his jeans and his deep breathing, he hadn't so much as twitched a muscle.

"Are you playing hard to get?"

He chuckled deeply. "I told you the other night— you call the shots."

Her blood surged, pooling directly between her thighs, and she instinctively pressed closer. "Which means what, exactly?"

"Which means—" he said, his gaze traveling down

her neck and over her breasts for a moment before he reached her eyes again "—ask me."

"Ask you?"

"Ask me to kiss you," he replied, the tiny pulse in his cheek throbbing madly. "Ask me to make love to you. Ask me to be inside you."

Nicola's libido surged, and she sucked in a sharp breath. "Kiss me?"

He draped a hand around her neck, anchoring her head, drawing her closer, and then his mouth was on hers. Not gently. Not softly. But exactly what she wanted, their lips together, their tongues together, fused by a need that was both thrilling and terrifying.

Then he pulled back abruptly, leaving her panting and wanting more. "And what else?" he demanded, skimming his hands down her sides and holding her hips. "What else do you want?"

She pushed closer, feeling him hard, and she reached down between them, pressed her palm against him through the rough denim. "Make love to me. I want to feel you inside me."

He groaned, kissing her again, his hands grinding her hips seductively, and then he pushed her dress up her thighs. Nicola met his tongue with her own, and they did a sexy dance in her mouth as his hand moved between her legs. She almost bucked off the couch when his fingers slipped beneath her panties, and he found her moist and ready for him. He touched her intimately, finding a rhythm within seconds, and she climaxed almost immediately, gasping his name as pleasure rocked through her, wave after wave pulsing across her skin, through her blood and deep down into the far reaches of her soul. Then his mouth was on her throat, his free hand gently kneading her breast before he effortlessly started undoing the buttons on her sweater. She ground her hips against him, feeling his hardness, wanting him inside her with such intensity she could scarcely breathe.

"You're so beautiful, Nic," he whispered against her throat, tracing his mouth around to the sensitive spot behind her ear as he plunged one hand into her hair, twisting the locks gently, before claiming her lips again.

Nicola grappled clumsily with the top button on his jeans and had just slipped it open when she heard a sound. A ringing. A cell phone. She had some faraway thought that it was Kieran's cell because he was probably on call for the hospital. But after a moment, she recognized the ring and groaned heavily.

"Is that you or me?" he muttered against her lips.

"Me," she said, agonized as she pulled back. "I have to get it. My father is watching the boys, and I—"

"Then, get it," he said softly and grabbed her hips, pushing her back until she was standing on unsteady feet.

Nicola straightened her dress and took a few wobbly steps. She grabbed her tote from the spot she'd left it and rummaged clumsily for her cell. It was still ringing, and she answered it in a breathless rush. Moments later, she ended the call and turned to face Kieran. He was now standing, his clothes back in perfect position.

"I have to go," she said, heat pricking the back of her eyes. "I'm sorry."

He frowned, stepping closer. "What's wrong?"

She shook her head, her thoughts completely jumbled. "That was Hank Culhane, the police chief," she explained and threw the tote over one shoulder. "Johnny's been arrested."

* * *

Breaking and entering. Theft. Willful damage. The list of offenses from Johnny's crime spree was long. Kieran knew that Nicola was barely hanging on by a thread as the police officer explained how her nephew had snuck out of the apartment after bedtime, had met up with a friend and broken into the bakery down the street. They had shattered two windows, damaged the cash register and sprayed paint in the kitchen. The fact that he hadn't acted alone and had the help of a friend was of little consequence. This was *her* nephew they were talking about.

She was hurting. She was angry. She was clearly unsure what to say or do. He also suspected she wasn't sure if she wanted him around witnessing the whole event. But he wasn't going anywhere. She needed someone to lean on, and he wasn't about to bail.

He stayed with her while she called her father and explained what had happened, and then spent several minutes speaking in Italian to her clearly distressed parent.

"Is Salvatore okay?" Kieran asked when she ended the call.

"Stressed out," she replied. "Like me. He had no idea Johnny had snuck out. Thankfully Marco is still sound asleep. Poor Papa…he'll be blaming himself for this."

"It's not your dad's fault," Kieran assured her. "Or yours."

"It sure feels like it," she admitted. "Maybe, but it's not."

"I can't believe he'd do this," she said, when they were alone and the police officer had gone to collect her nephew from an adjoining office. "What was he thinking?"

Kieran touched her hand. "He's acting out his grief, Nic. It's not so hard to understand."

"But stealing? And the damage. God, how am I supposed to pay for this?"

He squeezed her fingers. "The place is insured."

"How do you know that?"

"Because the baker, Mr. Phelps, is a reasonable man." He smiled. "And my family owns the building, so I know the landlords are fair. You can stop stressing."

She rolled her beautiful eyes. "Great… Liam's gonna have a fit."

"Liam won't do any such thing," he assured her. "I can handle my brother. Let's just get Johnny home and leave the other stuff for another day."

"Does that include you and me?"

"Yes," he replied.

"Doesn't my crazy life make you want to run a mile?"

Kieran didn't want to run. He wanted to help her. "Not at all."

She was about to respond when the door opened and the police officer ushered Johnny into the room. The boy had his head bent, his eyes downcast, his feet barely managing a shuffle across the linoleum.

"Johnny," she said and sighed. "How could you?"

The child shrugged. "What do you care?"

Kieran saw her tense, and she got to her feet. "I care," she insisted. "You're my nephew. Of course I care."

"You care about Marco," he said and looked up, tears in his eyes. "No one cares about me. My mom and dad are dead."

"I know they are. And I know you miss them. I miss them, too. But you have me, and Marco and *Nonno*, and we all care about you."

He shrugged and tugged his hoodie over his head. "Can we go home now?"

Kieran looked toward the police officer, and he nodded slightly, then looked at Nicola. "I'll get Hank to give you a call tomorrow. Bill Phelps might press charges and want damages paid for but, considering Johnny's age and how he hasn't ever done anything like this before, I'm sure we can sort something out."

They both thanked the officer and, once they were outside, Kieran said he'd follow her to the restaurant to collect Marco and then see them safely home.

"You don't have to do that," she said and shuffled Johnny into her car.

"I know I don't have to," he said and opened her door. "But I want to. Let's go."

They pulled into the driveway about twenty minutes later. Salvatore couldn't believe that Johnny had snuck out, and a confused Marco was happy to be home and to see Kieran. He had no idea what had transpired with his older brother, which was a good thing. It took another twenty minutes to get him to go to bed and, while Nicola did that, Kieran sat at the kitchen table with Johnny.

"I guess I'm grounded now?" the boy said and pulled back the hoodie.

"Probably," Kieran replied.

Johnny looked up and frowned. "Are you gonna marry my aunt?"

Kieran almost fell off the chair. "Uh…no, certainly not."

"Why not?" Johnny shot back. "I thought you liked her."

Kieran chose his words carefully. "Of course I like her. We're friends. But that's all."

"Then how is she supposed to get a boyfriend if

you're hanging around?" he asked, grunting the question out.

Kieran had to fumble for a reply. "You want your aunt to have a boyfriend?"

"Sure," he muttered. "Then she might get married. And we'd be a real family again."

Kieran relaxed in the chair. Johnny's childish logic made perfect sense for a ten-year-old. He wanted a family like the one he used to have. He wanted things to return to how they had once been.

Stand in line, kid.

"I'm sure your aunt will get married one day, if that's what she wants," Kieran said quietly.

Johnny shrugged angrily. "Not if you're here."

"So, you want me to stop coming around?"

Johnny made another grunting sound and twisted his hands together. "I didn't say that."

"So, it's okay if I come here to see you and Marco?"

Johnny shrugged again. "I guess. I mean, you're kinda cool."

Kieran smiled. "Thanks. I think you're cool, too."

Johnny twisted his hands together. "Would it be okay if I started hanging out with you and Marco?"

"Sure," Kieran replied.

"And you could come and see Aunt Nicola, too…if that's what you want. I mean, I think she'd like that."

"And you'd be okay with that?" Kieran asked quietly.

Johnny nodded. "Yeah…if you like her."

"I like her," Kieran said. "We're friends."

Johnny met his gaze, chewing on his lower lip. "I just want things to be different. I dunno… I want Aunt Nicola to be happy. And how can she be happy if she's gotta look after me and Marco all the time? And, if she's not happy, then maybe she won't want to look after us forever. And *Nonno*'s really old, so he *can't* look after us forever. But if Aunt Nicola got married, she'd have a husband, and we could live in his house, and she'd be happy all the time and wouldn't care if me and Marco were here, too."

The hurt in Johnny's voice could not be missed, and Kieran's insides contracted. "So, you don't want to live in this house?"

He shrugged again. "I don't like it here anymore."

Kieran's attention was diverted toward the door, and he spotted Nicola hovering at the threshold. Her eyes glistened, and seeing her pain made his chest ache. He fought the urge to rush across the room and hold her close, to reassure her that everything would be okay. But he didn't.

She came into the room and walked around the table, stopping behind Johnny. She placed her hands on his narrow shoulders, squeezed him gently and kissed the top of his head. "How about you head off to bed, okay? We'll talk in the morning." Leaning over, she wrapped him in her arms and hugged him tightly. "I do love you, kiddo," she whispered. "No matter what."

Johnny muttered a swift good-night and left the room quietly, wiping tears from his face as he walked away. Nicola dropped into the chair the boy had vacated, propped her elbows on the table and let out an agonizing sigh.

"I suck at being a parent."

Kieran smiled gently. "No, you don't. It's been a hard day, certainly. But not every day will be hard. Some days will be good. Other days will be great. Accept that you're going to make mistakes."

"Like staying in this house?" she said and shuddered. "I overheard some of what Johnny was saying. I guess

I thought I was doing the right thing. I thought…it was best for the boys. But all I did was try and make it easier for myself."

Kieran reached across the table and grasped her hand, entwining their fingers intimately. "It's time to have some compassion for yourself, Nic. You did what you thought was right. At the end of the day, that's all you can do."

She inhaled deeply and offered a tight smile. "You're good at this, you know."

"I've had some practice," he said and grinned. "Occupational hazard."

Her fingers tightened around his. "I'm glad you're here. I needed a friend tonight. Even one who is getting in the way of me finding a husband."

Kieran's eyes widened. "You heard Johnny say *that*?"

"I heard. He wants a family like he used to have. So, I guess I should start looking for a boyfriend," she said wryly. "Any ideas?"

He laughed softly. "Don't ask me to play Cupid. That's my mother's department."

"Maybe she could help?" she suggested and then looked in the direction of the doorway for a moment, before her voice dropped in volume. "But before she does, I think we need to finish what we started."

Kieran's stomach took a dive. "Are you sure?"

"Positive," she replied and rubbed her thumb along his palm. "Only, next time, we'll try and make it to the bedroom."

"Or not," he said and released her as he got to his feet and moved around the table. "And now I'm going to salvage what's left of my good sense and get out of here so you can get some rest. Good night, Nic."

He kissed her soundly, lingering a little to taste her

sweet mouth before he straightened and left. But he was still thinking about her hours later. And suspected it would take more than one night to get Nicola from his thoughts. He'd had fifteen years, and it hadn't worked.

Because she wasn't only in his thoughts. She was in his heart.

And he wasn't sure he would ever get her out.

Chapter Eight

Nicola had a hard week. She spent as much time with Johnny as she could, as well as working at the restaurant and making peace with Mr. Phelps. She found herself in the clear, with nothing owed and all charges against Johnny dropped. Of course, she knew why.

Kieran.

A veritable knight in shining armor.

He'd stopped by the house several times during the week. Once with Jonah on the phone to go over plans for the fishpond, and once to hang out with the boys—both of them this time—to watch a movie and help make a cart for Johnny's fishing tackle. And then again to bring takeout from O'Sullivan's because she'd had a particularly long day at the restaurant and both boys had been misbehaving one afternoon. The boys had made plans to go fishing, and Marco's enthusiasm was beginning to outweigh his nerves, or so it appeared. Her gratitude toward Kieran was growing daily. He had patience and showed genuine care for her nephews. And with every visit, every conversation, she felt just a little less alone. She knew he was working and fitting the visits in between his shifts at the hospital, and she appreciated his attention to both Marco and Johnny. The problem was she was getting used to him stopping by, and that in itself presented a problem. Because they were friends.

That's all...

He'd said as much to Johnny the night they'd collected him from the police station. The night they'd almost made love. The night she'd experienced true passion for the first time in forever and had responded like a woman who was hopelessly and completely in love. Except that she wasn't. She couldn't be. She'd stopped being in love with Kieran fifteen years ago. To go back to that...it was crazy thinking.

She'd made plans to sleep with him and then forget all about him.

Simple.

Not...

Because a woman could never forget the first man she'd loved.

"Everything okay, Nicola?"

She looked up from her task of peeling cling wrap off an assortment of dishes and smiled. Gwen O'Sullivan was on the other side of the counter, watching her, her brows angled curiously.

"Of course," she said and kept working. "And thank you for the invitation today. The boys are delighted to be here."

The invitation to attend Gwen's birthday celebration had come from Kieran—via his mother, she suspected—and, once the boys knew it was being held at the ranch and that there would be pony rides for the kids and an assortment of other activities, they had insisted on going. And, since Nicola was keen to see them happy, she hadn't been able to refuse the invitation.

"I'm delighted to have you here," Gwen said and

smiled. "Not that I'm keen on turning sixty, but I'm loving the fact that my children and grandchildren are here to celebrate it with me. And friends—old and new. And some, like yourself, a little of both."

Nicola smiled warmly. She genuinely liked Gwen, and being around the older woman made her miss her own mother so much she ached inside.

And the ranch held so many special memories for her. When she was young, she'd spent countless hours in the kitchen with Gwen, going over recipes, talking about fashion and music and favorite television shows. The big house had always been full of people and lots of love and laughter.

It seemed quieter now, somehow, even though there were close to fifty people beneath the tent set out on the back lawn. Kayla was in the kitchen, as was Connie, and Nicola was pleased to have her friend close on hand. Even if Connie seemed unusually tense for most of the afternoon, something she suspected had to do with the fact that Jonah Rickard had made an unexpected visit. He spent most of the time talking to Liam and Kieran and left after dropping a wrapped box onto the gift table. Nicola admired his gumption, since he had every reason to stay away. But he appeared to have genuine respect for Gwen, and she knew it was reciprocated.

Nicola was surprised to see that Sean had also arrived, since he rarely showed his face in town. Liz's daughters were also there with their father, Grady, and his wife, Marissa, who Nicola remembered from high school. As she mingled through the crowd that afternoon, she realized how small a town Cedar River was. Even though she'd been gone for over a decade and only back for a year, she knew almost everyone.

"Okay," Gwen said and ushered them all from the

kitchen. "We'll let the caterers do the rest. I want you all out in the tent and having a good time. Off you go."

A buffet lunch was served about fifteen minutes later, and Nicola was returning to the table alone when Kieran sidled up beside her. "Plan on saving me a seat?" he asked.

She shrugged and compared her modest plate with his overflowing one. "Only if you let me have a buffalo wing," she said and sat down.

He slid in beside her and dropped the chicken onto her plate. "You owe me."

"Don't I know it," she said and smiled, remembering how she'd fallen apart in his arms at his apartment while he'd gone without release. "I'll make it up to you."

"When?" he teased.

"Tonight?"

He shook his head. "Can't. Working." He checked his watch. "In fact, I'm out of here in about forty-five minutes."

"Oh…okay."

He gave her a heated look. "If you get a sitter Tuesday night, we could finish what we started."

She swallowed hard, fighting the nerves that suddenly filled her blood. "Sure."

"Unless you've changed your mind?"

"Of course not," she shot back and smiled extra sweetly. "I want to get you out of my system once and for all."

His gaze darkened. "It's a date," he said and then shrugged. "I know, I know…it's not a date. We don't date."

"That's right," she insisted.

She spotted Liam at the next table as he smiled and winked, like he knew exactly what was going on. She glared at Kieran, then jabbed him in the ribs with her elbow. "Did you tell your brother what's going on between us?"

"Of course not," he replied quietly. "I'm not indiscreet."

"He looks like he knows."

Kieran looked up, glared at his grinning brother for a moment and then focused his attention back on her. "He's just being a pain in the ass."

"Why?"

"Because he can be," he replied. "Ignore him."

"And I thought my family was weird."

He chuckled. "Gino used to antagonize you all the time. So did Vince. That's what families do. It's one of the reasons why I love mine so much."

Her heart contracted. "That's nice. You really are a soppy sentimentalist."

"Is that a compliment?"

"Definitely," she said, smiling. "You're still the sweetest O'Sullivan."

"Sweet?" he grimaced. "Gee...thanks."

"You know what I mean," she said and waved a hand. "It's like, if you and your brothers were lined up, Sean's the O'Sullivan who women avoid because he's the bad boy, Liam's the one who's pined over, Jonah's the moody, tortured one...and then you...the one the girls want to marry. Honest, reliable, faithful...sweet."

"That makes me sound as boring as a shoe."

Heat scorched her cheeks. She wanted to backpedal. She wanted to stop talking to Kieran about marriage and all his endearing qualities. Because the more she talked, the more chance he had of figuring out that she was on the brink of being halfway to falling in love with him again.

Because he *was* the kind of man a girl wanted to marry. The fact he'd told Johnny he would *certainly* not be marrying her pained more than she'd believed possible. Because Carl hadn't wanted to marry her, either. And the notion that she was not marriage material hurt right through to her bones.

"You're not," she said, unable to stop the words from pouring out. "You're rock-solid. The guy who gives women faith in men, even when they've had their heart broken."

His gaze didn't waver. "Now who's being sweet, huh?"

"I guess we both have a lot to offer," she said softly and shrugged. "It's just a matter of finding the right person to share it with."

"Yeah," he said and rested a hand on her thigh beneath the table. "There's that."

"I don't have any illusions about us, Kieran," she said, feeling her desire for him spike. "Once we get one another out of our systems, we can move on. It's what I want. What I need. What happened with Johnny last weekend made me realize I need to think about people other than myself. And once we're done, I can do that."

"Sure," he said and quickly moved his hand. "Whatever. I'll see you soon."

He pushed the plate aside, got to his feet and left the table. Connie, who was on the other side of the table, moved around and took his spot. "What was that all about?" she asked, her voice little more than a whisper.

Nicola sighed. "Just Kieran and I being *Kieran and I.* History makes it complicated."

Connie frowned. "Be careful, okay?

"I will be," she promised her friend. "Kieran's no more interested in anything serious than I am." She raised a brow. "Anyway, I'd much rather talk about you and Jonah."

Connie's cheek spotted with color. "Don't ask."

"You like him?"

"Not one bit," her friend said dismissively. "He's the most arrogant, self-centered jerk I've ever met."

"Love and hate," Nicola said and grinned. "You never did really tell me what happened all those months ago."

Connie shrugged. "I guess we all have our own history."

Nicola knew much about her friend's past, but it was never spoken of. Some things were best left unsaid. She patted Connie's arm and finished her meal, conscious of Kieran at the other end of the tent. He left about half an hour later, without speaking to her again, although she did observe him saying goodbye to the boys who were still bounding around on the bouncy castle. She had a chance to speak to Liam before she left, thanking him for running interference with the bakery owner.

"Not a problem," he said, his arms cradling his newborn son. "But I didn't really do anything. Kieran did the sorting. You know how he is."

Yes, she did. "He likes to help people," she said, heat rising up her neck.

"He likes helping *you*," Liam remarked. "And he's genuinely fond of your nephews. Don't mess him up, okay?" Liam said more seriously. "He's been through enough these past couple of years."

Nicola's eyes widened. "I don't know what you—"

"I know the two of you are skirting around the edges of something," he replied. "His words, not mine. But it's clear that something's going on. Just make sure it's for the right reasons." He looked toward the jumping castle and then glanced at his own son. "Kids have a way of changing things."

"I know that," Nicola said, straightening her shoulders. "But for the record, your brother isn't in any danger of being messed with."

"You've always been his Kryptonite, Nicola…that'll never change."

He walked off before she could reply. But that was just as well. The truth was she had no response to such a revelation.

Kieran was getting ready for his shift on Sunday night when he got a text from Nicola asking him to come over. Johnny wasn't feeling well and had asked for him. So, by seven thirty he was striding up her path, and she opened the door before he reached the porch step.

"Thank you for coming," she said and ushered him inside. "I said I'd take him to the ER, but he specifically asked if you would come here. I think he has a fever, but he's been running hot and cold all evening. I'm not sure what's wrong."

"No problem," he said and held up his doctor's bag. "I don't start work for another hour. Is he in his room?"

She seemed frazzled. In baggy gray sweats, her hair in an untidy top knot and her cheeks flushed, Kieran thought he'd never seen her look more beautiful, and he fought the urge to haul her into his arms and kiss her like crazy.

"I'll take you up," she said, and he followed her up the stairs.

Marco was on the landing, cheerfully saying how he wasn't sick at all. When they reached Johnny's room, the boy was in bed under the covers, one arm flung over his forehead. He groaned, then made some comment about how his head hurt. Marco was hovering, and Nicola quickly shooed him back to his own room. Kieran examined Johnny, conscious that Nicola was standing by nervously, looking determined to think the worst. She was biting her lip, arms crossed, clearly at breaking point. When the exam was done and Johnny was back under the covers, he looked around the room, making a few observations.

"Okay, I need to speak with your aunt," he told Johnny. "You stay put and we'll be back up in a little while."

Kieran packed up his stethoscope and ushered Nicola from the room. She jabbered on as they headed downstairs and, when they reached the hallway, she grabbed his arms, her fingers digging into his skin.

"Please tell me what's wrong," she implored. "Is it serious? Chicken pox? Measles? Or something worse? Don't tell me—it's something worse," she said and gripped him harder. "He's really sick, isn't he? Kids don't get fevers without a reason. Maybe I didn't make him dress warm enough." Her eyes glistened. "This is my fault. He's really sick, and it's my—"

"He's not sick," Kieran said and grasped her chin, tilting her face up. "He's faking."

Her eyes widened. "Faking?"

"Faking," Kieran said again, rubbing her chin with his thumb. "He has a heating pad tucked under his bed. A minute or two held against the temple and presto… instant fever."

"But why…"

Kieran looked up and spotted both Marco and Johnny at the top of the stairs. They were grinning and whispering and had clearly hatched the plan together.

"That's why," he said and kissed her soundly on the lips. The boys giggled and then raced back to their rooms.

Nicola kissed him back for a moment and pulled away. "Little monsters."

"They just want to see you happy," he said and released her.

"They don't know that you make me miserable."

She was smiling as she spoke, but the words still stung. He remembered what she'd said the day before—about forgetting all about them once they were done. That had stung, too. Enough for him to bail on the party earlier than he'd needed to. "Do I?"

"No," she admitted. "Not really."

"I'm glad," he said. "Now, I need to get out of here before I kiss you again. I'll see you Tuesday."

She wrapped her arms around her waist. "How about tomorrow?" she suggested. "I'm working, so why don't you stop by the restaurant and have dinner?"

Kieran's brows shot up. "That sounds like a date."

"A pizza and bread sticks with me and the boys? If you think that's a date, then you need to get out more," she said and grinned.

Laughter rumbled in his chest. "Ain't that the truth. Okay, tomorrow. See you then." He walked to the door and turned. "And you might want to remove the heating pad from his bed—don't want him burning anything."

She gasped. "God… I don't think I'll ever get this parenting thing right."

"Sure you will," he replied. "You're a natural. All they need is love. And you're good at that."

Something passed between them, a look that spoke volumes, a look that had everything to do with their past and their present. A look that made him want her more than he'd believed possible. She called it unfinished business. He knew that it was simple destiny. An inevitability since they were fifteen years old.

He spent the next twenty-four hours wrapped up in thoughts of her. Jonah called and talked through the proposal for the pond, sending him the plans via email. After an uneventful shift in the ER, Kieran headed to JoJo's around six thirty on Monday evening.

He spotted Nicola the moment he entered. Dressed in a black skirt and white blouse, black pumps and with her hair pulled back, she looked too beautiful for words. He stayed by the bar for a few minutes, watching as she effortlessly did her job, chatting to customers, taking orders, coordinating the staff. She'd left a successful career back in San Francisco, but the work she did now had so much value. Her very presence in the restaurant made people happy. She was in her element, and thinking of how she'd moved her life and embraced looking after her nephews made his admiration for her grow. She had a kind heart and a strength he suspected she didn't know she possessed.

She looked up and met his gaze, her mouth creasing into a smile, and his insides did a crazy leap. Seconds later she was by the bar and lightly pressed a hand onto his forearm. Even through his jacket and shirt, Kieran's skin burned from her touch. But he didn't pull away.

"You're here," she said and removed her hand. "The boys will be happy. They've become very fond of you."

"It's mutual," he admitted and felt the truth of his words hit deep down. "So, are you happy, too?" She shrugged and turned. "I'm happy, too. Come over to the booth, and I'll get you a drink."

"Just club soda," he said and followed her, slipping into the seat.

She smiled. "You're so hard core."

"Yeah, I think we've already discussed how I'm the sweetest guy on the planet."

Her smile widened, and she went to speak but was interrupted by the excited chatter from Marco as he sidled up into the booth, followed closely by his brother. Johnny wasn't quite so animated but managed a grin when Kieran asked how he was feeling now he'd recovered from his fever. Nicola disappeared, and Kieran spent some time chatting to the boys, talking about school and the fishpond and how they wanted a basketball hoop installed in the backyard.

"Do you like kids?" Marco asked, biting into a breadstick.

"Of course he likes kids," Johnny said quickly. "He's here with us. And he's a doctor."

The boy's logic made Kieran grin. "Johnny's right. I like kids."

"Do you like older kids or just babies?" Marco asked, biting his lower lip just like his aunt did.

Johnny groaned impatiently. "Everyone likes babies, stupid. Older kids are the ones who get left."

"Left where?" Marco asked seriously.

"At the place where they leave kids who don't have a mom and a dad," Johnny explained matter-of-factly. "Everyone knows that. There's a girl in my class, and she was festered."

"Festered?" Marco's eyes were as big as saucers.

Kieran bit back a grin. "He means *fostered*," he explained to the younger boy. "Sometimes children who don't have a mom and dad go and live with foster parents."

"But we don't have a mom and dad," Marco stated. "So do we have to go and live with other people?"

"No," Kieran explained quickly. "Because you have

your aunt. You have family who want you to live with them."

Marco relaxed a little. "So, even if Aunt Nicola had her own kids, we could still live with her?"

"Of course," he replied.

"And it doesn't matter that there's no dad?" Marco asked.

Johnny rolled his eyes. "If Aunt Nicola had a baby then there would be a dad—don't you know anything? You gotta have a mom and a dad to make a baby."

"Who says?" Marco asked.

"Everyone. Except for Sissy Culhane—she's another girl in my class. She doesn't have a mom," Johnny said somberly. "But I think her mom died or something."

Kieran had gone to school with Joss Culhane, Sissy's father. "You're right, Sissy's mom died a long time ago."

"I wish my mom hadn't died," Marco said, his lip wobbling. "And my dad. But we're lucky that we've got Aunt Nicola to love us. And when she gets married, we'll have a dad again. Won't we?" he asked, looking at Kieran.

Kieran saw the longing in the boy's eyes, and something uncurled deep down, a feeling he'd pushed away for two years because it hurt too much to think about. Losing Christian had nearly broken him, and he was reluctant to feel that again. But it was hard not to feel the emotional tug that came from spending time with two children who were clearly longing for a father to replace the one they'd tragically lost.

"Yes, one day, perhaps you will," he said quietly.

"You could marry her." Johnny suggested and shrugged.

Kieran's skin burned. Yes, he could. But he wasn't about to say that. "Well, I'm not sure I—"

"Don't you want to marry her?" Marco asked, eyes wide. "Why not? I mean, she's pretty, right?"

Kieran tugged at his collar. "Yes, she's very pretty."

"And smart," Johnny added. "And she makes the best spaghetti and meatballs ever."

"You're right," Kieran said in agreement. "She does."

"Do you know anyone else who could marry Aunt Nicola?" Marco asked and chewed his lip some more. "And it would have to be someone we liked. And who liked us."

"What about the guy who came to check out the yard for the fishpond?" Johnny asked and chugged on some soda the waitress had delivered.

Jonah? Yeah…maybe not. "I don't think so."

"Maybe the policeman," Johnny said and then cast his eyes down guiltily. "The one who phoned Aunt Nicola about me."

Hank Culhane? "No," Kieran said and sipped his drink.

"But policemen like kids," Marco mused. "So do firemen. Do you know any firemen?"

"Why do you need a fireman?" Nicola's voice instantly cut through the chatter. "Is there a fire?"

Only the one in Kieran's belly when he thought about Nicola being with another man. He plastered on a smile. "Just boy talk," he quipped and shrugged. "So, I thought we were having pizza tonight?"

The moment he spoke, a waitress appeared and a family-sized tray was placed on the table. Nicola slid into the booth beside him, and he caught the scent of her perfume as she edged closer.

"Okay, dig in," she said and grabbed a slice of pizza.

The boys followed suit, and then Kieran helped himself.

"So why were you three talking about firemen?" she asked.

"We're trying to find you a husband," Marco announced, and Kieran saw her jaw drop. "So that Johnny and I won't end up in that place where the kids without a mom and dad go."

"What place?" she echoed, and then her voice got louder. "And what husband?"

"A husband for you," Johnny said and shrugged. "One that can give you a baby."

"How would the baby get inside your belly, Aunt Nicola?" Marco asked, wide-eyed.

Kieran fidgeted in his seat. The conversation was going from bad to worse. He looked sideways, saw the mortified expression on her face and managed a wry grin. "Haven't had The Talk yet, huh?"

"Of course not," she replied. "They're eight and ten."

"And curious," he said quietly. "Better start talking."

"You're the doctor," she reminded him, a deep scarlet hue crawling up her neck. "And much more qualified for it than me."

"Oh, no...you're the parent. This one's all yours."

"Please," she begged. He looked at her, saw her lip tremble and took pity on her. "Okay. But you owe me for this."

Kieran spent the next fifteen minutes explaining conception and childbirth to the boys, answering their questions as they shoved pizza into their mouths and drank soda. When he was done, Marco looked at him thoughtfully and asked another question.

"So, could *you* give Aunt Nicola a baby?"

"Well, I... I..."

His voice trailed off, and she sucked in a breath and jumped in to save him. "Who wants more pizza?"

The question quickly forgotten, the boys shook their heads and pleaded to leave the table and head upstairs to watch television. Once they were gone, she leaned closer and spoke. "I bet right now you're wanting to call the fire department."

He smiled wryly. "Thanks for the help. Next time you're on your own."

She laughed and moved back. "Sorry about that... looks like the boys have you set in their sights."

"I could think of worse fates," he said and finished his drink.

"I guess that only means one thing," she said quietly.

He stilled. "And what's that?"

She slid from the booth and got to her feet. "That we're in big trouble."

Chapter Nine

Nicola was driving back from one of the local produce farms early the following afternoon, when she was delayed just before the bridge for over an hour while the police and paramedics cleared an accident scene. From the mangled vehicle being hauled by a tow truck, the amount of debris on the road and the wailing sirens, it looked bad and, when she finally picked the boys up from school, she gave them an extralong hug.

She headed to the restaurant, had a debrief with the assistant manager and did inventory on the bar. Once she was done, she left the boys with her father for the evening and then headed home to shower and change. She had a date with Kieran. Okay…not a date. A few hours of unfinished business. But she intended following through with it.

By the time she tapped on his door, it was nearly eight o'clock. The door swung back, and he looked surprised to see her.

"Oh…Nic. Hey."

He seemed distracted, out of sorts, and she frowned. "Everything all right?"

"Sure," he said and opened the door wider, ushering her inside. "Would you like a drink?"

He had already closed the door and was striding down the narrow hallway before she responded. "Okay. Wine if you have it."

"Of course," he said and rummaged through a couple of cupboards for a glass.

She stripped off her coat and dropped her tote, feeling the warmth of the central heating seep through to her bones. She got a good look at him and realized he was still wearing his work clothes. And he looked terrible. "Long day?"

He poured the wine and glanced up. "You could say that."

His weary expression was unmissable. "What happened?"

She took the glass he offered and waited. He let out a long breath, met her gaze and spoke quietly. "I lost someone today."

"Someone?"

"A patient," he explained. "A seventeen-year-old girl involved in an MVA."

Nicola's insides crunched up. "I'm so sorry. I think I was caught up in the traffic jam from that accident today. It happened just before the bridge, right?"

He nodded. "Single vehicle. Texting while driving. She sustained significant chest and head injuries." He ran a weary hand over his face. "God, it was just awful. There were two other girls in the car who survived... but damn, I couldn't save her. I tried. I tried so freakin' hard. But it wasn't enough."

Nicola's eyes burned, and she blinked the tears away. "I'm sure you did everything you could."

He shrugged. "Doesn't mean squat, though, particularly when I had to tell her parents. Her father was inconsolable. Her mother hauntingly silent. And, as the words were coming out of my mouth, I kept thinking, what do I know about real loss? Raising a child for seventeen years, then losing them because of a damned text message…that's about as real and extreme as it gets."

She nodded, because she had no idea what to say to him. And then she found her voice. "I imagine that it never gets easier."

His gaze narrowed. "Telling loved ones that they've lost someone? No, never. And while I was doing it, while I was watching these people suffer through the terrible news, I thought, is this what my parents felt when Liz died? Is this what your father felt when Gino was killed? And how did the person telling them really feel? I felt sorry for myself. And angry at this teenager whose heart was literally in my hands as I was trying to revive her. I kept thinking, how could she do this, how could she choose to send a text message and hurt these people so much?"

Nicola placed her glass on the counter, moved around to get closer to Kieran and rested her hands on his shoulders, looking up into his eyes. "Because that's what real life is. It's hurt and loss, and sometimes it just sucks. But I'll bet that someday, when they can look back on the moment clearly, her parents will be grateful that it was you who told them she had passed away and that it was done with compassion and kindness and with real feeling."

He sighed and dropped his chin to the top of her head, wrapping his arms around her. "Thank you," he whispered. "I'm glad you're here. You look amazing, by the way."

She smiled gently and pulled back, touching his face.

"You don't. You look wrecked. Why don't you have a shower and get changed, and I'll cook something, since you probably haven't eaten."

He nodded and expelled a heavy breath. "You're right. I need to get out of these clothes. Be back in ten."

Once he left the room, Nicola took a sip of wine and then rummaged through the refrigerator, finding eggs and peppers and cheddar, and set about making an omelet. As she cracked and whisked the eggs, it occurred to her how neat and tidy the place was. The apartment looked even tidier than when Kayla had occupied it. She found sourdough on the countertop and cut a few thick slices for toast and waited for him to return before she put the ingredients in the pan.

When he walked back down the hall about fifteen minutes later, he was showered, shaved and dressed. Well, half-dressed. He wore low-riding jeans with the top button undone and a white T-shirt that amplified the broadness of his shoulders and clung to a good portion of his muscular chest. His feet were bare, his hair damp, and the scent of whatever cologne he used assailed her immediately, shooting her libido up like a firecracker, and she tossed back the rest of the wine.

The temperature in the room seemed to hike a few degrees, and she waved a hand. "Um…food. It won't take long."

"Don't go to any trouble."

"No trouble," she insisted. "You know I like to cook. And my dad rarely lets me into the kitchen at the restaurant. He likes to supervise the chef," she said and grinned.

"You do a good job," he remarked and came around the counter. "Being in charge suits you."

"Because I'm bossy?"

"Exactly," he said and grinned. "Sorry I wasn't in a good place when I answered the door."

She raised a brow. "You forget I was coming over?"

He shrugged lightly. "Not really... I just didn't think, if that makes sense."

"Perfect sense," she replied and began making the omelet. "Incidentally, are you a neat freak or something? There's nothing out of place here."

He grinned. "Not quite. The old lady downstairs comes up and cleans for me every Monday. She has a daughter in Idaho who gives her grief and needs the money, and I..." His words trailed off and he shrugged again. "You know...just trying to help."

He really is the most perfect human being in the universe.

The moment the thought came into her head, Nicola wanted to get it out. But she couldn't.

"I wish you were flawed."

He laughed, and the sound warmed her blood. "I am," he assured her. "You know that better than anyone."

She shrugged one shoulder. "High school was a long time ago. We've both grown up since then. And I know why you did it the way you did."

"Because you wouldn't have accepted it any other way," he replied, confirming her suspicions. "I had to hurt you back then. I had to make you hate me. If we'd tried doing things long-distance, it would have dragged out and become a great big mess. I didn't want that for you, Nic. I cared about you too much."

"I know," she said, her throat closing over, her eyes burning. "We both wanted different things. I knew how important medical school was to you, and I know I would have made it difficult for you to concentrate on studying if we'd stayed together and were living in different states. We were too young for that kind of commitment."

He nodded. "But I am truly sorry for hurting you. And I'm sorry that your fiancé was a jerk and didn't realize what he had. You deserve better."

Tears plumped at the corners of her eyes, and she quickly blinked them away, skillfully flipping the omelet. "I guess I'm just not the marrying kind."

"Sure you are," he said and shrugged loosely.

"If only there was a fireman handy," she said and pushed the bread into the toaster.

Color slashed his cheeks. "I'm sure they're overrated."

"Yeah," she said and grinned. "All those muscles and rescuing kittens from trees. So overrated."

He chuckled, and the sound warmed her through to the soles of her feet. Despite the undercurrent of sexual awareness between them, there was something else, something even more powerful. Friendship. Trust. Companionship. It had built steadily over the past couple of weeks. And it wasn't new. It wasn't some passing fancy. It was built on the foundation of their teenage romance. It was about knowing they were so important to one another back then. And in some ways, that friendship hadn't faded, not through years apart, or angry words or bitterness and hurt. It was in a kind of limbo, waiting to be unwrapped and given new life.

She nibbled on a piece of buttered toast while he ate, not wanting to make him feel self-conscious. And they talked…about the boys, and their work now and the work they'd left behind. They talked about Gino and Miranda and Liz, and he admitted to finding it hard to forgive his father for betraying his mother and for

Jonah's very existence. And they talked about the accident and the patient he'd lost.

And then he talked about his son.

"I can't imagine how hard it was for you."

He sighed heavily. "Honestly…it was as though I had my heart ripped out. He was my child. Or so I believed. And it still hurts so much."

He bared his feelings in a way she suspected he'd never done before, and his blue eyes had never glittered more brightly.

"I'm so sorry."

He nodded. "When you love someone that much and they're taken from you, it's like a wound that never heals. And I'm terrified of…" His words trailed off and he shook his head. "You know."

"Loving anyone again?" she prompted. "Loving a child again?"

"Yes," he admitted.

Nicola's throat closed over and she swallowed hard. Then she grabbed his hand and got to her feet, dragging him with her. She didn't have to speak. They didn't need any more words. He linked their fingers intimately and led her down the hall and into the bedroom.

The huge bed filled the room, and the bedside lamp gave enough light to dapple his skin. He took an unopened box of condoms from the drawer and ripped open the box. Then he pulled off his T-shirt immediately and moved in front of her, undoing the buttons on her dress one at a time, the back of his fingers skimming over her skin. Once the buttons were dealt with, the dress slipped over her shoulders and onto the floor. Her breasts surged, spilling over the top of the white lace bra, her nipples straining through the soft fabric. His gaze swept over her, past her breasts, down her rib cage and stomach, over the white panties and down to her thighs and then back up.

"You're so beautiful, Nic," he rasped. "I feel like it's our first time all over again."

It was quite the admission, and she realized that he was just as vulnerable as she was. His honesty was a powerful aphrodisiac, giving her strength, but also grabbing like fingers around her heart. And she knew, in that moment, that it would never be just sex between them. There were too many feelings. Too much history. Too much love…

I'm still in love with him…

The realization should have sent her running. But she wasn't going to deny her body and heart what it craved. It was one night. A few hours. The two of them. Their past now meeting their present.

She slowly unclipped her bra, freeing her breasts, watching his visual appraisal with a surge of resolve and desire. Shoes and underwear quickly followed and, once she was naked, she tossed her hair back and took a long breath. "Make love to me."

He groaned, curling a hand around her neck and threading his fingers through her hair, anchoring her head. And then he was kissing her—long, hot and deep kisses that went beyond any they'd shared before. Nicola touched his chest, running eager hands all over him, feeling his smooth skin, seeking out sensitive places with her fingertips. She undid his fly and pushed the jeans down over his hips, and he took about two seconds to flick them off. And then they were naked together, breasts to chest, hip to hip, thigh to thigh. He kissed her again, slower, deeper, hotter and hotter with each passing moment. Nicola grabbed his shoulders, hanging on while he effortlessly carried her to the bed and, once they were lying together, his magic fingers went to work, finding her wet and ready for him.

But he took his time kissing her, anointing every part of her skin with his mouth, teasing her breasts with his tongue before taking an aching nipple into his mouth. Nicola pushed her hands into his hair, urging him, wanting him, feverish and desperate to feel him inside her.

"Please," she begged, dragging his lips to hers so she could feel the seductive thrust of his tongue in her mouth. "I want to feel you inside me."

"Soon, very soon," he promised, trailing his mouth down her rib cage and farther still, until finally he was between her thighs, driving her insane with such skillful prowess that she gasped his name over and over. It was insanely erotic, the most intense feeling she had experienced in her life. He continued his exploration, his hands gently stroking her breasts, his mouth on the most intimate part of her, and Nicola grabbed his shoulders and clung to him, shuddering as wave after wave of pleasure coursed through her.

And then, when the shudders stopped and her breathing came back to earth, he grabbed the foil packet he'd placed on the bedside table, ripped it open and rolled the condom in place. When he moved over her, resting his weight on his arms, his erection seeking entrance, she welcomed him, parting her thighs as she grabbed his hips and drew him intimately inside.

It was like it had always been between them. Two people who knew one another perfectly. He kissed her deeply, seeking out her tongue, tasting her as he moved, creating a steady, erotic rhythm she knew would bring them both release. But he took more time because, at that moment, it felt as though they had all the time in the world. No one would dare intrude. Their hips met each other, thrust for thrust, his hands in her hair, mouths hovering close together, sighing, breathing, faster and faster. And when they could take no more, they both rose up and into that place where only pleasure existed. They came together, sharp and intense and on a wave of white-hot release so overpowering it shook them both to the very core.

When it was over, he rolled off her, his breathing ragged, his chest rising and falling. He got up and disappeared into the bathroom, returning seconds later. Nicola didn't bother to hide her nakedness, since he'd seen all of her there was to see.

"Well," she said as he flopped back onto the bed and pulled the duvet up. "That was good."

"Good?" he queried, his eyes shut.

She chuckled. "Okay…great. The best ever. You've learned a thing or two since high school."

Laughter rumbled in his chest. "I needed to."

Nicola rolled and traced her fingertips through the light dusting of hair on his chest. "Oh, I don't know, we made out okay back then. Unless you have some other tricks in your repertoire?"

He gently grabbed a handful of her hair and found her mouth, kissing her. "I just might."

"Care to elaborate?"

He rolled, taking her with him, pinning her to the bed, his eyes never bluer. "You bet."

He spent the next two hours elaborating. They touched, they kissed, they talked and laughed, and Nicola experienced a connection she'd never felt before. It was rediscovery all over again—only this time, they were older, bolder and wiser. And finally, when they were both sated and exhausted, they fell asleep, spoon fashion. When she awoke, it was after six, and she caught a sliver of morning sun slicing through the curtains. She slipped out of bed and found her clothes, dressed quickly and then headed to the kitchen to make coffee.

And she thought long and hard about what she'd done.

She'd fallen back in love with Kieran. Big mistake.

She'd fallen back into his bed. Bigger mistake.

And now she had to work out a way to get out of it.

He'd made it abundantly clear that he was in no position to have a serious relationship. And she wouldn't accept anything less. She'd be a rebound relationship at best. And Nicola wasn't ever going to put herself in that place again. Because there was nothing nice about being someone's *convenience*. The next time she gave her heart, she wanted a heart in return.

He was still in bed when she returned to the bedroom, lying on his stomach, his face buried in the pillow. The duvet had slipped and exposed his back, and her fingers itched with the urge to touch him.

"I've brought coffee," she said and placed the mug on the bedside next to a significantly less full box of condoms. "It's time to wake up."

He groaned into the pillow. "Come back to bed."

"I can't," Nicola said. "I have to pick the kids up and get them ready for school."

He rolled and grabbed her hand, urging her to sit on the edge of the bed. "Can I see you tonight?"

"I'm working," she replied.

"Tomorrow?"

"Same."

His gaze narrowed. "So, you've had your wicked way with me, and now we're done?"

Nicola shrugged. "Well, that was the deal."

He pulled himself into a sitting position. "Seriously?"

She stepped back from the bed and propped her hands on her hips. "I don't want to have illusions about this, Kieran. I have to think about what's best for the boys and—let's face it—anyone you get involved with is going to be a rebound relationship."

"Rebound? That's ridiculous."

She shook her head. "It's not. Admit it. You only stopped wearing your wedding band a few months ago."

"Because of my—"

"I know why," she said, pushing air into her lungs, trying to stay strong. "Because it helped you stay connected to someone you loved. Someone you still love. I get it. But I've been that transitional girl before, and I don't want to be it again. I can't afford to, not when I have the boys to think about. They need stability, and they need me to be whole and functional and not in the middle of some messy, half-baked relationship with a man who still has feelings for someone else."

He swung his legs off the bed. "I'm not still in love with my ex-wife."

"Are you sure?" she shot back, aching inside. "Your body may be here, Kieran…but I think a big part of your heart is back in Sioux Falls."

"You're being—"

"Realistic," she said, cutting him off. "And this is what I want. We agreed to have sex and get each other out of our systems, and we did. It was great. It was fun. It was exactly what we needed to do."

He got up, grabbed a pair of sweats from the chair in the corner and slipped them on. "You didn't respond like you were trying to get me out of your system, Nic. You responded like you couldn't get enough. And I'll bet that if I took you in my arms and kissed you right now, we'd be in that bed within two seconds, and you'd be screaming my name."

"I can't believe you just said that."

"It's the truth."

"Your truth," she shot back.

He rolled his eyes. "Are we really going to have a fight about this?"

"Sei incredibile," she hissed. "I also can't believe I let you touch me."

"Believe it," he shot back. "I've got a half-empty box of condoms to prove it."

Nicola cursed at him again, grabbed her jacket, spun on her heels and strode from the room. By the time she reached the living room, she was so mad she was shaking. She grabbed her tote and headed for the front door. She slammed it on her way out—hard and with purpose—and barely took a breath until she reached her car. But she didn't expect to find Kieran chasing after her, wearing only his sweats, clearly stumbling over the gravel driveway for the last half a dozen steps.

"Would you stop being so ridiculous and come back inside?" he demanded. "It's freezing out here."

Nicola glared at him, ignoring the fact he was half-naked and standing on the sidewalk and that he had a mark on his neck that looked suspiciously like a hickey. Well, served him right!

"I'd have to be a fool to dive back into bed with you," she said and opened her car door.

"Nic...please?"

"Don't call me that," she said and glared at him. "Don't call me anything. Just don't call me!"

"You came here, remember?" he reminded her. "To my apartment. Twice in one week. And you asked me to make love to you. If anyone's done the chasing here, it's you."

She burned hot from head to toe. "You're such a conceited ass!"

He laughed humorlessly. "So, this is it? We're done?"

"Yes," she said, dumping her tote onto the passenger seat. "You couldn't be any more out of my system than you are right now."

Getting back into the car, she drove off, refusing to look back in case she spotted him in the rearview mirror. If she had her way, she'd never see him again.

She drove home, cursing that it was only two streets and didn't take long enough for her to have let off all the steam churning through her blood. She quickly showered and changed and then headed to JoJo's. The boys were eating breakfast with her father, and Salvatore immediately sensed something was wrong because he told his grandsons to stay in the kitchen and finish their breakfast.

"Everything okay, *bella*?"

"Fine, Papa," she lied. "Just a lot on my mind. Thank you for watching the boys again."

"Bad date?" he asked and grinned.

"The worst," she replied. "What makes you say that, though?"

He chuckled. "You have that look. Did you know your mama wouldn't go out with me the first time I asked her? She said I was too arrogant. Too sure of myself."

Nicola knew the story well. "But she chose you in the end."

"Exactly," he said, still grinning. "It's not where you start that counts…it's where you end up."

"That doesn't make any sense," she said.

"Of course it does, *bella*," he said more seriously. "You think all matters of the heart are logical. They are not. I saw you the other night with Kieran," he said, reminding her what she'd once felt—what she *still* felt— for the man she knew she had to get out of her system. "I saw you laughing and joking and looking like you used to…not like you have the world pressing down on your shoulders."

"I don't feel like that," she denied, heat burning her eyes. "I'm happy, Papa… I promise."

Her father, usually a man of few words, gently patted her arm. "You have done a good thing here. You have stepped up to care for your nephews, you have taken over running this place and you do a wonderful job. But remember that it is important to have a life of your own, too, hmm?"

"I will, I promise," she said, taking a deep breath.

Twenty minutes later, she was back home, and the boys were getting ready for school. By eight thirty, she drove them to class and had a quick meeting with Johnny's teacher. Even though the charges from the bakery incident had been dropped, she'd informed the school about his behavior, wanting to ensure he wasn't also misbehaving in class. And his teacher was understanding and supportive of her decision not to ground him. Johnny had been through enough. She made another appointment to catch up again with the teacher at the end of the week and once she had finished with the meeting, Nicola returned to town. There was a tour bus arriving at midday, and she talked through the menu with the chef before heading out to do the banking and settle a few accounts.

Her day dragged. Kieran was due to spend some time with Marco the following day, but she doubted he'd show. She suspected he'd pull out of the Big Brothers, too.

Good.

She didn't want to see him again. She didn't want any more reminders about how stupidly she'd behaved, or how *over* they really were. It was time she pulled herself together and forgot all about him. If she was ever going to move on, Nicola knew she had to let go of their past once and for all.

On Thursday morning, she had a coffee date planned with Connie and headed to the O'Sullivan hotel around eleven. Before she even made it to the elevator, she'd bumped into Gwen. She wondered if the older woman had some kind of sixth sense and she dragged an unresisting Nicola into the restaurant. Once they were seated and sipping cappuccinos, Gwen spoke, her expression kind and generous.

"You look like you need a friend," the older woman remarked. "Or a mom."

Tears sprang to her eyes, and Nicola swallowed hard. She didn't want to do this. She didn't want to fall apart in front of Kieran's mother. But good intentions flew out the window the moment Gwen patted her hand.

"I don't know what to do," she said and sighed. "I'm trying to keep it all together...to be a good parent to the boys, to run the restaurant, to have a life. But I feel as though I'm failing at most of those things."

"You're not," Gwen assured her. "Being a parent is hard work, but you'll get better at it as time moves along. Is there anything else?" the older woman asked. "Something else bothering you?"

"You mean a six-foot-two something," she admitted and expelled a heavy breath. "I don't know how to stop."

"Stop?"

"Being in love with your son," she said, her heart aching.

Gwen's mouth curled into a gentle smile. "Perhaps you're not meant to."

She shrugged. "Maybe. But it hurts when the person you love doesn't love you in return."

"Are you so sure that he doesn't?" Gwen asked.

Nicola nodded. "He's not ready for this...for us... for the boys. And I can't accept anything less than everything, not when I have two children to consider. If it was only me," she said and shrugged, "who knows, maybe I'd take the risk. But the kids already have him earmarked to make a great husband and father, and—"

"They're right," Gwen said and regarded her seriously. "My son is an incredible man. He's kind and compassionate and strong, and he *was* a good husband and a wonderful father. Losing all that broke something inside of him. But seeing you together...seeing him with your nephews and with you, it's obvious that the four of you belong together."

It was a nice, romantic idea, but Nicola wasn't convinced. She knew the boys would relish the idea, but it was a fantasy. They'd agreed to keep it casual, to purge any lingering feelings they had for one another. But it had spectacularly backfired. He wanted no-strings sex. She wanted a lifetime commitment.

"Liam said I was Kieran's Kryptonite," Nicola said quietly. "But I think that perhaps that's what we are to each other...it seems like a good idea but, for some reason, it just doesn't work."

"He's been hurt in the past," Gwen reminded her. "Badly. And he's terrified of that happening again. Can you blame him?"

"No," she replied. "But I don't want to be his rebound affair, either. I've been there before, and it's not a lot of fun."

"No, it's not," Gwen agreed. "I was married to a man for thirty-five years who was in love with someone else for most of that time…but I don't think that's your fate. I think you'll get the life you want."

Nicola wasn't so sure. "I want so many things. But right now, I'd settle for not feeling so unhappy."

Gwen smiled. "Don't give up on him, Nicola. He's worth fighting for."

"You're biased," she said and half shrugged.

"Of course. But you know I'm right."

She did. Because Kieran was worth fighting for. But she was, too…and that was want she wanted. His fight. His belief that they were more than simply a chemical reaction to one another. More than an itch needing to be scratched for a few hours. More than a memory.

She wanted his love.

But he had a mountain of insecurities to scale before she would let him into her heart ever again.

Chapter Ten

"So, are you and your girlfriend in the middle of some sort of crisis?"

Kieran stared his brother, ignored the question and kept walking around the garden. Nicola's garden. She was inside, working on the accounts for JoJo's. But knowing her as he did, there had to be steam coming out of her ears—he was sure of it.

Jonah grinned. "She's got spirit, that's for sure."

"She's not my girlfriend. She's not my anything," he said pointedly and waved the plans in front of his brother's face. "Can we get back to this?"

It was Friday afternoon and the second time he'd been at her house since Tuesday. The day before, he'd arrived to spend time with Marco, and she'd barely spared him a glance, muttering something about expecting him to bail. And he almost had. He'd almost pulled the plug on having anything to do with her, her nephews or the damned fishpond. But his conscience had given him grief and, in the end, he knew he didn't have the heart to disappoint the boys. It wasn't their fault that he and their aunt were having a…thing. And now they were happily shooting baskets through the new basketball hoop he'd fixed to the side of the shed the day before.

"Yeah…she's not anything. That's why you look as though you want to punch someone."

"Are you volunteering?"

Jonah laughed, which was unexpected, since he rarely looked anything other than moody and resentful. "Keep me out of your romance problems." He walked on ahead and then turned. "So, what did you do?"

"Do?"

There was another clang in the kitchen. "Yeah, *do*. You obviously screwed up."

Kieran's mouth twisted. "She's impossible."

"And you expected something different?" Jonah queried.

"I expect rational behavior. I expect to know what I've done wrong."

"From the woman you're in love with?" his brother said bluntly.

"I'm not in love with her," he denied and strode around the yard, standing in front of the spot where the pond would go.

"Sure you are," Jonah said and grinned for a second. "Not that it's any of my business. But Liam thinks you never stopped loving her. And since she's inside hating you, you should probably go in there and talk it out."

Kieran scowled. "Stay out of it. You *and* Liam."

"I'm out," Jonah said. "Just a little brotherly concern."

Kieran made an exasperated sound, shoved the plans into Jonah's hands and trudged up to the house, making his way into the kitchen. She was at the dining table, tapping keys on the laptop. Her hair was up, and he caught a glimpse of one shoulder as her loose sweater dipped to the left. He swallowed hard, trying to think about anything other than her skin, her scent, or the way she moved. But it was impossible. Everything about her affected him on some primary, soul-reaching level. If he had any sense, he'd ignore her bad mood, stride directly toward her and haul her into his arms and kiss her beautiful neck.

"What do you want?" she asked, not looking at him, but clearly sensing his presence.

Kieran moved into the kitchen and placed a hand on the countertop. "Just letting you know there'll be contractors here on Tuesday to dig out the hole for the pond."

"I'll write a check to cover it," she said, still not looking at him.

"It was my idea," he reminded her. "I'll pay for it."

"I'm not a charity case."

"No," he said, suddenly all out of patience. "At the moment you're a head case."

She jumped to her feet and jammed her hands onto her hips.

"Jerk."

Kieran sucked in a breath. "Why are you so angry?"

"You know why."

He shrugged. "If I did, I doubt we'd be having this conversation. You're the one who bailed the other day."

She glared at him. "*I'm* the one who bailed. *I'm* the one who chased you. I guess it's all on me."

"Let's get this straight," he said and moved closer toward her, crossing him arms. "You're angry because I pointed out the obvious?"

"I'm angry at myself," she shot back. "Not you."

"Sure doesn't seem like it."

"Not everything is about you," she said hotly. "I

realized I made a mistake and shouldn't have gotten involved, okay?"

"Is this because you think I'm still in love with my ex-wife?" he asked quickly. "Because I assure you, that's not the case."

"Then who are you in love with?"

Kieran rocked back on his heels, a rush of words surging through his blood, but none would come out. Suddenly he knew what she wanted…knew what she expected…but he couldn't admit what he was feeling. It was too early. Too raw. Too risky. And he wasn't ready for any declarations.

"Nic, I…"

"Exactly," she said and shrugged. "You can't. You're not ready. You're nowhere near ready. And as much as you want to deny it, you are still wrapped up in your ex-wife," she said and then raised a hand when he went to protest. "And, yeah, maybe it's not love. Maybe it's other feelings, other emotions…but they are still there. Still haunting you. Still making it impossible for you to move on."

Resentment sparked in his chest, heating his blood. "Okay," he said and waved an exasperated hand. "So, maybe I'm not ready for some huge commitment. But I'm ready to spend time with you and be with you and—"

"Sleep with me?" she added. "Yeah, I know. Just sex. No strings, remember."

"They were *your* words," he reminded her. "Not mine. You wanted to get me out of your system so *you* could move on. That's what you said. You wanted to get past us. That's why you came to my apartment. That's why you asked me to make love to you. And now you want—what? Something else? Something more? Or what?" He laughed humorlessly. "Consider yourself moved on, I guess."

She had tears in her eyes, but he wasn't swayed. He was pissed. He felt manipulated and betrayed. He'd trusted her to be honest and upfront, and now she was asking for something he wasn't ready to give. He'd had enough of this game.

"I'd like you to leave," she said and turned away. "I'll tell the boys you had to go. And take your brother with you."

"That's your answer? Kicking me out?"

She made a miffed sound. "I'm not going to waste any more time on you *or* us."

Kieran didn't hang around. What he wanted to do was go to O'Sullivan's and throw down a few shots of bourbon to help ease the rage and confusion coursing through his blood. But, since he was on call for the next three days, he headed home, slumped in front of the television and drank a cola.

His cell pinged, and he stared at the number. Nicola. He looked at the message.

Flowers would be nice. N

Flowers? Was she serious? Didn't they just break up? Not that they were together…but it sure felt like a breakup. He dumped the phone onto the sofa and stared at the television.

Damned if he'd be a part of anymore female manipulation. He'd spent too many years married to someone who had lied to his face over and over, pretending to want him, making him love a child who wasn't his. He wasn't going to be that stupid again. Or that gullible. His next relationship—if there was a next one—would be on his terms. And that meant he wasn't about to get sucked in by Nicola's hot-and-cold routine. She either wanted him or she didn't.

It would be his way or the highway.

He wouldn't be swayed. He couldn't be. Because he wasn't in love with her. Sure, he wanted her. And making love with her had been incredible. They had great chemistry.

And, of course, he *liked* her. They had a lot of history. A lot in common. He enjoyed being around her. He couldn't get enough of her scent, her smile, the damned sexy way she swayed when she walked. Kissing her was like nothing he'd ever experienced.

And he liked being around the kids, too, even though it was the last thing he'd imagined he'd want to do. And maybe the hurt he'd felt over losing Christian had lessened some since he'd been spending time with Marco and Johnny.

And maybe, the more time he spent with Nicola, his heart didn't feel like it was closed for business. Perhaps there were times over the past few weeks when he had stopped being afraid to actually feel something for someone, in case it was cruelly taken away.

He was conflicted. Because he wanted to be with her, but didn't know how to on her terms. She wanted so much more than he was ready to give.

Kieran glanced at the text message again. Was she trying to meet him halfway? To let him know they weren't as over as she had made out. It ignited something in his chest. Relief. Curiosity. Hope.

But I do not love her...

Still, that didn't stop him from heading to a florist in town first thing Saturday morning.

* * *

"Um…there's a big bunch on flowers on the bar with your name on them," Connie said early Saturday afternoon. "So, spill?"

Nicola shrugged and continued filling the salt grinders. Her friend had stopped by the restaurant to drop off more flyers for the rodeo, which was the following weekend. It was one of the major events on the calendar, with competitors coming from around the state to compete for their share of the purse and trophies. There would be a band and dancing and a variety of food and drink vendors, a Ferris wheel and fireworks later in the evening. Of course, the boys wanted to go. And she'd agreed to attend with one of the other parents at school—a single dad who seemed nice and had two young boys of his own. His name was Alex, and she'd bumped into him on Thursday evening at a parent-teacher conference at the school. They'd started talking and, before she knew it, she was agreeing to a date.

Not that it was really a date. But it would be nice to have some *new* adult male company for a change.

And it would help erase a *certain person* from her thoughts.

Because she was tired of thinking about Kieran. Exhausted from too little sleep and too many dreams.

"Nicola?" Connie prompted. "The flowers?"

She shrugged. "O'Sullivan. He's lost his mind."

"What does the card say?"

She mulled over the words for a few seconds. "*As requested.* And then just his initial. And before you ask, I have no idea what it means."

"Did you ask him?" Connie inquired, her eyes wide.

"Of course not," she replied.

"Why not?"

"Because I've misplaced my cell phone and don't know his number." She wasn't about to admit that she suspected she'd left her cell phone at his apartment.

Connie's mouth curved. "I have his number. I can give it to you. And you could always call the hospital?" Connie suggested.

"I know I could," she said. "But I don't want to. I don't want to see him. Talk to him. Touch him. Kiss him. Or anything. Ever again."

Connie's mouth twitched. "Those are some pretty specific things."

"Precisely. And I don't want his stupid flowers."

Her friend grinned. "It's kind of romantic."

Nicola rolled her eyes. "I thought you were on my side. Even though I know you adore the O'Sullivans."

"Not all of them," Connie said pointedly. "But I do like Kieran, and he clearly likes you."

Yeah, sure he does.

But that wasn't enough. Nicola wasn't going to be anyone's second fiddle ever again. Or anyone's consolation prize. He'd made it clear he wasn't up for anything serious and, with the boys to consider, she wasn't about to play roulette with their fragile emotions. Or her own.

"I hate him. End of story."

"Sure you do," Connie said, eyebrows angled. "You're completely in hate with him."

She scowled at her friend. "How about we talk about you and Jonah?"

Connie took about ten seconds to bail.

Nicola spent most of the weekend at the restaurant, other than Sunday afternoon watching a movie with Johnny. Her oldest nephew had opened up a lot in the past week and wasn't as moody and sullen as he'd been in the past. She'd made him apologize to the owner of the bakery, and the older man had agreed to Johnny doing some chores around the place a couple of afternoons after school when the repairs were complete. His accomplice had been forced to do the same thing. His friend didn't seem like a bad kid either, and she'd tentatively agreed to let the boys continue their friendship sometime in the future.

She took some time off on Monday and spent the morning doing a few errands. When she got home, there was a large basket on her doorstep filled with an assortment of candy and wrapped in clear cellophane. There was a card, and she recognized Kieran's scrawl immediately.

For you... K.

Flowers and chocolate? What was he thinking?

She fought the overwhelming urge to confront him but decided the best defense was to ignore him completely. The boys were delighted by the candy, giggling their way through a bar of peppermint chocolate when they got home from school. The babysitter arrived. Mrs. Holden lived down the street, was a widow and had no problem staying with the boys until Nicola returned from the restaurant the few nights a week she worked. It meant her nephews weren't constantly traveling back and forth between the restaurant and the house during school nights.

On Tuesday, the contractors arrived, and she knew Kieran had dropped by because he'd left a note taped to her door informing her of the contractor's schedule. He'd also left a copy of the plans for her and said he'd stop by on Thursday to spend time with Marco and Johnny.

That meant she should make herself scarce. When she arrived home from the restaurant on Thursday night, Mrs. Holden's green Ford sedan was nowhere to be seen. But Kieran's Jeep was parked out by the curb. She stalked up the path, opened the door and found him in the living room, television on, feet up on the coffee table.

And asleep.

She pushed his shoulder to wake him, and he opened his eyes instantly and pulled his feet off the coffee table. "Hey, you're back."

"Where's Mrs. Holden?"

"She had a bad headache, so I sent her home."

Of course he did. "Where are the boys?"

"In bed and asleep. School night, remember?"

Nicola's belly rolled over. He looked so gorgeous with his nut-brown tousled hair and whiskery shadow along his jaw. In jeans and a gray Henley shirt, he looked so hot he could have melted butter.

"You should have—"

"I tried to call your cell, but it went to voice mail," he offered and clicked the TV volume down as he got to his feet.

"I misplaced my cell last week," she explained. "I'm using my spare. I thought I might have left it at your apartment."

He frowned. "You texted me Friday *and* Monday on that cell."

"No," she insisted and searched for her spare phone in her tote. "I didn't."

"The flowers…" His voice trailed off. "You told me you liked flowers. And then I received another one saying you liked candy."

"I did no such thing," she said hotly. "I don't understand how that could—"

"Of course," he said quickly and ran a weary hand through his hair. "The boys."

She stared at him. "Huh?"

"You said you lost your cell phone. They must have taken it and sent the messages."

"They stole my phone?" She was horrified. "And sent you messages to buy me flowers and chocolate?"

"Looks like it."

He was smiling, but Nicola saw nothing funny about the situation. "It didn't occur to you that I would never do that?"

He shrugged. "I thought you were...you know...flirting."

"Why would I do that?" she demanded, turning hot all over.

"Because you want me," he replied casually. "Why else?"

Heat scorched her cheeks. "I don't want you. I don't want anything to do with you."

"Are you sure about that?"

"Positive," she replied. "And I noticed that you didn't take the check I left to cover the costs for the pond. And don't think, simply because you're here, that I—"

She didn't get to say anything more because suddenly she was in his arms and he was kissing her. No finesse, no soft seduction. Just a hard, passionate kiss that should have infuriated her—but instead it curled her toes and unleashed a fire in her belly that could have sent them both up in flames.

And then he released her just as quickly, color slashing his cheeks, his breathing ragged. "Sometimes you talk way too much."

Nicola glared at him. "I officially hate you. And

stop sending me flowers and candy. And don't kiss me again... I don't like it."

"Liar," he shot back. "I think you're really turned on right now."

Nicola stormed across the room, then headed down the hallway and opened the front door. She knew he would follow, and she made a dramatic gesture, ushering him outside.

"Thank you for watching the boys. Good night."

He lingered in the doorway. "God, you're beautiful when you're angry."

"Go to hell."

He laughed softly. "I've missed you."

"Well, I haven't missed you," she shot back, lying through her teeth. Because she had missed him like crazy.

"I could stay for a while. We could talk," he said and shrugged. "Or make out." His voice flowed through her like fine whiskey.

His audacity was astounding. "I'm not in the market for another one-night stand. I'm looking for real commitment," she reminded him. "And that's not something you can give me, is it?"

"Who knows what the future holds?"

"I do," she shot back. "I know my future. I know that you're not in it. I know that on Sunday I have a date for the rodeo with a very nice man who's not afraid of commitment."

His expression narrowed. "A date? I don't believe you."

"Believe it."

"I was hoping we could go together. I'm part of the medical staff for the event, but my shift is only for two hours in the afternoon. I know the boys want to watch the fireworks, and I thought we could spend some—"

"I broke up with you, Kieran. And I have a date," she said again. "Now, good night."

He left, and she closed the door before he was down the porch steps. Then she leaned against the door and burst into tears. God, how long had it been since she'd really cried? Forever. Not since Gino and Miranda's funeral. And she needed it. She needed the emotional release it gave her. She needed to embrace the grief and sorrow that came with it.

And she was still blinking away tears twenty minutes later after she'd closed up downstairs, and then she took a shower and dressed in her pajamas and went to check on the boys. She was just about to turn off Johnny's night-light when he rolled over and spoke.

"Has Kieran gone home?"

"Yes," she replied and tucked his duvet around his bony shoulders.

"Marco and I really like him."

"I know you do," she said and touched his hair. "Is that why you took my cell phone?"

He looked instantly guilty and then nodded. "We were trying to help."

She knew exactly what they were trying to do. "It's wrong to steal things."

"I know," he admitted. "I'm sorry."

Nicola sighed. "You also know my password?"

He shrugged a fraction. "I saw you put it in once. I just remembered." He dug between his mattress and bed frame and withdrew her phone. "I think the battery ran out," he said and passed it to her.

She looked at the phone, then knelt next to the bed

and said gently, "Don't do anything like this again, okay?"

"I won't," he said, his voice wobbling. "I promise."

Nicola ruffled his hair. "Good night, kiddo. I love you."

"I love you, too."

She said good-night, headed to the next room to check on Marco and found him fast asleep, and then walked into her bedroom. It wasn't Gino and Miranda's old room. It was a smaller guest room at the end of the hallway. She couldn't quite bring herself to occupy the master suite. In fact, as much as the house was lovely and well designed, it had never felt like a home to her. She stayed for the boys but knew she'd never feel as though it was her own. Maybe she should put the house on the market, start fresh somewhere. The very idea made her feel more alone than she'd believed possible. She walked into the bathroom to brush her teeth, caught a glimpse of her unruly hair, red-rimmed eyes and blotched complexion and grimaced.

How did I get here?

And suddenly, every yearning, every longing, every dream she'd ever had came rushing forward and fresh tears burned her eyes. Marriage, children, a career… things she'd once believed she would have, expectations she'd taken for granted. Now, those dreams seemed so far away…unreachable as the stars surrounding a distant planet. And she was sad…for herself, for Marco and Johnny, for the babies she feared she'd never have. Because she did want kids. She wanted a large family, she wanted Sunday dinners and picnics by the river. And she longed for someone to love her, a man whose arms were strong and whose heart was big enough for her, the boys and any children they had together.

A fool's dream, maybe. But she couldn't let it go. She saw her children vividly…with dark hair and glittering blue eyes. The image was overwhelmingly acute and made her ache deep in her womb. It was the same image she'd had since she was young. Because, in her heart, in the secret place where she allowed only dreams to linger, she'd always believed that she would have Kieran's child. Even when she was with Carl, creating a life together, planning a wedding and a future, the old dreams would occasionally resurface, reminding her that she'd already had her one great love.

And, for a moment, she'd gotten him back.

That was what hurt—the knowledge that they'd been so close to recapturing something special. Of course, the outcome was all her own fault. She'd known going in, when she'd spouted words about purging him from her thoughts, getting him out of her system, using sex to sate her old resentment—in her heart, she'd known it was a lie. A falsehood of epic proportions. The biggest of her life.

But on Sunday, when Alex arrived to collect her and the boys in his state-of-the-art minivan that might have impressed her had she not felt so desperately unhappy, Nicola knew she had to snap out of her funk and try and have a good time.

Because Alex was nice. Tall, fair-haired and handsome in a clean-cut, accountant kind of way, he was exactly what she'd expected. He had a good sense of humor, two well-behaved young sons, a good job, and he appeared genuinely keen to get to know her. Although a little younger, his sons went to school with Marco and Johnny and once they were all seated in the minivan, they headed off.

They arrived at the show grounds a little after four

and had to walk a few hundred yards from the designated parking area. The bronc-riding events had already started, and they watched for a while, before the boys pleaded to check out the variety of stalls on the midway. As they walked behind the kids, Alex chatted about his job as a surveyor and asked her about the restaurant and her family, and it was all very nice. They sat at one of the picnic tables and watched as the band set up on the stage, eating hot dogs and sipping sodas.

Yep…as far as first dates went, it was a good one.

Except for Johnny and Marco. They were clearly not happy with the arrangement. They weren't impolite because they knew she wouldn't have stood for it, but they didn't waste any time letting her know in private that they didn't want to hang around with Alex's kids or Alex.

Things got worse when his younger son Tim raced off and tumbled into an elderly couple carrying donuts and hot coffee. The child was scalded down one arm and, despite Nicola's attempt to run cool water over the burn, the boy was clearly upset, and Alex suggested they head to the medical tent set up near the bleachers.

And, of course, since the afternoon seemed to be going from bad to worse, the first person she spotted when they entered the tent, stethoscope around his gorgeous neck, broad shoulders superbly filling out his white coat, was Kieran.

Chapter Eleven

His gaze zoomed in on her the moment they stepped in front of the small reception table and then to Alex as he explained to the nurse what had happened to his son. Marco and Johnny couldn't have been happier, and they quickly skipped past reception and headed for him. But he was at reception in seconds, regarding them suspiciously.

"Is there a problem here?"

The nurse explained about the burn and, within a few minutes, the wound had been examined and treated, and Tim had a gauze dressing around his arm. While Alex gave a few personal details to the nurse and the boys picked out grape lollipops from the jar on another table, Kieran cornered her by the door.

"You're actually on a date?"

She shrugged. "I told you as much."

He flicked his gaze toward Alex and scowled. "Who's the stiff?"

True, Alex was wearing a shirt and tie and did seem a little out of place among the cowboys and horses and locals dressed in denim and plaid, but he was still a nice man. And Kieran had no right to question her about anything or anyone.

"I think that's self-explanatory."

"Where did you find him?"

She scowled. "He's a friend."

"A friend like I used to be, or a friend like I am now?" he queried, his voice little more than a ragged whisper.

The implication wasn't missed. "None of your business."

His gaze narrowed. "You really like this guy?"

"Sure."

"And he likes you?"

"Of course," she said irritably. "Why else would we be on a date?"

"To torture me maybe?"

Nicola stared at him. "Not everything is about you."

He shrugged. "Do the boys like him?"

"Why wouldn't they?" she shot back. "He's a nice man."

"He's not the right man for you," Kieran said quietly.

Nicola's glare turned upward. "And why not?"

He reached out and touched her hair. "You know why."

She got lost in his gaze, suddenly held captive by his glittering blue eyes. His fingers stroked her cheek and as she pulled away Nicola looked across the tent and met Alex's curious stare. He smiled, nodded, and then gathered up his kids.

She left Kieran and met Alex on her way out of the tent. He spoke first.

"I'm going to take the kids home," he said and placed his hands on his youngest son's shoulders.

Nicola didn't argue. "Okay. Thanks for…the ride in the minivan."

He laughed. "Will you be able to get a ride home?"

She nodded. "Yes. Thanks again. Take care."

She said goodbye with the vague promise to see him again. However, she didn't stay in the medical tent but collected the boys, ignored Kieran completely and headed outside, finding a spot on the bleachers where they could watch the bronc riding. She sat there for an hour, fielded a few texts from both Connie and Annie asking where she was and hid among the crowd like a coward. And she seethed. Because he had no right to question anything she did. One magical night together didn't mean he had a claim on her. If he wanted one, he had to give her what she wanted. And she knew he wasn't ready for that.

But he found her soon enough and squeezed in between her and the boys, who were happy to give *him* whatever he wanted, it seemed. He'd ditched the white coat and looked sexy as sin in jeans, checked shirt and jacket. He offered her the coffee he carried and she refused, staring straight ahead, watching some cowboy get flung off a frenzied colt and then get to his feet without a scratch.

The crowd cheered loudly, and Nicola jumped. "I wish you'd leave me alone."

He grinned. "No, you don't. And now that your date has bailed you don't have any excuse for us to not to hang out together," he said and grabbed her hand. "So, have you had enough of this bronc-riding thing? I told Liam I'd meet him and Kayla by the Ferris wheel in five minutes."

"You want to ride the Ferris wheel?"

"Sure," he said easily and tapped the boys on the

shoulder and said they were heading for the rides. They had moved on from the bleachers and were walking toward the midway when he spoke again. "The last time we rode the Ferris wheel together, I got to second base."

"First base," she corrected and called the boys back from running too far off.

He laughed. "I'm sure it was second base."

"First," she said again. "And it was a long time ago."

He nodded. "You look nice, by the way."

She glanced down at her jeans, bright red shirt, sparkly vest and high-heeled cowboy boots. "Thanks."

"I think I must have a thing for you in boots. But I like the other ones. You know. The black ones."

"Weirdo."

He laughed again, and the sound rumbled in his chest, making her heart skip a beat. "You know exactly what you do to me when you wear those boots."

"I'm not exactly the temptress type," she reminded him. "But I'm glad you like them."

"So, friends again?"

She shrugged. "I'll think about it."

When they reached the Ferris wheel, Gwen was there, hands on the stroller that held her grandson, Liam and Kayla looking on with pride. Strangely, Marco and Johnny declined the offer to ride on the wheel, instead assuring Nicola they'd prefer to remain with Gwen. And Gwen looked delighted by the prospect. Liam made some faintly crude remark that was meant for adult ears only, and Nicola knew she and Kieran were being observed as though they were under a microscope. She almost suspected that Kieran had put the boys up to staying behind but, before she could protest, they were both settled on the ride and it was moving upward. It was dark now and, as the Ferris wheel lifted them, the people on the ground became smaller. She waved to the boys for a while, until they lost interest.

"Everything looks insignificant from up here," she remarked and stiffened when his arm came around to rest on her shoulders.

"Relax, will you? I'm not going to pounce."

"Your family thinks we're back together," she said bluntly.

"I know they do."

The seat wobbled and his hand tightened on her shoulder. She wanted to brush his touch away. She wanted to stop imagining they were back where they used to be. Because that hadn't ended so great.

"Are you going to tell them that we're not?"

"Honestly, I don't know what to tell them."

She shrugged. "It's not like I want people talking about us anyhow. I hate gossip. You know, you broke my heart on graduation day, and everyone knew it," she said quietly, almost to the wind.

He nodded. "I have to live with it."

"You devalued everything we were that day," she said, her pain suddenly palpable. "I hated you for a long time."

"I deserved it. All that hate and anger, every bit. But time changes things, Nicola."

"Nothing's changed, Kieran," she said and shuddered in the breeze. "We're right back where we were. And I don't know if I'd have the strength to recover again."

"What if you don't have to recover?" he said. "What if this is exactly how it's meant to turn out?"

"Then I suffered for nothing," she said and shook her head. "Because I'm back here in the same place anyhow."

"Which is where?"

Loving you. Nicola's chest tightened, and she felt the words burn on the edge of her tongue. "Wanting you."

He reached out and cradled her jaw, rubbing his thumb across her bottom lip. "Is that all it is?"

Nicola rested her head against his shoulder and sighed. "No."

"Then that's gotta feel better than hating me."

"Sometimes it's the same thing."

"And if we're both feeling it?"

"But we're not," she said and pulled away. "We want different things."

"What if we don't, Nic? Let's just date for a while and see if we can make it work."

"That's the problem," she said, dying inside. "You need a backup plan. An escape clause. And I don't want that, Kieran. I want stability. I want—I need—everything. Not the easy part, like dating and making out and flowers and making up after a fight. I have two kids to think about now, and they also need stability. They need a home. So, I need commitment. Assurances."

"There are no assurances," he said flatly. "You should know that better than anyone."

"Because I've been dumped twice?" She tensed as the car swung, realizing they were almost down at the bottom again. "You're right, I do know. But the next time, I want to get it right."

He laughed harshly, but she could hear the pain underneath. "You want the impossible."

"Maybe I do," she replied. "But I'm not going to compromise simply to make it easy for you."

"Sounds like you're trying to make it easy for yourself," he said. "You're setting rules, making demands."

"So are you," she snapped. "Only you're doing it in your usual passive-aggressive way."

"Why? Because I don't generally let my temper get the better of me? And I don't dish out ultimatums? Isn't that how we broke up the first time?" He shook his head. "We were eighteen years old, and you were making plans for our future. Talking about getting engaged. It's no wonder that I bailed."

Humiliation coursed through her veins. "I thought we were committed to each other."

"We were kids, Nic. Teenagers who'd been talking about college and summer break. And then, all of a sudden, you were obsessed with getting me to sign on the proverbial bottom line. I felt trapped and caged like I had no other option than to end things."

"Trapped and caged?"

He shrugged. "I half expected you to tell me you were pregnant."

Rage and hurt clung to her bones. "That's why you broke it off? Because you thought I was going to try and trap you with a baby?"

"It crossed my mind."

"You think I'd do that to you? Even back then?"

"People do things…"

"People?" She frowned. "I think that's *your* past talking," she said, aching inside. "Because it's definitely not ours. I never lied to you or deceived you. But because of what happened with your ex-wife, now you think every woman will do the same thing."

"People say things to get what they want. And let's face it, you haven't exactly been transparent about this thing between us."

"What does that mean?"

"Two weeks ago, you said we should have an affair,"

he reminded her. "'Just sex,' you said. And we did. Then suddenly, the parameters shifted, and it wasn't just about sex. It was about something else...about you wanting what *you* want. You can sugarcoat it any way you want, but at the end of the day, it's still a kind of deception."

The accusation was obvious, and the hurt she felt quickly morphed into anger. "You think I've manipulated you with sex?"

He shrugged. "You brought another man here today, knowing it would bait me."

Nicola was furious. The audacity. The ego. The conceit. Like he was some great prize that she was secretly hunting, using her wiles and sexuality. When he had so many walls up, so much baggage about being deceived that he couldn't see what was right in front of his face.

The Ferris wheel stopped and, once the worker undid the seat, Nicola pulled her tote over her shoulder, jumped down and rushed off, wanting nothing more than to get away from him. Outside the safety barrier, she spotted Gwen and the boys, and Liam and Kayla close by with their son at the cotton candy stand. She was in no mood for company and quickly asked Gwen to watch the boys for a while, knowing they'd be safe with the older woman. She'd taken half a dozen steps when she felt Kieran's hand on her arm, and he twirled her around.

"Nic, wait up, let me—"

She shrugged him off, conscious that her nephews and his family was watching the entire exchange. "I was right to hate you! We are so over."

Then she raced off, finding solace in the crowds, her heart in tatters.

* * *

"So, that looked like it went well."

Kieran glanced sideways, frowned at his brother and then sighed. "Yeah, just great."

His brother laughed. "I remember when Kayla and I first got together. I don't think I slept for a month." Liam clapped a hand on his back. "You'll figure it out."

Kieran wasn't so sure. Every conversation they had morphed into an argument. Every admission seemed to make things worse.

"I'm not so sure."

"Well, go and apologize."

Kieran scowled. "For what?"

"Anything," Liam replied. "Everything.

He turned around and saw the boys standing beside his mother, looking at him with serious, yearning expressions. Looking at him as though he'd screwed up…big-time.

"How're you ever gonna get her to marry you if you guys keep fighting all the time?" Johnny said and pulled the hoodie over his head.

Kieran turned hot from head to toe. The kid certainly had a way of getting everyone's attention. He looked at his mother, saw she was shaking her head slightly and guilt quickly swam in his gut.

His family moved off, heading toward the main stage where the band was playing. Knowing the boys were very safe with his mother, Kieran headed back to the medical tent to collect his bag and make sure he wasn't needed any longer. He grabbed his belongings, quickly put them in his car and then walked back to his family.

His brother was seated with Kayla, and they were completely focused on their son. His mother was talking to the boys, their expressions serious. He watched the exchange for a while, seeing the way they listened attentively and were nodding. Gwen was a wonderful grandmother, just as she'd been a wonderful mother. As he watched over the boys he realized he'd developed real affection for them. The knowledge that he'd become attached to the kids so quickly shocked him to the core. For two years, he'd avoided feeling anything. Avoided people. Avoided relationships. The very idea of getting involved with anyone after his divorce had been unthinkable. That he'd allow himself to care for a child again was unimaginable. And yet, watching Johnny and Marco sitting with his mother, talking to her so earnestly, Kieran realized that he did care.

He cared about them. And he cared about Nicola.

He'd never stopped.

Not after graduation. Not during college. Not through medical school and his residency. And not even through his marriage and divorce. He'd simply tucked the feelings away, wrapping them up because there was no point in dwelling on something that was part of his past.

But the past was over, and he was very much in the present.

Kieran walked over to the kids and sat on the bench. There was a lot of noise around them. A lot of families. Some sitting at picnic tables. Some stretched out on blankets with picnic baskets. Some were simply couples, holding hands, embracing, sharing a kiss or two. Even with all the activity—with the midway sounds, the band playing, the rodeo caller blaring over the PA system, and the sound of children laughing and squealing—Kieran experienced an almost surreal sense of intimacy with his family in that moment. He looked at his brother, so happy and content with the woman he loved and their baby son. Liam had fought hard for his happiness and his family and, despite the difficulties they had faced, he and Kayla had pulled through and made a family together.

Kieran thought about Jonah, who was fighting so hard to *not* be a part of them, but who had agreed to help his newfound brother build the ridiculous fishpond with little resistance. And watching Marco and Johnny together, seeing their bond the way he had a bond with Liam and Sean, Kieran realized he wanted that same bond with his half brother. They were family. Blood. And he needed to work harder. To stop avoiding getting close. Sure, Jonah could be a pain, but Kieran knew he needed to make more of an effort to break down his brother's defenses.

Thinking about Jonah turned Kieran's thoughts to their father. He'd spent very little time with J.D. since he'd returned to Cedar River. True, Kieran had always been closer to his mother than to his dad, but he was man enough to admit that he'd steered clear of J.D. because he was ashamed of his father's past. His dad had cheated and lied and kept his son a secret for three decades…and there was enough deception in his behavior to remind Kieran of his own failed marriage.

Nicola had accused him of still loving his ex-wife. But that wasn't it. True, while he was married, he'd believed that he'd loved Tori, but it wasn't losing her that had broken him inside.

It was failing. *His* failure.

He'd failed at his marriage, and he'd failed the child he had believed was his son. Because if Tori had truly loved him and he'd loved her, if he'd tried harder, been more attentive, given her what she'd needed, maybe Christian *would* have been his. Of course, it was moot now. And the pain, he realized, *had* lessened. Being home, working at the hospital, hanging out with his family had helped ease the ache in his heart.

It made him see that he could feel again. And trust again. He could live an authentic life and not be afraid that it would all be stolen away. Sure, it had taken effort. But with effort, he grasped as he watched his family, came reward.

Which meant one thing—he needed to make an effort with Nicola.

They were good together. They worked. They made one another laugh.

And she'd loved him once...maybe she would again.

He sent her a text message asking her to come back to the picnic table so they could talk. When she didn't respond in a few minutes, he sent an emoji of hands begging. When nothing came back within ten minutes, he took a selfie with the boys. When she still didn't respond, he sent another selfie with the kids, only this time they were wearing the fake nose-and-mustaches that he quickly went and bought from a vendor on the midway.

Of course, the kids thought it was hilarious at first. But when she didn't respond after half an hour, their delight turned to obvious distress.

"Has she left us?" Marco asked, clearly upset.

Kieran cursed his stupidly in involving the kids in his scheme to get her attention and managed a smile. "Of course not. She probably can't hear her phone's ringtone with all the noise here."

"She has it on vibrate," Johnny said, and Kieran glanced at his mother and shrugged.

"Maybe she got lost?" Marco suggested, his lip wobbling.

"Or maybe she doesn't want to look after us anymore," Johnny said and nodded, as though he had all the answers. "*I* wouldn't."

"Does that mean we'll be festered?" Marco asked, clearly unhappy.

"Fostered," Kieran corrected and then cursed himself. "And no, that won't happen. She's not answering because she's mad at me, not you guys. She loves you both very much. And I'm sure she'll be back soon."

"If she doesn't, we'll have to go and live with Uncle Vince," Johnny announced. "Coz *Nonno* is too old to look after us."

"But I don't want to leave my school," Marco wailed and began to cry.

Kieran grabbed his hand reassuringly. "You're not leaving your school. You're not moving in with your uncle. You're staying right here."

"Can't you do something to make sure she's not mad at you anymore?" Marco asked and hiccuped.

"Sure he could," Liam said and laughed, ignoring how Kayla jabbed him in the ribs. "Nothing makes a woman less mad than a..." his brother paused for effect *"...diamond."*

"A diamond?" Marco echoed.

Kieran glared at his brother and shook his head, but Liam was clearly enjoying his discomfort.

"Yes," Liam said, still grinning as he wiggled the third finger on his left hand. "One that goes right here."

"Would you stop—"

"Oh, for God's sake," Liam said, clearly exasperated. "Just admit that you're in love with her and want to marry her and want to be a father to these two great kids."

Pandemonium broke out. His mother started laughing delightedly. Kayla admonished her husband. And the boys were suddenly jumping up and down excitedly and then began whispering to one another. Kieran shot to his feet, when without warning, both boys suddenly raced past him and headed directly for a large oak tree. Before he could register their intent, they were both swinging from a couple of limbs and then scaled up the tree about twenty feet.

Kieran strode to the base of the tree, ignoring the curious stares and whispers from several onlookers. His mother and brother were soon at his side. He looked up, and relief overwhelmed him when he realized the kids were safe. He and his brothers had climbed the same tree many times when they were kids. Which didn't mean they could stay up there. There was a lot of noise around them, and he raised his voice so they could hear.

"Come on," he demanded. "Get down here."

"Not until Aunt Nicola gets back," Johnny announced defiantly. "We want to talk to her."

"She's going to be furious if she gets back and you're up there."

"But it's you she's mad at," Marco reminded him. "Not us."

Kieran sighed heavily. "I'm not joking…get down now."

"Do you really want to be our dad?" Johnny asked, eyes wider than Kieran had ever seen. "Because that would be okay if you did."

"I want you to get down out of the tree," Kieran said tersely. "You've got five seconds."

Both boys laughed at him. "Now you sound like our dad," Marco said and giggled.

Frustrated, Kieran pulled his cell from his pocket and sent Nicola a text.

They're up a tree and won't come down. Stop sulking and get your ass back here now.

It took two seconds to get a reply.

On my way.

Four minutes and thirty-six seconds later, she returned. And she didn't look happy. She ignored Kieran completely and looked up at her nephews, hands on hips, chest heaving.

"What's going on here?" she demanded.

"We're *pro-venting*," Marco announced proudly.

"Huh?"

"I think he means *protesting*," Kieran supplied and came up beside her.

There was laughter around them, particularly since the crowd had grown. In fact, there were about thirty people standing around the tree.

"Protesting what?" she shot back, arms now waving.

"Their right to get what they want," he said and shrugged.

"Which is what, exactly?" she asked, her eyes narrowed.

"Me," he replied. "And you. Together."

Her mouth fell open. "What are you talking about?" she demanded and then looked up at the boys before he could reply. "I want you out of that tree, right now!"

"Not until you stop being mad at Kieran," Johnny said matter-of-factly.

She glared at him. "Did you put them up to this?"

"Of course not. But they want what they want."

"This is ridiculous. Johnny, Marco…climb down now."

"Not until you two make up," Johnny said and almost lost his balance. A petrified hush came over the group.

"Do something, will you?" she hissed in Kieran's direction. "This is all your doing."

"I wasn't the one ignoring the text messages."

She scowled. "I needed to be away from you. I needed to think."

"Are you about done?" he inquired and watched her, bewitched by her beautiful hair and pouting lips. And then clarity washed over him like a great wave.

"I'm done."

"Good," he said and grabbed her hand and then promptly dropped to one knee. "Then, marry me?"

Chapter Twelve

Nicola wondered if she'd stepped into a dream. Kieran was in front of her, proposing marriage. There was a crowd of people around them, who were now cheering, and she could hear Johnny's and Marco's excited whoops from their spot in the tree.

She tried to tug her hand away, but his grip was firm. "What?"

"You heard. Marry me. Be my wife. Let me be your husband."

Not a dream. A nightmare. "Stop it," she demanded. "This isn't helping."

He shrugged, still on his knee, still holding her hand, still looking up at her. "It's what they want."

What the kids wanted. Of course. Not what he wanted. And she knew he was saying it only to defuse the situation with her nephews. "But it's not what I want. Get on your feet this minute."

"You don't want to marry Kieran?" Marco said from his spot up the tree. "We thought you liked him."

She did like him. *She loved him.* And she was furious with Kieran for making a mockery out of her feelings. She twisted her hand free and stepped back, looking around helplessly, searching for an ally. Gwen was smiling widely and nodded, and then she glanced toward Liam, who winked at her. So, they were all in on it together. A ruse to get the boys out of the tree. She swallowed hard, grabbed Kieran's arm and dragged him to his feet. Of course, she had to play along, to make out like it was what she wanted, too. And afterward, she never wanted to see him again.

"Okay," she said and looked up at the boys. "Sure, we'll get married. Now, can you two come down from there please."

She heard cheering and clapping, but it was suddenly drowned out by the white noise screeching in her brain. Humiliation coursed through her blood, and she swallowed the heavy lump in her throat. While it was clearly a great joke to the O'Sullivans, Nicola hurt so much she could barely breathe.

"You gotta kiss each other first," Johnny announced, tottering on a thick branch.

Nicola's heart lurched. If he fell…if anything happened to either of the two precious children she'd been bestowed custody of, she would never forgive herself. And they needed to know she had their back and that she would do anything to keep them safe and protected.

She took a breath and leaned toward Kieran. His arm looped around her, settling on her hip, and he drew her closer, his intent obvious. Nicola looked up at him, her eyes burning.

"I'll never forgive you for this," she whispered.

"Sure you will," he said and inched closer. "You just agreed to marry me."

"I wouldn't marry you," she said on a sigh, his mouth hovering above hers, "if you were the last man on the planet."

"Wanna tell them that?" he challenged, his gaze darting upward for a moment.

Her denial was smothered by the soft touch of his lips, and the crowd cheered again. Nicola swayed, felt his hand tighten, and she sighed against his mouth. His kiss reminded her of everything they had once been to one another, of everything they'd rekindled in the past couple of weeks and then of everything she knew they had lost. Because they had no future. The kiss was just for show. His proposal was a joke.

Suddenly, Liam was by the tree trunk helping them down, and the boys were racing toward her. Marco began jumping around them excitedly, and Johnny gave a thumbs-up sign. Nicola pulled herself away from Kieran's embrace and hugged both boys.

"Don't ever do something like that again. You scared me!"

"We've climbed that tree a hundred times," Marco announced. "*Nonno* brings us to the park all the time."

She made a mental note to talk to her father about his activities with the boys.

"I think we should go home now," she said, grateful that some of the crowd had begun to dissipate. "There's been enough excitement for one evening."

"But we haven't seen the fireworks yet," Marco wailed and then pouted. "You promised."

"And people should always keep their promises," Johnny added. "Right?"

"Of course," she said. "The rodeo event will be finished soon, so we can go back to the bleachers and find a good spot to sit."

"We'd rather stay here," Marco said and rushed over to clutch Gwen's hand. "I wanna stay with my new grandma."

Nicola moaned inwardly. Things had gone from bad to worse. She was about to explain that Gwen wasn't actually going to be their grandmother, when the older woman spoke.

"I think that's a great idea. Let's go and find a place to sit so we can talk about how great grandmas are and how little boys shouldn't climb trees without permission."

"See," Kieran said as Gwen walked back to the picnic table with both children. "All fixed."

"I really hate you right now."

His mouth curved at the edges. "Is that any way to talk to your fiancé?"

She laughed humorlessly, aware that they were now alone, standing by the tree. "I'm not going to marry you."

"'People should always keep their promises,'" he said, reminding her of Johnny's words. "Right?"

Nicola glared at him. "You know I only agreed to get them to come down. Stop being ridiculous. You don't want to marry me any more than I want to marry you."

"I don't?"

She waved a dismissive hand, torn between hating him and loving him, because he was talking about marriage like it was a casual thing, and to Nicola it was precious and something she had dreamed about. "They'll have forgotten all about it by the time they get home."

"Don't be so sure," he said, his blistering gaze unwavering. "They're terrified you're going to leave them."

She gasped. "I would never do that."

"I know that…but that's a child's logic. It's why Marco is so emotional, why Johnny acts like the tough guy. Those are their coping mechanisms for what they believe is inevitable. Being left. Being alone."

Heat filled her chest, and she glanced toward the boys. "But I'll never leave them. They're my nephews. My family. They're my children now. How could they possibly think I'd leave them?"

"Because when people are hurt, when they experience grief and loss that seems unimaginable, they get scared. And afraid. Afraid to…believe. Afraid to hope that something great is actually possible."

An odd expression came into his eyes, and for a moment, the tiniest of seconds, Nicola wondered if he was talking about the boys or himself. But the look was gone in a flash. And they were back to their usual stance… their usual wall of resistance.

"I should take them home and talk to them, reassure them," she said, almost to herself.

"It's not words they want, Nicola. It's actions."

She stiffened. "You mean, like pretending that we're getting married."

"I'm not pretending."

She made a disbelieving sound. "Are you saying you actually *want* to marry me?"

"Of course."

Of course. Just like that. He was about as romantic as a rock. "That's crazy. And impossible. Marrying you just because my nephews think you hung the moon is out of the question. I've told you before, I'm not in the market to be anyone's rebound relationship. Particularly yours." She inhaled a shuddering breath. "The boys are confused enough by what's going on between us."

"Are we back to the rebound thing again?" he shot back irritably.

"It's not a 'thing,'" she insisted. "It's the truth. It's

how things are because of what happened to you in your marriage, and—"

"My marriage is over," he said and ran a hand through his hair. "It's been over for two years. And if I'm honest, it was never much of a marriage to begin with. Something was missing, and—"

"I really don't want to hear the details about your marriage, Kieran," she said.

"You brought up the subject," he reminded her.

"Because I—"

"Because it's an easy target, I guess. Blame my lousy marriage for everything, and we don't have to face what's happening here, right now, between us."

"There's nothing between us," she said and grabbed her tote. "I'm going to tell the boys the truth."

"They'll be hurt."

She tilted her chin. "They'll get over it. They'll get over you." She took a breath, stronger, deeper. "Like I did."

She left him by the tree and walked toward the picnic table. Gwen must have sensed something was wrong and that Nicola needed space and time alone with her nephews because she gave her a gentle smile and patted her arm and then walked off to stand near Liam and Kayla, who were huddled close together and keeping a discreet distance.

"Boys, we need to talk," she said as she sat down and grabbed each of their hands, squeezing them gently. "I want to make something very clear to both of you. You are the most important thing in the world to me, and I'll never leave you. We're a family, and we'll always be together."

Marco's bottom lip did its familiar wobble. "We were a family with Mommy and Daddy, and they left us."

"I know," she said gently, her insides aching. "They had an accident, and they died. And it's okay to be sad about that. It's okay to cry sometimes."

"But not all the time," Johnny said and elbowed his brother in the ribs.

Nicola smiled, her heart breaking. "No, not all the time. But sometimes. And we should think about them and talk about them and always remember how special they were and how much they both loved you guys. But we have to make a new family, just the three of us."

"What about Kieran?" Marco asked. "Isn't he gonna be part of our family, too?"

Johnny rolled his eyes. "They just said that to get us out of the tree—right?"

Nicola couldn't deny it. "I don't think we should—"

"But he wants to marry you," Marco said, his face pained. "He said so."

"When two people like each other, they should get married," Johnny said and shrugged. "It makes sense."

"And he's building us a fishpond, and he put up the basketball hoop, and he fixed my hand when I got the fishhook in it," Marco added. "And he's taking us fishing soon so I won't be afraid of the water anymore. He must like us to do all that. Is it because he didn't have a diamond?" Marco asked and jumped up. "Because he could get one."

Dazed, Nicola shook her head. "A diamond? What are you talking about?"

"For right here," Marco said and shook his left hand vigorously. "So you won't be mad at him anymore. See?" he said and peered over her head. "You just have to get one, and then she won't be mad at you anymore."

Nicola turned her head and saw that Kieran was standing behind them, barely three feet away, and he'd obviously heard the entire exchange. She met his gaze, and her insides contracted. He had an odd look on his face, something unfathomable, and she could have sworn there was a smile twitching his mouth.

"They know," he said and smiled. "You can deny it. But the kids know the truth."

"What truth?"

"Our truth," he replied. "They can see it…even if you can't."

Nicola sucked in a long breath. "I have no idea what you're talking about."

"No?" he queried. "Then ask them. They'll tell you what you're too scared to face. Kids are surprisingly direct that way."

Nicola got to her feet and moved in front of him, keeping a discreet distance from her nephews, but close enough that she could still see them. "Listen up, Doctor Charm. Stop using the boys to get what you want… whatever that is. I'm not interested. Not in you or us. You had your shot fifteen years ago and you blew it."

As she said the words, as she felt them leave her mouth on a breath, Nicola experienced an ache deep within her chest. Because, suddenly, she was seventeen again, and her heart was breaking. And in that moment, she knew she'd never really recovered from his rejection. Knowing he'd believed she might try and trap him with a baby back then only amplified that hurt tenfold.

He stared at her, meeting her gaze. She watched as he swallowed hard and then took a step back. "I see. So, okay."

And then he turned and left, walking off, his broad shoulders disappearing into the crowd.

Heat burned her eyes, her lungs, her skin. And she

couldn't breathe, couldn't think, couldn't do anything but stare after his retreating figure.

Stay and fight for me...stay and fight for us...

But he wouldn't. Because he was afraid to really feel anything. He could make all the insincere marriage proposals he wanted...that didn't prove anything. He talked about dating her, about their insane chemistry but, at the end of the day, the words were empty because they didn't contain what she needed the most. His heart. His love.

"I see that you did exactly what you said you wouldn't do."

She glanced sideways. Liam. The man had all the stealth of a jungle cat. He was beside her, and she noticed that Gwen and Kayla were now with the boys.

"What?"

"Mess him up," he said bluntly.

Nicola wrapped her arms around herself. "He's not messed up."

Liam gave a shot of humorless laughter. "He's about as messed up as it gets."

She shrugged. "You're imagining things."

His brows rose. "I know my brother."

"Maybe not as well as you think."

His mouth curled. "I know he's crazy about you and your nephews. I know that over the past couple of weeks he has actually returned to the land of the living. And I know that the only thing that's changed is you. So, ease up, okay?"

Heat burned her eyes and she blinked. "I don't know what you think I've done, but you are way off the mark."

"Didn't he just ask you to marry him in front of fifty or so people?"

Her back straightened instantly. "He wasn't serious."

Liam sighed. "Really? Looked pretty serious to me," he said and shrugged. "But if you don't love him…"

"But I do," she said quickly and then gasped, humiliated that she'd admitted the truth to Liam when she could barely admit it to herself. "I mean… I mean…"

"I'm glad. You guys belong together."

They did…yes. "Except that he left," she reminded him.

"Isn't that what you wanted?" he asked.

"Yes." She swallowed hard. "No."

He chuckled. "Well, looks like you've got some thinking to do."

Then he left her, walking back toward his wife and son.

Nicola remained where she was, aching through to every part of her soul, watching as Marco and Johnny hung out with the O'Sullivans as though it was the most natural thing in the world.

Five minutes turned into ten, ten into twenty, until nearly forty minutes had passed, and she realized she'd hadn't spoken a word to anyone. Weeks ago, her life had been about routine and monotony and getting through each day. And then Kieran had returned to town, and suddenly she was back feeling a whole pile of old feelings. And she also found new ones.

Like friendship.

And companionship.

Bitterness turned into forgiveness. Resentment turned into understanding. She thought about the kindness he'd shown toward the boys, and her heart ached. She thought about the support he'd offered her, the wisdom, the shoulder to lean on. Things she was sure she would never have.

I'm such an idiot…

Because she'd set rules. She'd made their relationship about sex and nothing else, when the reality couldn't have been further from the truth. She desired him, she wanted him more than she'd ever wanted anyone. But it had always been more than that. It had always been love. Even when she'd hated him, her love for him hadn't disappeared.

She'd wanted him to fight for them and had despaired when he didn't. But she was just as guilty of *flight* instead of *fight*.

She'd left him after they'd made love, she'd run like a scared rabbit because she was afraid to believe it could be something more than simple attraction. Because jumping in meant risk. And risk meant vulnerability. Risk meant surrender.

And surrender had let her down in the past.

Nicola let out a weary sigh just as the band started playing again. Gwen said she wanted to sit closer to the stage, so they grabbed their belongings and found a table near the dance floor. The fireworks would be starting soon, and the boys promised to sit quietly and share Johnny's gaming console until then. Liam and Kayla hit the dance floor for a slow, moody cover of a George Strait classic while Gwen watched over the baby and her nephews. Suddenly, Nicola felt so alone she could barely stand being in her own skin. There seemed to be couples everywhere, and she stood by the table, arms crossed, heart aching, wanting his arms around her so much every part of her hurt.

And then she saw him.

He stood on the other side of the dance floor, and the throngs of people seemed to do a kind of instant divide. He was watching her, and she couldn't have looked away if she'd tried. He took a step the same time she did, until they were both in the center of the dance floor.

"You came back."

He nodded. "We had some unfinished business."

"I know. But I wasn't sure if you thought it was worth fighting for.

"It is," he said. "Turns out, it's the only thing that matters. Unless you really think I've blown it for good."

She shook her head, trying not to cry. "You haven't. I was so upset, so angry, and…I think I just said that to hurt you."

"It worked."

"I guess we've hurt one another a lot over the years."

"I have more than you," he acknowledged. "I guess you owed me one. But I got your point, Nic."

"You know you make me crazy."

"Ditto," he said and smiled a fraction, holding out his hand. "Would you dance with me?"

She smiled. "No point in wasting a good George Strait song."

He chuckled and drew her close. "You know how I said there was something missing in my marriage?" he said and took her hand, raising it to his mouth and kissing her knuckles softly. "Do you want to know what that was?"

She nodded, in a trance. "What?"

His gaze burned into hers. "You."

Nicola's heart leaped in her chest. "Me?"

He took a long, shuddering breath, stared deep into her eyes and spoke. "You're the love of my life, Nic. You always have been."

Her racing heart skipped a beat, and then another. "Are you sure?"

"Positive. And this is not a rebound thing. This isn't

about sex, although making love to you is out of this world. The truth is I love you. I can't imagine loving anyone *but* you."

Nicola's world spun, and she pressed closer, feeling the heat and strength that emanated from him seep deeply into her bones, and she said what was in her heart. "I love you, too."

Kieran had spent two years in a kind of emotional wilderness, afraid to open himself up. Now he was feeling closer to Nicola than he ever had to anyone, ever. Her words filled his heart and soul. Her words made him feel alive and whole. They chased off every fear he harbored about intimacy and closeness.

The song ended and another began, and he rocked her in his arms, feeling her pressed against him, happier than he ever remembered being in his life. She swayed, and his hand traveled down her back, resting on her hip. With his free hand, he reached into his pocket and pulled out a small box.

"What's this?" she asked.

He grinned. "Where do you think I've been for the last hour?" he said and deftly flipped open the lid, exposing the antique diamond ring. "Marry me?"

"Oh, it's beautiful," she said with a sigh. "But where did you get it?"

"It was my grandmother's," he explained and kissed her forehead gently. "She gave it to me when we were first dating. I guess she thought I might have a use for it one day. So…is that a *yes*?"

She smiled and nodded. "Yes. One hundred percent yes."

He slipped the ring on her finger, and it looked as though it had always belonged there. "That looks good."

"Are we really doing this?"

"You bet," he said and kissed her mouth. "Let's go and tell the boys."

She touched his cheek and then gently moved his face in the direction of the tables. "Um, I think they might have figured it out already."

Kieran spotted Marco and Johnny standing with his mother, Liam and Kayla, and they all looked delighted. He laughed, looped an arm around her waist and walked her off the dance floor.

"So, when's the wedding?" Liam asked and patted him on the shoulder.

"No idea," Nicola replied and showed off her ring to Kayla. "But soon."

Marco tugged on Kieran's coat. "Does that mean you get to live with us now?"

"It sure does, kid."

The little boy grinned happily. "And does that mean you'll give Aunt Nicola a baby now?"

He laughed, seeing Nicola's embarrassment and loving her for it. A baby. A child with Nicola. Weeks ago, the idea would have made him run a mile. But now, he wanted it. He wanted the whole package—marriage and kids and sticky fingers and pet hair and chaos. He wanted to feel every emotion, every joy, every single day.

"I'll see what I can do," he said and kissed her.

The boys whooped and laughed, and his mother hugged them both.

Kieran felt the rightness of it though to his bones. Nicola had always been his. He had always been hers. The years they'd been separated slipped away, and now they were exactly where they were meant to be... together.

Marco was jumping up and down, and Johnny came forward and held out his hand. Kieran took it, and the boy unexpectedly hugged him. And then Marco hugged Johnny, and Nicola hugged them all, and he experienced so much love for all three of them he wondered if his heart might actually burst.

My family...

His family to cherish. His family to protect. His family to lay down his life for if he had to.

"I love you so very much," he whispered close to her ear, his throat tightening, his hands trembling at the realization that he'd finally found his home.

She held on to him, her hands keeping his steady. "I love you back. *We* love you."

And that, he thought as the kids laughed and he kissed her, was the best news he'd ever heard.

Epilogue

"So, where's your mom?" Nicola asked as Kieran grabbed her hand and walked her around the back of the house and through the small orchard. "I thought she'd be here today."

The boys were racing on ahead, searching for adventure. Or *misadventure*, she thought and grinned, watching as they circled a different tree each and laughed. It was four days after Kieran had spectacularly proposed at the rodeo, and Nicola had never been happier in her life. They'd spent time together as a family. At her house. At the restaurant. And he'd taken the boys fishing and Marco had felt safe and relaxed under Kieran's care. He was so incredible with the kids it made her heart sing every time she thought about it.

The wedding was planned for mid-November, which was just a few weeks away, but she didn't want to wait any longer. Neither did the boys. They insisted that she and Kieran marry straightaway, and even though she knew their request was half fear, half excitement, she wasn't going to disappoint them. Her dad had expressed some early concerns about their intentions but, in the end, he agreed that she and Kieran had been waiting for this for fifteen years—which was like an overlong engagement. Connie had stepped in to help with all the preparations, and Nicola was amazed how quickly something could be planned with the right people arranging things. She had a dress fitting planned for the following Tuesday, the flowers were ordered, the family's hotel was catering, and now they were walking around the garden, making final decisions on where the tent and reception area would be situated.

"I wanted to do this with just us," he replied and looped an arm over her shoulder.

It was a chilly afternoon, but Nicola was as warm as toast, wrapped up in his love. She nodded and pointed to a spot as they circumnavigated the house and ended up around the front again. "I think the tent should go there."

He nodded, looking at the flat lawn. "Good spot."

"And the band there," she said, gesturing to the left. "We'll have to set up a parking area, as well. I'll talk to Connie about seating arrangements, and you still need to give her a list of anyone you want to invite who isn't on the list we made up together."

He smiled at her obvious enthusiasm. "Are you sure you're okay with this happening so fast?"

"Positive," she said and nodded and motioned to the boys, who were chasing one another. "They're so excited. And they adore you. So do I," she added and pressed close into him. He was warm and welcoming and familiar, and she looped her arms around his waist beneath his sheepskin-lined jacket, snuggling close. "Is Sean coming back for the wedding?" she asked.

He nodded. "He's agreed to be a groomsman alongside Jonah."

"That's good," she said. "And I'm so happy your nieces will be flower girls."

"It was good of you to include them. It would have meant a lot to Liz. And Grady and Marissa were delighted for the girls to be a part of the day. And of course, Liam is the best man."

She shook her head playfully. "Not a chance. You're the best man I've ever known."

He laughed, and the sound warmed her blood. "That's very sweet."

"It's the truth," she said, loving him, needing him, wanting him. "Every moment I spend with you I realize that more and more. I love you, Kieran. And it feels so good to say. So good to feel."

He turned her around, grasped her chin and titled her face to meet him. "No regrets."

"Not one," she said on a sigh. "Only that we didn't do this a long time ago."

He kissed her mouth softly, lingering at the corner, his hand coming around her nape seductively, with a promise of what was to come. "I guess we both had to work out a way to get back to one another. But I promise you, Nic, I will love you and cherish you and always keep you in my heart. And whatever we face, we'll do it together."

She sighed and touched his face. "That's what you should say," she said and smiled when he frowned a little. "Your vows…you said you were wondering what you should say. And *that* was perfect."

He kissed her again, deeper, with every ounce of love she knew he felt. "Okay."

"I feel like I'm dreaming. It's all happened so fast. So much change."

He grasped her chin. "Feel like a bit more—hmm?"

"Huh?"

"Change," he explained and smiled. "Well, you see, my mom is moving out."

"Moving out?"

"From here. She wants to live in town. She has friends there, and she reckons this place is too big to have only her rattling around in it. So, I was thinking, this would be a great place to raise our family."

Nicola's heart stopped. *Their family.* They were the sweetest words she had ever heard.

"Live *here*?"

She looked at the boys, still racing around, laughing and having a wonderful time. They looked so happy. She glanced around, taking in the huge home, the perfectly landscaped gardens, the wide driveway, the barn and stables, the acres of pastures crisscrossed with white fences. From the orchard to the pool to the tennis court around the back, the place reeked of luxury and wealth.

But that was not what drew her to it. It was a home. Despite their own rocky marriage, Gwen and J. D. O'Sullivan had raised their children here with love, and it showed in every nook, every garden, every hall and every room in the big house. And Nicola could think of nothing better than raising a family in such a place.

She smiled warmly. "Yes."

"Yes?" He grinned. "No argument? No discussion?"

"Nope," she replied. "I think it's a great idea."

"Really? But your brother's house…"

"I should never have stayed there," she admitted. "You were right when you said it was filled with memories of all they had lost. In a way, I was selfish, thinking about how it would be easier for me by living there, not disrupting the boys' routine."

"You're the least selfish person I've ever met," he said gently.

"I'm not, really," she said and sighed. "Being surrounded by the memory of Gino and Miranda, their belongings, even driving their old car. I took the easy way out. But no more. I want to sell the house and put the money into a trust for the kids."

"Of course," he said gently. "And how about we find a spot here on the ranch and create a kind of memorial for them, somewhere the boys can have a special place to remember their parents."

Tears plumped at the corners of her eyes. "That's a lovely idea. And I would love to live here with you and raise the boys in this wonderful place. Just the four of us. Or five or six," she added. "In case anyone else comes along."

She watched as he swallowed hard, his smooth throat closing over. She knew it was a hard subject for him. Maybe the hardest they would face. Finally, he spoke. "You really want children?"

She nodded. "Yes… I'd like to have a child with you. Are you okay with that?"

He squeezed her hand. "Even though I can't guarantee that I won't be insecure at times?"

She knew how hard it was for him to feel and say that. And she loved him more for having the courage to face his fears. "So…that's a *yes*? We'll have kids if we can?"

He smiled. "Well, I did promise Marco I would give you a baby…and a person should always keep their promises."

She laughed, loving him so much she could barely breathe. "I can't wait to marry you and have your baby and live in this beautiful house."

He hauled her into his arms and twirled her around.

She laughed and, once her feet were back on the ground, she nodded and called for the boys to come closer. "You tell the boys. I mean, they already think you hung the moon. Once they find out they'll be living here permanently, they'll think you've given them the stars, as well."

He called the boys over and began to tell them about the house. And Nicola knew she had all she'd ever dreamed of. And more. They were a family. Which was everything.

* * * * *

SOARING ON LOVE

JOY AVERY

Dedicated to the dream.

Chapter 1

Roth Lexington leaned against the banister of the upper-level balcony inside The Underground Jazz House—The Underground, for short—nursing a glass of bourbon. The amber liquid had always been his drink of choice, ever since he'd taken his first sip at thirteen. "It'll make you a man," he'd been told. He was definitely a man, but he wasn't sure the bourbon had anything to do with it.

Taking a swig, he savored the earthy notes. A fire flared in his chest, but it wasn't from the whiskey. This inferno ignited from envy. With a tight jaw, he observed the partygoers below. He soaked in their laughs, their smiles, their congratulatory hugs and handshakes for the future bride and groom.

Normally, nothing soothed him like a smooth beverage and the silky sounds of jazz, but neither did much for him now. And he knew why. The reason stood several feet below him in the form of the sexiest woman in the room. Also, the guest of honor at this engagement party he'd reluctantly attended.

Tressa Washington.

Since the first time he'd laid eyes on the ravishing ER nurse several months ago in his best friend's living room, she'd danced in his thoughts. Danced sensual moves. Provocative moves. Seductive moves. Moves that had forced him awake in a hot sweat on several occasions. In his thirty-six years, he couldn't recall a woman ever having this kind of effect on him.

He didn't like it. He didn't like it at all.

Stunning in a fitted off-white jumpsuit, Tressa stood out among the sixty or so people in attendance. Tiny curls framed her round face, lightly touched with makeup. Though she didn't need any makeup at all, really. That was how stunning she was.

Engulfed in conversation with a group of women, her lips—the ones he craved to leave kiss swelled and aching—curled into a smile, and those dimples he'd grown to adore pierced her chocolate-brown cheeks. His gaze burned a heated path along her voluptuous body, stopping briefly to appreciate her ample breasts. They'd fit in his grasp perfectly.

It took a real man to handle dangerous curves like hers. And as he'd stated before, he was a man.

A knot tightened in his stomach. How he'd love to suckle nipples he'd teased with his thumbs to tautness. He curtailed his thoughts when he felt a tightening in his boxers. Wearing a hard-on for the bride-to-be in the middle of her engagement party would be a shit thing to do. But dammit, he couldn't help that Tressa turned him all the way on. He wanted her so badly he ached. Forbidden fruit was always so damn tempting.

Loud laughter drew his attention to Tressa's fiancé. *Cyrus Williams.* Even the thought of the man's name put a sour taste in his mouth. A cornball name for a cornball. Damn he hated that man. Or more accurately, envied him. Cyrus had something he wanted—Tressa's warm body pressed up against his.

Pushing his envy aside, Roth still got a bad vibe from this Cyrus character. He'd always been good at reading people and something about Tressa's soon-to-be husband screamed *shady.* Roth blew out a heavy breath. But Cyrus was none of his business, and neither was Tressa. And if he told himself that a few more hundred times, maybe he'd actually be convinced. He slid his eyes back to her.

As if sensing his ogling, Tressa shifted in his direction. The instant their gazes locked, a lightning bolt of desire seared through him. She smiled at him in that warm, welcoming manner he'd become accustomed to. A smile like that wasn't easily forgotten. But that was exactly what he needed to do. Forget. Forget that soul-stirring gesture and the woman donning it.

Tressa's best friend, Vivian—his best friend Alonso's wife—said something that drew Tressa's attention. Tressa slid her gaze away, allowing him to breathe again. Maybe he was being absurd, but he'd got the feeling she'd regretted ending their connection just as much as he had. Yeah, absurd.

Alonso clapped him on the shoulder. "Careful. The way you're staring at the bride could give someone the wrong idea. Namely, her soon-to-be husband." He laughed.

She wasn't a bride yet.

Roth and Alonso had been friends since way back. Over the years, Alonso had kept him out of so much trouble and got him into his fair share, as well. He didn't trust many people, but he trusted Alonso with his life.

Roth continued, still coveting something he'd never have, "You know if this was back in the day, she'd be mine, right?"

Yes, it was a cocky statement but also a true one. When he was young and dumb, he would not have hesitated to pursue Tressa at full throttle, regardless of her *situation*. Luckily for Cyrus, he'd become a far better man than he'd once been.

Alonso chuckled. "Trust me, I know. I'm surprised you came. You sounded a little iffy when we talked earlier."

Roth pulled his attention away from Tressa before he overheated. Taking another swig from his glass, he paused for a moment to savor the rich flavors. "Figured I'd swing by on my way out of town."

"Out of town?"

"Headed to my place in the mountains."

Alonso quirked a brow. "Alone?"

"That's a good question." Powerless against it, he sought out Tressa again. When their gazes locked, electricity—raw and powerful—slammed through him, causing a puff of air to escape. *What in the hell was that?* Alarm triggered his defenses, sending flares up like Fourth of July fireworks. He needed rescuing.

"You all right, man?" Alonso asked.

No, he wasn't. He wouldn't be all right until he'd got Tressa out of his system.

* * *

As one of the women went on and on about something, Tressa slid an inconspicuous glance to her watch—a flashy piece packed with diamonds—that Cyrus had given her as an engagement gift. He was good at giving expensive gifts. She just wished he were as generous with his time. In the past two weeks, they'd barely seen one another. As an investment banker, he should understand the importance of investing in the future, as well as in the right commodities.

She gave an occasional nod and displaced smile, just to present the illusion of listening. *Will this party ever end?* It'd only been an hour since her family and friends had all gathered to celebrate what should have been one of the most exciting nights of her life.

It wasn't.

There were a number of reasons she could have rattled off as to why, but the most severe one hovered above like a sexy gargoyle watching over the city.

Roth Lexington.

Simply thinking his name made her insides flutter. Then she scolded her body for the defiant act. Plenty of times she warned her system against responding to Roth. And plenty of times it'd disobeyed her.

Don't look at him. I repeat, do not look at him.

As if her body would choose today of all days to start listening to her. *Defiant.* Her brain sent her gaze to the balcony. The man was as tempting as the glowing hot-doughnut sign at Krispy Kreme. Who in the hell could resist? Definitely not her. But in this case, she had to. She was getting married.

Roth stood chatting with his best friend, Alonso. The mere sight of him pounded her insides like a sensual jackhammer against stubborn concrete. From any angle, he was gorgeous. Tall, a few inches over six feet, a body that would be the envy of any athletic trainer, skin the tone of the best imported cocoa beans and a gleaming smile that rivaled the sun. *That damn smile.* In a quiet setting, it could hypnotize a woman into doing reckless things. Trust her, she knew.

When Roth's attention slid to her, she gasped from the shock of awareness that scorched her soul. He flashed a half smile. She returned the gesture, then yanked her focus away from him before she melted into a puddle of lust in the middle of her own engagement party.

Damn. Why did that man cloud her better judgment and distort her common sense? *Stop it, Tressa! You're getting married in one month. February 18*, she reminded herself. But looking was okay, right? As long as she didn't touch. She gnawed at the corner of her lip. But she had touched. Oh, God, how she wanted to touch again.

She'd never been the unfaithful type, but when Roth had pulled her into his arms and kissed her senseless, she hadn't done a damn thing to break free. A reel of the kiss in her best friend's kitchen played in her head. Recalling how good his mouth had felt pressed against hers caused her lips to tingle. She touched two fingers to them.

It'd been the best damn kiss she'd ever experienced in her life. They'd both agreed that what had happened had been a huge mistake and had vowed to never mention it again. But a kiss like that haunted you. It wasn't something easily purged from your system. But, Lord, had she tried to purge it, along with this ornate desire to... *To what?* What did she really want from Roth?

Everything, she ruefully admitted. So why in the hell was she about to marry another man? *Because Cyrus is the right choice.* She eyed the gaudy diamond on her finger. So why didn't she feel the same exhilaration when she looked at Cyrus as she did when she eyed Roth? *It'll come*, she told herself. *Give it time.*

The air in the room grew thick, and she struggled to breathe. Was she having a panic attack? Fresh air. She needed fresh air. Weaving her way through the crowd, she escaped unseen through a side door. On the massive stone patio, she sucked in a few deep breaths. After several minutes her pounding heart returned to its normal steady beat. But she still felt as if she were plummeting.

The chill of the winter night air jarred her, making her regret not grabbing a jacket. She cradled herself in her arms to generate some heat. Closing her eyes, she appreciated the stillness of the night. But even the tranquil setting couldn't silence her thoughts and they popped right back open, the world rushing in.

Fools rush in.

She wasn't sure why the phrase blared at full volume in her thoughts. *Fools rush in.* Was she rushing into this? At thirty-four, shouldn't she be married? Some of her friends were already married with several kids. Her mother's voice played in her head and she smiled. *If your friends jumped off a roof, would you jump, too?*

No, Mommy, but... She sighed. Her biological clock was tick, tick, ticking away. She wanted kids. A houseful of germy, whiny, adorable, lovable kids. She thought about Jamison and her eyes burned with impending tears. Pushing thoughts of the boy away, she refocused.

Cyrus is a good man. An honorable man. A respectable man. So why did it feel like she was about to make the biggest mistake of her life?

Tilting her head heavenward, she whispered, "God, please give me a sign."

"Escaping your own party?" The voice came from behind.

Tressa flinched. *That was fast.* Ignoring Roth as the sign—for now—she turned toward him. No man should have been allowed to look that damn good in a simple black suit. On any other man, it would have been forgettable apparel. Something told her this image would linger in her thoughts all night.

Finding her words, she said, "Um…no. Not escaping. I just needed some fresh air. So many people inside. It's a bit stuffy. How'd you know I was out here?"

Roth leaned against the banister, crossing his legs at the ankle. "Instinct, I guess."

Instinct, her ass. She'd felt the caress of his eyes on her all night. She may have escaped everyone else, but she hadn't escaped his watchful eye. "And here I am, believing I'd made a clean getaway."

"Getaway, huh? What—or who—are you running from?"

Curious eyes probed her. "No one."

"Hmm."

Why did that *hmm* sound so accusing? Roth straightened to his full height. They stood in silence for a moment, simply staring at one another. The intensity in his eyes made her knees wobble, but she refused to turn away. If he wanted to assert dominance, he'd have to find a less willful opponent.

Then he folded his arms across his chest and the

move rattled her, because his biceps blossomed into cannonballs and strained against the tailored suit coat— it fit him far too well to be off-the-rack.

"So, fresh air is the only reason you're out here?" he said.

Regrouping, Tressa said, "What other reason would there be?"

He shrugged one wide shoulder. "I don't know. It looked like you were having some kind of anxiety attack. I came out to check on you."

Tressa released a nervous laugh. "What? No. An anxiety attack?" She brushed his accurate words off. "No." How was he diagnosing her with anything? He was an aerospace engineer, not a doctor. But the fact that he was concerned about her warmed her insides. "I'm fine. Like I said, it was stuffy in there. I came out—"

"For fresh air," he said, completing her sentence.

"Yeah." A corner of his mouth lifted into a sexy smile and she chastised herself for staring so hard at his lips. Lifting her eyes to his, she mumbled, "I'm just fine."

"Good. You're going to catch your death out here, Nurse Washington." Roth removed his suit coat and draped it over her shoulders. "Better?"

Lost in his manly scent, she mumbled, "You smell fantastic." Immediately realizing she'd actually said the words out loud, her cheeks burned with awkwardness. "Um, yes. Better. Thank you. W-what about you? Now you're going to catch your death or at least pneumonia." She'd been around Roth plenty. Why now was she turning into a bumbling fool?

"I don't get sick," he said.

Roth slid his hands into his pockets. The move

caused his biceps to flex again, and she imagined wrapping her hands around them as he made slow, sweet love to her. "I see. You muscle—muscle—*must*," she spit out. "You must have a strong immune system." *Bumbling fool.*

"I guess so. You and your fiancé seem happy together."

The odd timing of his words took her by surprise. "Thank you." She shifted away from him before he saw the uncertainty in her eyes and stared out into the darkness. Were she and Cyrus a doting couple? Was that what people saw when they looked at them—happiness?

Roth leaned in slightly. "Are you happy?"

Alarmed by the question, Tressa snapped, "Yes. Why would you ask that?" Then she regretted the sharp bite in her tone.

Roth pulled one hand from his pocket and flashed a palm. "I didn't mean to upset you. It's just..." He shrugged. "It's just that most women seem over the moon when they're about to walk down the aisle."

Was he suggesting she wasn't over the moon? She was plenty over the damn moon. "Yeah, well, I'm not most women."

"Oh, I definitely know this."

A glint of something flashed in his demanding brown eyes and it smoothed her ruffled feathers. Again, their gazes held for a long, quiet, intense moment. Were these probing glances power plays between them, or was it that when they looked at each other, they simply became lost in each other's souls? There was something soothing about the way Roth looked at her, a look that could polish rough edges.

"Well, I'll let you get back to your fresh air. Congratulations again on your engagement. Good night."

Tressa's brow furrowed. "Wait." The word came too urgently. "You're not leaving, are you? The party, I mean." Why did the possibility bother her so much?

"Shortly. I promised two of your aunts dances, and I don't make promises I can't keep. Then I need to get on the road before it gets too late."

Yeah, her aunts—and several other of her female family members—had grown quite fond of Roth. Alonso, too. But Vivian had intervened on that one, crushing all of their dreams about her man. "On the road?"

"I have a cabin in Silver Point. The mountains," he clarified. "About four hours away."

"Huh."

"Don't look so surprised."

"It's not that. I just took you for more of a city dweller."

"I love being in the mountains. No one near for miles. Absolute peace and quiet. I can go on my deck and play my sax as early or as late as I want without disturbing a soul." His brow furrowed. "That reminds me. I don't think I locked my vehicle." Obviously, he noticed Tressa's where-did-that-come-from expression. "Juliette's in there—my saxophone."

"You call your saxophone Juliette?"

"Yes."

"Okay." Tressa recalled the first and last time she'd watched him play his sax. It was the most alluring thing she'd ever witnessed. He'd made absolute love to the instrument. The way he'd held it, caressed it, wrapped his lips around it… Her cheeks heated just thinking about him playing her like a saxophone.

What is wrong with you? You are about to be a married woman. Her mother would be so disappointed in her for lusting over one man while engaged to another. She massaged the side of her neck. "So, the mountains?"

Roth continued, "Mountain air is great for clearing the mind and rejuvenating the soul."

Sounded like her kind of place. "You sound like a travel brochure. I've never been to the mountains." The declaration sounded as if she was trolling for an invite. She kicked herself.

"Really?"

She nodded.

"Well, anytime you and your husband want to get away, let me know. You're more than welcome to use my place. It's not much, but it's cozy and intimate. The perfect escape for a couple in love."

A couple in love. Boy, he was laying it on thick. Tressa returned her attention to the darkness.

"Tressa, are you sure—"

Whipping toward him, she said, "Yes, I'm sure I want to marry Cyrus. Why does everyone keep asking me that?"

"I…was actually going to ask you if you were sure standing in this cold was a good idea."

She eyed Roth dumbly, her level of embarrassment soaring to unprecedented heights. "Oh." Compassion danced in Roth's eyes as he scrutinized her. No doubt he saw right through her. How was that possible?

Standing dangerously close to her, he said, "If you ever need someone to talk to, I'm a great listener."

"Thank you, but I'm—"

"Fine," he said, completing her sentence for the second time tonight.

"You're getting pretty good at finishing my thoughts."

The corner of his mouth lifted into a sexy smirk. "If I thought that had been a compliment, I would say thank you."

He was getting pretty good at reading her, too, because it had been a cynical remark. When she attempted to remove his coat to return it, he stopped her.

"Just leave it with the hostess when you're done. She'll make sure I get it. Good night, Tressa. Enjoy the rest of your party."

"Enjoy the mountains."

When Roth disappeared through the doors, she tightened his coat around her, inhaling his delicious scent. Had Roth's intrusion really been her sign? She laughed at herself. No. Tilting her head again, she said, "God, if you send me a sign, please make it a pronounced one. I don't want to miss it."

Twenty minutes later Tressa found herself on the dance floor with her soon-to-be husband. With her thoughts still stuck on her encounter with Roth, she barely processed Cyrus's presence.

"Should it bother me that my fiancée smells like another man's cologne?"

This snagged her attention. Reeling back, she stared into Cyrus's probing green eyes. "Excuse me?"

"You smell like *him*."

Playing coy, she said, "*Him*, who?"

Cyrus's features hardened and deep lines etched into his caramel-toned forehead. "You know what *him* I'm referring to. Don't try to play me for a fool." His expression softened. "I love you, Tressa. I want to spend the rest of my life with you. But I need to know."

She searched his sad eyes. "Need to know what, Cyrus?"

"I need to know… I need to know if you're sleeping with him."

Tressa froze, stunned by Cyrus's question. Her lips parted, but nothing readily escaped. Why in the world had Cyrus asked her that?

"I see the way he looks at you. Hell, he's been staring at you all night. Every damn move you make. I don't want to lose you. I don't want to lose you to him."

Cyrus's words broke her heart. At that moment she realized how unfair she'd been to him. Cradling his smooth face between her hands, she said, "I would never hurt you like that, Cyrus. You're the man I'm marrying, remember?"

A smile curled his lips and he eased his forehead against hers. "I love you, baby. I love you so much." His expression turned somber and he rested his hands on either side of her neck. "I've made mistakes, Tressa. But I swear I'm going to be a good husband to you."

Mistakes. What mistakes had he been referring to? Before she got the opportunity to ask, clapping sounded behind Cyrus. Tressa glanced over his shoulder, her gaze landing on a brown-skinned woman in a very revealing black gown. She wore a black fishnet veil that made her look as if she was in mourning.

"That was so beautiful," the woman said, nearing them. "Too bad it's nothing but a bunch of bull—"

"Natalie!" Cyrus barked. His nostrils flared and a vein pulsed in his neck. "What in the hell are you doing here?" he said through clenched teeth.

Fine lines etched into Tressa's forehead. "*Natalie?* You know this woman, Cyrus?"

"Yes, he does. *Very* well." Natalie placed her hands on her hips. "We had an *intimate* work relationship until a few days ago," she said with a smirk.

Cyrus looked as if he could snatch the woman's heart out with his hand. Spittle flew from his mouth when he said, "Shut the hell up, Natalie," through teeth gritted so tightly they should have all been ground to dust.

Whispers and words revealing shock among the small crowd now circling them, swirled around her. Tuning it all out, she zeroed in on Cyrus. "You should probably start talking right now. What's going on?"

"Yes, Cyrus. We'd both like to know what the hell is going on," Natalie added.

This time ignoring their party crasher, Cyrus turned to her. "Tressa. I made a mistake. We can—"

When he reached for her, she backed away. This was the mistake he referenced earlier. "How long?"

When he didn't answer, Natalie did. "Four months."

"Four—" The air seized in her lungs.

"Baby—"

Tears stung her eyes, but they were more angry than sentimental ones. "You lying, cheating, no-good, trifling bastard." She wrenched the ring from her finger and tossed it at him. Eyeing Natalie, she said, "He's all yours. The wedding is off."

Cyrus grabbed her arm. "No, you don't mean that."

A second later Tony—her three-hundred-pound ex-lineman cousin—clapped a large hand on Cyrus's shoulder. The look in his eyes suggested Cyrus release her now.

Obviously, Cyrus got the silent message, because his grip on her arm loosened, then fell away.

Several family members—including her visibly livid mother—swarmed around Cyrus like bees on the attack. They stung him with their not-so-gentle words of disapproval. As the room erupted in utter chaos, Tressa made her escape. She'd asked for a sign and, boy, had she got it.

Chapter 2

Amid all of the chaos, Roth eyed Tressa weaving her way through the room and toward the exit. She brushed past the outstretched hands of individuals undoubtedly offering their comfort and support. He tore down the stairs after her, but by the time he made it outside, she was nowhere in sight. Where in the hell had she vanished to so damn suddenly?

He squinted against the dark for any sign of movement. Nothing.

When the door banged open behind him and Cyrus's snake ass slithered out, dragging his hideous mistress behind him, Roth's jaw tightened in disgust.

Cyrus slid a razor-sharp glance in Roth's direction. Roth readied himself for a confrontation, but Cyrus only flashed a scornful expression, then escaped in the opposite direction.

After hanging around another half hour or so—just to see if Tressa resurfaced—he decided to head out, leaving instructions for Alonso to call him the minute he heard anything. Yanking open the door of his SUV, Roth slid behind the wheel and slumped in the seat. A part of him wanted to start the engine and follow through with his plans to leave, while another part of him—a much greater portion—wanted to hang back to make sure Tressa was okay.

He abandoned the idea of staying. Tressa definitely didn't need him to further complicate her life. Given what she'd just gone through, he was certain he was the last person she wanted to see. Not because he'd been in any way responsible for the debacle that had taken place, but because he was a man. And at this point she more than likely hated the entire male species.

And who could blame her? He'd certainly held a discord for the female population when he'd got his heart broken several years ago. Then he'd met Tressa a few months back and feelings he'd long abandoned rushed him like water released from a dam.

Four months.

Roth shook his head. That slimy bastard had cheated on Tressa almost their entire relationship. Via Alonso, he'd learned Tressa and that clown Cyrus had only dated a short time before they'd become engaged. Why even propose if he knew he had no intentions of being faithful?

Why would any man in his right mind sacrifice a woman like Tressa?

Roth recalled the expression on Tressa's face as she darted from the room. A mix of confusion and pain danced in her usually sparkling eyes. At that moment he really wanted to hurt Cyrus, if for nothing more than dimming her glow.

"Are we leaving?"

Roth jolted, then whipped around to see Tressa stretched across his back seat. *What the...* How in the hell had he missed seeing her when he'd got in? *Pre-occupied*, he told himself. *Damn.* She'd nearly given him a heart attack.

Activating the interior lights, he scanned her body as if looking for any damage. When he saw her red, puffy eyes, he fought the urge to climb over the center console and pull her into his comforting arms. And though she had every right to cry, he wanted to advise her not to waste her tears on a lowlife like Cyrus.

Roth's words were gentle when he spoke. "Everyone is looking for you."

She hugged her arms around her body. "I don't want to be found. I can't handle the looks and whispers right now."

Being the voice of reason, he said, "People are worried about you, Tressa. They just want to know that you're all right. You really should—"

"Roth, please. Spare me the lecture. I don't have my car here. I need to go. Can you just get me away from here? Just drive. Please." Her voice was low, but screamed of exhaustion.

Tressa's sad, pleading eyes tugged at his heart. Who could blame her for wanting to avoid being poked and prodded like a lab rat by people's stares of pity? Facing forward, he cranked the engine, popped the gearshift into Drive and pulled away.

Silence filled the car for the first few minutes. Roth avoided plying her with the usual pacifiers: it's going to be okay, the pain will go away, look on the bright side. Instead, he stayed quiet because no words could ease the sting of betrayal. Only time could do that.

Roth adjusted the rearview mirror so that it settled on Tressa's face. He hated seeing her this way, a sad replica of her customarily jovial self. "Maybe we should call Vivian to let her know you're okay. She was really worried about you."

Tressa's eyes landed on his. Even through the reflection, their connection rang intense. Everything and nothing had changed. Though she'd ended her engagement, she was still off-limits. Maybe even more so now.

"I will," was all she said before sliding her gaze away.

"Should I take you home?"

"No. He'll probably be at my place. I don't want to see him. Ever."

Roth washed a hand over his mouth as if he was ironing his goatee. All he wanted to do was make her smile—laugh even. But he doubted anything he could have said or done would have accomplished that.

"Were you going to the mountains alone?"

An hour ago the answer would have been yes. But once he'd walked away from her on the balcony, he'd discovered a need for something—or in this case, someone—to take his mind off her. Still, he responded, "Yes, I'm going alone."

"You don't have a very good poker face."

Damn. She'd read him. Now he felt like a complete ass. All she needed was another man lying to her. "Why?"

"I guess because you don't lie enough to pull it off."

He chuckled. She was right. Since lying was what

people had done to him most of his life, he valued the truth more than most. But that wasn't the *why* he meant. "Not that. Why did you ask if I was going alone?"

Her gaze fixed on his again. She didn't need to answer for him to know she wanted an invite to his cabin. If her goal was to hide from the world, it would be the perfect escape for her. No one would find her in Silver Point. An hour ago the idea of him and Tressa *running off* together would have been damn appealing, but now it reeked of trouble. "Maybe you'd prefer a hotel? You wouldn't—"

"You don't want to be saddled with a jilted ex-bride-to-be. I get it."

Damn. Why did she have to make it sound so morbid? "That's not it, Tr—"

"Just drop me off at the nearest hotel. I've dealt with scarier things. I'll be fine."

Scarier things? What scarier things had she dealt with?

Ten minutes later they pulled up in front of the De Lore Hotel in downtown Raleigh. The sprawling building was the epitome of luxury. He'd heard nothing but great things about it. It even looked fancy. Concierge, bellmen, greeters. Tressa would be comfortable here. Much more comfortable than at his cramped cabin.

Why in the hell did he sound like he was trying to convince himself? And why did the idea of leaving her here alone bother him so damn much? It wasn't like he was abandoning her. She would be okay, right?

Once she was checked in, he'd call Vivian to come and comfort her. Her best friend was who she needed, not the man who constantly fantasized about making love to her. Roth brushed a hand over his close-cut hair.

A young man who'd been standing at what looked

like a podium and dressed in a black overcoat and gloves approached his SUV. When Roth lowered the window a gust of cold air rushed in. He welcomed the brisk breeze because it felt as if his system was over-heating.

"Good evening, sir. Welcome to the De Lore Hotel. Will you be staying with us this evening?"

"Ah…" *Shit. Spit it out, Lex. Say yes, she will. Say it.* His gaze slid to Tressa. When she rested her hand on the door handle to open it, his heart raced. *Don't do it, man. Don't do it.* "Actually, no. Maybe another time. Thank you." The window rose and he pulled off, leaving the man standing there.

Roth swiped his thumb back and forth against the steering wheel. *What in the hell are you doing? This woman of all women should not be in your back seat. And taking her to the cabin? The cabin's your sanctuary.*

A significant thought occurred to him. *What about the nightmares?* His past had a way of haunting him in his dreams. All he needed was to wake up scream-ing at the top of his lungs. It would scare the hell out of Tressa and embarrass the hell out of him. An occur-rence like that would break two of his cardinal rules: never show vulnerability and always maintain control. He'd learned a long time ago that being vulnerable got you hurt and losing control made you rash.

Her being at the cabin with him *period* would break the third: always wake up alone.

Two days. He could handle two days cooped up with the woman he'd dreamed about, fantasized about since the first day they met. *Two days.* No problem. Hell, it wasn't like he could actually make a move now anyway.

That would be a shit thing to do. She was vulnerable, grieving and probably out for a little sexual revenge.

The last point gave him pause. *Sexual revenge.* A woman scorned was capable of anything, right? Well, he'd never played the role of the rebound guy, and he wouldn't start now. Not even for Tressa. That alone should keep his libido in check.

"Thank you, Roth. I promise I won't get in your way."

He met Tressa's tender gaze through the rearview mirror and his heartbeat kicked up just a notch. *Oh, you're already getting in my way.* Influencing him to make bad decisions, testing his resolve, reminding him how it felt to crave something unattainable. "You'll like Silver Point," was all he said.

Roth swiped his thumb back and forth across the steering wheel, lost in his thoughts. This was the stupidest thing he'd done in a long while. Reckless, even. He couldn't be alone with Tressa. Yes, he had self-control, plenty of self-control. But this would require a whole lot of self-discipline.

His eyes slid to Tressa, who'd been watching him through the mirror. For a split second, he didn't regret pulling away from the hotel. Her eyes slid away, and after a short time, his did, too.

Four hours later they arrived at the cabin on the hill, as the townsfolk often called it. He popped the SUV into Park, then glanced back at Tressa. She'd fallen asleep two hours into the drive—or had pretended to be to avoid having to talk.

His insides did a shimmy watching her. She really was asleep now, because in the stillness, he could hear her soft snores. As far as bad decisions went, bring-

ing Tressa here was the Grandfather Mountain of poor
judgment calls. He just hoped it wouldn't backfire in
his face.

Tressa assumed Roth's gentle touch was only in her
dreams until his voice penetrated her slumber, and she
realized he was trying to wake her. She cracked her
eyes and squinted to focus. His handsome face slowly
materialized. "How long have I been asleep?" she asked
in a groggy voice.

"A couple of hours. Come on, Sleeping Beauty."

She took Roth's outstretched hand, the spark giving
her the jolt of energy she needed. Gravel crunched under
her feet as she stepped out of the vehicle. One of the
first things she noticed—excluding the bone-chilling
cold—was the quiet. No horns. No traffic. No bustling.

Yeah, this was the perfect place to rejuvenate her
soul. Being here would be good for her. It would give
her the time she needed to think and clear her cluttered
thoughts. Inhaling a deep breath, she blew it out slowly.
Already she felt...free.

The only light radiated from the full moon. She tilted
her head and scrutinized a sky so clear it could have
been a flawless oil painting. And the stars... Had she
ever seen them twinkle more brightly?

And then there were the oversize trees. She performed a slow turn. Trees, trees and more trees surrounded them. Roth hadn't exaggerated about the
privacy of this location. Not a single soul would be
able to hear them scream if they were attacked.

The quaint cabin caught her eye. What it lacked in
size, it made up for in charm. Built completely of logs,
seven steps led to a nicely sized wraparound porch. A

cobblestone chimney protruded from the roof. Several hours ago she would have tingled at the idea of her and Roth cuddled intimately in front of a wood-burning fireplace. Not now.

Roth startled her when he draped his coat over her shoulders. He'd obviously changed out of his suit at The Underground because now he wore a thick black sweater, jeans and a pair of black mountain boots. Despite her current state of mind, she could still appreciate how devastatingly attractive he was. "Thank you. I'm freezing." She shivered for effect.

"We can go into town in the morning and grab you some clothes. I'm sure you don't want to wear this the entire weekend." He fingered the thin fabric of her jumpsuit. "Regardless of how beautiful you look in it."

Disappointment flashed on Roth's face that suggested he regretted saying the words. Regardless, the compliment brought a lazy smile to her face. "It's gorgeous. Your cabin. Thank you again for bringing me here with you. I won't get in the way."

What she really wanted to say—ask actually—was why had he seemed so reluctant to bring her here at first, and what had changed his mind? But she decided against it. She was just happy she wouldn't have to be alone.

"Thanks. Like I said, it's not much, but I love it."

Tressa opened and closed her mouth several times.

"Ears popping?" Roth said.

"Yes."

"It's the altitude. You'll get used to it."

Moving to the back of the vehicle, Roth removed a bag and a large black case she assumed was his saxophone—Juliette—before they made their way inside, out of the cold. Or so she'd thought. It was as cold inside the cabin as it had been outside. Possibly a degree or two colder. She pulled the wool coat tighter around her shoulders.

"I believe it's warmer outside."

"I'll build a fire," Roth said. "It shouldn't take it long to warm up in here."

The interior wasn't at all what Tressa had expected. A mocha-colored leather sofa and a matching chair sat in the living area. Several pictures of airplanes hung throughout the room. A flat-screen television was mounted on the wall above the fireplace. A bookcase packed with books sat in one corner. Was it for decoration, or did Roth enjoy reading?

Her eyes trailed to the kitchen outfitted with all stainless steel appliances. A small dining area seamlessly melted the space together. A set of stairs led to what she assumed were the bedrooms. This was nice. Really nice.

The sound of the fire crackling curled Tressa's lips. It took her back to when she was a child and winters spent at her grandparents' house. Good times. Roth's voice faded Tressa's memories.

"Unfortunately, there's only one bed, but it's yours. I'll camp out on the sofa." He patted the plush-looking piece. "We're highly acquainted. I've fallen asleep in her warm arms many nights."

"No, Roth. I can't let you do that. I'll take the sofa. No argument," she said when protest danced in Roth's mesmerizing eyes. "Truly, it's fine." No way would she inconvenience him after he'd been so kind as to bring her here.

After a few seconds of scrutiny Roth shrugged. "Okay, but you're going to hate me in the morning."

As if that was possible. The perplexed look he gave her rattled her a bit. What was he attempting to decipher? How she was holding up? Why she'd wanted to come here with him? Would she be okay? She didn't know the answer to any of it.

To end his exhausting scrutiny, she said, "Please tell me you have food in this place. I'm starving."

"Yes, we do. I have someone who looks in on the place for me. When I let her know I'm coming, she always stocks the fridge."

She?

Jealousy was the last emotion Tressa expected, but a hint of it crept in. Could this have been the mystery woman he'd intended to spend the weekend with before she'd come along and derailed his plans? Was it selfish that she didn't regret spoiling his rendezvous? Yes.

"Well, let's just see what *she* brought, shall we?" If nothing else could, cooking relaxed her. It'd always been her first love, with nursing a close second, of course.

"In a minute. But first—" he captured her hand and angled his head toward the sofa "—let's sit a second."

Tressa studied their joined hands as they moved across the room. A simple act of kindness should not have felt so damn good. A soothing sensation tingled in her palm. At the sofa, Roth released her hand and guided her down, taking the spot next to her. The way he eyed her made her feel as if she'd sneaked the last piece of key lime pie, and he was simply waiting for her to confess before he had to accuse her.

Tressa straightened her back to give some semblance of strength. "Is everything okay?"

He leaned forward, rested his elbows on his thighs and intertwined his fingers. "You tell me."

Tressa arched a brow. "I…don't…know what you want me to say." Though she had a good idea he wanted her to mention something about what had taken place at The Underground. She'd hoped to avoid discussing her disastrous engagement party, but it seemed she wouldn't get off that easily. Couldn't he have waited until morning when she'd got a decent night's sleep before he approached the thorny subject?

"You've had a rough evening. If you—"

"I'm fine, Roth," she said, pushing to her feet. Subtlety obviously didn't work with him.

Before she could stalk away, he captured her hand again. This time he didn't let it go when she sat. His large hand completely swallowed hers, but she loved the feel of his warm flesh caressing hers.

"You keep saying you're fine, but I don't believe you."

"And I'm not trying to convince you." Instantly, she regretted being so callous. But dammit, she didn't want to discuss what had happened between her and Cyrus. Especially with Roth, of all people. She was hurt, embarrassed and still processing it all.

Her cruel tone appeared to have little effect on him. That same sympathetic expression remained on his attractive face. They stared at one another for a long time. Roth refused to turn away, and so did she. It felt as if he were trying to peer into her soul, but it was too dark for him to see inside. Beyond his strict and unwavering gaze lingered compassion. Mounds and mounds of compassion. And a hint of pity.

Tressa bent to the idea and turned away. "Don't feel sorry for me, Roth."

"I don't. I feel sorry for the bastard who didn't recognize what he had."

Tressa brought urgent focus back to Roth, her eyes lingering briefly on his mouth before climbing to latch onto his draining gaze again. Was he the reason she wasn't feeling the all-out dismay Cyrus's betrayal should have caused her? She was hurt—and angry—but she also felt something else. Relief.

Roth's cell phone vibrated and she flinched. "You should get that," she said, seeing her opportunity to escape this overwhelming and confusing moment.

Without even pulling the device from his pocket, he said, "It can wait."

After a couple more seconds of buzzing, either the call rolled to voice mail or the caller hung up. Tressa couldn't help but wonder if it was the woman Roth had planned to spend the weekend with. Before she'd dozed off on the drive up, Roth had sent several calls directly to voice mail. A part of her was happy to be here, away from her own problems, but another part of her felt guilty for potentially causing some for Roth, and for ruining his plans. Even if the idea of him making love to someone else bothered her more than it should have.

"I appreciate what you're trying to do, Roth. I truly do. But I don't want to talk about it now. I just… I just want to get through the night. I just want to get through the night," she repeated.

Roth brought her hand to his lips and kissed the inside of her wrist. It was the most intimate and soul-stirring move he could have made. The energy delivered through the sensual and delicate act sent a shock wave of desire sparking through her system. Everything about being there with Roth felt so right and so wrong all at the same time.

Chapter 3

When Tressa had volunteered to *whip something up*, it didn't take long for Roth to discover that they had two totally different definitions of the term. While he'd suggested preparing peanut butter and jelly sandwiches—to which she'd laughed hysterically—Tressa had taken the reins and created a spread that looked as if it belonged in a magazine for culinary professionals.

How in the hell had she managed to turn generic grocery items—a block of cheddar cheese, a can of Southern biscuits, beef hot dogs, thin-sliced pepperoni, club crackers, kettle chips and French onion dip—into a work of edible art? She truly was amazing in the kitchen.

"*Wow.* This looks scrumptious," he said, his growling stomach loudly approving. "A nurse and a chef. How in the heck did that happen?"

"I grew up watching my family help others. My father was a policeman, my mother a teacher. I had aunts, uncles and cousins who were firemen, clergy, counselors, doctors, lawyers, you name it. If there is a position out there geared toward helping people, one of my family members held it. Now, my love for cooking…I got that from my Poppa. My grandfather," she clarified and beamed with pride.

Roth envied her, envied anyone who'd grown up surrounded by family. As a youngster, he'd dreamed of growing up, getting married and having a thousand kids. Somewhere along the way, that vision had faded. Tressa's voice snatched him out of his thoughts.

"Do you mind if we eat in front of the fireplace?" she said.

"Sounds good to me."

After arranging everything on the brown shag rug, Roth returned to the kitchen for two hard black cherry lemonades. It'd actually been Tressa who'd introduced him to the drink. He usually went for the harder stuff—whiskey—or the occasional beer. With her feminine wiles, she'd convinced him to try the sweet beverage when they'd both been at Alonso and Vivian's place at the beach. He'd got hooked. On Tressa and the drink.

Roth recalled that beach trip. Watching Tressa wade through the water in an ocean-blue bikini, her skin glistening under the rays of the sun, had been torture in its most pleasurable form. On several occasions he'd wanted to ignore the fact that she was seeing someone and seduce the hell out of her, but he'd resisted. Looking back, he wished he had taken a risk. Maybe it would have spared her some heartache.

"Earth to Roth."

Tressa's voice pulled him back to reality. "I'm sorry. Did you say something?"

"Yes. I asked if you could bring some napkins."

Roth grabbed a stack of napkins off the counter and fanned them through the air. "Got it." He passed her one of the bottles, then eased down next to her.

Tressa eyed him curiously. "Are you okay?"

"Yeah. Yeah," he repeated when she didn't look convinced. "I drift sometimes. Growing up in foster care, I rarely got privacy. Sometimes escaping inside my own head was my only refuge."

Damn. Why had he shared any of that? His past was typically something he kept to himself. Not because he was ashamed of it, but because the second people learned he'd been a foster kid, they showered him with unnecessary sympathy. He hated that with a passion.

"I was a foster mother to a six-year-old once. Jamison," she said absently. "I'll never do it again."

"*Wow.* That bad, huh?"

Tressa grimaced. "God, I made that sound so harsh and insensitive. Let me clarify. I wouldn't do it again because I grew so attached to him in the short time he was with me. Watching him leave was the hardest thing I'd ever had to do. I cried like a baby for days."

He'd picked up on Tressa's nurturing side the first time he'd met her. It was one of the things he found so attractive about her. Nursing was the perfect profession for her. "Why didn't you adopt him?" Roth asked out of curiosity. She seemed to have cared for the child.

Tressa stared into the crackling fire. "I wanted to."

"Cyrus? Is he why you didn't adopt Jamison?" Roth wasn't sure why he'd come to that conclusion, but when

Tressa faced him again he knew he'd been spot-on. He hated the man even more.

She slid her gaze back to the fire. "Pathetic, huh?"

Roth wanted to say something encouraging, but he couldn't find the words. Growing up, every single day he'd wished for someone to care enough to want to adopt him, but it had never happened. But Tressa could have been the answer to the prayers Roth was sure Jamison said every night. She could have saved him from the hell of the foster system. But instead, she'd allowed that bastard Cyrus to convince her to send Jamison back into…hell.

Anger swirled inside him. He wasn't sure if it was geared more toward Cyrus or Tressa. He took a long swig from his bottle.

"After two weeks without the sound of Jamison's laughter, I realized the mistake I'd made. I contacted the agency, but I was too late. A family was interested in adopting him. I know I should have been ecstatic he'd found a permanent home. I was and I wasn't." She shook her head. "I had no right to be upset. I'd had my opportunity and blew it. I was being selfish. Which is typically *not* me, might I add."

She'd redeemed herself.

"He would have been lucky to have you as his mother."

A lazy smile curled her lips. "Thank you, Roth. That was kind of you to say."

Tressa's lips parted, then closed as if she'd reconsidered what she was about to say. The move drew his attention to her mouth. A knot formed in his stomach when she thought about how badly he wanted to lean over and kiss her. *Not a smart move. Fight this, Lexington.*

"I asked for a sign."

Scrambling his thoughts of ravishing her mouth, he said, "Excuse me?"

"Tonight. Right before you joined me on the balcony. I asked God to send me a sign if I was making a mistake by marrying Cyrus."

Was she suggesting he'd been her sign? Something warm and prideful blossomed in his chest.

"I guess your fiancé's mistress crashing your engagement party was a fairly obvious one, huh?"

And just like that, it wilted. "You don't seem too distraught about it." Roth pressed his lids together. "*Shit.* I'm sorry. That was an insensitive and stupid thing to say. I'm sure you're plenty upset."

"I'm not, actually. I mean, I'm angry as hell and hurt, but not in a debilitating manner, if that makes sense."

He hadn't expected that response. "Why?"

A beat of silence played between them.

Tressa lowered her head as if to hide her face in shame. "Because deep down, I knew Cyrus wasn't the right one for me. I just hung on in hopes of my feelings changing. I guess I kinda brought this whole mess on myself."

Roth knew it was a statement that didn't need a response, so he remained quiet. Before he'd even realized what he was doing, he draped an arm around her shoulder and pulled her against his chest. Tressa rested against him without any hesitations. Maybe he couldn't have her in the way he truly wanted, but he could be a friend in her time of need.

* * *

Tressa tossed and turned, unable to find a comfortable position. When she moved, it felt as if she were stuck to the smoldering leather. Kicking the quilt off that Roth had given her, she sat up and dragged the back of her hand across her forehead. It had to be three thousand degrees in here. And since heat rose, she was sure Roth was cooked to a crisp.

She sent a gaze to the loft. Though her view was obstructed, she imagined him sprawled out across the bed, his body sweat-dampened and glistening. A tingle in her belly slowly traveled to the space between her legs. As usual, her body was clearly on a mission to destroy her.

The popping embers brought her attention to the fireplace. She thought about their time in front of it earlier and how Roth had pulled her into his arms, and how safe she'd felt there. He'd wanted to kiss her, she was sure of it. So why hadn't he? Because he was too much of a gentleman.

She'd wanted Roth to kiss her, do more than kiss her, and it irked the hell out of her that he hadn't. But it'd probably been for the best. What kind of woman wanted a man to seduce her mere hours after finding out her fiancé has been sleeping with another woman? *A woman out for revenge*, she thought to herself.

No, that wasn't it. She blew a heavy breath. Her desire, need, want for Roth, weren't fueled by any of those things. Her longing for him was as authentic as it got. Which was why she had to fight it.

Tressa allowed her head to fall back against the cushions. Why did she always choose the wrong men? That included Roth. She wanted to believe he was a good guy, but the fact he could so easily push one woman aside—

who probably believed she had a position in his life—for another, even if the other was her, suggested otherwise.

Pushing everyone else aside, she focused on herself. "Will I ever find love?" she whispered to the universe, a tear sliding out the corner of her eye. "True love." That kind of ridiculous love that made you suddenly smile for no reason at all. She deserved that and wanted it. Wanted a husband who loved her beyond words. Wanted a family, a house full of kids—biological, adoptive or both. She wanted dogs, family dinners, vacations. "I want it all," she mumbled.

"You got it."

Tressa bolted forward to see Roth standing at the edge of the stairs in a navy blue tee that hugged his solid frame nicely and navy-blue-and-white pajama bottoms that sat just right on his lean frame. "What?"

"Insomnia?"

Tressa laughed at herself and wiped her eyes. "Um… sometimes. I didn't wake you, did I?"

"Ah, no, you didn't. I have trouble sleeping some-times, too."

Roth studied her. No doubt he wanted to address her tears, but she prayed he wouldn't. Then, as if he'd read her mind, he turned his attention to the kitchen.

"Hot cocoa usually helps. Would you like some?" he said.

Although she teetered on the edge of spontaneously combusting, she said, "Sure." She could use the con-versation, as long as it wasn't about her.

When she rose, her muscles protested the move.

Roth chuckled. "So, how's the sofa? Hate me yet?"

"Ha ha." Making her way across the room, she said, "Can I help?"

"No." Roth pointed to the small dining table. "Sit, woman."

Tressa saluted him. "Yes, sir."

Lounging in a chair, Tressa gleefully watched Roth move about. There was something alluring about a man working in the kitchen, especially this man. Even if all he was doing was heating milk.

Roth chatted about something, but truthfully, she had no idea about what. Lost in her own thoughts, she chuckled when she recalled the animated expression on his face when she'd nixed his PB&J sandwich suggestion.

"Don't laugh. It could happen," Roth said.

Breaking free from her thoughts, she said, "Um… what exactly could happen?"

He rested a hand on his hip. "You haven't heard a single word I've said, have you?"

Tressa bit at the corner of her lip and shook her head. "Sorry. I drift off sometimes."

He barked a laugh. Obviously, at the fact she'd used his own words against him. "Prepare to be impressed." He approached the table with two steaming mugs, set one in front of her, then lowered into a chair next to her at the square table with his in his hand.

Tressa took a sip and moaned. "*Mmm.* Real milk. And the cinnamon is a delicious touch. You did well."

"See, I can do a little something-something in the kitchen, too."

She imagined he could do a lot of something-something elsewhere, as well. After taking another sip, she said, "So, what is it that could happen?" Referring to his comment from earlier.

Roth's eyes slid to his mug, but only briefly. "While you're here with me, I plan to cater to your every need."

This sobered Tressa rather quickly. Cater to her every need? The possibilities made her stomach flutter and her body bloom. God, she prayed her nipples didn't bead underneath the oversize T-shirt Roth had given her to sleep in.

Scattering the illicit images hijacking her thoughts, she lowered her eyes to the steam rising from her cup. "Why—" She cleared her throat. "Why would you want to do that?"

"Because you deserve it. You've been through a lot. I think you need to be reminded that you're still a queen. And queens get served." He tapped her foot playfully with his own.

Tressa dared her body to give one damn indication of how much his words had affected her. Finally, someone saw and acknowledged her worth. But why did it have to be the man she was determined to resist?

Roth continued, "Plus, something tells me you never really abandon nurse mode. That you're constantly taking care of others and rarely focus on yourself, doing what makes Tressa happy."

Doing what makes Tressa happy. That should become her new motto. She shrugged one shoulder. "I like helping people," she said, in lieu of confessing that he was 100 percent correct. She rarely took time for herself.

"This weekend… It's all about you, lady. Got it?"

Roth crossed one ankle over the opposite knee, rested his hands in his lap, tilted his head and eyed her as if asserting his authority. She propped her elbow on the table, rested her cheek against her palm and eyed him back.

That seemed to be their thing—staring at one another for long, heated moments.

"Got it." What else could she say?

"Good."

Roth was a lethal combination: successful, sexy, charming. And he used it all well. Though a future with him was impractical, was a night of passionate, no-strings-attached sex out of the question?

What the hell was she saying? Roth struck her as the kind of man who molded into your system and stayed there, the kind of man who made women lose their minds. *One night?* Something told her one night with him would spiral her out of control. Her world was topsy-turvy enough. Still, everything about him intrigued her. *Stay away.*

Tressa circled her finger around the rim of the mug, ignoring his alluring aura. "I apologize if I caused any problems between you and your weekend companion." A corner of Roth's mouth lifted and her eyes fixed on his lips. Had anyone ever told him how damn sexy his mouth was? She was sure they had.

"Don't apologize," he said.

"I ruined your plans."

"Shit happens."

"Yes, it does." And there was some other *shit* she would love to happen right then.

Shit like him leaning over and kissing her long and hard.

Shit like him gliding his large hands up her bare thighs and underneath her shirt.

Shit like him pushing her panties to the side and curving two long fingers inside her.

Yes, all of that.

"Drifting again?" Roth said in a low, sensual tone.

Straightening her back, she said, "Um...why do you ask?"

Roth's eyes lowered to her chest and lingered there several seconds before rising. "Seemed as if you were... daydreaming."

The prickle on her skin told her she would regret looking down, but she tilted her head forward anyway. Yep, regret. Blazing-hot, flesh-searing regret.

There was no hiding those high beams of her beaded nipples. If she could have utilized one superpower at that very moment, it would have been the ability to make herself invisible. She pushed to a stand, urging the floor to swallow her. "I'm really tired. I'm..." Instead of finishing her thought, she forced her feet forward and willed her body to deactivate like she was a Transformer.

"You haven't finished your cocoa."

"It worked." She forced a yawn. "I don't think I need any more."

"Wait," Roth said.

Tressa froze as if he'd pointed a gun at her. When he moved toward her, she felt a wave of nervous tension. His head pointed toward the stairs. "Take the bed. I'll take the sofa."

As tempting as the offer was, she shook her head, then snuggled back onto the sofa.

A beat later Roth climbed in behind her. "Anyone ever told you you're too damn headstrong sometimes?"

Tressa stilled, her body going berserk from Roth's closeness, his solidity, his heat, his scent. Processing it all scrambled her brain. Her nipples tightened even more, her breathing grew clumsy, the space between her legs throbbed and begged to be touched. Sparring with her out-of-control body, she glanced over her shoulder and said, "Many call it being passionate. And what do you think you're doing?"

"If you're on the sofa, so am I. We suffer together."

"Roth—"

He made a snoring sound, which made her laugh. "Okay, suit yourself. But I'm not moving. I've grown very fond of this sofa. It's extremely comfortable. And for the record, no one falls asleep that fast."

Another round of snores caused her to laugh again.

Who was being the headstrong one now? If he wanted to stay there, then so be it. But there was no way she was getting off this sofa. Not because she was trying to prove how stubborn she could be. It was because Roth snuggled behind her felt too damn good to simply walk away from.

Chapter 4

While Tressa showered, Roth scrounged up something for her to wear shopping. He placed the T-shirt and sweatpants on the bed, then went back downstairs. Removing Juliette, he went out onto the deck to free his trapped emotions through music notes. He played and played hard. A rigid and rough tone that would be considered too edgy for most. This soothed him.

Several minutes later he stopped abruptly and snatched the instrument from his lips. He deserved every damn bothersome emotion swirling around inside him. The harder he tried to deny the pull Tressa had on him, the stronger it became, like a spiteful monster taunting him with its power over him.

If he had just allowed Tressa to get out of his SUV at the hotel, all of this could have been avoided. Why had he brought Tressa here?

Dammit. He was losing control. He never lost control.

The scene from that morning played in his head—waking up with Tressa fast asleep in his arms. For an hour he'd simply watched her sleep, not moving a single muscle and risking waking her. She felt right in his arms. Too damn right.

At one point he'd been so damn hard he was surprised he hadn't pushed her off the sofa. And when she subconsciously ground her ass against him, he thought he would die a slow and painful death. One thing was for sure, he didn't stand a chance in hell against Tressa Washington.

He was good at hard and cold. So why did he keep dispensing soft and warm around her. *Cater to your every need?* Had he really said that shit? He chuckled. *Yep.* And the funny thing about it, he'd actually meant every word.

He raised Juliette to his lips again but reconsidered. With the mayhem inside him now, playing would terrify the wildlife.

Tressa was right here. Right here for the claiming. Why was he hesitating?

From the deck, he heard her cell phone vibrate again. The tenth time in the past hour. Cyrus's no-good ass, no doubt. Tempted to answer the phone and tell the bastard to never call Tressa again, Roth resisted. Hell, for all he knew she wanted him to keep calling. She hadn't actually taken any of his calls to tell him otherwise. Wouldn't that have been the logical thing to do?

Wow. Wasn't that the pot calling the kettle black? He hadn't exactly jumped to take India's calls, either. Well, at least she'd had the good gumption to stop calling, obviously realizing he'd rescinded her invitation to the cabin.

Venturing back inside, he stored Juliette, then fixed himself another cup of coffee while he waited for Tressa so they could go to the store. Roth chuckled. Tressa's presence was definitely going to shock the hell out of Glen. He hoped the man didn't jump to any conclusions. He and Tressa were just friends. And that was how it had to remain. At least for now. At least until he was sure she was over her ex. And right now he wasn't so convinced that she was.

Tressa and Roth arrived at The General Store. Tressa originally assumed it was what Roth called it, but that was actually the name. The General Store. Couldn't get more generic than that. The airy barnlike structure resembled something from an old Western movie from the outside, but the inside was anything but old-timey.

Everything occupied the large store, including clothing. That was great because, though she was grateful, Roth's baggy St. Claire Aeronautics T-shirt and oversize black sweatpants didn't exactly make her a walking fashion movement. Nor did the stilettos she wore with it. And the mountain jacket swallowed her whole. But that part was okay, because Roth's scent saturated it. It was like having his warm arms swaddled around her all over again.

Her thoughts went to waking in his arms that morning. She couldn't recall ever experiencing a more peaceful night of sleep—well, until Roth started flinching in his sleep. Whatever he'd been dreaming kept him active.

Falling asleep on the sofa with Roth was one mistake she would not make again. The lapse in judgment had pushed her body to the brink of sexual insanity. Stubborn, passionate, whatever you wanted to call it, that had definitely been one battle she hadn't picked wisely.

"Lord, look who the mountain lion done dragged in."

Tressa followed the raspy voice to a short, round man. His long-sleeved denim shirt was buttoned all the way to the top and tucked into a pair of faded jeans held in place by green suspenders. With a head full of wiry salt-and-pepper hair, the older man kind of reminded her of her grandfather. God rest his soul.

A very docile dog with paws the size of saucers ambled up to Roth and brushed against his pant leg in the same manner an adoring cat would do. Roth rubbed his large head. "What's up, Shank?"

Shank's appreciation of the attention was clear, his back leg pumping harder the more Roth rubbed him. If Tressa hadn't known any better, she would have sworn the dog had smiled.

Tressa hung back while Roth, the gentleman and Shank socialized, but she could hear their conversation.

"Nettie told me you were coming to town. Since you're gonna be here a week, make sure you stop by for supper before you leave. You know Nettie will be hurt if you don't."

"I don't think I'll get by this trip. I'm only here for the weekend."

Confusion crinkled the man's aged dark brown skin. "I thought Nettie said you were here for the week."

Roth clapped him on the shoulder. "Change of plans."

Was the change because of her?

"Well, shucks. It's probably for the best. They're calling for snow Monday. Could be a headache." For the first time, his swamp-green eyes trailed to Tressa. "Or romantic. 'Pends on how you view it, I suppose. Hello, beautiful." He brushed past Roth.

"Glen, this is my friend Tressa," Roth said.

Tressa wasn't sure why Roth's use of the word *friend* bothered her, because it was exactly what they were. Friends. Just friends. "Hello." She offered her hand, but Glen pulled her into an embrace that suggested they'd known each other for years. *Okay, then. A hug it is.* Unlike with Roth, Shank had little interest in her and disappeared behind the counter.

When Glen held her at arm's length, his round cheeks blossomed. "Well, it's a pleasure meeting you, friend Tressa." Glen cut his eyes in Roth's direction. "And any friend of this man's is definitely a friend of mine."

Tressa noted Glen's obvious admiration for Roth.

Glen continued, "I know you haven't gone through all of that food my Nettie took to your place." He clapped a hand on Roth's shoulder. "My wife likes to make sure this joker is taken care of. And when she heard it might snow…she packed like a famine was coming." Glen sounded a huge laugh that made his stomach jiggle.

Ah. Nettie was Glen's wife. The information sent a hint of satisfaction through her.

"Nettie left plenty," Roth said. "We just need to gather a few other things."

The front door chimed, drawing their attention.

"All right. Well, holla if you need me," Glen said and moseyed away.

Tressa glanced up at Roth. "You were supposed to stay a week?"

He shrugged. "Yeah, but it's—"

"It's not okay." Normally, he was the one finishing her thoughts. "Don't let me disrupt your plans again. I already feel bad enough. We're staying the week. I, for one, wouldn't want to disappoint Nettie."

Roth laughed. "You did hear the part about snow, right? We could get stuck here beyond a week. Frankly, I'm not sure I can put up with you for more than a week."

Tressa's mouth fell open, and she swatted him playfully. "How rude."

"I'm just kidding. You're great company."

She was in no rush to get back to Raleigh. The more time she could spend in Silver Point, getting her thoughts together, the better. "I'm okay with getting stuck here. I have nothing better to do."

Roth folded his arms across his chest. "What about your job?"

"Twelve days on, twelve days off. I'm in my twelve-days-off stretch. And I don't start new culinary classes until the spring." Man, she was really pleading her case. And for the first time, she considered that maybe Roth's plans had changed because he *hadn't* wanted to spend a full week with her. Backpedaling, she said, "But you're probably right. Staying a week is probably a bad idea." When Roth laughed, she shot him a disapproving look. "What's so funny?"

He shook his head. "Nothing."

"What?" she repeated, adding a hint of bass to her voice as if it would force this rugged man to yield to her demand for information.

"You're delaying the inevitable, Tressa," he said plainly.

Delaying the inevitable? Inwardly, she sighed. Of course, they were back on the engagement party again. "I'm not delaying anything, *Roth*. I'm—"

"Running?"

Tressa shot him a narrow-eyed gaze. "Excuse me?"

He flashed his palm. "You know what? It's none of my business."

"You're right. It's not any of your business. So please stick to designing airplanes and refrain from trying to analyze me." She rolled her eyes and stalked off. *Running? Ha.* The nerve of him to make such an outlandish assessment simply because she wanted to enjoy the beauty of the mountains. Just like a damn man.

Running.

She wasn't running from anything. She planned to face her situation head-on, but not until *she* was ready.

A few steps from Roth's SUV the lights blinked twice, letting her know he'd unlocked the vehicle. Yanking the door open, she hurled herself inside. A second later the doors locked and Roth activated the auto-start feature. It wasn't long before warm air blew through the vents, and she closed them in protest, then laughed at herself. The only one who would suffer if she froze to death would be her.

Why was Roth so damn considerate? Why was he being so damn nice to her? It made it that much harder to be angry at him. And why was she so annoyed with him anyway?

Because he's right. She was running.

She'd ignored every phone call, text message, email and IM Cyrus had sent her. But she didn't have to explain herself to anyone. If she wanted to refrain from adulting for a while, it was her choice. No one else's. She glared toward The General Store. Not even to the man who'd altered his life for her.

Tressa closed her eyes and allowed her head to ease

back. Pressing two fingers against her temple, she attempted to knead the pain away. What was going on with her? She was usually more in control than this, a warrior. Now she simply felt like a battered peasant.

She chastised herself for not at least grabbing a piece or two before storming out of the store. Now she would have to wear the same outfit the entire weekend. Well, it served her right for being so juvenile.

Time ticked by. Why hadn't Roth emerged yet? Was he waiting for her to return? Recalling how she'd reacted filled her with regret. He clearly had her best interest at heart and had told her what she needed to hear, whether she wanted to hear it or not. Wasn't that what friends did for each other?

Friends? Could she even classify them as friends? Acquaintances probably worked better. How about potential cuddle buddies? This made her laugh.

Roth finally exited the store, carrying several overstuffed bags. When he opened the back door, a gust of cold air rushed in. He unloaded his haul, then slid behind the wheel.

"I grabbed you a few things," he said.

Grabbed her a few things? "You don't know my size."

"Twelve."

Or maybe he did. She tossed a glance in the back seat. A few things? It looked as if he'd outfitted her for the entire month. Even after she'd treated him like crap, he'd still looked after her. Who was this man? "Thank you," she said in a low, yielding tone. "I'll pay you back."

"That's not necessary." He sighed. "When you stormed off, I had to make an executive decision about what to get. You probably won't be runway ready, but you'll be warm."

God, she felt horrible about how she'd acted. "Roth—"

"If you're going to apologize, don't. I was out of line. You're a grown woman. You don't need me to hold your hand."

Maybe she did. Maybe that was exactly what she needed. For someone to simply hold her hand.

"I have this overwhelming need to protect you," Roth said.

The words almost seemed painful for him to admit. Had she just got a glimpse at a vulnerable Roth Lexington? The flash of weakness was endearing. Her lips twitched, but she didn't want to smile. Just like him, she needed to play it cool. But the fact that he wanted to protect her melted her heart into a big, messy puddle. No man had ever said anything like that to her. How did she respond?

Roth continued, "Big brother instinct. At least that's what my foster brothers would call it." Roth blew out another breath. "I should be the one apologizing. From this point forward, I will mind my own damn business. You have my word."

Big brother instinct? Was he suggesting he saw her as a kid sister?

Hell, no. No man would look at a sibling the way he looked at her.

"Still, I overreacted. You didn't deserve that. I'm sorry."

Roth studied her for a moment before he spoke. "I accept."

They fell into comfortable silence, staring at one

another in *their* way. She needed to give this thing they did a name. Something with fire in it, because every time they latched onto one another in one of these passion-swirling stare downs, flames burned through her as hot as lava.

Before she was completely consumed, she searched for something monumental to say, something that would convey her sentiment, a line that would reveal some things, but conceal others. Unfortunately, her brain was fried.

Chapter 5

Roth stood staring out at Silver Point in the distance, recalling the conversation he'd had with Tressa that morning outside the general store. He'd given her too much. Why in the hell had he told her about his need to protect her? *Way too much.* But what he'd seen in her eyes suggested it'd been just enough. For her, at least.

Why did this damn woman leave him feeling so exposed?

Tressa's reflections danced in the glass as she moved down the stairs. He wanted her in the worst way. There was truly no more denying that.

Tressa stood at the door alongside Roth. "God, this view is amazing. You can see the entire town below." When he didn't respond, Tressa glanced up at him. "Hey, are you okay?"

He flashed a low-wattage smile. "Sorry. I drifted off."

They shared a laugh at their inside joke.

"So, what do we have planned for this gorgeous Saturday afternoon? Now that I have clothes that fit—perfectly, I might add—I'm down for whatever."

"Whatever, huh?" That was a risky statement.

"Yep," she said with confidence.

"Well, let's get out of here, then." He had the perfect outing. And the more time they spent *out*, the less time he'd spend daydreaming about being *in* her.

Twenty minutes later they entered the Blue Ridge Parkway. The drive along this stretch was stunning, even with the leafless trees and absence of color. Hands down, fall was Roth's favorite time of year here with the vibrant reds, yellows and oranges.

Taking a quick detour, he veered off to the Grandview Overlook. Tressa stood staring out at the miles and miles of rolling mountaintops, clouds swooping low as if they were there to welcome the formations into heaven.

"If I'd known how beautiful it is here, I'd have come a long time ago," Tressa said.

While Tressa took in every inch of the scene surrounding them, he took in every inch of her. Everything about her was so delicate, yet alluded strength. Definitely strong willed. He laughed to himself. It took a helluva woman to have gone through what she had and still be able to smile as bright as the sun. He admired that about her. That resilience. It was attractive as hell.

"Come on," he said, leading her back to the SUV. "If you liked that view, you'll love where we're headed next."

The road leading to the top of Grandfather Mountain was narrow, winding and steep. When they made it to the top, Tressa blew out a sigh of relief. He remembered his first time taking the trip and understood her reaction. "What's wrong?"

Tressa rested her hand over her heart. "A couple of times I thought we'd topple over the edge. Especially when another vehicle was coming from the opposite direction. I feel like I should get out and kiss the ground."

"You were never in any danger." He glanced into those tender eyes. *Turn away, man. Turn away.* Tressa's eyes were like puddles of brown desire that chipped away at the fortress around his heart every time he peered into them. At this rate she'd reach his center in no time. That troubled him. His heart was off-limits. Even to Tressa.

Exiting the vehicle, they stood in the parking lot for a moment, appreciating the view.

"Those houses look like they're sitting right on the edge of the mountain. One bump and *boom*, they're tumbling to the bottom." She leaned forward as if to gauge exactly how far they were from the bottom. A ways.

Roth decided to not mention the fact that if she looked up from town, his cabin would appear the same way.

When they finally made their way to one of the mountain's main attractions—the Mile High Swinging Bridge—Tressa mounted a protest. "No way, no how are you getting me on that." She jammed a finger at the metal structure. A passing couple laughed and she shot death rays at the backs of their heads.

"Trust me. It's not as bad as it looks," he said.

"No, it's probably worse. I don't do bridges. Not since—"

Her abrupt stop made Roth curious about what she was holding back.

"I don't do them, and no way in hell would I ever do a *swinging* bridge. *Swinging*, Roth. That means it moves, right?"

"Yes, but—"

She tossed her hands up. *"No way. No how. Let's go."*

When she tried to walk away, Roth hooked her by the waist. It was faint, but he swore Tressa moaned. Or maybe it'd been him. Damn, he hoped it hadn't been him. But it was possible. Touching her always triggered something in him. He willed himself to let go, but his arm didn't budge. "Baby, you can't—" He stopped abruptly. *Shit.* Had he really just called her *baby*? Releasing her, he took a step away.

Tressa turned to face him, a look of uncertainty in her gaze. Clearly, he'd spooked her with the accidental use of the term of endearment.

Clearing his throat, he started again, this time dropping *baby*. "Um...you can't come all the way to Grandfather Mountain and not cross the bridge. It's... sacrilegious."

Tressa studied him. "Okay. I'll do it, but on one condition."

"Name it." Because, really, how bad could it be?

"We stay in Silver Point the entire week."

Real bad. What she considered a condition, he considered a blessing. However...there were forces greater than him at work here, and those forces suggested he not tempt fate any more than he already had.

"I know you think I'm running, Roth. I'm not. It's

just that being here with…" Her eyes moved away briefly. "I feel at peace in Silver Point. I haven't felt this way in a long, long time." Her lips curled slightly. "And I kinda like it and selfishly want more."

How in the hell could he argue with that? "Okay."

"Really?"

Like him, she obviously couldn't believe his answer, either. He nodded.

"Good. Well, then…let's do this." Tressa stopped shy of taking the first step onto the bridge. "And you have to hold my hand."

This was getting worse and better by the second. He splayed his gloved fingers and Tressa locked hers with his. It was a damn good thing there was a barrier between their hands. From experience, he knew their current would have surely fried everyone on the bridge.

Tressa's grip on his hand tightened when the bridge swayed. It wasn't a vicious movement, but it could be felt. For a moment he thought she'd pull away and run back to steadier ground. But surprisingly, she kept soldiering forward.

The farther they walked, the more hesitant her steps became. Then she stopped.

"Wait, wait, wait, Roth. I've changed my mind. I don't want to do this. I can't…"

Her voice cracked as if she was about to cry, and what he saw on her face was genuine fear. They backtracked, went straight to the vehicle and headed back to the cabin. Tressa didn't utter a word the entire drive, simply stared out the window and bounced her legs in quick succession.

As bad as he wanted to, Roth didn't push her to talk. When she was ready, she'd tell him what had frightened her so much the color had drained from her face. Roth didn't know what had happened, but he was convinced it hadn't been anything good.

Damn. Had he pushed her too hard? He should have respected her wishes.

It was a little after six in the evening when they pulled into the driveway. Inside, Tressa removed her gloves, coat and hat, then eased onto the sofa and hugged her knees to her chest. Everything inside him wanted to go to her and cocoon her in his arms, protect her. Instead, he lit a fire.

"Can I get you anything? Hot chocolate, maybe?" he asked.

Tressa shook her head. "No. I'm sorry for ruining the day."

Roth eased down next to her and took her hand into his. "You didn't ruin anything. I had a *great* time." Simply because he was with her, but that part stayed with him.

"Yeah, until I spazzed out."

"That was my fault. I shouldn't have pushed you."

Tressa swallowed hard. "When I was a child, I spent summers with my grandparents in the country. One day my childhood best friend, Cammie, convinced me to go with her to The Spot."

"The Spot?"

"A place where all of the *cool* kids hung out."

For some reason Roth got the feeling this story wouldn't end well.

"We were only ten and shouldn't have been hanging out with sixteen-year-olds, but we thought we were grown."

Didn't all kids at that age?

"It was all a lure. The cussing, smoking, drinking." She chuckled. "Of course I was always the one too scared to do any of it. My grandmother didn't play. She was old-school and wholeheartedly believed in ass whoopings."

At sixteen, he'd done all of those things she had mentioned. However, he wouldn't have classified himself as a *cool* kid. More like a menace.

"I begged Cammie to leave, but she wanted to stay. 'Just a few more minutes.'" Tressa's grip on his hand tightened as if she remembered something awful. "This boy Cammie had a crush on, Kevin Marshall—" she said the name with a scowl "—convinced her to jump off the bridge and into the river below, which wasn't a big deal. Everyone did it." Her voice cracked as she continued.

Tears welled in her eyes.

"Cammie hit the water wrong. By the time anyone got to her, it was too late."

A tear slid down her cheek, and Roth brushed it away. A second later he draped an arm around her shoulders and pulled her against his chest. Tressa wrapped her arms around him and held on to him tightly.

"It was twenty-four years ago, but when I got out on that bridge, it all came rushing back."

Roth stroked her arm. "You have no idea how horrible I feel for forcing you out there."

"You didn't force me, Roth. We made a deal, which I assume is void now."

"Nah. I'll still honor it."

A beat of silence fell between them.

Tressa tilted her head to look at him. After several

beats of silence, she said, "Thank you, Roth. For everything. You're a good friend."

"You're welcome." And before he knew it, he'd pressed a kiss to her forehead. When she reared back, their gazes held.

For the thousandth time, he told himself this had to stop. All of it. Especially this thing they did, this silent, powerful connection. It was too invasive. If it continued, she'd be in a place no one was allowed. Not even her, especially not her.

"What do you see?"

Roth's brow furrowed. "What do you mean?"

"When you look at me that way, like you're trying to read my mind, what do you see?"

The question was loaded and dangerous. "A beautiful, strong, compassionate, selfless, intelligent, sometimes-stubborn woman, who I wish would have come into my life at a different time. A time when things were less… complicated." He'd fallen on his own sacrificial sword.

Tressa's gaze left him briefly. "I see," was all she said.

Forcing his eyes away from her hypnotic stare, he kissed the inside of her wrist. This was something he had to stop doing, too. But he did it again. Suddenly, her wrist wasn't enough for his lips.

His mouth covered hers in a slow, cautious manner. Maybe he was giving her the opportunity to pull away since he clearly lacked the ability to do so.

She didn't.

Instead, Tressa's lips parted to accept his greedy tongue. He probed every inch of her wet, delicious mouth. For months, he'd longed for this opportunity again, ever since he'd kissed her in her best friend's kitchen.

Then, just like that, he snatched his mouth away. What in the hell was he doing? She wasn't available to him. Not yet. Not in the way he wanted and needed her.

Staring into her uncertain eyes, he said, "I should start the stew." Amid great personal protest, he stood up and walked away, leaving her alone on the couch.

But being the sometimes-stubborn woman she was, Tressa didn't allow the conversation to simply end there. Perhaps because he'd said a lot, but had left even more unsaid and she wanted—possibly needed—to know what.

How did he tell her that after only a day with her, he was falling harder and faster than he'd ever fallen before, and *not* sound insane?

"You or me?" she said.

Roth avoided looking at her, despite his confusion by the question. "You or me?"

"Less complicated for you or for me?"

"For the both of us, Tressa."

"I see. Have you considered the possibility that this is truly simple, but we're the ones choosing to make it too hard?"

"Poetic, but what's real—"

"Are your feelings for me real?"

This brought his eyes to hers. His shoulders slumped, defeat fighting its way in.

"I thought they were. Mine are, too, Roth." She sighed. "Maybe a week here is not such a good idea, after all. You're right. This is complicated. We shouldn't risk things getting any more confusing or complicated for either of us." She stood from the couch. "I'll be ready first thing in the morning. If you don't mind, I'll take the bed tonight."

He stared at the back of her head as she climbed the stairs. Any more complicated? As if things between them could get any more complicated than they already were.

Chapter 6

The following morning Roth stared out the kitchen window and sipped his coffee. Just when he thought things couldn't get any more complicated, things got more complicated. His eyes swept over the snow-covered landscape. At least six inches had fallen overnight, and snow was still falling. Six inches. How in the hell was this even possible? The snow wasn't supposed to have arrived until tomorrow, not today.

Maybe Tressa had asked for a sign. He laughed to himself. *Signs*. This was a sign, all right. A sign that *shit happens*. And most of the time for the worst.

He massaged the tension in his neck. This was a complication. A colossal complication. Still, the snow was beautiful.

And speaking of beautiful things…

Tressa ambled down the stairs and he almost laughed

at the sight of her in the floor-length grandma gown he'd purchased at the general store. The plaid fabric did little to accentuate her assets, which had been his intent. Since the air was already tense between them, he kept his amusement to himself.

Boy, had she challenged him the night before. And what had he done about it? Not a damn thing. What he'd wanted to do was race across the floor, snatch her into his arms and kiss the hell out of her again. Let her taste and feel him. It'd taken all his strength to fight it. But he had.

Their kiss had left him exposed and put his feelings for her out there. Though he hadn't confirmed them, he hadn't denied them, either. *Lord, the balls on this woman.* Yeah, she was the type of woman who could ruin him or cause him to ruin himself.

"Good morning," she said, barely making eye contact with him.

"Morning."

Picking up the Not Before My Coffee mug she seemed to be fond of, she said, "I'm all packed. What time are we getting on the road?"

"That might be a little difficult," he said.

She eyed him for the first time since she'd come down and said, "Difficult?"

With a head tilt, he directed her to the glass door leading onto the deck.

When she slid open the thermal curtains, she gasped. "Oh. It's snowing. A lot."

The hint of excitement that danced in her tone made him smile.

Turning to him again, she said, "I thought it wasn't supposed to start until tomorrow."

Exactly what he'd thought, too. That was what he got for falling asleep on the sofa before the weather report aired. He shrugged. "Guess Mother Nature changed her mind. Unfortunately, going down the mountain is not an option for the next few days. Sorry."

"We're stuck?"

He couldn't readily decipher what flashed in her eyes. It wasn't anger, but not quite elation, either. "Don't worry. We're good. There's plenty of food, water and firewood. And if the power happens to go out, I have battery-operated lanterns." Of course, he doubted any of that impressed her, especially since she'd clearly been looking forward to leaving. Her words rang in his head. *I'm all packed.*

"You sound prepared." Tressa folded her arms across her chest and bit at the corner of her lip. "So, how long do you think it'll be before we can leave?"

"It's hard to say. Wednesday? Thursday? But you might luck out and can get away from me before then."

"I'm not trying to escape you, Roth."

"*Hmm.* Really? You seemed pretty determined to get away from me last night."

"I retreated. That's what people do when they're losing a battle, right?" She turned away and focused out the door again.

Well, she was right about one thing; there was a battle being fought, but she was wrong about who was losing.

"Do you have a sled?"

"A sled?"

She shrugged her flannel-covered shoulders. "Might as well take advantage of our situation, right? God, I miss playing in the snow."

A sled? "No, but I have trash bags. They work just as well."

For the first time since she'd come down the stairs, she smiled. "My friends and I used to use trash bags when I was younger."

"So did we." Mainly because no one he knew could afford a sled. He shuddered at those hard times. He never wanted to know how it felt to go without again.

"Do you want to eat first? I can whip us up something real quick."

"Later. After sledding—trash bagging."

They shared a laugh.

Okay, this was good. Laughter was good.

His eyes raked over her body. "Are you going to change? Could get a little chilly in places." *Damn.* Why had he gone there? He didn't need to add sexual innuendo to their already-delicate situation.

Tressa smiled in a way that suggested she'd caught the sly remark he'd tossed.

"Give me ten minutes," she said and left the room.

Roth pressed his palms against the countertop, leaned forward and shook his head. The logical portion of his brain warned him away, while the irrational part kept steering him toward Tressa. Either he stopped, or he would crash and burn.

Moments later, the sound of Tressa descending the stairs pulled him from his thoughts.

"Okay, I'm ready," she said.

Even wearing a black toboggan, black earmuffs, a black mountain jacket zipped up to her chin and black subzero gloves, she was breathtaking. Grabbing his winter gear and the bags, they headed out the door.

Outside, Roth squinted against the blinding landscape. Snow still fell in a steady shower of plump flakes. The crisp air burned his nostrils on inhale. Too long out here and he'd be a Popsicle.

When Tressa slid her hand into her back pocket, his eyes lowered to her butt. That plump rump filled those jeans nicely. His imagination took hold, warming him rather nicely. A stir below the waist forced his gaze away.

Lines of heated air danced like smoke clouds in front of him when he said, "Be careful going down the stairs." He hadn't thought to salt them until now, when the risk of Tressa slipping and injuring herself became a factor.

At the bottom Tressa waved him on. "Go ahead. I need to fix my sock." She knelt and fiddled with the black all-terrain boots she wore.

The second he moved past her, a snowball clocked him in the back of the head. "Ouch." He turned, nursing the area where he'd been hit.

Tressa covered her mouth and bent at the waist in laughter.

"Oh, you think that's funny, huh?" When he scooped up a glove full of fluffy snow, Tressa's eyes widened and the laughter ceased.

"You wouldn't."

He stalked toward her like a lion that was seconds from pouncing on its prey. "Oh, I would."

"But my snowball was the size of a gumdrop. Yours looks like a bowling ball."

"Don't fault me for having large hands." Large hands he wanted to use to explore every inch of her body.

"But…but…I owed you that."

Roth didn't bother asking her why she felt she owed him a snowball to the back of the head. Instead, he kept stalking toward her. If they were playing eye for an eye, he owed her, too. Owed her big. Owed her for making him experience all these crazy and confusing feelings.

The snow crunched under her feet as she took cautionary steps back. A beat later she took off running. "You won't take me alive."

Aiming, he chucked the snowball, hitting Tressa smack-dab in her left butt cheek. When it wiggled a little, he groaned to himself.

Tressa yelped, then grabbed her behind. "Ouch! That hurt."

"Oops," he said. "I was aiming higher. Really, I was." He'd have probably been more convincing if he'd have said it slipped.

Her face lit with laughter. "I'm going to get you for that, Roth Lexington."

"Take your best shot." He did a fake right, then a fake left.

For close to an hour, they ran around the yard like kids, blasting each other with snow. It was the most fun he'd had in years. This was how he wanted to spend his time with her. Having fun, not at each other's throats about a bunch of feelings.

"Time, time," Tressa said, forming snow-covered, gloved hands into a T. A blink later she fell back into a pillow of snow, flapping her arms and legs.

"Woman, what are you doing?"

"Making a snow angel. You have to make one, too."

She was crazy if she thought he was getting down there. "I'm not lying on that cold-ass ground. Have you ever heard of frostbite? Hypothermia?"

"Wimp."

Roth barked a laugh. "Name-calling won't force me to change my mind."

"Pretty please with a cherry on top."

All it took was one look into those spell-casting eyes. *Dammit*. "Okay, okay."

Roth wanted to pretend the idea of making snow angels didn't excite him, but it did. As a kid, he'd always seen it done on Christmas movies and had secretly wished it were him sprawled out in the snow, enjoying the time with his parents like the laughing children on the television.

"Closer, Roth. I won't bite."

A corner of his mouth lifted. Too bad. Biting could be fun.

"What just ran through your mind?" Tressa said.

"Um, how cold the ground is." His response sounded more like a question, rather than an answer to hers.

"Mmm-hmm."

She truly didn't want to know what had raced through his mind, what always raced through his mind when he was with her. Finding the nearest hard surface, and the ground would do to make love to her. By the time they left Silver Point, he'd need counseling.

They moved their arms and legs simultaneously. With angels formed, he made a motion to get up, but Tressa stopped him.

"Tressa, this ground is hella cold, woman."

"Two seconds." She reached into her pocket and pulled out her cell phone. "We have to take a selfie."

A selfie? He was freezing his balls off, and she wanted to take a selfie? "Are you serious?"

"Yes. Lie back and smile, you big brute."

Tressa positioned her head close to his. He had to

admit, onscreen they looked great together. After several snaps—some of them smiling, some of them making silly faces—Roth couldn't feel his ass.

"Three more and we're done," she said.

But before she could press the red dot on the screen, the phone vibrated in her hands. Cyrus's ugly mug filled the display. Roth snarled at the phone, then caught himself.

"I'll give you some privacy," he said. He'd wanted a reason to get off the hard, cold ground, and now he had one.

Tressa swiped her thumb across the screen, sending the call to voice mail. "I don't need it."

"Why?" Catching himself, he swallowed his words. After the general store incident, he'd vowed to mind his own damn business. "Can we get up now? I can't feel my legs."

"Quit complaining," she said.

A blink later Tressa smashed a handful of snow in his face. He heaved as if she was drowning him.

"Suck...er."

She tried to make a smooth getaway, but he was too fast. "Oh, no, you don't." He snagged the back of her coat, pulled her back and pinned her to the ground. Miraculously, his temperature rose several degrees.

Tressa squirmed and laughed as if Roth was tickling her. "I'm sorry. I'm sorry," she squealed, her laughter floating in the cold air.

"*Sorry* is not going to work. You have to pay for that. Do you see my face? My cold, wet face?" He scooped up a mound of snow and held it inches from her. "I'm sorry. This has to be done. It's going to hurt me more

than it hurts you. But every action has an equal or opposite reaction. Any last words?"

Still rolling with laughter, she said, "Yes, yes."

"Okay. Spit them out before I exact my revenge."

Tressa laughed some more. "Revenge is best served
cold."

Roth laughed, bringing the snow closer to her face.

"Wait. Wait. My last words."

His hand continued to close in on her. "You better
make it quick."

Tressa sobered. "Kiss me."

Damn. He hadn't expected that. The expression on
her face was firm, so he knew she hadn't said it by accident. "You don't want that, Tressa. If I kissed you,
this time I wouldn't stop kissing you. Not until one or
both of us froze to death out here."

"Death is inevitable. Wouldn't you prefer to die
happy?"

Roth's jaw tightened. Did she have any idea how
much delicious trouble teasing him could get her in? He
tried his damnedest to pull away. Unfortunately, he lost
all control. Lowering his head, he allowed his lips to
brush hers. The heat that radiated through him burned
hot enough to melt the snow off the entire mountain.
"Are you sure this is what you want?" he asked against
their sparsely touching lips.

"Oh, yeah. Kiss me, Roth Lexington. And kiss me
like you mean it."

"And after the kiss ends?"

"We're both adults, Roth. It doesn't have to end at a
kiss. One time or a hundred. I just want to be with you."

Roth growled at the implication, his erection swell-
ing. *One time or hundred?* The thought was enough

to make him shudder. He brushed his lips against hers again. "Do you know what you're asking for?"

"All of you. Now, enough teasing. Kiss me. With the same intensity you did last night."

"Okay," he said in a you've-been-warned tone. But before he could capture her mouth in the hellish manner he wanted, that damn cell phone interrupted them again. True, it could have been anyone in the world calling her, but instincts told him it was that rat bastard.

"Just ignore it," she said against his wanting mouth. "Kiss me."

The intrusion brought him back to his senses. He couldn't just ignore it. When he slowly pulled away from her, disappointment danced in her eyes. "You're not ready for me, Tressa. You have unfinished business. And every time you run from your fiancé—"

"*Ex*-fiancé," she corrected with unsubtle irritation in her tone.

"Is he really?" Roth regretted the terse response.

"You were there, Roth. You saw what happened, what he did to me. Do you really think I would still want to be with Cyrus after that? He's no longer a part of my life."

"Then you should quit avoiding the opportunity to tell him that, because right now he believes he still has a chance with you. And I'm not sure he doesn't. I'm not sure I'm not just your way of getting back at the man who wronged you."

Hurt filled Tressa's eyes and he knew he'd cut deep. He started to apologize but reconsidered. Yes, he felt horrible for hurting her, but as long as he kept this doubt wedged between them, things couldn't get out of focus again. He needed twenty-twenty vision to handle this situation.

Roth pushed himself from the ground, dusted the snow from his clothing, then offered Tressa his hand. Surprisingly, she allowed him to help her up. On her feet, her lips parted, then closed as if she reconsidered whatever she was about to say.

The next several hours were quiet ones. Tressa hadn't said ten words to him since they'd come in from the snow and he hated it. The silence was torture. Mainly because he enjoyed talking to her. It was always like a conversation with an old friend—unforced and effortless. Well, he guessed he could be grateful that she hadn't retreated upstairs.

Roth couldn't concentrate on the Walter Mosley novel he'd been reading, so he dog-eared the page and placed the book on the sofa beside them. He slid a glance at Tressa, whose eyes were pinned to the television screen.

Maybe he'd gone too far earlier. Who was he kidding? He'd gone way too far. Attempting to warm the frigid air around them, he said, "What are they saying about the weather?"

"It's snowing."

And the temperature in the room dropped several more degrees. Deciding not to poke the hornet's nest, he stood. "I'll start dinner." He waited to see if she would offer her assistance. Nothing. Yep, she was pissed at him. And she probably had a right to be. Again, he'd overstepped his boundaries. God knows he was the last person who should tell anyone how to manage their love life.

Tressa stood. "I'm really not all that hungry. I'll be upstairs if you need me."

Roth scrubbed a hand over his head and groaned. This woman was going to be the death of him. And judging by the amount of friction between them, something told him he wouldn't die happy.

he honestly believe that? Even thinking he did frustrated her even more.

Being honest with herself, maybe a small part of her had wanted to feel as if she were getting a small amount of revenge against Cyrus. God, was she really this screwed up?

She released a humorless chuckle. Could she actually blame him for not wanting to get involved with her? Her life was a mess right now. Who wanted that kind of...*complication*?

A smile curled her lips when she closed her eyes and recalled their time in the snow together. They'd been having so much fun. Then Cyrus had ruined it. Disdain flowed through her. Cyrus was getting too good at disrupting her life.

She eyed the ceiling and replayed Roth's words in her head. *You're not ready for me. If you only knew how ready I am.* Why in the hell was he fighting this so hard? Oh, yeah. He believed Cyrus still had a chance with her. He was so far from the truth a compass couldn't have guided him back. Roth was right, she needed to talk to Cyrus. And she would. But for now, she'd make Cyrus wait for her to decide when she wanted to talk to him.

A thought occurred to her and she sat. One she should have seen before now. Roth wouldn't be intimidated by Cyrus. A man like Roth would welcome the challenge of claiming her for himself. Maybe a part of him did believe what he'd said. But there was more to it. Some other reason why she couldn't reach him. Something else he was hiding behind. But what?

A heavy sigh left her lips. Why should she drive herself insane trying to figure it out? He wanted nothing to do with her. She'd honor his wishes.

Just a few more days.

All she had to do was refuse to look into Roth's eyes, avoid sitting too close to him, quit appreciating his manly scent, stop enjoying the way her skin tingled when his dark eyes raked over her and keep her nipples from beading every time she thought about him caressing her breasts.

Yep, piece of cake. Which was exactly what she wanted now, Roth caressing her breasts and a piece of cake. Too bad she couldn't have either.

When her stomach growled again, she headed to raid the kitchen. She moved down the stairs like a cat burglar, but froze like an ice cube at the sight of Roth sprawled on the sofa fast asleep with an open book flat on his shirtless chest.

Whoa. Now, this was a sight for sore eyes, not-so-sore eyes, eyes of all states. The flickering flames washed him in an amber glow. It was the most alluring thing she'd ever seen. *Stop it, Tressa. Consider him the enemy. A well-put-together, devastatingly appealing enemy. But the enemy nonetheless.*

With his mouth partially open, soft snores poured out. Helpless against it, her eyes trailed over his smooth chest, appreciating the one pec peeping out from under the book. She would love to run her tongue over his nipple and those faithful-to-his-workout-routine abs. *No, you wouldn't.* Nor did she want those muscled arms to close around her in a snug embrace. *Nope. Not at all.*

A fine line of curly black hairs disappeared beneath the waistband of the gray sweatpants he wore. Her system hadn't been ready for the imprint at his crotch. She squinted to make sure her eyes weren't playing tricks on her. *Nope.* The man was packing, with a capital *P.*

Before the sight blinded her with desire, she slid her eyes away. A blanket lay in a multicolored puddle on the floor beside the sofa. Had it fallen off or had he kicked it off? Probably the latter. It felt like 710 degrees in there. In her case, she suspected the scorching temp had less to do with the fire and more to do with her reaction to all of that hot chocolate before her.

Tressa reached for the book, then reconsidered. Okay, now she was being silly. Even though he was now in the enemy category, what harm could come from her removing it?

The second she touched it, Roth's eyes popped open. In a flash, he grabbed a fistful of her shirt. Startled, her legs wobbled, then buckled, causing her to collapse on top of him.

The surge that coursed through her entire body had to be what it felt like to touch a live wire, minus the threat of certain death. Then again, by the magnitude of which her heart pounded, cardiac arrest couldn't be far behind.

Eyeing Roth dumbly, she said, "I… The book…" Her eyes traveled to his mouth, posed in a straight line. "I'm sorry." But when she tried to shimmy out of his hold, he held her in place.

As usual, they eyed each other for a long suffocating moment. Roth's eyes lowered to her mouth, and his jaw tensed as if he was fighting not just a desire to kiss her but a need.

His gaze rose to her in a manner that suggested he struggled with what to do next.

"Did I frighten you?" he said.

"Um…no."

"Why are you trembling?"

Desire. "Okay, maybe a little," she said instead.

"I'm sorry. I didn't mean to scare you. In one of the facilities I lived in for a while, you always had to keep one eye open. Falling asleep guaranteed you'd have your belongings stolen. I learned to sleep lightly. Some habits are hard to break."

"It's okay, really." To even imagine the hell he'd been exposed to growing up hurt her to the core. There was no wonder he didn't have a lot of faith in people. If she had to guess, he viewed her as one of those thieves in the night just waiting for him to doze off. But the only thing she would ever be interested in stealing from him was his heart.

Unsure why, Tressa rested her head on his shoulder. Maybe because she felt a tremble in him, too. Comforting the enemy was the noble thing to do, right?

To her surprise, Roth circled her in his warm, strong arms. She exhaled. *This is how it's supposed to be.* Closing her eyes, she relaxed and enjoyed being the object of his affection. This was how she liked things between them, comfortable, easy. So why was she about to make things bumpy?

"Something clearly exists between us, Roth. Something that gives me so much peace it scares me."

He hummed a sound that could have been interpreted as understanding or confusion, then his arms tightened around her a hint more. Was that his way of saying he felt the same way? She needed him to use words.

"Why are you afraid of me, Roth?" That was the only logical explanation. The only thing that made sense.

Roth chuckled a smooth, sexy sound that caressed her ears.

He placed a finger under her chin and tilted her head up. "Woman, do you really think I'm afraid of you?"

There was no need to be, but yes, she did.

"I'm not afraid, Tressa. Just cautious."

"Am I a risk?"

"Yes," he said without blinking.

Now they were getting somewhere. "Am I one worth taking?" She could tell by the way he studied her that the question had caught him off guard. Bringing her mouth within inches of his, she teased him in the same way he'd teased her earlier. "Am I a risk worth taking, Roth?"

His jaw tensed, relaxed, then tensed again. "Yeah, I think you are," he said in a low tone of surrender. "But it's not that—"

"It truly is that simple." Tressa pushed out of his arms and straddled him. She grabbed the hem of her shirt and lifted it over her head. Roth sucked his bottom lip between his teeth. His hardness swelled between her legs and pressed against her warmth. "Do you want to make love to me, Roth?"

"Yes." The sound of surrender danced in his voice.

"Good." And triumph danced in hers.

Lowering again, she glided the tip of her tongue slowly across his moist bottom lip, then dragged it between the split. He parted his lips and gently sucked her tongue into his mouth. They kissed for a long time. Slowly, tenderly.

Roth's hands explored her body, gliding up her arms, over her shoulders, down her back and came to rest on her ass. She moaned when he squeezed gently, then not so gently. The not so gently caused the throbbing between her legs to pulse even more ferociously.

She snaked a hand between them and rubbed Roth's hardness through the fabric of his sweatpants. A guttural sound rumbled in his chest. Venturing farther, she inched her hand beneath his waistband and wrapped her eager fingers around his hot, hard flesh and stroked gently.

In a swift move, Roth freed himself from her grasp. Like a child who'd been denied her favorite toy, she whined, "I want to feel you, Roth." She kissed one corner of his mouth. "I want to stroke you." She placed a kiss to the opposite side. "I want to bring you to the brink of exploding."

Roth didn't respond to her risqué words. Instead, he entangled his fingers in her hair, held her mouth to his and kissed her, hard and raw. Draping a strong arm across her back, he sat forward, shifted, swung his legs off the couch and stood.

When he took a step toward the stairs, Tressa broke their kiss. "In front of the fireplace. I've fantasized about making love to you there since we arrived."

Dark desire danced in Roth's eyes. Her head spun from the anticipation of being the recipient of the massive amount of passion she saw swimming in his hard stare.

Roth lowered them to the rug and blanketed her body. "I've craved making love to you since the very first time our eyes met months ago."

"That's a whole lot of bottled-up yearning."

"You have no idea." A corner of his mouth lifted into a wicked smile. "But you're about to find out." Roth pecked her gently, then stood.

"Where are you going?" she asked with shameless alarm in her tone.

"Nowhere, baby."

Tressa ogled with delight as Roth removed his pants. She gnawed at the corner of her lip, waiting for the fitted boxers to fall.

Roth hooked his thumbs inside the black fabric, then paused. "You're staring. Do you see something you like?"

Tressa sucked her bottom lip between her teeth and nodded seductively. At least in her mind she was being seductive. In actuality, she probably resembled a bobble-head doll. It didn't matter, as long as Roth gave her what she wanted.

Roth teased her, inching them down with no regard to speed. "Think you can handle it?"

"There's only one way to find out."

Tressa fought the urge to shout when Roth revealed himself. From the feel she'd copped earlier, she'd got a good idea of what to expect. But actually seeing his impressive manhood only thrilled her more. How much longer would she have to wait to experience it?

"I should warn you, I'm an unselfish lover. I like to give. And I'll keep giving until I'm sure you're satisfied."

Had he any idea how much his words turned her on? "I've never been known as a taker, but I guess I can make an exception and gracefully accept everything you're offering. That's the least I can do."

Roth smirked. "Close your eyes. And keep them closed until I say open them."

Her lips parted with mounting protest, but when Roth shook his head, clearly warding off her objections, she followed his directions. Once her eyes were shut, Roth blanketed her body again. The feel of his solid flesh meshed against her was foreplay all by itself.

Roth tilted her head to one side, then placed a delicate kiss just below her earlobe, then whispered in her ear, "All I want you to do is just feel. Can you do that for me?"

Oh, she was feeling already, so that shouldn't be a problem. "Yes," she said, mimicking his tone.

Roth kissed her in the same spot again. A blink later, what felt like hundreds of feather-soft kisses peppered her tingling skin: her neck, her jawline, her shoulder, her collarbone. Then it all stopped. Her lids fluttered, the desire to open her eyes as intense as the sensations swirling through her entire body.

Roth's soft lips tasted her skin again, kissing a line between the valley of her aching breasts. Dragging his tongue over one mound, he sucked a hardened bead between his lips. The intensity of the act caused Tressa to gasp, then smile with delight. He worked his tongue slowly, twirling circles around her tender nipple and flicking it gently. "Mmm."

He took his time exploring her body, kissing, licking, suckling, driving her mad. Inching down, Roth alternated between tender kisses and delicate nips to her skin. When he positioned her legs over his shoulders and claimed her core, she cried out in bliss. His tongue lit a raging blaze that threatened to consume her.

A bead of sweat trickled down her neck, taunting her already-sensitive skin. There was not one word that could effectively describe the havoc Roth was wreaking on her body.

As if he thought his tongue wasn't bringing her enough pleasure, he introduced his fingers. The second he glided them inside her wetness, curled them upward and worked them in and out of her, she lost all control. Fists clenched the soft material beneath them, blood whooshed in her ears and her body temperature rose several degrees.

Vicious waves of intense pleasure crashed through her. Never had she experienced an orgasm so powerful, so consuming. Her legs shook, her entire body folded to the delicious torture Roth was subjecting her to.

After what seemed like an eternity, her body calmed. Roth made his way back up her shivering torso in the same manner he'd gone down, still as gentle as before. He, again, feathered her burning skin with delicate kisses. His caring manner only made her want him more.

Roth's stone-like hardness pressed against her trembling thigh. At her mouth, he placed a soft kiss on her lips. The idea that her essence lingered on his lips aroused her again.

"Open your eyes," he said.

Beyond the heated look of desire, there was something more. Hesitation? She hoped not. If he denied her now, there was no doubt she'd die.

"Finish what you started," she said as motivation.

Roth reached for something. His wallet. Then a condom.

On his knees, their gazes held as he tore into the gold foil. She broke their connection in favor of watching him roll the latex down his impressive length. Her body supercharged at the notion of him satisfying the raging hunger inside her.

Roth blanketed her body and captured her mouth in a heady kiss. Without using his hand, his manhood effortlessly located her opening. She drew in a long, sharp breath, then released it in a shaky moan.

"Did you feel that, baby?"

Tressa whined, *"Yes."*

"Did it feel good?"

"Yes. Yes!"

Tressa couldn't ever remember a man filling her, stretching her, going as deep as Roth. And his gentleness… Sex with Cyrus had always been so urgent, so stiff, so swift. Not discounting the satisfaction obtained from the occasional urgent, stiff, fast interlude, because sometimes that was exactly how she wanted it, but this—the way Roth chose patient over rushed, gentle over rigid, unhurried over quick—was what she needed right now.

He'd wanted her to *just feel*. And, goodness, was she feeling.

She felt everything.

Passion.

Pleasure.

Delight.

Hunger.

Greed.

The clench of another orgasm.

Another.

What was Roth doing to her? Whose body was this? Multiple orgasms had never been a thing for her. And when she'd listened to her girlfriends boast about their back-to-back releases, she'd assumed something had been wrong with her. Now she knew better.

The orgasm tore through her far more potently than the last. Roth's name rolled off her tongue in a loud, pleasure-filled cry.

"Mmm." He hummed. "Say my name again, baby."

When he drove himself even deeper, she dragged her nails across his damp back. "Roth, Roth, Roth... Oh—I'm—"

More sensations swept through her, collecting the fragments the last release left behind.

Roth's rhythm increased but remained tender in delivery. A moan, groan, growl combination rumbled in his chest. A second later she felt him throbbing inside her. He stroked until he obviously had no more to give, collapsing next to her.

Their chests rose and fell in sync. Silently, he pulled her spent body into his arms. The soothing thump of his heartbeat lulled her. One thing was for sure. Roth knew how to make her feel like a woman.

Chapter 8

Roth catapulted himself off the floor, his heart hammering in his chest. Where the hell was he? Dizziness set in and he stumbled, but regained his balance before falling. Urgent eyes swept the room. The cabin. He was at the cabin.

Beads of sweat lined his forehead. Sucking in one lungful of air after the other, he still couldn't catch his breath. He bent at the waist, resting his sweaty palms on his knees. What the hell was—

"Roth?"

Though he recognized Tressa's voice, his brain couldn't process which direction it'd come from. "*Tressa*. I can't… I can't breathe," he said, dropping to one knee.

"I'm right here, Roth. I'm right here, baby. Just focus on my voice." Tressa knelt in front of him, cradling his face between her hands. "Just breathe. You're having a panic attack. Look at me. Come on. Look at me."

"I—" He heaved. "I can't—"

"Yes, you can. Just relax and look at me, Roth."

When he finally trained his focus on her, she took his trembling hand and placed it over her beating heart. The level *thump, thump, thump* had a near-instant calming effect on him.

"That's it. Just breathe. Slow and steady."

His brain shot on a hundred cylinders, but he processed her comforting tone. After several minutes he was back to normal—or as normal as he could be after something like that. Drained, plus somewhat embarrassed, Roth lowered himself to a seated position, propped his arms on his bent knees and lowered his head. Tressa moved behind him and kneaded his tight shoulders. Nothing had ever felt better.

"Bad dream?" she said in a near whisper, her words delicate.

"Nightmare." He scolded himself a second later. The door had just been opened to her questioning. And just as expected, she walked through.

"About?"

She continued to manipulate his tired muscles.

"Come here." Roth secured Tressa's naked body in his arms with one swift motion. His eyes combed over her ample breasts, and he fought the desire to dip low and suck one of her dark nipples into his mouth. His hunger stirred, but he tamed the beast.

A moment later his eyes slowly climbed to meet her gaze. He stared down into her sympathetic eyes. "Would you be upset if I said I didn't want to talk about it right now?" The unwanted memories that occasionally haunted his dreams weren't easily discussed.

Tressa fingered the cross around his neck. "Of course not." Her eyes slid to the pendant. "This is beautiful."

"It was a gift from a very special woman." *He* witnessed the flicker of confusion and/or concern on her face and flashed a half smile. "My ninth grade math teacher." He admired the piece. "I was actually pretty smart in school. Some would even say gifted. But I rarely applied myself, because no one ever influenced me to do so." Her expression turned serious. "Until Mrs. Sanders." Roth laughed. "She pulled me into her classroom one day, literally by my ear. She sat me down and said she saw something in me, something good. And that since I wanted to act like a wild mustang, she'd stay on my behind until I was tamed."

Tressa burst out laughing, then covered her mouth.

"Go 'head. Laugh at my pain."

"Sorry," she said through her fingers. "Continue, please."

"The next day Mrs. Sanders gave me this necklace. She said it was a reminder. A reminder that she and God would always be in my corner."

"Wow." Tressa blinked back the tears the powerful words summoned.

Roth brushed a stray hair from her brow. "Thank you, Tressa."

"For what?"

He captured the hand she'd used to place his over her heart and kissed the inside of her wrist, then her palm. "For sharing your energy with me."

"It was the least I could do. You gave me a lot of

your energy earlier." Her beautiful mouth curled into a delicate smile.

"Some moments from my past…" He paused. "I carry a lot of them with me, Tressa. It gets heavy sometimes."

"You carry the load well. You're one of the strongest men I've ever met, Roth Lexington. You may have gone through hell, but you managed to come out on the right side. Your past haunts you, but…I ain't 'fraid of no ghost."

Roth barked a laugh. "Beautiful, funny and sexy as hell." And one hell of a woman, because, in so many words, she'd told him she had his back.

"Yeah, you lucked out, sir. I'm the whole package. If I had a collar, I'd pop it."

Roth dragged an index finger down the center of her chest. "If you had a collar, that would mean you were wearing a shirt. I much prefer you butt naked and screaming my name."

"You up for showing me how much?"

"If you're up for taking it."

Tressa sat forward and hurried her mouth to his. He tried his damnedest to consume her whole. Roth avoided labeling what was happening between them. This powerful, intense, amazing chemistry that held him prisoner to her. Whatever it was, he prayed it never ended.

After experiencing the warmth of Roth's arms all night, Tressa didn't need to crack her eyes to know she was in bed alone. The chill confirmed it. Reaching for the sky, she stretched her tired muscles. She and Roth had made love in front of the fireplace several times, found their way to the bed and made love several more times.

Swinging her legs over the side of the bed, she sat there for a moment, recalling her night with him. A wide smile curled her lips. The smile dimmed when she thought about the panic attack he'd had. By the look on his face, he'd been embarrassed. He never had to be ashamed in front of her. Especially over anything in his past. The light and the dark moments, she'd embrace them all.

After a trip to the restroom, Tressa slid on one of Roth's shirts, tossing her nose up at the grandma gown he'd purchased for her at the general store and headed downstairs.

Roth was out on the deck, wearing nothing but a pair of pajama pants and a thin long-sleeved shirt. Was this the same man who'd nearly turned into a Popsicle when they'd played in the snow?

Strapping into her winter apparel—a toboggan, gloves, coat—and her boots, she joined Roth. The snow continued to fall in a steady shower, but not as heavy as the day before, suggesting it was nearing an end. The fact saddened her.

"Roth, where is your coat? You're going to catch pneumonia out here."

Roth bunched her coat in his hands and pulled her to him. Against her lips, he said, "I don't get sick," then kissed her senseless. Pulling away, he said, "Good morning."

It took a second or two for her brain to reboot after that spine-twisting kiss. "Good morning."

Tressa initially contributed the target warmth heating

her cheeks to her body's reaction to Roth, but then she noticed the black box affixed overhead. "What is that?"

Roth followed her stare. "An infrared heater."

"Huh." Why hadn't she noticed it before? Her attention slid to the stacks of colorful construction paper scattered on the tile-top table. "Is this arts and crafts hour?"

Roth barked a laugh. "No. I like making paper airplanes."

Considering his profession, that made sense.

"It helps clear my mind."

Tressa was tempted to ask him what had his mind cluttered, but figured it had something to do with his nightmare. Maybe soon he'd feel comfortable enough to talk to her about his past.

"Pick a color," he said.

She pressed her index finger into her chin. "Hmm." Then she settled on a steel blue color. Roth folded, tucked and creased before handing a fully formed plane back to her, along with a fine-point black Sharpie marker. "What's the marker for?"

"For writing a message on the inside of the plane."

"A message? What kind of message?"

"Anything you want."

Tressa hesitated for a moment, attempting to understand the purpose of this whole message-writing-on-the-plane thing. She laughed to herself. That sounded like a movie. "Who's going to read it?"

"No one."

Okay, now she was really confused. "We're writing a message that no one will ever read?"

"Yes. That's the beauty of it. It's like confession without the priest."

Roth scribbled something on his paper. She shrugged. What the hell. If no one was ever going to read it, what could it possibly hurt? *Hmm.* She tapped the marker against her bottom lip. What could she write? Something funny? Something ridiculous? A quote? *So many choices.* Her eyes slid to Roth. *Something intimate.* He had said it was like confession.

After she was done, Tressa refolded the paper, unsure if she should have written a love note to him. But the fact that no other human eyes would ever see it helped to put her mind at ease. "What now?"

"Now we exchange."

A hint of alarm rushed over her. "But you said—"

"Don't worry. I'm not going to read it."

A second or two passed as she debated whether or not to trust him with the plane. Reluctantly, she passed it over. "And now?"

"Now we throw them."

Before Tressa could even process what was happening, the steel blue paper soared through the air. Her mouth fell open and her eyes went wide in disbelief. "What— You— Why did you do that?"

A quizzical expression formed on Roth's face. "Do what?"

"Throw it." Her voice rose an octave.

Roth laughed. "That's typically what you do with paper planes." He flashed her a suspicious look. "What in the heck did you write on there, your Social Security number?"

That actually would have been better. "Um, an…old family recipe. It's top secret. I could be tossed out of the family for revealing it."

She bit back a laugh, but Roth didn't. He burst into laughter, then wrapped her in his arms from behind.

"Don't worry. Your recipe is safe. We're in the middle of nowhere, and bears can't read. I don't think." He kissed the back of her head. "Your turn, gorgeous. Just aim and fire."

It took a second, but she realized how ridiculous she was being and laughed at herself. Why was she so worried? Roth was right. They were in the middle of nowhere. Who did she think would come across her plane way out here? *No one*, she assured herself. *No one*, she repeated for good measure.

It was probably just lying out in the wet snow, waiting to be consumed by a mountain lion. Heck, even if someone did happen upon it, who would know it was from her? *No one.* Yep, that last *no one* made her feel so much better.

She released Roth's plane. *What did he write?* she wondered. Guess she'd never know. "Wow. Those little suckers sure did glide through the air."

"I hope your, uh, *recipe* wasn't too explicit," he said.

She wasn't sure she liked the sound of that. *Scratch that.* She was *sure* she hadn't liked the sound of that. "Why?"

"The last time I released planes, several made their way all the way into town. Imagine my surprise when I saw one pinned up in the general store. Good thing it was only a motivational quote."

Tressa's stomach dropped to her knees. "All the way into town, huh?" Her gaze slid through the trees and to Silver Point in the distance.

"Yep. I got skills. I'm reigning champ for longest distance and airtime in the Southeastern Paper Plane Competition. Skills." He kissed the back of her head again and pinched her butt. "I'll make us some breakfast."

Reigning... Paper Plane Competition? Forget food, she needed a shot of something strong.

Chapter 9

Roth lowered the book he'd been reading and peered over the top at Tressa sitting at the opposite side of the couch, engulfed in a Maya Angelou book of poems. He smiled. Man, she was engaged. The only other time he'd seen her this intense was when he'd sent her airplane sailing away the day before.

And speaking of airplanes... What in the hell had she written? Was it something about him? He recalled the way her body had tensed in his arms when he'd mentioned the possibility of her plane reaching town. Yep, it'd been about him.

He laughed to himself. That was presumptuous as hell, but he was rolling with it. "What did you write about me?"

Tressa's eyes slowly rose to his. "Excuse me?"

"On your plane. What did you write about me?"

Tressa placed the book facedown on her lap and folded her arms across her chest. "That's awfully presumptuous of you, sir."

"Well, ma'am, it's obvious you have a thing for me."

She tried to suppress a smile that broke through despite her efforts. Sobering, she said, "Oh, really?"

"Yep."

"And how, Mr. Lexington, did you come to this conclusion?"

"Well, Ms. Washington, first, it's the way you look at me."

She laughed. "And how do I look at you?"

"Like no woman has ever looked at me before. Like you truly see me."

Tressa's expression turned serious and so did his. The tender ways she looked at him revealed she saw something more than a vessel for sex.

"I do see you," she said. "Even the parts you try to hide."

And that was what he feared, her seeing the parts he wanted to keep hidden. He didn't want to scare her away. He also didn't want to give too much, too soon. Just in case. Throughout the years, he'd been used to far more things *not* working out than actually working.

Conversation seized, and they gaped at one another.

Tressa was the first to break the silence. "You said *first*. Does that mean there are more reasons?"

There were, but did he want to list them? *What the hell?* "The way you touch me." He interpreted the expression on her face and answered the question before she asked. "Like you're trying to heal me, despite having no idea how deep my wounds run."

"I will."

"You will what?"

"One day I'll have an idea."

And she was probably right. Especially if he kept giving her pieces of himself. It was like he couldn't stop, like Tressa was meant to free him of some of the baggage he lugged around. Now seemed like the perfect time to ask an important question. "Should we talk about what's happ—"

"No," Tressa said.

Her tone held its signature levelness. The reply surprised him. He thought for sure she'd jump at the opportunity to discuss or define this beautiful magnetism. He arched a brow. "No?"

"We should just let it happen naturally. *Just feel.*"

"That's my line." And it brought back some damn good memories.

"Is it copyrighted?"

Roth lunged forward, blanketing Tressa's body with his. "Copyrighted? I'll show you copyrighted." He tickled her until she laughed so hard she snorted, which made him laugh just as hard.

Roth couldn't remember the last time he'd been so amused. He laughed so hard his sides began to hurt. By the time they settled, they both had tears running out the corners of their eyes. Instead of returning to his side of the sofa, he nestled against Tressa. She rested a delicate hand on his cheek.

"I see you, Roth Lexington, and I like the view."

He shifted his head to kiss her palm. "I'm not finished showing you who I am. Just be patient with me."

"Okay." She kissed the tip of his nose. "You're warm."

"Being this close to you makes my temperature rise," he said.

"Flirt."

Roth intended to kiss her, but before he made contact, Tressa pinned him with accusing eyes. "I think you're catching a cold."

He sighed. "Like I told you before, Nurse Washington, I don't get sick."

Several hours later Roth felt as if he'd been dragged up the entire mountain by a raggedy snowplow. Instead of Tressa saying, "I told you so," she instantly shifted into caregiver mode, forcing him upstairs and into bed, despite his protest.

He stared at the ceiling, bored out of his mind and lonely. "Tress... Baby, where are you? I miss you."

Damn. They'd only been apart twenty minutes. Plus, she was only a flight of stairs away. Yet, he missed her. Then it dawned on him. He didn't have a cold; he was experiencing symptoms of withdrawal. He laughed at the silly analogy. This was definitely a cold, and he felt like crap.

"Men are such babies when they're sick," she said, nearing the bed with a steamy bowl of something.

He pushed himself up onto his elbows. "What's that?"

"Chicken-and-rice soup."

He really didn't feel like eating, but she'd gone through so much trouble. To show his gratitude, he could surely get down a few swallows. "It smells delicious."

Tressa took a seat on the edge of the bed, scooped up a spoonful of the fragrant liquid, blew it to cool it down, then fed him.

"Mmm. Woman, you do have some major skills in the kitchen."

"Just in the kitchen?" A mischievous grin spread across her face.

Oh, if he had the energy—and a cootie-free status—he'd have taken her right there. "Tease."

After he'd got his fill, Tressa placed the bowl on the nightstand, butted her back against the headboard and directed his head onto her lap. She stroked a hand over his cheek. Why did her touch soothe him so much?

"Just rest."

Relaxed, Roth allowed his eyes to close. In his adult life, there had only been one woman he'd allowed his guard down around, and she'd hurt him. He'd sworn to never allow himself to be in that position again. And he'd managed to stick to his vow. Until now. Until Tressa. She'd become the exception to his ironclad rule.

With his ex, the connection had never been as strong as the one he felt with Tressa. Not even after the two years they were together. A part of him wanted—knew he needed—to pull away from this thing blooming between them. But the part of him that liked the way she looked at him, liked the way she touched him, loved how he felt when he was with her, beckoned him to stay, to risk.

"You're supposed to be resting, Mr. Lexington, not stewing in your thoughts."

"Huh?"

"I've noticed that whenever you glide your thumb back and forth across my skin like that, you're in deep thought."

Damn. He hadn't even realized he was doing it. He shifted to eye her.

Tressa smirked. "You're not the only observant one around here. I told you I see you. In vivid color." She winked.

Overwhelmed by the emotions storming inside him, all he could say was, "Oh, yeah?"

"Yeah."

Well, since she saw so much, did she see how hard he was falling for her?

The following morning, Roth was still fast asleep when Tressa snaked from the bed. She didn't readily move away. She watched him sleep. He looked so adorable.

Mr. I Don't Get Sick.

The nighttime elixir she'd prepared and given him—a mix of bourbon, because he had no rum, honey, lemon juice and cayenne pepper—had put him out cold. Recalling the expression on his face when he'd tasted the concoction nearly made her burst out laughing. It definitely wasn't the best-tasting remedy, but it worked wonders. He would feel like a new man when he woke up. Well…better than he did before he'd taken it, at least.

Moving away, she headed downstairs to prepare them some breakfast. Before making her way into the kitchen, she threw a few more pieces of wood on the fire. A glance out the window revealed the snow had finally stopped. *God, this place was gorgeous in the snow.* Probably even more beautiful in the spring when everything was in bloom. The idea of returning brought a smile to her face.

She'd got her wish to spend the week at the cabin. The only problem…Roth was sick. She shook her head at the quirk of fate. Actually, that wasn't all bad. Well, bad for him, but she actually enjoyed his relying on her. That built trust, which was the foundation of any relationship.

Collecting a few items from the fridge, she laid them out on the counter. They could remain at the cabin for several months and never run out of food. Mr. Glen's wife had stocked the place as if she'd been expecting a famine and didn't want Roth to suffer the fallout.

Nettie. Tressa laughed to herself. For a split second at the general store, she'd thought Nettie had been the woman Roth was supposed to spend the weekend with. That conjured another question. Who was the woman she'd replaced? And what had been their status? A friend with benefits? A booty call? An on-again, off-again lover?

Well, whatever was taking place between them was not just a passing fling. She was all-in and needed to know that Roth was, too.

Coffee. She needed coffee. Without caffeine, she never thought clearly. Abandoning the bacon and eggs, she brewed a pot of the morning roast. Once it was done, she poured herself a cup, leaned against the counter and trained her gaze through the window.

Enjoying how the first sip of the hot liquid pleasure warmed her nicely, she closed her eyes and moaned in delight. This would certainly help with clarity.

"I'm jealous."

Tressa opened her eyes to see Roth propped against the wall, watching her. How had she not heard him come down? His voice was raspy and his usually brilliant eyes weak. He still wore his pajama pants. Instead of a shirt, a thin blanket draped his shoulders. "What are you doing out of bed, young man?"

"I feel better. Not 100 percent, but much better than I felt last night."

He sneezed into the crook of his arm, paused, then sneezed again.

"Bless you." Nope, definitely not 100 percent. She felt so bad for him.

"Thanks," he croaked. Ambling to the sofa, he snagged a box of tissues and collapsed down onto the cushions. "My esophagus still burns from that poison you forced me to drink."

"I'm about to cook breakfast. Any special requests?"

He coughed, sneezed, then blew his nose. "I'm not really hungry."

"You have to eat something, Roth. Even if it's only a couple of bites of toast. It'll help you get your strength back."

"Yeah, I need my strength."

If she could see his face, she knew there'd be a roguish grin spread across it. She hated not being able to at least kiss him, but she didn't want the cooties, too, though her training told her she probably already had them. Maybe she'd better double up on the orange juice. They both couldn't fall ill.

"Okay. I request a couple of bites of toast," he said.

It sounded as if his face was buried in a pillow when he spoke. Even sick, he still found a way to make her smile. "A couple of bites of toast it is. And some orange juice," she added.

"And some orange juice." He peeped over the back of the sofa, then collapsed out of sight as if he didn't have the energy to maintain the position. "I'm supposed to be taking care of you, remember, beautiful?"

Tressa dropped four slices of bread into the toaster.

"You are taking care of me, handsome. You have been taking care of me since the moment you found me in your SUV."

Roth lazily chuckled. "I'm glad you chose my SUV to stow away in."

A smile touched her lips. "So am I."

After a hearty breakfast of bacon, egg, toast and juice for her—half a piece of toast and several sips of OJ for Roth—he fell asleep with his head in her lap. She used this time to continue the book of Maya Angelou quotes and poems she'd started.

Love is like a virus. Tressa snickered to herself. Maybe Roth didn't have a cold virus; maybe he was falling in love with her. *Wishful thinking.* With thoughts like these, she obviously hadn't had enough coffee. In her defense, the text did state love could happen to anybody at *any* time. *But after only a few days? Nah.* She wasn't buying it.

Then it dawned on her. This thing between her and Roth hadn't just grown wings at the cabin. It'd been soaring for months; she'd just chosen to ignore it. *Had* to ignore it. Her gaze lowered to Roth. "It took flight the moment I first laid eyes on you," she said in a whisper.

"What took flight?" Roth asked, his eyes still shut.

"*Um*…nothing. Just something I read in the book. Go back to sleep. You need your rest."

"And what do you need?"

Besides forever with you… "For you to get better."

Chapter 10

A day or so later, Roth felt almost back to normal. However, Tressa was still making a fuss over him taking it easy. He'd never had someone make such a big deal over his well-being. It felt…good.

The worst part of being sick hadn't been feeling like the tennis ball in a match between the Williams sisters; it was not being able to kiss Tressa in the deep, passionate manner he craved. He shot a glance toward the stairs. She'd been up there for an awfully long time. What was she doing? Taking a nap?

Pushing off the sofa, he climbed the stairs. When he heard Tressa on her cell phone, he stopped.

"*Fine.* I'll meet you. I have to go."

Her words were low but sharp and cold. That had to mean only one thing. It'd been her ex on the line. By her own words, they were done. So why had she agreed to meet him? A ping of jealousy rippled through him, followed by mounds of concern.

Taking a deep breath, he tried not to jump to conclusions. Continuing the climb, he said, "Hey." Tressa flinched at his words. He noted the look of distress on her face when she turned to him.

"Um, hey. Everything okay?" she asked.

"Yeah. Everything's fine." When his eyes briefly slid to the cell phone in her hand, she tossed it on the bed. "Everything okay with you?" A part of him wanted her to tell him she'd been on the line with her ex, while another part of him simply wanted to ignore what he'd heard and *trust* that there was no reason to be concerned. For him, trusting was far more easily considered than applied.

"Perfect, now that you're here."

Tressa closed the distance between them, wrapped her arms around his waist and rested her head on his chest. Her grip was snug, as if something had her rattled. What in the hell had Cyrus said to her? Anger tightened his jaw, diluting the emotions he'd previously felt. All he experienced now was that insistent need to shield her. He cocooned her in his arms, giving her the comfort he suspected she sought.

"Mmm. Your arms feel so good." She tilted her head upward. "How do you feel?"

"Like a new dollar bill. Thanks to your TLC."

"You know what would make you feel even better?"

Yes, he did. Making untamed, insanely hot love to her. But he decided to get her answer first. "What?"

"A hot bath."

Oh, he liked her suggestion even better.

Taking his hand, she pulled him toward the bathroom. As the tub filled, she poured several capfuls of rubbing alcohol into the water. This woman loved her rubbing alcohol. Since he'd got sick, she rubbed his chest down every night in the stuff. "Something my mother used to do," she said.

He didn't know if her home remedies actually worked, but between the rubbing alcohol and the potion she'd made him drink, he'd experienced very little chest congestion. Guess he couldn't discount them completely.

Stripping and climbing into the steamy water, he protested when Tressa said she wasn't joining him. Instead, she sat on the edge of the claw-foot tub, lathered a rag and began to wash his back. He hummed in satisfaction. "That feels amazing. A brother could get used to this kind of treatment."

"And a sister could get used to giving it to him."

When silence filled the room, he toyed with the idea of mentioning he'd overheard her conversation. Okay, eavesdropped, if one was being technical. Instead, he went a different route. "Have you talked to Vivian? You know she likes you to check in. I guess she wants to make sure I haven't fed you to a bear or something."

Tressa swiped the rag over his shoulders. "There's not a bear in North Carolina that can handle me."

Well played, he thought, considering how she'd craftily deflected his question. Maybe he was being a fool, but something deep inside him said he had nothing to worry about. He just hoped that *something* was right. "Really?"

"Yes, really."

"Well, this chocolate bear can handle you." In one swift motion, he had her in the tub with him. Her arms flailed as if she'd fallen into shark-infested waters.

"Roth Lexington! I can't believe you just did that. I'm soaked."

He closed his arms around her, causing her back to nestle against his chest. "Quit fronting, woman. You know you wanted to be in here with me."

"Whatever."

He could hear the smile in her voice. Tressa cooed as he pressed a kiss to her shoulder, the crook of her neck and the edge of her ear. "Thank you," he whispered softly. "Thank you for taking such good care of me."

Growing up in the system, he never got the luxury of homemade soup, specialty elixirs or back washes. And he sure as hell hadn't encountered anyone as selfless as Tressa. She was unlike any woman he'd ever bedded.

Bedded? That sounded so cold. Tressa wasn't just warming his bed; she was thawing his damn heart.

He honestly couldn't recall the last time anyone had shown him such compassion without wanting something in return.

Tressa glanced over her shoulder. "You are very welcome. Plus, I feel partly responsible for you being sick. It was my idea to play in the snow."

Now that she mentioned it… "Partly?"

"Ah, yes. *Partly.* I mean, you are a grown man. You could have said no."

Roth pinched her playfully on the thigh.

"Ouch," she said through laughter.

"As if I could have said no once I saw the way your face lit up. *'Ooh, snow,'* " he mocked.

She swatted him playfully. "I don't believe those were my exact words, and I definitely don't sound like that." Easing her head back against his shoulder, she smiled. "Snow reminds me of my grandmother. My father's mother," she clarified. "Gram used to make snow cream every snowfall. Never the first snow. The first snow washed away all the germs." She frowned as if the memory ushered in a great deal of sadness. "I miss her."

"How long has she…?"

"Almost six years. Old age. She was ninety-seven."

Roth whistled. "Ninety-seven. She lived a long life."

"A long and vibrant life. After my grandfather's death, she didn't sit around depressed and withdrawn. She traveled, she explored, she adventured, she fell in love over and over again. Though she once said she'd never love a man the way she'd loved my grandfather."

He kissed the back of her head. "Tell me about your grandfather."

She perked up. "My grandfather was as royal as a king to me."

She said it with so much passion Roth envisioned a *Coming to America* scene.

"He spoiled me and my brothers, but not with just material things. He spoiled us with knowledge and wisdom. He was a family *and* a community man. My grandfather was the man any and everyone in the neighborhood knew they could come to if they needed anything. Help with their mortgage. Help with utilities. Food for the dinner table. Clothing. School supplies for the kids. Anything." She sighed. "He's the reason I love to cook."

When Tressa blinked rapidly, he knew she was blinking back tears. He tightened his grip around her. "You're lucky to have grown up surrounded by so much love." He kissed the back of her head again. "You're so lucky. The only *l*-word I've ever truly known is loss. My mom died when I was three. My dad gave me to his sister to raise, then disappeared. When I was seven, my aunt died in a car crash. That's how I ended up in foster care. No one wanted me."

Tressa turned around to look at him. Tenderness blazed in her adoring eyes. "I want you," she said in a delicate voice.

"Why?"

She straightened and rested against him again. "Because this feels right. Us. We feel right. Things for me haven't felt right for a very long time, but this…this feels right. My life is not picture-perfect, Roth, but I really want you in it."

"The last time I…" He stopped short of saying *fell in love* in fear of spooking her. "I was hurt once. I've had my guard up ever since."

"What happened?"

"She cheated on me."

"Oh."

"From the start, I knew we hadn't been right for each other. But I wanted someone to love. And someone to love me," he added. "I entered into the relationship for all the wrong reasons. I wasn't the man I should have been. I was closed off and sometimes cold. She sought comfort elsewhere."

"And now? Are you still closed off and sometimes cold?"

"That was five years ago. I've done a lot of growing since then. I'm still a work in progress, but I'm here." Allowing his hands to glide up her body, he cupped her breasts and squeezed. "Don't you feel me?"

Tressa moaned a sound of satisfaction. "Yes," she said in a sultry tone. "I feel you all through my system."

Pinching her nipples through the wet fabric caused

her to shiver against him. When he rolled them simultaneously between his fingers, she moaned. "Woman, I want to kiss you so badly I can taste it. But since I can't right now, I'll find pleasure in making you come. Can I make you come?"

"O...kay."

After a couple more minutes teasing her taut nipples, he peeled the shirt from her body and dropped it into the water with them.

"You're not wearing any panties," he said, his tone laced with desire. "I like that." His hand snaked between her legs, gliding between her folds. When he started to massage her clit—first slowly, then with much more gusto—she gripped the sides of the tub.

"Yes, Roth. I want to come. Make me—"

She cried out, her body jerking forward. Water sloshed as if they'd activated jets. By the quickness of which he'd brought her to a climax, she'd wanted this. When she settled, her hand slinked into the water, her fingers wrapping around his painful erection.

"Shit," he growled through clenched teeth. She pumped up and down. Slow, then fast. Her grip tightened and a lightning bolt of pleasure sparked through his entire body. When her thumb swiped back and forth over the head of his shaft, he exploded.

His seed spilled into the water. Tressa continued to milk him. Several expletives flew past his lips as he throbbed in her hand.

Once they'd both gathered enough energy to move, they got out of the tub and moved into the bedroom to dress. Something had been missing from his life for a long time and he knew what. More like *who*. Tressa was that missing something. How did he know? Because he'd never felt so whole in his entire life.

Still, somewhere in the back of his mind, a tiny amount of doubt about whether or not she was truly over her ex lingered. But a relationship required taking chances, and he was willing to take one with Tressa. He just hoped he wasn't making a mistake.

Roth admired everything about this strong, vibrant, gentle woman. His gaze followed her around the room and watched as she dressed in a purple sweater and jeans. What he admired most about her wasn't the strength she displayed, her vibrancy or her gentleness. What he truly admired about her was her gigantic heart.

He'd always heard when you'd found "the one," you'd know.

He knew.

But despite all of that, all of the deep emotions she elicited, he still had to be cautious.

"What?" Tressa asked, a warm smile curling her lips.

He shook his head. "Nothing, beautiful. Nothing at all."

She neared him, then playfully tugged at his red long-sleeved shirt. "There's something. You just don't want to tell me. But you will." A look of triumph split across her pretty face, then she sauntered away.

Yep. The one.

Chapter 11

Tressa wasn't sure how she felt about leaving Silver Point. Usually when she traveled, her desire to return home grew after two days of being away from her own bed. But this time she wouldn't have minded a few more days at the cabin with Roth.

She eyed him as he locked up the cabin, then headed toward the SUV. The man resembled a sleek and sexy black stallion. When he opened the driver's-side door, the scent of his cologne rushed in and triggered all kinds of wicked memories.

"So, are you ready to explore Silver Point a little before we leave tomorrow?"

Tressa shifted toward him and bit at the corner of her lip. "Yes, but first…"

"I'm listening."

"I want to try the Mile High Swinging Bridge again. I think I'm ready."

Roth arched a brow. "You sure?"

She nodded. "As long as you're with me, I'm good."

"I'll be right there," he said, leaning over and placing a gentle kiss on her lips. "Let's do this."

Forty-five minutes later, they arrived at the entrance to Grandfather Mountain. While remnants of snow remained, their drive up the mountain was clear.

Instead of taking the stairs from the parking lot, they accessed the bridge using the elevator located inside the Top Shop. It felt as if the temperature had dropped several degrees from the time they'd left the cabin until now. She zipped her coat higher.

"You ready?" Roth asked.

Staring across the lengthy structure, Tressa experienced a brief moment of hesitation, then she glanced up at Roth and an instant calm washed over her. "Yes."

Roth splayed his fingers and she joined her hand with his. They took several steps until they were standing on metal. Her grip on his hand tightened.

"You know you don't have to do this, right?"

"I know. But I want to." Needed to, actually.

Several moments later, they stood in the center of the bridge. Though her heart thumped in her chest a little harder than normal, her temperature rose despite the cold and the slight tremble of her body. The 360-degree, panoramic view of the mountains was amazing.

She closed her eyes and inhaled the cool, crisp air, but popped them open when the bridge swayed harder than it had before. Gripping the rail, she gasped.

"You're okay," Roth said.

When they finally reached the opposite side, Tressa

blew a sigh of relief. Roth wrapped his strong arms around her, and it felt as if she'd been awarded a medal of honor.

"You did it," he said, lowering his mouth to hers.

They shared a celebratory kiss. Briefly, everyone and everything around them disappeared, and she forgot they were standing a mile above sea level. Her connection with Roth made her feel invincible. That's how she knew this thing they shared was real.

The trip back across the bridge was a breeze. You never would have known that just twenty minutes prior, she'd been a bundle of nerves. Making their way back to the car, Roth pulled her hand to his mouth and kissed her wrist.

"I'm proud of you," he said.

The simple affirmation lit her soul. "Thank you."

Once she was settled inside the vehicle, Roth rounded the vehicle and slid behind the wheel.

"I hope you don't mind, but I told Nettie and Glen we'd stop by for lunch. I hate coming to Silver Point and not spending a little time with them."

"I don't mind, but I look a mess. I need to change."

Roth leaned in to kiss her on the cheek. "Baby, you look fine. You always look fine, fully clothed or naked."

"Flirt."

He bounced his brows twice.

When they arrived at Nettie and Glen's place, Tressa admired the ranch-style brick home. A wide porch spanned the entire length of the front of the house. Four white rocking chairs rocked faintly against a bitter breeze. In the distance sat a barn and a stable. She wondered if there were horses inside.

Roth got out and rounded the vehicle. When her door

opened, a hint of nervousness fluttered in her stomach. For some reason she felt as if she was about to meet his parents for the first time.

"What's wrong?"

She imagined saying, "What if they don't like me?" in a whiny voice. Instead, she smiled and said, "I'm really going to miss Silver Point."

"We'll come back anytime you want." He placed a kiss on her forehead, then led her to the front door.

Glen made a thunderous sound of excitement when the door opened. If nothing else, the man was jolly. He gave Roth a manly handshake, then pulled Tressa into his arms.

"I'm glad y'all could make it. Come on in."

Glen stepped aside and they entered. Instantly, Tressa had her answer about whether there were horses in the barn. The spacious sitting room was like a horse museum. Cowboy hats, pictures of horses and horseshoes all claimed space on several walls. Horse figurines, medals and trophies were on display in a well-lit wooden cabinet.

Yep, there were horses. Or at least there used to be.

Tressa eyed a picture of a group of men posing at what looked to be a rodeo. Her eyes narrowed on one of the men in the frame. Though he was several years younger and several pounds lighter, the wide smile was unmistakable. *Glen.* Had the man been a cowboy in his youth?

"Yeah, that's me," Glen said as if he'd read her thoughts. "Sure do miss the thrill of it all. You ever been to a rodeo?"

Tressa shook her head.

Glen clapped Roth on the back. "You should take her, Pilot. She'd enjoy it."

When Glen moved away, Tressa mouthed, "Pilot?"

Roth leaned in close. "I don't just design planes. I sometimes like to fly them."

"Fly—"

Tressa's inquiry was cut short. She assumed the stocky woman who rushed toward them was Nettie. She wrapped her chubby arms around Roth and hugged as if squeezing him gave her life. With her short stature, she barely made it to Roth's pecs.

"I didn't think I'd get to see you this trip."

When Nettie finally released Roth, she set her eyes on Tressa, then Roth, then Tressa again. "Oh, Glen, you were right."

Tressa's brow furrowed. *Right? Right about what?*

Nettie didn't elaborate; she simply pulled Tressa into her arms and hugged her just as affectionately as she had Roth. One thing about Nettie and Glen, they sure knew how to make a person feel at ease.

Lunch consisted of the best stew Tressa had ever put in her mouth, homemade sourdough rolls and a lemon meringue pie that practically melted in her mouth. When Glen asked to see Roth in his study, Tressa and Nettie tidied the kitchen, then sat at the table and thumbed through Nettie's recipe box.

Tressa was like a kid on Christmas morning. Some of the recipes had been passed down through Nettie's family from generation to generation. Tressa made a stack of all the ones she wanted to photocopy. There was only one she wasn't allowed to even glance at. When she'd reached for the flimsy aged once-white paper, Nettie moved it out of reach.

"Tradition," Nettie said. "You have to be family for this recipe. Glen's mother passed this along to me when we were first married. She said every woman should own one recipe of love." Nettie beamed as if remembering the moment. "It's brought years and years of Sanders love."

Tressa's mind worked overtime, guessing what kind of recipe it could be. A beverage, appetizer, main dish, then she settled on it being a dessert. An extremely decadent dessert. *Fine chocolate, maybe? Orange liqueur? No, raspberry.*

Suddenly, something Nettie said replayed in her head. *Years and years of* Sanders *love.*

Nettie wasn't just the food delivery woman; she was much more. "Sanders? You were the teacher who gave him the necklace."

Nettie smiled. "He told you about that?"

Tressa nodded. "Yes, he did. I laughed at the mustang part," she admitted.

Nettie laughed. "Lord, that boy was a handful. Cutting class, fighting, getting into all kinds of trouble." She frowned. "Glen and I could never have kids of our own. My students became my kids and I poured as much love into them as I could. For some reason, I really took to Pilot, and he took to me."

"You saw something in him," Tressa said, repeating what Roth had told her.

"Yes, I did. He had both book and street smarts. There was no limit to what he could accomplish. He just needed someone to believe in him. We would have adopted him, but we could never cut through all of the red tape. Seems they based their decisions on the amount of money one has, rather than the amount of love."

"Thank you for believing in him." Tressa had said the words before she'd even realized her brain was forming them. But gratitude for such a selfless act was warranted.

Nettie cupped Tressa's hands. "Pilot must really like you. He's always been so guarded when it came to his past. Be good to him. You have an extraordinary man."

Nettie wasn't telling her anything she didn't already know. "I will."

Once they'd said their goodbyes and made promises to return soon, Tressa and Roth ventured into town.

Their first stop was the Silver Point Coffee House. When they walked through the door, Roth was greeted by several individuals. Obviously, he was well-known by the locals.

Just like The General Store, the coffeehouse gave an old-timey impression from the outside, but the inside told a different story. Exposed brick and aged wood gave the quaint shop a modern feel. There was ample seating with bistro and four-top tables scattered about. What caught Tressa's eye was the two oversize empty burgundy recliners positioned in front of a tall crackling fireplace. It was the perfect spot for them.

Roth joined her by the fireplace with two steaming soup-bowl-sized mugs of hot chocolate. "Wow. That's a lot of hot chocolate."

"They do everything big in Silver Point."

They sipped and chatted for hours. She couldn't remember the last time she enjoyed herself just talking. Roth told her about his time spent at The Cardinal House, a group home for boys, and she shared with him things from her childhood she'd never told anyone else. Like the time she'd broken the neighbor's window and her brother had taken the fall for her. He still held it over her head 'til this day.

When they finally left the coffeehouse, they ventured to the thrift store next door where Roth had purchased them several books. Their last stop was a unique card-slash-gift shop.

Inside the vehicle, Tressa pulled a small box from her purse and passed it to Roth.

"What's this?" he asked.

"Open it."

Roth lifted the metal bookmark from the wrapping. "Don't judge a book by its cover or a man by his past."

"It's not much. I just wanted to say thank you."

"For what?"

"For…everything. This week has been incredible, Roth. You have been incredible. You made what should have been the very worst week of my life, the best week of my life. I want you to know I appreciate you."

Roth reached over, placed his hand behind her neck and pulled her mouth close to his, but he didn't kiss her. Staring into her eyes, he said, "Thank you."

"You're welcome."

The following morning, Tressa and Roth finally got on the road back to Raleigh. Roth had been silent since they'd pulled away from the cabin. Was he regretting returning home, too?

The way he brushed his thumb back and forth across the steering wheel told her something occupied his thoughts.

"I'm really going to miss Silver Point," she said.

Roth didn't respond. He simply eyed her briefly, smiled and returned his gaze to the road ahead.

What was going on with him? She wanted to think the best—that things weren't changing now that they'd left the close quarters of the cabin. But the worst crept in—that just maybe she had been only a temporary replacement for Roth.

When they pulled into her cul-de-sac several hours later, the fact that Cyrus's car wasn't parked in her driveway brought her relief. Not that she cared if Cyrus saw her and Roth together. It was a well-deserved ass whooping she knew Cyrus would have surely talked himself into. She would have felt awful if Roth went to jail for assault on account of her.

Inside, Tressa watched as Roth took in his surroundings. His eyes moved from the open living room decorated in brown and teal, to the kitchen outfitted with stainless steel appliances.

"You have a nice place," he said, folding his arms across his chest.

"Thank you. Is everything okay, Roth? You seem to have something on your mind."

He directed her to the chocolate sofa. "Sit. We need to talk."

She wasn't sure she liked the sound of that. *We need to talk* were typically words of doom. "Okay," she said, ignoring the quiver in her stomach. She eased down and stared up at him. "I'm listening."

Roth took a seat on the leather ottoman directly in front of her and cupped her hands. She saw the signs. When he dipped his head, she decided to make this easier for him. "I get it, Roth. You're not ready for a commitment. You thought you were, but now…I get it." Her heart crumbled a little more with every word she spoke. "We had a great time at the cabin, but we're back in the real world and things don't look as clear for you, right? You just want to be friends." She forced a smile. "I get it and…it's okay."

Roth brought his gaze to her with urgency. "Can you let me go so easily?"

Now she was confused. Wasn't he trying to get away? "I don't want to let you go, but I don't want to hold on to you if you don't want to be held. I'm giving you an easy out."

"Giving me an easy out? I don't want an out. I was trying to give you one."

Her brows bunched. "Why would you think I wanted an out? I'm crazy about you, Roth Lexington. You have to know that by now."

Roth's head dipped again. "I heard you on the phone yesterday. You were agreeing to meet with someone. To talk things over. I assumed it was your ex."

Shit. He'd overheard her. Why hadn't he said anything before now? Well, he was half-right. She had agreed to meet with Cyrus, but only to give him all his junk she planned to pack up tonight. "I promise you, Roth, he's not the man I want in my life."

"Tressa…"

He paused as if whatever he needed to say pained him. Anything this difficult to declare couldn't be good.

"For years," he continued, "I've avoided romantic attachment like the plague. Being hurt once was enough for me. I was content with my bachelor lifestyle. Then you stowed away in the back of my SUV and forced me to whisk you off with me to my cabin."

"Forced? Really?"

"Whose story is this?" Roth said, followed by a lazy half smile.

"Fine. Carry on with your tall tale."

"Not many people have ever seen me beyond what I've wanted them to see. I keep trying to hide from you…" He sighed heavily. "I can't."

"Why would you want to hide from me, Roth?"

"You know how they say every man has a weakness?"

She nodded.

"You're mine. And honestly, I hate that shit, Tressa. You scare me. You scare me because you make me too vulnerable. Vulnerability gets you hurt. Vulnerability is a sign of we—"

She pressed a finger against his lips. "Vulnerability is a sign of being human. And being human looks excellent on you." She smiled but Roth remained stone-faced. "There's something you're not saying. What is it?"

"I need to fall back, Tressa. Not because I don't want to be with you. Trust me, I do. But I need you to be 200 percent sure I'm who you want."

Her heart sank to her feet. Where was all of this coming from? He wanted to be with her, but he wouldn't? It made no sense. How in the hell had things dissolved so quickly between them? "Roth—"

"Please, baby. It's hard enough letting…" His words faded. "Don't fight me on this."

Tressa snatched her hands away as frustration kicked in. "Don't *fight* you on this? You claim you want me, but it sure as hell doesn't feel that way to me. You asked me if I could let you go so easily. Can you let me go?"

When he didn't respond, she stood. "We spent an

amazing week together, one that I'll never regret, but obviously, you do. If you want to walk away, Roth, I'll let you. But you will not, *will not*," she repeated, "put your cowardliness on me."

When she tried to walk away, Roth placed his hands on either side of her waist to keep her from escaping. She blinked rapidly to keep her tears from falling. "I'm giving you *your* out, Roth. Just take it."

He didn't utter a word, didn't budge. Instead, he pulled her close to him and rested his forehead against her trembling stomach. She couldn't explain, but she could feel his fear as if they were one cell. Instinctively, her hand smoothed over his head to comfort him. This was one of the strongest men she'd ever encountered, but at that moment she truly believed she was his weakness. What she desperately needed him to know was she would also be his strength.

Lowering to her knees, she positioned herself between Roth's legs and cradled his face between her hands. A look of exhaustion played in his features. The sight clenched her heart.

Neither of them uttered a word. Words would have only bottled something too powerful to contain. Besides, none were needed. All that needed to be said was conveyed by a method they'd seemed to have perfected.

The stare.

That stare.

Their stare.

His eyes said he knew. And she was sure he saw the same knowledge in hers. Nothing was accidental. Where they were on this journey was exactly where they were both supposed to be.

Chapter 12

It'd been a week since she'd returned from Silver Point, and Tressa missed her time there already. She and Roth were still going strong, and she'd been the happiest she'd been in a long time. Every time she thought about him—which was quite often—her heart skipped a beat.

She glanced at the clock. Ten o'clock. A second later the house phone rang like clockwork. Without even looking at the caller ID, she knew it was Roth. He'd called her every day for the past week at the exact same time. Ten o'clock sharp.

"Hello," she croaked.

While it had taken a few days, she'd finally succumbed to Roth's cooties. In bed with a pounding headache, stuffy nose, congestion, a sore throat and a fever had not been how she'd envisioned spending her remaining time off.

However, there had been a silver lining to this dark cloud, and he'd waited on her hand and foot. Every morning he'd dropped by with breakfast on his way to work. Every day at lunch he'd either personally delivered or had food delivered to her. Every afternoon after a long day's work, he was at her front door ready to nurse her back to health.

Roth's smooth tone poured over the line. "Hey, beautiful. How ya feel?"

Tressa groaned. "*Ugh.* How do I sound?"

"Like a world-renowned opera singer."

"If you were trying to make me smile, it worked."

"That's always my goal," he said. "Have you had any of the remedy I mixed for you?"

"Um…yes. Several ounces, I believe."

Immediately, she asked forgiveness for the lie she'd just told. Roth had attempted to remake the home remedy she'd whipped up for him at the cabin when he'd fallen ill.

Unfortunately, what he'd brought to her bedside had been the color of dirty pond water and tasted like a lukewarm mix of turnip-green juice and hot sauce with a twist of lemon. But she'd taken several sips because he'd gone through the trouble of preparing it.

She made a note to pour a few ounces down the drain before he arrived later that evening. Had to keep up appearances.

"I wish I were there with you," he said.

"I wish you were here, too."

"I have several things here at the office I *have* to complete before I leave, then I'm all yours. Are you hungry? I can have something delivered."

She loved how this man took such good care of her. "No. My appetite is a bit wonky today."

"Well, get some rest and I'll be by tonight."

"You've been spreading yourself thin, Roth. Go home and get you some rest. I'll be fine. I am a nurse, remember?"

Roth chuckled. "Don't worry about me. And I'm perfectly aware of your profession, Nurse Washington, but I'll see you tonight anyway."

She wasn't going to argue. They said their goodbyes and Tressa snuggled against her pillow, wishing it was Roth's chest instead.

A beat later her cell phone chimed, indicating a text message. Eyeing the screen, she frowned. *Cyrus.*

Can't make the meet tomorrow. Something came up. Need to reschedule.

"Again, huh," she said to the screen, then sighed. This was the second time he'd squandered the opportunity to collect his things. Not giving him any more of her energy, she tossed the phone aside. She'd deal with him later.

Tressa got her wish several hours later when Roth undressed and slid into bed next to her. Despite her low-grade fever, his warm body was just the remedy she needed. She felt so guilty taking up so much of his time, but craved spending every available minute with him. She prayed this new relationship excitement never wore off for either of them.

Nestling under his chin, she wished she could smell his manly scent, but her clogged nose made it impossible. "I've missed you," she said.

"I seriously doubt more than I have you." Roth placed a finger under Tressa's chin and tilted her head upward. "Kiss me, woman. Just a little peck. I can't stand my lips not touching yours another day."

"You want my cooties?"

"Wasn't it you who told me I can't catch the same cold twice?"

"Yes, but we can't be certain you're the one who gave me this cold."

Roth's eyes narrowed in animated accusation. "Let me find out you've been out here, kissing other men and collecting their cooties."

Tressa kissed Roth under the chin, his five-o'clock shadow pricking her lips. "There is only one man's lips I'm concerned with. But I'm also concerned about his well-being. So…" She kissed the tip of her fingers and pressed them to his forehead, the tip of his nose, his cheek, then his chin. "That will have to do for now."

"I'll take what I can get, but just so you know, my lips are going to wither up and fall off if I can't kiss you soon. And not just your neck and shoulders."

Tressa laughed, which turned into a ferocious coughing fit. Roth retrieved the glass of water from the nightstand and offered it to her once she'd settled. "Sick sucks," she said, claiming her position back on Roth's chest.

Roth glided his hand up and down her back. "You'll be 100 percent soon."

Tressa closed her eyes, but remembered the package she'd received earlier. "I have a gift for you," she said, coming up with one elbow.

Tressa sent Roth to the kitchen for the package on

the counter. If there was one thing she was good at, it was one-click shopping.

Roth slid back into bed with her, then removed the crystals. "Um…you got me coal? Have I been a bad boy?"

She swatted him playfully. "They're called black tourmaline." One of her coworkers had told her the stone, along with amethyst, was supposed to help ward off negative energy. "It's a protective crystal. Place it by the bed, and it'll ward off nightmares. We'll keep some here and some at your place." Tressa ticked off the other benefits of black tourmaline: promotes detoxification, balances the chakras, relieves stress, improves mental alertness. "And there are a few more. I just can't remember them all. I think it's supposed to be good for memory, too. That'll—" She smiled when she saw the way Roth eyed her. "What?"

Roth's expression was unreadable. Was he trying to process all of the uses or was he thinking she was bat shit crazy? A second later he smashed his lips to hers. He didn't try to gain entry into her mouth with his tongue; he just held his lips against hers.

When Roth finally pulled away and looked at her, he didn't have to say a single word, but he did. "I've never met anyone like you. You are an amazing woman, Tressa Washington. Your heart…" He shook his head. "Come here." He pulled her into his arms again and lay back on the bed. "Woman, you're the answer to all of my unspoken prayers. I'm a damn lucky man."

And she was a damn lucky woman.

Roth glanced over at the black torpo… Black toma… The black crystals Tressa had got him. He didn't know

whether or not he should put much stock into their pow-
ers, but the fact that Tressa had been thoughtful enough
to purchase them gave him incentive. His heart had
swelled even more from her kindness. When he'd said
he was a lucky man, he'd meant every word.

He glanced down at her, fast asleep in his arms. Her
hair was strewed, she didn't have on any makeup and
she snored—loud. But in spite of all of that, she was the
most gorgeous woman he'd ever seen. All he wanted
to do was take care of her, protect her. In his head, he
knew he needed to slow down, but Tressa made him
want to move at the speed of light. His feelings for this
woman grew more powerful every single day.

Lifting her arm, she squirmed but didn't wake. He
gingerly snaked out of bed. If he fell asleep at seven in
the evening, he'd pop up in the middle of the night, wide
awake. Moving from the bedroom to the kitchen, he
snagged a banana, laughing at the two monkeys climbing up the arm of the aluminum banana holder.

Though he'd probably not have been ambitious
enough to choose the color, the pear-green-themed
decor in the room played well with the cherry cabinets
and stainless steel appliances. He wondered if she'd
specifically chosen this house because of the spacious
kitchen. Roth imagined her there at the oversize island,
chopping, dicing, smiling as she prepared for him and
their kids.

Their kids. He chuckled and washed a hand over
his head. "Slow down, Lex," he mumbled to himself.
There was no guarantee Tressa would give him the
football team he wanted. At least six. Even more if she
agreed. Possibly even adopt. There were a lot of kids

out there who needed a good home and love. He had a lot of love to give.

Abandoning the thoughts of his imaginary family, he moved from the kitchen and into the living room and dropped onto the chocolate sofa. Grabbing the tablet he'd brought with him, he tapped in his pass code. *Might as well use the time to get some work done.*

With Tressa right in the next room, maybe he could actually focus with her so close. He laughed when he considered how one minute he could be positioned at the design desk in his office, working away, the next he'd abandoned all thoughts of work and had replaced them with Tressa.

Damn, that woman is potent. She was all woman for sure. But she was also a flame that blazed through him constantly. *A man on fire*, he thought.

Setting the tablet aside for a moment, he went back into the kitchen for a bottle of water. When he decided the banana wasn't going to be enough to hold him, he grabbed the bag of sour-cream-and-cheddar chips from the top of the refrigerator.

Taking the last paper towel, he moved to the storage room where Tressa kept additional rolls. A cardboard box sitting on the floor caught his eye. For whatever reason, he lifted the top and looked inside.

The box was crammed packed with male toiletries. Obviously, Tressa had got around to packing Cyrus's shit, but hadn't got around to giving it to him. The idea of her meeting with the weasel bothered him. No doubt the slimy bastard would try to slither his way back into her life. His jaw tightened, then relaxed. He wasn't worried about that loser.

Or should he have been? Would seeing him awake

any dormant feelings Tressa still had for the man? There had to still be some, right? Roth shook his head. He couldn't stress over that. He had to trust Tressa, trust what they had.

Replacing the top, he grabbed the roll of paper towels, dropped it onto the wooden holder, then returned to the living room. Instead of working, as he'd intended, he found himself scrolling through the pictures of his boys—young men, he corrected—from the community center where he gave saxophone lessons to disadvantaged kids. They had been so excited about performing for their families at the Duke Energy Center for the Performing Arts in downtown Raleigh. And not just the younger kids, but the sixteen- and seventeen-year-olds, too.

They looked all *GQ*'d, decked out in their tuxedos and fedoras. He laughed at some of the jailhouse poses. He planned to do all he could to make sure none of them ever found themselves posing that way in a real jailhouse.

"My bed gets awfully lonely without you."

Tressa ambled across the floor and he directed her onto his lap. Kissing the side of her head, he said, "I had intended to get some work done since you were sleeping, but I started looking at these pictures."

"There better not be any big-boobed blondes on that device." She managed a lazy smile.

"Jealous?"

"Maybe."

He nuzzled her neck, then kissed it gently. "Your big boobs are the only ones I'm interested in. And I can't wait until you're better so I can show you just how interested I am." Redirecting his wayward thoughts, he positioned the screen so that they both could see the images.

"Are these the young men in your saxophone academy?"

"Yeah. A good-looking bunch, huh?"

"Yes." Tressa pointed to one of the younger kids. "Aww, he's a cutie-pie. Those glasses make him look like a young philosopher."

"Sebastian. He's smart as a whip and doesn't miss a doggone thing. He's a little timid, but will say whatever is on his mind. No filter. He's a good kid, though."

Tressa swiped through the pictures, commenting on most of them. "God, I can't wait to have a house full of kids running around. It's going—"

Tressa stopped as if she'd realized a mistake she'd made. Maybe she thought the mention of kids had spooked him. It hadn't. They could talk about kids all night long, because as far as he was concerned, she would be the mother of his football team.

Chapter 13

Tressa usually didn't wake at the crack of dawn when she didn't have to work. But Roth had shown up at her door at six that Saturday morning—*six in the morning*—blindfolded her and whisked her away to an undisclosed location. At least he had the common courtesy to bring her coffee.

In the month they'd been dating, every day was an adventure with him. What she truly valued was the fact that he always made time for her. Whether it was whisking her off to dinner and a movie, or challenging her to a game of bowling. He truly made her feel like she was an important part of his life.

"Are we there yet, Roth?" Tressa tussled with the silky fabric over her eyes. "This blindfold is chafing me."

"Hands off," he said, swatting her playfully. "We're almost there."

A short time later Roth activated the turn signal and made a right. He parked, then moved around to her side of the vehicle and helped her out onto the hard surface. Where were they? Using her available senses, she tuned in to her surroundings.

She smelled…exhaust, maybe? No, gasoline. Definitely gasoline. A racetrack? No. If they were at a racetrack, she would have heard the roaring engines and cheers from a crowd. Plus, she seriously doubted anyone raced this early.

What did she hear? Wind. Lots of it. And she felt it, too. A windmill farm? That made her laugh. Why in the world would Roth bring her to a windmill farm?

Roth took her hand and led her forward. She remembered the last time he'd held her hand for support. The Mile High Swinging Bridge at Grandfather Mountain. That trip to Silver Point had been the start of something beautiful.

Tressa's steps were now just as hesitant as they'd been walking out on the bridge. "Don't let me fall, Roth." Although, she knew he'd never allow that to happen.

"Do you think I'd allow you to hurt a pretty little hair on your head? Stand right here," he said, placing his hands on both her shoulders as if to steady her. "Don't move."

"And risk breaking my neck?" Her ears perked when she heard what sounded like a key being inserted into a lock. Then it sounded as if he'd opened a metal garage door. It clanked and rattled so loud it startled her. She reached out, her wiggling fingers searching for the comforts of his. "Roth?"

"I'm right here, baby." He stood directly behind her. "You ready?"

"Been ready." When Roth removed the blindfold, her eyes adjusted to the light. Squinting, she blinked several times, but the small personal aircraft was still there in all its massive glory. "What…"

Roth placed his hand on her lower back and ushered her forward. "Meet *Zoom*."

Tressa's eyes scanned the black-and-silver plane, then the hangar where it was being housed. If it was any brighter in the all-white, pristine space, she would have needed sunglasses. *"Zoom?"* she said absently.

"You ready?"

She whipped toward him, confused by the question. "Ready for what?"

"Part two of your Valentine's Day. We'll only be gone overnight."

Still confused, she said, "Part two…?" Her words trailed off.

Part one of her Valentine's Day had been pretty damn fantastic. Roth had had four dozen red roses delivered to the hospital. When he'd arrived at her house to pick her up for dinner, he'd given her the largest box of chocolate she'd ever seen. After a dinner fit for a queen, they'd returned to his place and made love for hours.

"Where are we going?"

"It's a surprise."

Roth strapped her into the two-seater aircraft. She'd be lying if she said she wasn't a little nervous about Roth flying them to wherever it was he was flying them to. And it wasn't the fact that it was Roth, per se; she would have been nervous with anyone behind the wheel—controls—of this intimate craft. Plus, when she flew, she was used to having far more space, and far more pilots manning the controls.

"Um, is your pilot's license up-to-date?"

Roth flashed a stunned expression. "You have to have a license to fly? The video game simulation never stated that." He smirked. "Don't worry, baby." He cradled her chin, leaned over and kissed her gently on the lips. "I got you. A champion, remember?"

"Of flying *paper* planes." She hadn't actually meant to say the words aloud.

"Look at me," Roth said. When she did, he continued, "Not only do I always want you to feel happy with me, I want you to feel safe, too. If you don't want to do this, we don't have to. I won't be offended."

Tressa inhaled and exhaled slowly. "Let's do this."

Several moments later, they taxied down the runway, then ascended.

Tressa marveled at the view below them. The cars and houses resembled pieces in a board game. Roth seemed so comfortable, so at-home handling *Zoom*, that all of her earlier concerns melted away.

"How long have you had *Zoom*?" Tressa felt as if she was screaming into the aviation headset.

"I built her a little over two years ago."

Built? Okay, she hadn't heard that right. Adjusting her earpiece, she said, "Did you say *you* built this plane? Like…with a hammer and screwdriver?"

Roth laughed. "I had a few more tools, but yeah, something like that."

A second later she released a shaky chuckle. "You're not serious."

The look he gave her said he was. Who in the hell

was this man? More important, was he any good at building planes?

Roughly five hours later they touched down in Arizona, took an Uber to the car rental location, grabbed a bite to eat, purchased more temperature-appropriate clothing, then checked into the Renaissance in downtown Phoenix.

The spacious hotel room was decorated in blues and browns. A king-size bed rested in the middle of the spacious hotel room. A wall-mounted TV, a dresser and two nightstands outfitted the space. Their location boasted an amazing view of mountains in the distance.

"This bed is cozy. You should come and try it out," Roth said, sprawled across the plush mattress.

Tressa turned away from the window. One of the first things to catch her eye—excluding her man—were the black tourmaline crystals on the nightstand. He'd brought them with him. For some reason, it made her smile.

"Come over here, woman. There are some things I need to do—I mean, say—to you."

She moved toward the bed, slowly removing her clothing piece by piece. Roth came up on his elbows and sucked his bottom lip between his teeth, watching her eagerly. First, her shirt dropped to the floor, then her bra. Next, her jeans and panties. Raw desire danced in his eyes.

"I want that. All of that," he said, his heated gaze burning a line up and down her body.

In a seductive voice, she said, "And you can have it, baby. All of it." She smirked. "After I get a hot shower." She took off for the bathroom.

"Woman! Oh, you will pay for that."

A couple of hours and orgasms later, Tressa had been eager to stay in bed with Roth all day long, exploring new ways to please one another. Unfortunately, he'd insisted there was someplace they needed to be by seven, but he wouldn't give her any other details beyond that. What in the heck did he have up his sleeve? Whatever it was, she knew she'd like it.

On the drive to their destination, Tressa grilled Roth, but he remained tight-lipped. Thirty minutes later they crossed the line into Chandler, Arizona. A short time after that, a sign read Rawhide at Wild Horse Pass. "Where are—" Tressa's eyes widened when she saw a second billboard-type sign. Popping Roth in the arm, she said, "Arizona Black Rodeo?"

"Glen said I should take you to a rodeo, right? Here we are."

"No. I mean, yes. But no, I can't believe we're here." Tender eyes admired him. "You flew all the way to Arizona to bring me to the rodeo." Tressa's heart did a pitter-patter in her chest. "You're all right with me, *Pilot*."

Hundreds of people appeared to be in attendance in the large arena. Tressa had never seen this many people dressed like cowboys and cowgirls in one place in her life. Young, old and everything in between. A group of mature women passed by and she laughed at the purple shirts they wore—Saddle up! Shut up! Hold on! She had to score one of those. And a cowgirl hat.

Roth held her near as they made their way through the crowded arena. The noise inside the place was thunderous, the lighting intense and the smell...interesting, but she loved it all.

Ooh, la, la, she thought when a group of cowboys

passed them, several tipping their hats at her. "I think you'd look good in one of those outfits, baby. What do you say we do some role-playing tonight?" When Roth didn't respond, she glanced up at him. "Roth?"

Roth's hard stare left the group who'd just passed them and settled on her. "You like that, huh?"

Something was off with him. He lacked the warmth that had been present just moments ago. What had changed? Then it dawned on her. *The group.* Had the men tipping their hats at her bothered him? As if Roth could read her thoughts, he smiled and nestled her closer against him.

Leaning in close to her ear, he said, "I'll show you a real cowboy when we get back to the room," then winked.

There was her naughty man. Still, what had prompted the shift she'd seen in him? He'd never displayed any hint of jealousy before. Not wanting to ruin the moment, she didn't address it. But she would when they returned to the hotel.

For the next two hours they occupied seats in the VIP section, directly above the chutes, and watched bull riding, tie-down roping, steer wrestling and undecorating. Tressa cooed during the mutton busting, where children raced sheep. Though it was quite entertaining, her nerves took a beating. Her worst fear was of one of them falling and breaking something. Luckily, it didn't happen.

After all of the main events had ended, they decided to do the vendor stroll. Hand in hand, they moved along the trails of vendors peddling everything from wallets to horse saddles. She joked about getting one of the saddles and strapping it onto Roth's back. He was all for it.

"So, what did you think?" Roth asked, draping his arm around her shoulders and pulling her close. "You think you want to add cowgirl to your résumé?"

"Heck, yeah," she said. "And tonight I'll show you how good I ride."

"Let's skip the vendor stroll and the Rawhide Steakhouse. We need to get back to the room right now."

Tressa bumped him playfully. "You are insatiable."

"I can't help it. You bring out the hungry beast in me. And the hungry beast has to pee. I'll be right back." Roth started away, but stopped. Backtracking, he pressed a hard kiss to her lips. "Don't move."

"I'll be right here."

Once Roth disappeared around the corner, Tressa leaned against the metal railing and watched the remainder of the kids' calf scramble. She laughed aloud as a dozen or more kids chased black calves. And she'd thought the mutton busting was amusing.

Tressa glanced up when something brushed her elbow. A tall, attractive, dark-skinned man wearing a black cowboy hat smiled down at her. Something happened in the arena and the entire place erupted in cheers and applause, drowning out whatever the man had said.

"What?" she yelled.

He leaned in uncomfortably close. "I said cowboys and cowgirls in the making."

"Looks that way."

Instead of him leaving, like she would have preferred, he continued chatting her up.

"You're not from around here," he said.

Curious, she asked, "Why do you say that?"

"There is close to a thousand people in this arena and you're the only one not wearing a cowboy hat."

Tressa sent a glance around her. He was right. She tossed her head back and laughed. "I am not. My *boy-friend* and I flew up today for the rodeo."

The man made a pained face, then placed his hand over his heart as if he'd been stabbed. "Oh, the *b*-word. You just killed me with seven letters."

"Nine, actually. But who's counting?"

Dead Man Walking continued to go on and on about something, but Tressa tuned him out. Then as if there had been a shift in the atmosphere, she glanced to see Roth standing several feet away.

Thank God. Maybe now this chatterbox would move on. But instead of Roth joining them, Roth's steel-cold gaze assessed Dead Man Walking, and judging by Roth's body language, *walking* was about to be dropped from the title.

Extreme turmoil clawed through Roth when he turned the corner to see some man bent over, whispering something in Tressa's ear. When she laughed, jealousy—a quadrillion times greater than anything he'd ever felt before—tore through him. His throat tightened and pain drummed in his temple.

What the hell had he said to her?

Roth shuddered, resisting the urge to charge like a bull and knock the bastard over the metal rails. He'd never been an insecure man, so he couldn't explain why the scene in front of him rubbed him so raw. But it did. His jaw tightened and every breath he took was drawn out and heavy, almost like fire in his lungs.

The cowboy kept yapping about something, but Tressa didn't seem to be paying a great deal of attention to him. Still, she hadn't sent him packing and that bothered him. Roth's hands tightened into fists when the cowboy stole a glance at Tressa's backside.

As if Tressa could sense his anguish, she turned toward him, the smile on her face melting into a frown. She shot him a worried glance, and he shot her a look right back—one of displeasure.

What in the hell was Tressa doing to him? He'd always prided himself on his ability to remain in control and be levelheaded, even during the direst of situations. Now here he was, acting like a rabid dog.

Composing himself, he held Tressa's probing gaze as he approached. The closer he got to her, the longer their eyes held, the less rage he felt.

"Hey, baby," she said, placing her hand on his back and ironing it up and down. "This is…"

"Frank," the man said, extending his hand to Roth.

Roth didn't really give a damn who he was, but he shook Frank's hand anyway, applying a hint more pressure than necessary. It'd been a warning—man code for *get the hell away from my woman*. One he was sure Frank got, because he pretended to see someone he knew, then hurried away.

Roth set his stone gaze on Tressa, but didn't speak.

"I think Frank's a zombie. He died when I told him I had a boyfriend, but he came right back to life," Tressa said and laughed. "He's awfully talkative for a zombie."

Roth knew she was trying to lighten the mood, but it didn't work. "Really? Well, at what point did you decide to tell him you had a boyfriend? When your head was cocked back in laughter or when he was whispering in your ear?" He instantly regretted his words and his pointed tone. What the hell was wrong with him?

Then it hit him. It hadn't been wholly about the cowboy. But the incident had triggered something already nagging him. It was seeing Cyrus's packed box still sitting in Tressa's closet when he'd gone to pick her up that morning. Why was she still holding on to the items? It was like she couldn't bear to rid herself of them.

Tressa's head jerked in what Roth took to be shock. Her jaw dropped and she stared at him as if he'd grown a second head. Recovering, she said, "I'll meet you at the car," and then stalked off.

Dammit.

Back at their hotel room, Roth tossed the door key, wallet and car fob on the dresser. The drive back had given him plenty of time to cool off, not to mention Tressa's cold shoulder. In that time he realized he'd acted like a jackass. Now he needed to make things right.

Tressa stood in front of the dresser, removing her jewelry. When he walked up behind her and rested his hands on either side of her waist, she flinched. He kissed the back of her head. "I'm sorry."

Her tired eyes met his through the mirror. "Okay." She pushed his hands away and escaped to the bathroom, slamming the door behind her with so much force the abstract painting hanging over the bed rattled.

Roth trailed her as far as the bathroom door but didn't enter. He started to move away until he heard her sniffles. Scrubbing a hand over his head, he pinched his lids together tightly, hating himself for bringing her to tears. "Baby, please don't cry."

Tressa didn't respond.

Blowing out hard, he rested his hands on either side of the door frame. "I saw red when I saw you with Frank. When I saw the way he was looking at you, checking you out…I felt threatened. I've never been an insecure or jealous man, Tressa. *Never.*" He paused. "But when it comes to you… I don't know. I'm different." He refrained from adding Cyrus's box to the mix. He knew that would only make things worse.

Tressa sniffled several more times, and he thought his heart would explode from regret. All he wanted to do was burst into that room, pull her into his arms, kiss every tear away and make her forget he'd ever hurt her. Which, clearly, he had.

"I'm sorry, baby."

On a whim, he tried the door. Surprisingly, it was unlocked. When he stepped inside, Tressa was sitting on top of the closed toilet seat, dabbing at her eyes with a tissue. It ripped chunks from his heart. He guided her to stand, then wrapped her in his arms. "I'll never make you cry again."

Several tense minutes ticked by, her silence driving him insane. Why wouldn't she just say something to him? Anything. And as if the universe had heard his innermost desires, he got his wish.

"I can't—" Tressa's voice cracked, but she soon continued, "I can't be with you, Roth."

Roth's chest tightened and a sharp pain shot down his arm. He swore he was having a heart attack. Was Tressa ending things? He prayed he'd heard her incorrectly. Rearing back, his worried eyes searched hers.

Tressa continued, "Not if you can't handle me talking to other men. I'm surrounded by men. All day, every day. You need to decide right now, before this goes any further, whether or not you can handle that. I want to be with you, Roth. But I won't be in a relationship where I have to walk on eggshells."

At the thought of losing Tressa, fear filled every cell in Roth's body. He didn't know what to do, what to say. He'd just got her. There was no damn way he would lose her over this, over his own insecurities. He cradled her face between his hands. "I don't want to lose you. Tell me what I need to do."

"You need to trust me. Trust that what we have is real and that I'd never do anything to hurt you, Roth. I get you've experienced a lot of heartbreak and disappointment in your past and it has lessened your faith in people. I can't be one of those people. Not if this is going to work. For this to work, you have to believe in us. I'm *crazy* about you, Roth Lexington, but I didn't like the man I saw tonight." Her eyes clouded with tears. "He scared me."

Jesus. What had he done? "I would never harm you. *Never.* Please tell me you know that." Several seconds that felt like several eternities ticked by.

"I know," she finally said.

Roth snatched Tressa into his arms and held her like he'd never held her before. He greedily claimed her energy. It gave him strength. "Be patient with me, baby."

"I will." A second later she pulled away. "You won't always get to simply say *I'm sorry* and expect everything to be okay. *I'm sorry* won't always be enough."

He nodded his understanding. "Is it enough now?"

When she nodded, he pulled her back into his arms. He may have denied it before, but there was no way he could any longer. He was falling in love with this woman. And the thought of *ever* losing her scared the hell out of him.

Chapter 14

Tressa checked her watch again. The third time since she'd occupied one of the tables inside Tender Hearts Memorial Hospital's café. Cyrus had dodged this moment long enough. If he didn't show up this time, she would take his things to the incinerator and burn them. The junk had cluttered her storage closet and life long enough—two and a half months to be exact. She'd been dead serious when she'd given him an ultimatum: either meet her to collect it *today* or it would be ashes.

He'd chosen the former.

He was officially twenty minutes late. No call. No text. No nothing. *So typical.*

Was he calling her bluff?

Well, he had ten more minutes to show, or she was out of there. If he missed this opportunity, he wouldn't get another.

Choosing to meet in a public place had been a great idea. She was glad Vivian had suggested it. Vivian had also suggested bringing a Taser, but she didn't feel that was warranted. Cyrus wouldn't harm her. However, her mother used to say you just never knew what desperate folks were capable of, especially when pride and ego were involved.

Tressa scattered the troubling thoughts. *Ugh.* She just wanted to get this over and be done with Cyrus, so she could focus on better things. An image of Roth filled her head. Just the thought of that man calmed her. She couldn't wait to see him tonight. Just like with the rodeo trip a month ago, he was being just as tight-lipped about where he was taking her on their date.

She ran her fingers through her shockingly short hair, still unsure how she felt about the new cut or going natural. Change, she reminded herself. The fact that Roth had loved it brought a smile to her face.

A crackle of lightning was followed by a deep rumble of thunder that shook the building and caused her to jolt. When she glanced up, Cyrus was strolling through the café doors. Had the ferocious weather been announcing his arrival?

Cyrus's unhurried steps suggested he had no idea that he was already late. Tressa shook her head in disgust. Oh, he knew; he just didn't care how his actions would inconvenience her. It was amazing how much clearer you saw things once someone had deceived you.

Once he finally approached the table, Tressa skipped a customary greeting. "I don't have long."

"And hello to you, too, sweetheart. Yes, I'm well, and I hope you're the same. My day? Oh, it was lovely."

Tressa rolled her eyes at his smugness. Why in

the hell did he believe she'd offer him any type of cordialness?

"What the hell happened to your hair?"

Tempted to say her man liked it, she ignored the question instead. "Thank you for finally showing up." Cyrus unbuttoned the caramel-colored, ankle-length wool coat he wore and placed it on top of the box containing his belongings. Why in the hell was he getting so comfortable? After removing his hat and scarf, he placed them with the coat, then eased down into the chair opposite her.

Tressa motioned toward the box. "I believe that's everything. If anything is missing…" She shrugged.

His eyes leveled on her. "You don't care, right?"

"Right."

Cyrus clasped his hands in front of him and leaned forward. "Why are you being so damn difficult? I made a mistake. Aren't I entitled to one?" His tone was a mix of frustration and impatience. "You've always been so damn stubborn."

"Well, my stubbornness is no longer your problem now, is it?"

Those steel-gray eyes darkened. "You were supposed to be my wife and just like that you want to walk away. I was good to you. You never wanted for anything. I loved you, still love you," he said through gritted teeth. "Even despite the way you've treated me the past few months."

She stood, refusing to sing this same old song with him. "I truly wish you nothing but the best, Cyrus. Enjoy the rest of your afternoon."

Cyrus stood with such urgency, his chair fell over. The swiftness of his action took her by surprise. In a blink, he was in her face. She'd never been fearful of him until this moment. The hardened expression he wore unnerved her. Maybe she should have given the Taser suggestion a little more consideration.

Cyrus grabbed Tressa's wrist and positioned his mouth close to her ear. "Are you sleeping with *him*? Don't think I haven't driven by your place and seen his SUV parked in the driveway. In my damn spot."

Tressa's eyes widened. "Driven by my place? Are you stalking me?"

Cyrus ignored the question, his tone softening. "Baby, please. Just give me another chance. I swear I'll be the man you need. I'll do right by you this time."

"You had your only chance to do right by me. Now, let go of my arm, Cyrus, before I scream bloody murder."

Instead of loosening, his grip tightened and Tressa thought he'd snap her wrist.

"Is there a problem here, Nurse Washington?"

Tressa recognized the voice and blew a sigh of relief, thankful for the intervention. Cyrus loosened his grip, and she yanked her arm away. Facing Dr. Benjamin Pointer, one of the cardiothoracic surgeons at the hospital, she said, "No, Dr. Pointer, everything is fine."

Dr. Pointer slid his gaze to Cyrus. If she had to translate Dr. Pointer's expression, it stated: *though I might be Ivy League–educated, I'm from the streets.* Obviously, Cyrus was good at nonverbal communication, because he backed away, collected his things and left with no further complications. But she had a feeling this wasn't over.

Several hours later Tressa and Roth were led to one of the many tables inside Tegria's, the Brazilian steak house she'd heard only great things about.

Roth pulled out her chair, and she eased down onto the burgundy leather. The aromas wafting around the room made her stomach growl. The fact she hadn't eaten since one that afternoon—seven hours ago—didn't help.

"This place is gorgeous," she said, scrutinizing the lengths of burgundy fabric draped from the high ceilings, the modern decor and the eclectic light fixtures.

"You're gorgeous," Roth said, taking her hand.

Though the lighting in the restaurant was dim, Tressa feared he would see the nasty bruise Cyrus's tight grip had left behind. Icing the area had done little to reduce the bruising. The chunky bracelet masked the black and blue for now, but she couldn't hide it forever.

Maybe she could say it was from a disgruntled patient. It was plausible. She'd been socked in the jaw once. No, she wasn't going to lie. Their relationship couldn't be plagued with lies. She had to tell him about her encounter with Cyrus. *No secrets,* she told herself. But not tonight. Tonight she just wanted to enjoy a beautiful evening with her man. Her trifling ex had ruined her afternoon; she refused to allow him to ruin her evening, too.

Tressa reclaimed her hand. "Mr. Lexington, are you trying to seduce me in this restaurant full of people, then entice me to join you in the restroom?"

"Don't give me any ideas, woman."

When he winked at her, a few naughty thoughts ran through her mind.

Roth dragged a finger along her forearm. "How was your day?"

"Long."

Concern spread across his face. "Did something happen?"

Tressa waved off the words. "No. Nothing out of the ordinary. Everyday stuff. A normal day in the ER. I just need a long, hot soak." To stop her babbling, she lifted her water glass to her lips.

He leaned in close. "I think I can manage a long, hot bath. A nice rubdown afterward. How does that sound?"

"Excellent. I'd like that a lot."

Over the next couple of hours Tressa and Roth enjoyed mouthwatering appetizers, several varieties of fire-roasted meats and sampled countless side dishes. To say she was stuffed would be a gross understatement.

"So, Chef Washington, does Tegria's get your seal of approval?"

"Absolutely. I am officially in love with this place."

"Did you save room for dessert?"

"Are you kidding me? If I eat one more thing, I'll explode. Are you getting dessert?"

He nodded like an overly anxious child who'd just been offered free rein in a candy shop.

Tressa laughed. "Where do you put it all?"

"I have plenty of space left. I didn't eat as much as you did."

Tressa swatted him playfully. "I can't believe you just said that."

Roth snagged her hand and brought it to his lips. "You know I'm only playing with you." He kissed the back of her hand, then her palm. When he slid her bracelet to kiss her wrist, he went still. He squinted as if he didn't believe what his own eyes were seeing. Fine lines crawled across his forehead.

"What happened to your wrist? How'd you get this nasty bruise?"

Tressa's heartbeat increased slightly. This was not where and how she wanted to tell him. "Today…um… Today, I…um…" She cleared her throat. "One of my patients… He was high on meth and had a psychotic break. He thought I was an alien coming to abduct him." *So much for the truth. It was just one lie for the greater good*, she tried to convince herself. Still, she felt awful and guilty.

Roth's features hardened. "How in the hell did they allow that bastard to manhandle you like this?"

Tressa glanced around to see if Roth's words had drawn any attention. Luckily, the place buzzed with so much chatter, she doubted anyone even gave them a sideways glance. "Roth, sweetie, calm down. It's really not that serious."

He made a sound similar to what a tortured animal would make. "Not that… It is that serious, Tressa. I don't like the idea of anyone putting their hands on you, especially aggressively enough to leave a mark like this."

To ease the mood, she said, "You know, I bet if you kiss it, you'd make it all better." She flashed a warm smile.

"Tressa, this is no joking matter. I—"

"Please." She batted her eyes for effect.

Roth studied her long and hard, his displeased expression finally softening. A beat later he peppered her wrist with delicate kisses.

"See, it's better already."

Roth flashed a lazy smile, then slouched back against his chair. She'd seen the fury that had danced in his eyes. Thank God she hadn't told him what had really happened. There was no telling what he would have done.

Continuing to give credibility to her story, she said, "I'm an ER nurse, Roth. I deal with the unpredictable day in and day out. Sometimes—" she lifted her arm "—things like this happen."

His tone sounded weary when he spoke. "Yeah, well, I don't like them happening to you."

In that moment Tressa had never felt so protected in her life. She kind of liked it. Too bad it was based on a lie. The greater good, she reminded herself.

Chapter 15

On the drive to his place, Roth wanted to be elated that he was getting quality time with Tressa, but what she'd revealed at the restaurant had dampened his mood and he just couldn't snap out of this funk. If he could just have five minutes with the asshole who'd done that to her wrist, he'd pulverize him.

Another wave of anger crashed through him. Sliding a glance in Tressa's direction elevated some of his rage. He squeezed her hand. "Hey." When she looked at him, he lost himself in the delicate expression on her face. How could anyone want to hurt her? "Have I told you how beautiful you look in that little black dress?"

"Only a hundred times, but a hundred and one couldn't hurt."

"You look beautiful."

"Thank you. And you are looking dapper yourself. I love that sweater on you."

"This old thing?"

A smile curled her lips before she turned away and slid her gaze back into the darkness outside the window. Something was bothering her. He could tell by the fact that she'd seemed distracted ever since they'd left the restaurant. But what? Then it hit him. The way he'd blown up when he saw her wrist. Had he scared her? *Damn.*

"Hey?"

"Hmm?"

This time Tressa didn't bother looking in his direction. "At the restaurant… I apologize if I overacted. If I frightened you."

Tressa turned toward him, a look of confusion on her face. "Frightened me? You didn't frighten me. You actually made me feel shielded. And I'm grateful that you have my back."

Roth brought her injured wrist to his lips. "I do. Don't ever forget that."

To his credit—and fault—he was a natural protector. If you messed with someone he loved, you messed with him. That had been the case with his foster brothers, waging war on anyone who'd done them dirty. Now it was the case with Tressa. And there was no limit to what he would do for her.

A short time later he pulled into his garage and shifted into Park. Hopping out, he moved around the vehicle to open Tressa's door. The fact he would fall asleep and wake with her in his arms lightened his mood considerably. Before he allowed her to escape from the vehicle, he leaned in and gave her a soul-shaking kiss, tasting and savoring every inch of her mouth. The sweetness from the mint she popped into her mouth right after leaving the restaurant still lingered and he tried his damnedest to rid her mouth of all its flavor.

When he finally pulled away, his lips ached. Damn, he had to have her. His erection made that painfully clear. Instead of a look of desire on Tressa's face, she donned one of concern. Enough was enough. He wanted to know what the hell was going on with her and he wanted to know now. Obviously, she'd witnessed that on his face.

"Roth, I need to—"

His cell phone vibrated, causing Tressa to pause. "I'll send it to voice mail."

"No, take it. It could be important. We'll talk inside."

Nothing was more important than she was, but it was late for anyone to be calling. He fished the device from the holder on his side. *Alonso.* A smile crept across his face. He and Vivian had been trying to get pregnant. Was Alonso calling to tell him he was going to be a godfather?

If so, that would mean Roth was about to be out of 50K. Years ago they'd agreed that whoever had a kid first, the other would establish a college fund. It'd started out as a joke because at the time, neither of them could have put their hands on that kind of money. But they knew one day they would be able to.

"What's up?" Roth greeted him, pushing open the door from the garage for Tressa to walk through. She mouthed that she'd be in the living room and he nodded with the promise to be there in a second.

"Shit, man. Vivian just got home from the hospital

and told me what happened today. That shit is foul. Is Tressa okay? Are you okay? I know you blew a gasket."

Roth figured Alonso was talking about Tressa's incident with the meth head. His jaw clenched at the ugly visual that filtered into his thoughts, some big, burly biker type slinging her around the room by the wrist. 'Course if he was a meth head, he couldn't have been so big, right? Still, that didn't pacify him. Roth opened the refrigerator door for a bottle of water. "Yeah, everything is good."

"It's a good thing Tressa didn't marry that lowlife. Any man who puts his hands on a woman is a punk."

Roth stilled and his brow furrowed. His jaw clenched tight enough to crush his teeth. He slid a glance to Tressa, who was walking around the pool table using her hand instead of a cue to sink balls in. Had her ex done this to her?

"Let me call you back, Lo."

"Okay, man. Peace."

Peace? Peace wasn't exactly something he was feeling at the moment. Taming his mounting outrage, he joined Tressa alongside the pool table. "Tell me what really happened to your wrist, Tressa." He kept his tone as steady as possible. "The truth this time."

Tressa tensed but relaxed a moment later, refusing to look at him. "Obviously, you already know the truth, Roth."

"Why did I have to hear it from someone else? You looked me directly in my eyes and lied to me."

Whipping toward him, she said, "What would you have done if I'd told you Cyrus did this, Roth?" She lifted her arm.

"Don't you mean what I'm *going* to do to his ass?

Right now, in fact." He turned to move away, but Tressa snagged the hem of his sweater, then moved around to block his path.

"Baby, he's not worth it."

"Why?"

"Because he's irrelevant."

Roth already knew that, but Cyrus's irrelevance wasn't what he was inquiring about. "Why did he grab you?" Tressa's eyes lowered, which told him what he'd suspected. "He knows about us?"

"He has an idea," she said, barely audible.

"And that's why this happened?"

When she didn't respond, he had his answer. He made a fist so tight his knuckles cracked. He was the one the bastard should have come for, not Tressa. But Roth would make sure he felt every ounce of that mistake.

Tressa rested her hands on his chest and he flinched. "What are you going to do, Roth?"

He flashed her a do-you-really-want-to-know look.

Her words were sharp when she said, "You're not a monster, Roth."

His words were equally as pointed and urgent when he said, "No, I'm not. But I am a man who loves a woman and will be damned if I let—"

"Wh-what did you just say?" Tressa interrupted.

It took him a second or two to realize what he'd allowed to slip. *Shit!* This was not how he imagined saying those three words to her for the first time. He massaged his forehead. When he spoke, his tone was much calmer than it had been moments before. "I said—"

"You said you love me."

He scrubbed a hand over his head, handling her

trifling ex no longer seeming so urgent now. A lazy chuckle floated from him. "I guess I did."

"Did you mean it?"

She seemed almost hesitant to ask.

"Yeah, I did."

"I love you, too."

Roth crushed his mouth to hers and kissed her long and hard. Without breaking their connection, he hoisted her into his arms and climbed onto the pool table. "Do you have any idea how much I want you right now? I want you so bad I'm bordering delirium."

"Well, I can't have the man I love going insane. I guess that means you better take me."

Roth rolled her onto her stomach, then slowly unzipped the sexy-ass dress he'd fantasized peeling her out of all night. Leaning forward, he peppered tender kisses over her vanilla-scented skin. She always smelled so damn delicious. Maybe that was why anytime they were together he wanted to eat…her.

"You're always so gentle," she whispered.

Kissing his way to her ear, he said, "Not tonight, baby. Not tonight."

"I think I like the sound of that."

Roth made his way down her body, pushing her dress to her hips and exposing the black lace panties she wore. Her butt cheeks peeked from under the material. The sight was arousing as hell.

Dipping forward, he placed a kiss to her lower back. Tressa shivered, then moaned a low hum of delight. The sound made him all the more eager to please her. "You like that, I see."

"I like it anytime you touch me."

A confident smile spread across his face as he slid

her panties down her legs and over the sparkly black stilettos she wore. Those stayed on. Starting at her lower back, he dragged an unhurried finger across the dip, along the split of her buttocks and to her core.

Tressa squirmed when he teased her with a bent finger, gliding his knuckle up and down her clit. She moved her hips in sync with the movement of his finger.

"Faster, Roth."

Instead of doing what she requested, he stopped.

"*Nooo*. What are you—"

She drew in a sharp breath when he slid his thumb inside her canal and moved it in and out of her. Slowly at first, then faster. Tressa rode his finger, her ass bouncing in his face. He smacked one cheek, then the other, causing her to purr.

"You're so damn wet I could swim inside you," he said.

"I...I told you I like your touch."

"Oh, I'm going to be doing a lot of touching, teasing, tasting. I might drown tonight."

"I'll give you mouth-to-mouth."

Shit. He couldn't take this. Yanking his finger out of her, he climbed off the table and brought Tressa with him. "Let's get rid of this," he said, pulling the dress over her head and slinging it off to the side. Taking a step back, he admired her gorgeous body and thought about the sinful things he was about to do to it. His tongue glided across his bottom lip.

Tressa smirked. "You like what you see?"

"*Love* what I see." He motioned with his head. "Come here." Tressa glided toward him like a runway model. When they stood toe-to-toe, he said, "Kiss me."

She wrapped her arms around his neck and pulled

his mouth to hers. Their tongues fought a passionate battle. He walked her back until her body was pinned against the pool table. Lifting her, he placed her on the edge. Breaking their kiss, he said, "Lean back, but not all the way."

Once Tressa had propped herself up, Roth dipped forward and kissed her collarbone, then dragged his tongue down the column of her neck. Working his way down her torso, he sucked one of her hardened nipples through the lacy fabric of her bra.

"Roth, please."

"Please, what?"

"Make love to me. Make love to me now. Please."

Hearing her beg for him made him throb even harder. Whether she knew it or not, he was inflicting as much glorious torture on himself as he was on her. "Soon, baby. I promise." The reassurance was for them both.

Removing her bra, Roth pushed her ample breasts together and pulled both nipples into his mouth at once. He urged Tressa back, until her entire body was stretched out on the pool table. "Bend your knees." She did. "Now, spread yourself open for me."

Instead of her hand going directly between her legs, she put on a show for him. She started from her shoulders and slowly glided her finger down, teasing her own nipples along the way. He massaged himself through his pants, a primal sound rumbling in his chest.

Her hands continued their descent. When she spread her glistening lips, she dipped the tip of her finger inside herself, pulled it out and circled her wet index finger around her bead.

Roth intervened. "No. That's all mine."

"But I want you to watch me come."

"I want to make you come."

With that, he leaned forward, hooked his arms under her thighs and pulled her heat to him. Tressa's cries tore through the room the second his mouth touched her. He twirled his tongue around her clit, savoring the divine taste of her essence. Tressa held his head in place with her hands and ground against him.

"Roth..."

Her labored breathing told him she was close to exploding. When he suckled her clit, she fell apart. She slapped her hands against the table, her nails dragging across the fabric. Her back arched and her body bucked. He didn't pull away until Tressa's body had relaxed. In a flash, he was out of his clothes and into a condom. Joining Tressa, he rested her legs on his shoulders, leaned forward and drove inside her.

"Yes!" she cried out over and over again.

Roth delivered powerful thrusts, one after the other. Tressa screamed, cried, stuttered his name. Her nails dug into the backs of his arms, but the pain didn't hinder his performance. Hell, she could have ripped out a chunk of his flesh and he wouldn't have stopped, couldn't have stopped. Her wetness, her warmth, held him captive.

"I love you," he said. Why he'd said it at this particular time, he didn't know. But it felt like it needed to be said at that moment. Tressa tried to say something, but he crushed his mouth to hers. His words were the last ones he wanted her to hear before she plunged into ecstasy.

A beat later Tressa pulsed around him as an orgasm claimed her. Her cries were captured by his mouth.

Her body shook under him. The more she pulsated, the closer he came to his own release.

There wasn't an image on the face of the earth that could keep him from tipping over the edge. He wanted this too badly. But he tried to stave off the impending release, imagining shit like a cuddly koala bear nibbling on a leaf, a giraffe urging its calf on wobbly legs, even an orange-and-white-spotted koi fish eating its meal.

Nothing helped.

The orgasm slammed into him like an out-of-control semitruck. He roared like a lion declaring war on a territory invader. Pumping until he couldn't muster another damn stroke, he collapsed down next to Tressa and pulled her into his shaky arms.

Once his breathing calmed, and he regained the ability to speak, he said, "I need you to trust me, Tressa. And I need to be able to trust you. This can't work if either of those major components aren't in place."

Tressa came up onto her elbow and eyed him quizzically. He answered before the question escaped.

"You lied straight to my face, baby. I get why you thought you had to, but I need honesty, Tressa. I've been lied to my entire life. I need the woman I love to love me enough to always be truthful with me, no matter how much it might hurt. I need that."

Tressa slowly nodded. "And I'll give that to you."

It would be one of the best gifts he'd ever been given.

Chapter 16

Tressa lounged on the white leather sofa in the VIP section of The Underground. The place hadn't changed since the last time she'd been there. She remembered several months back and cringed. Though the night of her engagement party had ended in disaster, something much more beautiful had emerged.

Her gaze sought Roth on the stage. Damn, he was sexy as hell when he played that sax. Obviously, she wasn't the only one who thought so. Every woman in the place seemed drawn to the mesmerizing sound of his instrument, but Tressa noted one in particular.

Her eyes narrowed on the exotic-looking beauty in the very revealing emerald green cocktail dress. All night the woman had seemed more captivated with Roth personally than his playing abilities.

She'd never been the jealous type, but a ping of resentment prickled her skin. Dismissing the woman as simply an adoring fan, she trained her gaze on Roth again. A rush of heated desire coursed through her. Damn, she couldn't wait to get him naked. She bit at the corner of her lip. The black fedora could stay.

As if he'd sensed her undressing him with her eyes, he glanced in her direction. Their gazes met and held. Something sparked in his eyes that needed no translation. Longing. Clearly, she wasn't the only one with sinful things on her mind. The man had turned her into a sex piranha. She nibbled on him any chance she got.

Roth ambled down the stage stairs and cut his way through the sea of two- and four-top tables until he stood directly in front of her. He serenaded her and, boy, did he do his thing.

Every note that escaped from his saxophone danced through the air and crash-landed directly in her heart. Just as if it were his touch, she could feel the passion in his music. A brilliant smile touched her lips. By his actions, he'd told the entire room one thing…she was his. The enormous gesture filled her with pride.

When Roth finished his soulful melody, he took her hand, guided her to her feet and pressed a gentle kiss to her lips. The entire place erupted in applause.

The band continued to play, drawing the crowd's attention away from them.

"That was beautiful, baby." A tear she could no longer contain escaped her eye. Roth swiped his thumb across her cheek, causing her skin to tingle.

"Don't cry," he said.

"Sorry. Beautiful things make me do that."

"Huh. I've never seen you cry when you look in the

mirror." He kissed her again. "I'll join you shortly. I love you."

Tressa smoothed a hand along his cheek. "I know."

"How?"

"You just played me a love song."

He smirked, then started away.

"And I love you, too," she said.

"Forever." He winked and continued toward the stage, accepting handshakes and compliments.

"Forever," she mumbled to herself.

Tressa escaped to the bathroom to check her makeup. *Not too bad*, she thought, removing the tube of ruby-red lipstick from her clutch to freshen her lips. A toilet flushed behind her and she jerked. She'd assumed she was there alone. A young woman walked out. Gayle, if she remembered the woman's name correctly. She'd been the hostess at the entrance when they'd arrived.

"Hey," the woman said, pumping several squirts of soap into her palm.

"Hello. Gayle, right?"

The woman nodded. "Oh, my God, Roth's performance was amazing. You must feel like a queen."

Actually, she did feel quite regal. "He's a talented musician. And yes, I do feel majestic."

Gayle dried her hands. "Girl, if I had a man who serenaded me, I'd probably have twenty kids."

They shared a laugh.

Tressa and Roth wouldn't be making any babies tonight, but they would definitely be performing some baby-making actions.

"I know India hates the day she let that one slip away. Even if she was too dumb to recognize what she had, as she put it."

The words snagged Tressa's complete attention. *India? Who in the hell was...* "India?"

"India Breemer. She owns The Underground," Gayle said as if Tressa should have known this. "I'm surprised the two of you haven't met."

Not as surprised as she was by these revelations.

Gayle shrugged. "Well, she has been traveling a bit lately." She checked her watch. "Uh-oh. I better get back on the floor before India notices I've been gone more than five minutes." Gayle laughed. "She may look all gentle in that green dress, but she's a queen cobra in disguise."

Tressa forced a bye as Gayle exited the room.

Green dress? A knot looped and tightened in her stomach. The woman who'd taken so much interest in them—*him*, she corrected—was Roth's ex. Why hadn't he mentioned any of this to her? Why hadn't he told her he played at the exact same club owned by his ex? *His ex.* An ex who *clearly* still had a thing for him. He'd had plenty of opportunities, including on the drive here.

She shook her head, never recalling Roth ever uttering India's name. Her first instinct was to stalk out of that bathroom, stroll right up to India, stick her hand out and introduce herself. "Hi, I'm Tressa Washington, Roth's girlfriend." Then stick her tongue out for good measure.

Tressa laughed at her own childishness. There was no need to go that route. Heck, after Roth's performance, Tressa was sure everyone in attendance knew she and Roth were more than just friends. That put her a bit at ease.

Still, why hadn't he told her? This kind of information should have come from him, especially when he was all about being completely honest. She scrutinized the red-and-black era-specific decor inside the posh room. *This damn club.* She shook her head. *This damned club is a curse.*

Roth stored his saxophone in the case, then snapped it shut. Now that his set was over, he could concentrate all of his focus and attention on his sexy muse. He stirred below the waist when he summoned an image of Tressa in that off-the-shoulder wine-colored dress. Yeah, he planned to drink her up tonight.

Judging by the expression on her face when he'd played for her, she'd loved every second of his attention. He loved seeing her smile, especially if he was the one putting the smile on her face.

"Now I guess I know why I never received the text containing directions to your cabin."

Shit. He turned to see India standing behind him. The form-fitting, low-cut dress she wore should have done something to him, but it didn't. Yeah, Tressa had ruined him. And he was okay with that.

Roth's spontaneous decision to invite India to his cabin had been a result of desperation. That night—the night of Tressa's engagement party—he'd needed something to take his mind off the fact that Tressa would never be his. He recalled his foolish words to India. *If I text you the address to my cabin, would you show up?* Her answer had been a sultry, "I'll be waiting." Inwardly, he chastised himself for having been so damn brainless.

"She's beautiful," India said. "Is it serious?"

He nodded. "Yeah, it is."

India's face lit into a bright smile. "Congratulations."

She draped her arms around his neck. "I'm happy for you."

When her glittered lips pressed against the side of his neck, he snatched away and held her at arm's length. "No."

India smirked. "I'm just making sure." She winked and sashayed from the room.

Grabbing up a hand towel, Roth scrubbed at the side of his neck, making sure there was no remnant of India's lipstick remaining. Satisfied with the results, he left the room to join Tressa. As irrelevant as it was, he should probably mention his past with India. He hadn't before because the past was the past, right? But now, he didn't want to feel as if he were keeping anything from Tressa.

Before Roth could escape from the back, Gayle stopped him in the hallway.

Gayle bit at the corner of her lip as if she dreaded whatever she needed to say. "I may have got you in hot water. I'm sorry."

His brows bunched. "Hot water with whom?"

"Tressa," she said hesitantly. "I was chatting with her in the bathroom and may have mentioned India." She rested her hands on either side of her face. "I'm sorry, Roth. It never dawned on me that she didn't know about the two of you."

"Thank you for letting me know, Gayle."

She apologized again, then hurried off.

Roth could read Tressa well enough to know what she'd learned about him and India bothered her, because this was not the jovial woman he'd walked away from several minutes ago. Easing down beside her on the leather sofa, he captured her hand and kissed the in-

side of her wrist. "What's wrong?" he asked, fishing to
see if she'd tell him about her conversation with Gayle.

"Nothing."

"Dance with me, beautiful."

"Roth, I don't really feel—"

"Please." He kissed her wrist several more times.
"Pretty please."

Tressa sighed. "One song."

If she was only giving him one song, he'd better
make it a good one. On the way to the dance floor, he
whispered to Ernest—one of the guys on stage. The
man gave him a nod.

"What did you say to him?" Tressa asked.

Enveloping her in his arms, he flashed a half smile.
"I told him I needed a special song for a very special
woman. I dedicate this song to you."

A moment later the band performed John Coltrane
and Johnny Hartman's "My One and Only Love."

They swayed to the soothing melody. When Ernest's
regal baritone voice poured through the room, Tressa
relaxed in his arms. Roth had to give it to Ernest; he
could melt ice when he crooned. The man could sing
his ass off, really sing. Not any of this new age stuff
you could barely decipher from shrieking.

Roth and Tressa never broke eye contact.

While he'd been lost in her dancing brown eyes
plenty of times before, this time was different. He was
swimming in her soul and experiencing all the effects
of being there. Giving her the opportunity to come clean
with him, he said, "You want to tell me what's going
on?"

"Maybe you should tell me, Roth. I know about you
and India. What I don't know is why I had to hear it

from someone else. It feels like you're trying to hide something."

"Tressa…" he said coolly, "India and I happened a long time ago. I'm not trying to hide anything from you. I honestly didn't think my past—which is exactly what it is, the past—with her was all that relevant. Any interaction we have is *strictly, strictly*," he repeated, "business." Except for the part where he'd invited her to his cabin in a moment of despair. But he had sense enough to keep that to himself.

"Is the fact that she's still in love with you irrelevant, as well?"

Roth threw his head back in a laugh. "Baby, now you're being ridiculous. India and I haven't been a couple in, what, five years."

"Is she the one who hurt you?"

He eyed her but didn't respond.

"I thought so. I've seen the way she looks at you, Roth. You may be blind to the fact, but she still has a thing for you. I'm a woman. I know the signs, and hers is a flashing big-ass green neon light."

"And I have a thing for you," he said, hoping to deviate from this topic. If India still *had a thing for him*, he didn't care. Nor was it any of his business. Tressa was his business. The only person's feelings he could control was his own. And all his feelings were wrapped up in Tressa. "Do the signs show you how much I love you?" He nuzzled her neck. "What color is that big-ass neon sign?"

Still stone-faced, Tressa rolled her eyes at him.

Placing a finger under her chin, he turned her head back to him. "Do you trust me, baby?"

"Yes, but I don't trust her."

"And you don't have to. Your trust should be with me, not her." He captured her hand and placed it over his beating heart. "Do you feel that, woman?" he asked, his expression serious.

"Yes," she said, some of the bite gone from her tone.

"Every beat belongs to you and you alone, Tressa Washington. Every woman in this building could strip naked right now and throw themselves at me, and I would throw them all back. Why? Because I'm not going to do shit to jeopardize what we have. You're the best thing that has *ever* happened to me, woman. The very best thing."

Tressa blinked rapidly, but it didn't keep the tears from falling. For the second time that night, he swiped a thumb across her cheeks.

"You keep messing up my makeup."

"If it all ran down your face, you'd still be the most beautiful woman in here."

"Flirt," she said with a lazy smile.

"Are we okay? Really okay?"

Tressa studied him for a moment, then nodded. "We're really okay."

He tilted her head back and kissed her tenderly. "Good."

Chapter 17

Tressa sat alone at one of the two tables inside the nurses' lounge, forking at the now-wilted lettuce in the bowl in front of her. Pushing the grilled-chicken salad away, she cursed the thoughts that tortured her. Two weeks had passed since she'd learned about Roth and India's past, and it'd been all she could think about—*obsess over*, she corrected.

Though she'd told Roth his continuing to play at The Underground didn't bother her, it did. It bothered her a lot. When in the hell had she become so damn insecure? The answer came quickly—when her ex's mistress crashed their engagement party, and at the same club owned by Roth's ex.

A thousand times she'd reminded herself that Roth was absolutely nothing like Cyrus, and she believed it. Still, she couldn't stop thinking, *What if?* Yes, she trusted Roth, but this had nothing to do with trust and everything to do with the idea of history repeating itself. Tressa recalled the things Roth had said to her that night in the club and smiled, the memory lightening her heavy thoughts. Roth was a good man. She had nothing to worry about.

Tressa hadn't asked for any details about his and India's history—and he hadn't offered any—but she remembered their conversation from the cabin. They hadn't been right for each other and she'd cheated on him. He'd never mentioned they'd remained friends.

Then it hit her.

Could her true issue be the fact that Roth hadn't offered to stop playing at The Underground? She wouldn't have let him, but shouldn't he have at least offered?

The door swung open, and Vivian sauntered in. "I am not going to miss these crazy hours," she said, dropping into the chair opposite Tressa.

Vivian had decided to resign from her position at Tender Hearts Memorial Hospital to focus more of her time on the project her husband, Alonso, was developing downtown geared at helping the homeless and disenfranchised. She was going to miss working with her best friend, but Tressa truly understood and supported Vivian's decision.

Vivian's eyes slid to the discarded salad, then slid to Tressa. "Everything okay? You usually don't let food go to waste."

They laughed.

Sobering, Tressa said, "Should I feel some kind of way about Roth not offering to quit playing at The Underground?"

"I don't—"

"He didn't even say, 'I'll find another club to play at, because I know it bothers you that India is my ex.'" Saying it aloud, Tressa accepted how selfish she sounded, but wasn't she making a genuine point?

"Why do—"

"I mean, he didn't even take my feelings into consideration by not offering to leave. But really, why should he? He's been playing there far longer than we've been dating. Why should he alter his life for me?"

"It really—"

"But isn't that what people do for love? Make sacrifices?" *Ugh.* She buried her face in her hands. "What is wrong with me? I've never been this weak."

"Take a breath, Tress. You're not weak, you're in love, ladybug."

Tressa didn't dispute Vivian's words.

"You should talk to Roth. He'll respect your concerns. That man loves the hell out of you."

A slow smile curled Tressa's lips. "I've never loved any man the way I love Roth. It's like this beautiful, pleasurable, terrifying plane ride. At times I desperately want to plant my feet on the ground. But at others, I love how he makes me feel like I'm flying, soaring so high in the clouds I feel like I'm in heaven. The way I love him scares me, Vi. I can feel him in my soul. He's brought so much joy, so much happiness into my life. I can see myself spending the rest of my life with him."

"I wish you could see your face right now. You are glowing." Vivian narrowed her eyes at her. "Are you pregnant?"

Tressa tossed a balled-up napkin at her. "No." However, the idea of her stomach swelled with Roth's child—his children, as many as he wanted—wasn't a bad one.

"You're afraid because of what happened with Cyrus, but you can't let fear dictate your steps. I believe you told me something similar once." Vivian smiled, then continued, "I read something once that said sometimes the greatest love of your life comes after the biggest mistake of your life. Would you agree Cyrus was the biggest mistake of your life?"

"Oh, yeah. Without a doubt."

"Then that means Roth is the greatest love of your life." Vivian took Tressa's hand. "I've noticed such an amazing change in you, Tress. Every single day you walk through that door confident and sure. I hadn't seen you that way in a long while. Trust me, I know loving someone with everything inside you is daunting as hell, but do it anyway. It's so worth it."

Tressa released a heavy sigh, allowing her worries to escape with the warm air. Vivian was right. Love— this kind of love—was worth it.

Roth and Alonso sat at the round conference table inside Alonso's office, neither uttering a word. Roth drummed his fingers over the polished wood as if he was playing his sax, even humming a melody in his head. John Coltrane and Johnny Hartman's "My One and Only Love." So fitting. Alonso spoke, pulling him from his thoughts of what he'd done.

"Tell me again what happened."

A sly grin spread across Alonso's face, then he laughed. Well, who could blame him? The story was so damn bizarre, it was hilarious. One minute he'd been sitting behind his own desk, in his own office, the next… His gaze fell back to the shiny black ring box placed in the middle of the table. "I went inside the jewelry store to purchase Tressa a cross necklace—"

"And you came out with a mammoth-size rock."

Alonso laughed and so did he. "Man, I swear to God that ring called my name. The next thing I know…" He pointed to the five-carat emerald-cut diamond ring. "I'm walking out with that and without a single regret in the world."

"Well, I for one had no doubt you were going to make Tressa your wife. The two of you are meant for each other. I don't think I've ever seen you happier than when you are with her. You know I support this 100 percent. I'm happy for you, man."

Alonso stood and Roth followed suit. After exchanging a brotherly hug, they both dropped back into their seats.

"So when are you going to pop the question?"

Roth ran his hand over his head. "I was going to do it tonight, but decided to wait until this weekend. I want it to be special, something memorable. She deserves that."

"Are you doing it at the club?"

"Hell, no," Roth said. "Tressa would say no for sure. She's convinced that place is a jinx." And could anyone blame her? But he was about to leave her with at least one good thought of the place. "You guys should come out for the show on Saturday. It'll be my last."

Alonso's head jerked back in what Roth took to be surprise. "What? You're leaving The Underground?"

Yeah, he couldn't believe it either, but it was time. "Tressa says she's okay with me being there, but I can tell it bothers her. And honestly, if the shoe was on the other foot, I might be a little leery about her working so closely with her ex, too. I know she trusts me, but I don't want to give her any reason to worry." The fact that India had started acting oddly after seeing him and Tressa at the club had been another reason, but he didn't mention that one. After Saturday, it would no longer be an issue.

"Are you going to play elsewhere?" Alonso asked.

He'd contemplated it but decided he'd much rather spend his free time with Tressa. "Nah. I'm going to chill for a while."

"Speaking of exes. Whatever happened with that situation with Tressa's?"

Roth shrugged. "Strangest thing. He left her a voice mail message apologizing profusely for manhandling her at the hospital, then said he was moving out of state and that he wished her the best."

Alonso barked a laugh. "Did you have anything to do with his decision to flee the state?"

Roth sat back in his chair and crossed an ankle over his leg. "Come on, man. Tressa forbade me to confront that slimy bastard."

"Uh-huh. What did you do?"

Alonso knew him too damn well. "I may have contacted him to say I would ruin his career and his life, if he ever contacted Tressa again."

Alonso gave a knowing smirk.

And they left it at that.

Alonso fell back against his chair and intertwined his fingers behind his head. "We've come a long way, man. We got lucky. I think about all the shit we've been through…" His words trailed off. "We're two blessed brothers. Good—scratch that—*great* women. Love.

Happiness. Success. We did it. Just like you always said we would."

Yep, he had said it, over and over again. Believing life had far more to offer was what had got him this far. He couldn't agree with Alonso more; they were blessed and happy and in love with great women. And soon, he would ask his muse, his lover, his heartbeat, to be his wife.

Yeah, life was good. He eyed the ring box. And it would only get better.

Chapter 18

By the time Saturday rolled around, Roth's nerves were shot, so much so he'd walked out of the damn house and forgotten Juliette—his tenor sax. The one thing he hadn't left behind, the black ring box. In less than two hours, he planned to lower to one knee and ask Tressa to spend the rest of her life with him.

A tiny voice whispered, *Will she say yes?*

Confident, Roth answered with a swelled chest. Of course she was going to say yes. Why wouldn't she? If he wasn't sure of anything else, he was sure Tressa loved him. A second later he frowned. But what if…

Roth shook the negative thoughts away, but somehow they fluttered right back. Her last engagement hadn't exactly gone off without a hitch. What if she'd decided marriage wasn't for her? What if he proposed and she said no? What then?

Arriving at The Underground, Roth pulled into a space in the back lot. The same space he'd occupied the night he'd discovered Tressa in the back of his SUV. The night that had patterned his feet on this glorious journey toward love. This had to be a good sign, right?

Of course it was.

So why did he have that nagging feeling?

Roth considered calling Tressa to make sure she hadn't got held up at work or, worse, changed her mind about meeting him there. This wasn't exactly her favorite place. Just to see the look of surprise on her beautiful face, he needed her there to hear his announcement that tonight would be his last performance.

If she didn't show, it would definitely put a hitch in his arrangements. He'd have to scrap the plan to propose on a carriage ride through downtown. It didn't matter where he proposed. All he knew was he had to do it tonight. He couldn't wait another moment.

As if he'd sent some kind of vibration across town to Tender Hearts Memorial Hospital, his phone rang, Tressa's name flashing across the screen. Actually, the words *My Queen* scrolled across the screen, because that was what she was to him, his queen. "Hey, beautiful."

"Hey, handsome. I only have a second."

Alarmed, Roth said, "I hope you're not calling to stand me up, because that would really suck." *Really suck*, he repeated to himself.

"No, but I may be late. Thirty minutes, an hour tops. I'm sorry." Her words dripped with regret.

"Is everything okay?"

"Yes, just a madhouse here. Full moon. I gotta go.

Love you to pieces and I'll make my tardiness up to you in countless sinful ways."

"I'm definitely going to hold you to that. Love you, too." And tonight she'd know just how much.

Tressa had some hell of apologizing to do. Her one hour, *tops*, had stretched into two. And of course she'd missed Roth's performance. Inside, she squinted and scanned the room for him, but he was nowhere in sight. He was there because his SUV was still parked out back. Plus, he wouldn't have left without calling to tell her. If there was one thing her man was, it was considerate.

A swamped Gayle, the hostess she'd met her last visit there, pointed her toward the back of the building. "Try the back. I saw him walk that way earlier," she said, then bustled away. "Oh," she called back, "tell him I said I'm really going to miss our old-school R & B chats."

"Going to miss—" Gayle was off before Tressa could finish her thought. Was Gayle leaving The Underground? Probably so. She'd got the impression the woman didn't care very much for India.

India.

Just the thought of her name grated Tressa's nerves. Pushing the raw feeling aside, she headed in the direction she'd been pointed.

The sconces affixed to the beige walls provided minimal lighting along the hallway. Fortunately, Tressa didn't need any illumination to locate Roth; she simply followed the boom of his elevated tone. And he sounded pissed.

Approaching the partially opened door, she reached

for the handle, but froze when she heard a woman's voice.

"You are full of shit, Roth."

Her tone was just as heated as Roth's had been.

"I don't owe you shit, India."

India? Tressa's eyes narrowed as if she was trying to see through the door. What in the hell were they arguing about? A lover's quarrel came to mind, but she debunked the term.

"But why, Roth? Why now? Was it the kiss?"

The air vacated from Tressa's lungs. Had they kissed? Her heartbeat kicked up a notch or two and her breathing grew ragged. She wanted to burst through the door right then, but her need to hear more was greater.

"When I was in jeopardy of losing this place, it was your performances that saved it. We built this place together, Roth. We're a team. Now what? You're going to walk out on me? Just like that? No notice, no explanation, no nothing? Just some tonight-will-be-my-last-performance bullshit announcement you made to the entire club without having the decency to let me know first."

Tressa rested a hand on her trembling stomach. Roth was leaving The Underground? India's tone softened to a pitch that could be considered seductive, and rage shot through Tressa. Still, she held a level head.

"We're good together, Roth. You know we are."

For whatever they'd shared to be in the past, Roth and India sounded mighty cozy. Tressa's cheek burned with outrage with the possibility that she'd been played for a fool. Again. Now she really wanted to explode into the room, but her heavy feet were rooted to the tile floor, making her unable to crash their party or flee the building. The urge to do both overwhelmed her.

"I'm sorry, India."

Roth's tone sounded sympathetic, as if in some way he regretted what he was doing.

India continued, "You can't leave."

Roth's tone sounded exhausted when he said, "What do you want from me, India? What the hell do you want from me?"

"Everything. I love you. I never stopped loving you, Roth. After all these years. I want you to admit you still have feelings for me, too."

Tressa's stomach knotted as she waited for a response from Roth. Did his silence mean he still loved India or that he didn't feel the question warranted a response?

When he finally spoke, his tone lacked sentiment. "I don't love you and haven't for a long time. We had our chance. It just wasn't meant for us."

When India spoke again, her tone was crammed full of emotion, and Tressa was almost certain she was crying.

"Then why in the hell did you invite me to spend the weekend with you at your cabin a few months ago? Was it just about sex?" she spat.

Tressa's brows furrowed. *Invited her to his cabin?* India had been the woman… Her chest grew heavy and bile burned the back of her throat.

A beat or two of silence lingered before Roth said, "Yes, it was."

"You liar. Do you think I don't see how you look at me when I walk past? Do you think I don't know what ran through your mind when I undressed in front of you earlier?" Her tone grew soft again. "You wanted me then, Roth, and I know you want me now."

Instead of Roth refuting the claim, he said, "Goodbye, India. Have a great life."

The door flung open with so much force, Tressa flinched. Her lips parted, but nothing would escape. She dragged a hand across her cheek.

"Tressa?" Roth's hard expression melted to one of shock.

Sure of the questions racing through his mind, she said, "I heard everything. I—" The words snagged in her throat. "I have to go. I…"

She closed her eyes briefly to subdue the queasiness she was feeling. When Roth touched her, she shoved his hand away. Forcing her feet to move, she took several clumsy steps back until she bumped into the wall, then made haste down the corridor.

As she fled, Tressa felt like she was in one of those fun houses at a carnival. Everything ran together into a hazy blob of shapes and colors. Her head spun, forcing her to stop and rest her hand against the wall to regain her equilibrium.

"Baby—"

Standing behind her, Roth rested his hands on her waist, preventing her from getting away. She lacked the energy needed to push him away. "You lied to me, Roth. Everything was a lie," she said more to herself than to him. "You told me there was nothing between the two of you, that I could trust you with my heart, that I would never regret falling in love with you." Tears clouded her eyes. "You lied, because I regret it plenty."

"Please don't say that, Tressa. Please." He kissed the

back of her head several times. "I never lied to you. I swear, there's nothing—"

Needing to look into his eyes, she turned toward him. "Did you invite her to your cabin for sex?"

"Just listen, baby, please. I—"

"Did you invite her to your cabin for sex, Roth?" Tressa spewed the words like venom.

Defeat danced in Roth's eyes. "Yes."

"Then there's something."

Tressa's gaze slid past Roth and leveled on India propped against the door frame, watching them like her favorite sitcom. For a brief second Tressa considered barreling down the hall to knock that condescending smirk right off her face. But what would be the point?

"Can we talk?" Roth said.

Drawing her attention back to him, Tressa refocused on the visibly exhausted man in front of her, the man she loved, the man who'd changed, rocked and shattered her world. "No."

Chapter 19

Instead of immediately leaving the community center where he taught saxophone lessons to disadvantaged kids, Roth stood with his arms folded across his chest, staring out the fogged-up window. The darkness outside mirrored his soul. A single ray of light hadn't penetrated through him since… He refused to even give life to what had happened several days ago at The Underground.

By giving Tressa her space, he hoped she'd realize how ridiculous she was being. Yes, what she'd heard was bad, really bad; he'd be the first to admit that, but she'd refused to even give him the opportunity to explain. She'd simply jumped to conclusions.

Waiting for her to come to her senses, he'd gone through a myriad of emotions. Today he'd welcomed anger. *How in the hell could she believe I'd ever do any-*

thing to hurt her? Roth sighed heavily. Watching that woman walk away from him had been like watching an alligator gnaw off your leg and not doing anything to stop it because you had no idea what to do.

Dammit, you should have done something.

"Mr. L?"

"Yes!" *Damn.* Roth massaged his temple, took a deep breath, then turned toward a stunned-faced Sebastian, one of the kids in his class. "I didn't mean to snap at you, Sebastian. I apologize."

Sebastian ambled toward him, his hands tucked inside his tattered jean pockets. The ten-year-old was as timid as an abused puppy, but Roth saw something in the kid. Maybe a little of himself at that age. Roth had quickly outgrown his timid stage. Maybe Sebastian would, too.

"What's up, man?"

Sebastian lowered his head, lifted it, then lowered it again. "I wanted to make sure you were okay." He dug the tip of his worn tennis shoe into the scuffed industrial tile, his gaze never meeting Roth's. "You always tell us to practice, practice, practice at the end of each class, but you didn't say that tonight. You say it after every class. And before dismissing us, you always make us say, 'We're strong black men, and we matter.' You didn't do that, either."

Roth chuckled. *Damn.* He guessed he had been a little off tonight. Sebastian paid attention to everything, so it didn't surprise him that the inquisitive boy had picked up on his turmoil.

"So, is everything okay?" Sebastian asked. "You're not leaving us, are you?" He finally glanced up, pushing his wire-framed glasses up his nose.

The kid reminded Roth of a young philosopher. With the right guidance, he would do great things. Adjusting his mood, Roth said, "Dude, no, I'm not leaving you guys. You know how much I love teaching you knuckleheads how to play. Even though I think the only reason most of you come is for the pizza on Thursdays."

Sebastian lowered his head, but Roth could see the smile that played on his lips. Every young man who participated in Roth's twelve-week-long academies were required to sign a pledge to take their lessons seriously. While each Tuesday and Thursday they showed up faithfully, he suspected the reward was what kept most of them so dedicated.

But he didn't care what it took to get them through the door. If they were in class with him, they weren't out in the streets causing or getting into trouble.

Then there were the two or three he had like Sebastian, who truly enjoyed learning to read music and play the saxophone. Their eagerness alone made this all worth it.

Roth placed a hand on Sebastian's shoulder and jostled him playfully. "I apologize for straying away from routine. I'll have it together by Thursday. I promise. Thank you for keeping me on my toes, man. I owe you."

"My dad stopped doing things he used to do right before he left me and my mom." Sebastian shrugged a scrawny shoulder. "I don't want you to leave, Mr. L. You're a great teacher and you don't treat us like kids. Plus, you buy us pizza." He smiled, revealing a missing bottom tooth.

"Don't worry. I'm not going anywhere," Roth said.

Sebastian's words hit home. If nothing else, Roth

understood abandonment. He would never do that to his boys. Or someone he loved.

For the past week Tressa had hidden her pain behind forced smiles and work. Still, no matter how brilliantly she smiled or how many hours she strolled the halls of Tender Hearts Memorial Hospital, Roth eventually invaded her thoughts. And when that happened, her heart shattered all over again.

Vivian grabbed another mozzarella stick off the table and crunched into it, drawing Tressa's attention. Tressa smiled at her best friend opposite her on the couch, who'd arrived at her place an hour ago with an overnight bag and comfort food: mozzarella sticks, chicken wings, pizza, garlic knots, fried ravioli and vanilla ice cream to wash it all down.

"You do know I'm trying to lose a couple of pounds, not gain," Tressa said, reaching for another one of the meat-filled ravioli and popping it into her mouth. She'd start fresh tomorrow.

Vivian grabbed another piece of pizza. "Tonight, calories don't count."

They shared a laugh.

Tressa appreciated what her friend was doing, but it wasn't necessary. "You don't have to babysit me, Vi. You're a married woman. You should be home with your husband."

"I want to be here. Alonso won't be home till late. He's supposed to be meeting Ro—" Vivian stopped abruptly.

"You can say his name. I won't go ballistic." Though she might just burst out crying. It truly could go either way.

To think a few weeks ago she'd been the happiest woman alive. Now look at her, wrapped in a blanket on her couch stuffing her face with food. *Pitiful.* Happiness was clearly reserved for individuals who didn't let the likes of love get in their way. *Love.* She growled at the low-down, trifling emotion that had brought her far too much pain.

"You know what's funny, Vi? I really thought this was it. I really thought I'd get my happy-ever-after. I thought Roth was the one." Her voice cracked with unintended emotion.

"Roth *is* the one."

Did Vivian not recall all the things she'd told her, all the things she'd overheard that night, backstage at the club? How could she still believe in Roth? Tressa blew out a heavy sigh, choosing not to address Vivian's words. "I'm done."

Vivian eyed her quizzically. "Done with what?"

"Love, men, relationships. I'm done with it all. Obviously, this is a sign I'm meant to be alone."

Vivian barked a humorless laugh. "You don't mean that, Tress."

Yes, she did. "I trusted him, Vi. I trusted every kiss, every touch, every intimate moment I shared with him. I trusted him." She shook her head. "I should have known better. I know the games men are capable of playing. I just never thought Roth—" She stopped at the onset of emotions she felt. No way would she cry. *No. Damn. Way.* Her head tilted back against the cushion. "I'm done."

"I can't believe what I'm hearing. From *you*, of all people. You are the freaking ambassador for all things love."

"Maybe once. Not anymore."

Vivian sat up ramrod straight. "When I foolishly wanted to run from Alonso, it was you who gave me a swift kick in the ass and brought me to my senses."

"And I'm happy for what you and Alonso have, Vi, but I'm beginning to think love is just not meant for me."

"So you're just going to give up?"

Tressa folded her arms like a defiant child. "Yes."

"The Tressa *I* know wouldn't just bow down and take it. She would fight for what she loved, *who* she loved. And trust me, I *know* you love Roth just as much as he loves you. And another thing, you may be *done with love*—" she made air quotes "—but love is not done with you."

Tressa eyed her best friend. Why in the hell was Vivian so distraught? She was the one going through the perils of love.

Tressa ached to stress just how wrong she thought Vivian was. But since Vivian was clearly the new poster child for love, Tressa kept her comments to herself. And just for the record, she wasn't giving up; she was giving in. Love had taken her through too damn much.

No, she didn't care what anyone said. She was done with love.

Chapter 20

Roth had thrown himself into his work—arriving at the office at the crack of dawn, not leaving until pitch dark. Why? Because designing a new aircraft was the only thing that kept him half-sane and his mind off Tressa. That and playing the sax, but somehow, playing always brought his thoughts back to her.

When his cell phone rang, he tossed a glance at the clock. *Eight. Shit.* He was late. Taking the call from Alonso, he said, "I lost track of time. I'm on the way."

Alonso rattled off something about it being packed and he'd go ahead and grab a table. Ending the call, Roth logged off his computer before midnight for the first time in days, gathered his belongings and headed out to meet Alonso—who would undoubtedly spend the evening trying to cheer him up. Why? Because that was what best friends did for each other.

A half hour later Roth sat inside the Flaming Arrow Bar and Grille, nursing a glass of top-shelf bourbon. Conversation swirled around him, people happy and celebrating life. He envied them, because at this moment his life was shit. Without Tressa, his…life…was…shit. He was man enough to admit that.

So why in the hell hadn't he done anything about it?

Scanning the room, his eyes lingered on blissful couples hugged up in booths, whispering sweet nothings to each other. He saw people on their way to being happy couples, offering enduring gestures in hopes of solidifying their positions in each other's lives. Then there were the individuals obviously searching for that love connection, exchanging interested glances and warm smiles. Lastly, the handful clearly looking for just an evening with no commitment.

Him, in a past life.

Roth grumbled and damned everyone around him for carrying on with their lives while his life was falling apart around him. What had love done to him? And why had he allowed Alonso to talk him into coming here against this backdrop of happiness?

Alonso claimed another one of the habanero wings from the platter. "Have you called her?"

After giving her some time to come to her senses—which hadn't happened—he'd decided to help her along by reaching out. She'd shunned him like a leper. "A hundred times. I feel like a stalker." He took a swig from his glass. "She hasn't blocked me yet. I guess that's a good sign."

"She will come around," Alonso said.

Roth wasn't so sure about his friend's optimism. The anger he'd suppressed came back with a vengeance.

"Why in the hell am I sitting around, moping? I haven't done anything. I never touched India. If Tressa can't trust me, then maybe..." His heart wouldn't allow him to complete the sentence.

"Tressa loves you, Ro. She's just hurting. Give her time to sort all her feelings. She will come around."

"Yeah, well, I'm hurting, too. She tossed me away, man. She tossed me away just like every other—" Stopping abruptly, he finished the contents of his glass and motioned to the waitress for a refill. Enough of this feeling-sorry-for-himself bull. "I'm good. How do I even know it's worth it anyway?"

Alonso pushed his plate away and wiped his hands. "What if Tressa walked in with another man right now?"

Alonso's words ignited an inferno inside Roth, and lava flowed through his veins. His jaw clenched so tightly he thought the bones would shatter. The mere suggestion of another man getting any of Tressa's time caused him to see red.

Alonso jabbed a finger at him. "That reaction, my friend, is how you know it's worth it."

Roth's brow furrowed.

Alonso barked a single laugh. "You looked like you were ready to kill over a woman who hasn't spoken to you in over a week. That's love, man. And love is always worth it."

Roth's heart rate slowly decreased. He massaged the tension from the back of his neck. "Could you have thought of another way to make your point?"

Alonso flashed his palms. "Hey, I did what I had to do. You were there for me when I had given up any hope of getting Vivian back. You had my back. Now it's time for me to repay the favor."

Alonso clapped Roth on the shoulder. Roth couldn't be mad at his best friend for getting his blood boiling. That's what true friends did. They said and did whatever they needed to do to keep each other from making devastating mistakes.

"Thank you, man," Roth said.

"My pleasure. Now, let's strategize on how you're going to get your woman back."

There was no need. Roth knew exactly what he needed to do.

Tressa rolled her head to the side to glance at the clock sitting on her nightstand. Four o'clock. In two hours she had to be up, bright eyed and bushy tailed. Unfortunately, she wouldn't be either. She'd be surprised if she'd got four full days' worth of sleep total in the past two weeks. One thing was for sure; she couldn't keep going like this.

Her eyes landed on the black tourmaline on the nightstand, and she thought about Roth. He hadn't had a nightmare since she'd given him the crystals. She'd attributed it to the tourmaline; he'd attributed it to her. Recalling how grateful he'd been by her gesture warmed her, along with words he'd said. *Woman, you're the answer to my unspoken prayers.* The amount of compassion that had glowed in his eyes…

Tressa swallowed down the building emotions. She hated to admit it, but she missed Roth like hell. The way he touched her—as if she were a rare stone. The way he kissed her—with so much intensity it left her breathless. The way he made love to her—as if he was giving her chunks of his soul.

Tressa pinched her eyes together to fend off her tears. Her head suggested she needed to get over Roth, but her heart gave other advice; sound advice, she chose to believe. So why was she lying there in bed alone and not beside the man she loved?

Because you are a stubborn fool, Tressa Washington. And it has cost you the best thing that's ever happened to you. A beat later, tears rolled from her eyes.

She cried.

She cried long.

She cried hard.

She cried ugly.

She cried for the pain she'd denied feeling over her loss.

She cried for the many times she'd rejected how much she missed Roth.

She cried for the countless moments she'd told herself she no longer loved him.

She cried for…for the mere fact there had been no laughter in her soul since she'd walked away from him.

She cried until there were no more tears left.

Had losing Roth truly been a sign she deserved to be alone? She certainly believed in signs, especially ones she'd asked for. But she hadn't asked for this. She would have never asked for her heart to be ripped from her chest. She would have never asked for this type of pain.

But had she?

She'd been the one who'd refused him the opportunity to explain. She'd been the one who'd walked away, her hurt overshadowing the guidance of her heart. She'd been the one who'd, for the past few weeks, refused to reach out to him. Had she asked for this?

Two hours later the alarm sounded and Tressa slammed her hand onto the snooze button. She draped her arm over her eyes, cursing the light penetrating her blinds.

It can't be six already.

Dragging herself from the bed, she charged through her morning bathroom routine, then headed for the kitchen to consume a trough of coffee. The fragrant java smell greeted her the second she opened her bedroom door. *Thank God for coffee machines with timers.* The first sip of the strong brew caused a twitch in her lips that would have normally blossomed into a smile.

Today she didn't feel like smiling. Would she ever again? Feel like it or do it?

Leaning against the counter, she steadied the cup between her hands. She just couldn't continue like this. Her job performance was taking a hit and so was her health. Over the past two weeks she'd experienced elevated blood pressure and heart palpitations. She blamed it on sleep deprivation and stress. Her eyes lowered to her mug. Of course, her increased caffeine intake could be a contributor, as well.

Relinquishing the mug, she grabbed her insulated tumbler and filled it to the brim. Checking the time, she grabbed her purse and headed for the door. If she was late again, Ms. Kasetta, the toughest charge nurse in the South, would have her head—and her job, no doubt.

Stopping abruptly, she cursed, veered back to the kitchen and lifted her keys from the hook. "Can't go anywhere without these." Satisfied she hadn't forgotten anything else—like her brain—she hurried out the door.

The second she stepped foot on the porch, Tressa gasped and dropped the tumbler. The top popped off and hot coffee ran everywhere. The mess only fazed her for a millisecond, sending her gaze back to her lawn.

Stunned by the display, her eyes swept her front yard. "What the…" Countless airplanes littered her grass. Stepping over the spilled coffee, she descended the stairs. Her purse slid from her arm and *thunked* to the ground. There was only one person who could have accomplished this. Roth.

Her eyes brushed from one side of the yard to the other. Where was he? Was he still there? Watching her, maybe?

Collecting one of the lavender planes, she unfolded it. Sure enough, a message was scribbled inside, just as she suspected. "Memories are priceless. One of the best ones I have is making snow angels with you." A smile touched her lips. It was one of her best, too.

She lifted another lavender plane. It, too, contained a memory message. "We don't remember days, we remember moments. I'll never forget the exact moment I fell in love with you." Tressa flipped it over, expecting more to be written. Disappointed that there wasn't.

She wanted to know when.

She swallowed hard and blinked back tears. Choosing a white airplane this time, she pulled it apart as if gold coins waited inside for her. This one was a Maya Angelou quote.

"'People will forget—'" Her voice cracked and she recited the rest in her head. The last line, *people will never forget how you made them feel*, was written in all caps. Roth's penned words followed. *You make me feel invincible.*

Tressa clapped her hand over her mouth, a single tear sliding from her eye. *Oh, my God. Oh, my God.*

A red plane caught her eye. Scanning, she realized it was the only red plane there. Moving to the center of the yard to collect it, she took a deep breath before unfolding it. *I promise* was the only thing written. Tressa brows bunched. *I promise?* What did he promise?

Before she got the opportunity to ponder the cryptic message any further, a paper plane soared overhead and landed a foot or two in front of her. She turned urgently, expecting to see Roth standing there. Nothing. Where in the heck was he?

"Roth?"

Her eyes scanned the yard again, even kneeling to look under her vehicle. Bemused, she gave up her search for him and collected the steel blue plane. She gasped, recognition setting in immediately. This was *her* plane, the one she'd crafted at the cabin. She studied her handwritten words—smeared, but somewhat still legible—on the warped piece.

"How—"

"When I first read your words, *he makes me feel like I'm soaring*, I swore I'd do any and everything in my power to always make you feel that way."

The soothing sound of Roth's steady tone caressed her like tiny fingers exploring every inch of her body. Gathering her thoughts, she turned to face him. The sight of him sent a *boom* through her system, reviving every part of her that felt as if it'd died since they'd been apart. For the first time in what she labeled forever, she felt alive again.

Her eyes took in every inch of him. His handsome face, his thick shoulders, the brown short-sleeved shirt he wore, the jeans that hung perfectly from his toned frame, even his all-black tennis shoes. *I've missed you*, she said, but only in her head.

Lifting the plane, she said, "How did you get this?"

"Glen."

Her eyes widened. "It made it to town."

Roth chuckled that beautiful sound she'd missed so much.

"Almost. He came across it when he was searching for his dog who'd run off into the woods. And since I'm the only one known for crafting paper planes, he put two and two together."

Dumb luck or fate. She wasn't sure which, and she didn't care. All that mattered was that it'd brought Roth back to her.

Roth cupped his hands in front of him. "I have something to say. Just listen. Please."

Tressa nodded.

"Baby—" He paused as if he'd suddenly recognized an error he'd made. When he started again, he dropped *baby*. "*Tressa*, I get it. It's not always about what happened. Sometimes it's about perception, appearance. The things you heard… I get it. They were awful and they hurt you. But there are two important things I need for you to know, then I'll leave."

Leave? The word rattled her.

"First, I have never, ever been unfaithful to you. The things you heard…" He shook his head. "I never did anything that would disrespect you. I put that on my life."

"What about the kiss—" The idea of Roth kissing another woman froze the words in her throat.

"She kissed me on the neck. It wasn't provoked, nor

wanted. That's the only time in five years her lips have ever touched me."

So much passion radiated from Roth's words that all she wanted to do was drape her arms around him. But she resisted. "You said you had two things to tell me."

"The second thing… I love you more than life itself. You are my life. I'll never stop fighting for you, for us. Because that's what I do, baby. I fight for what I love, for who I love. I'll never stop fighting. That's my promise to you."

Tressa swallowed hard, her chest aching with emotion. Roth reached up to touch her but abandoned the thought.

"That's all," he said, his voice cracking. "I won't take up any more of your time." He backed away, then turned to leave.

"When—" She took a deep breath, then started again. "When did you know?"

Roth turned slowly. Asking for no reference, no clarification that they were even talking about the same thing, he closed the distance between them. "When you took my hand at the cabin and placed it over your heart. My heartbeat fell in sync with yours at that very moment. And I knew I would love you for the rest of my life. These past two weeks—" he lowered his head as if to hide shame "—let's just say my heartbeat has been irregular."

Tressa thought about her own suffering. She'd contributed her palpitations to sleep deprivation, stress and caffeine. But could it have been from Roth's absence? Could their hearts truly beat in such harmony?

Obviously.

"I owe you an apology, Roth. I was closed-minded

and judgmental. I never gave you the benefit of the doubt or the respect you deserved. I let fear guide me. But that's no excuse for how I treated you. I'm sorry. I'm so sorry. And I would do anything, *anything*, to have you back in my life again." Tressa's heart pounded against her rib cage and tears rolled down her cheek. "I don't deserve a second chance, Roth, and I'm not sure I deserve you, but I want—I *need*—you." She took a deep breath, then continued, "You are that spark that ignites everything good in me. I should have been the one fighting, Roth. I should have been the one fighting for you, for us. I'm fighting now."

This time when Roth reached out to touch her, he didn't pull back and neither did she. When the pads of his thumbs swiped across her skin, she closed her eyes, feeling as if her entire spirit recharged from his touch.

Roth rested his forehead against hers. "I'm lost without you."

"I love you, Roth Lexington. I love you with every cell in my body. Do you forgive me for hurting you? Can you—"

His mouth crashed against hers, the feel of his lips causing a surge through her entire body. They'd kissed plenty of times before, but this time was unlike anything she'd ever experienced with him. She gladly accepted every urgent swipe of her tongue, meeting his urgency with eagerness of her own.

They kissed long, hard and for what felt like an eternity. Then reality kicked in. Tressa jerked away from his addictive mouth. A look of pure desperation flashed across Roth's face.

Tressa laughed for the first time in far too long.

"Work." She laughed again, this time at the ridiculous timing of her words.

Roth's brow furrowed. "What?"

"I have to get to work."

The pained expression slid from Roth's face. A second later he scooped her into his arms. "You're going to be a few minutes late."

"If I'm late again, I'm going to be in the unemployment line."

Roth carried her toward the house. "Then you can focus on opening your own culinary studio. Or be a stay-at-home mom."

Tressa's jaw fell open, but she couldn't find her words.

"Keys," he said, climbing the stairs.

Unscrambling her brain, she said, "Somewhere on the ground."

A minute later they pushed through the front door. Roth slammed the door shut and pinned her against it. Again, his mouth claimed hers, but only for a short time. With urgency, he snatched her shirt over her head, then her bra came off. Untying the strings of her scrub pants, he pushed them down over her hips. Pressing his body firmly against hers.

"You feel that?" he asked against her mouth.

"Yes. And I want it."

A sexy sound rumbled in his chest seconds before he snaked a hand down her panties. He massaged her slowly, gently. Intense moans rolled past her lips.

Roth kissed her gently on the lips. "Tell me you love me more than any other man walking the face of the earth and that you always will."

Did he really expect her to form a sentence? As

good as his hand felt between her legs, all she could do was moan.

"Say it, baby. Please. I need to hear it. I desperately need to hear it."

"I…" The tingling sensations of an orgasm stalled her words. "I love you…more than any…"

"Any other man," they said in unison.

"Walking the face of the earth, and I always… I always will. *Oh, God!*"

The orgasm nearly crippled her, shattering her into a thousand pieces of useless matter. Her knees buckled, and she fell against Roth's solid chest. Scooping her into his arms, he carried her to the bedroom, laying her partially on the bed, and finished removing her clothing. Dropping to his knees in front of her, he claimed her core with his mouth. It wasn't long before another powerful orgasm overtook her.

Like lightning, Roth rid himself of his clothing, blanketed her body with his and drove himself into her, hard and deep. Tressa cried out in pure ecstasy. He delivered wild, delicious strokes that fogged her brain. It felt good. It felt so good.

"Don't stop, Roth."

Roth pinned her legs back and drove into her even harder. "Woman, don't ever make me suffer without you again."

Jesus, it felt so good. "Okay."

Roth growled a primal sound, his body trembling. A beat later he throbbed inside her, sending her over the edge once again. Delivering four or five more lumbering strokes, he collapsed onto her. Their heaving chests rose and fell in tandem. Roth's sweat-silken forehead wet the crook of her neck and his labored breath tickled her skin.

"That was…amazing," she said.

Roth raised his head, eyeing her with admiration. "You're amazing. Are we good, baby? I mean, really good?"

Tressa smoothed a hand down the side of his face. "We're good. Really, really good."

Finally wrangling herself from Roth's arms, Tressa darted into the bathroom, took the fastest shower she'd ever taken, threw on her bra and panties and barreled from the room. "I'm so—"

She stopped so suddenly, she nearly toppled over. Her jaw dropped, staring at the bed. "Roth?" she said, scanning the room for him. Taking a few steps closer to the bed, she rested a trembling hand over her mouth, while the other pressed into her quivering stomach.

Tressa reached for the black box sitting in the center of the bed, withdrew as if it would bite her, then reached for it again. Popping the top, she gasped at the huge diamond ring inside. Her hands trembled so badly, she nearly dropped the box.

"I want to spend my life with you, Tressa Washington."

She turned to see a fully dressed Roth standing behind her. How did he keep sneaking up on her like that?

"I want to share with you my hopes, my dreams, my ups, my downs, my fails, my successes. I want to share it all with you."

Somehow, her brain formed a sentence. "You want to marry me?" She wasn't sure if it had been a comment or a question.

"Yes. I was supposed to do this the night we…" His words trailed off. "I've made plenty of mistakes in my life, Tressa. But the one thing I got right was falling in love with you."

Her eyes clouded with tears at his sweet words. Falling in love with him was something she'd got right, too.

Roth claimed the black box and removed the ring. "I know this is probably not the most ideal moment, but…" He lowered to one knee. "Tressa Nycole Washington, will you marry me? I'll make you happy, baby. I'll make you so happy."

Tressa half sobbed, half laughed. "I'm in my underwear, Roth. But yes! Yes, yes, yes, a hundred times. I'll marry you."

Roth slid the ring on her finger, stood, hoisted her into his arms and kissed the past few weeks without him away. Pulling back, he said, "You should probably call to let someone know you won't be in today and possibly tomorrow, either. We have lost moments to make up for."

"Forty-eight hours is an awful lot of time. What do you have in mind, Mr. Lexington?"

"Well, soon-to-be Mrs. Lexington—" he kissed the ring on her finger "—I plan to spend all of that time reminding you how it feels to soar."

Oh, she didn't need a reminder. "I remember. In fact, I'm soaring on love at this very moment." But she'd make the call anyway, because the idea of spending the next forty-eight hours, plus the rest of her life in his arms, was too damn tempting to pass up.

Epilogue

Tressa stared into Roth's concerned eyes, not recalling a time in the past couple of years she'd ever seen her husband so shaken. Though she was the one in the hospital bed, he seemed to be suffering far more.

Roth blotted the sweat from her forehead. "Breathe, baby. Just like we learned. You got this and I've got you. What you go through, I go through, remember?"

"Okay, trade places with me," she said through labored breaths.

One of the labor and delivery nurses chuckled.

"All right, Tressa, one big push and your bundle of joy should slide right into the world. Ready?" Dr. Fiona asked.

After nine hours of labor, hell, yes, she was ready. "Let's do this."

Several hours later Tressa watched Roth with their

son, Shiloh Randall Lexington. The way he admired the newborn brought tears to her eyes. Thinking back, she remembered how tears had run from Roth's eyes when she'd told him she was pregnant.

A week after their engagement, she and Roth had married at the only place she would consider—the cabin. At that time she hadn't believed her life could get any better. It had.

Maybe she should give partial credit to Nettie and the top secret family recipe she'd shared with Tressa as a wedding gift. "Because you're family now," Nettie had said.

Turned out, it wasn't a food recipe at all. It'd been a recipe for a happy marriage. It was an interesting tradition, and she planned to pass a copy down to her boys when the time was right and hoped they committed each ingredient to memory and prepared the dish every day, just as she had.

2 cups of romance.
2 cups of laughter.
2 cups of trust.
2 cups of respect.
2 cups of sharing.
2 cups of tenderness.
2 cups of courtesy.
2 cups of consideration.
2 cups of attention.
4 cups of patience.

She'd altered hers a tad, adding 16 cups of great sex.
"Knock, knock."
The door creaked open and a very pregnant Vivian

waddled through, holding Justen's hand—Tressa and Roth's three-year-old son. She never used the word *adopted*, because she felt just like she'd given birth to him. Justen's thick black curls bounced as his short legs carried him across the room to Tressa's bedside. He stood on his tiptoes to see her.

"Mommy, okay?" he asked in his tiny voice.

To be so young, the child always showed such empathy for others.

"Mommy is fine, my sweet boy." She brushed a finger over his caramel cheek. "Let me look at you. I think you've grown two inches. Do you want to meet your brother?"

Roth waved Justen over.

Justen patted Tressa's hand. "Justen be right back. 'Kay, Mommy? I'm a big brother now."

"Yes, you are, son." Tressa blinked back tears. God, she loved that little boy. What had started out as a temporary emergency foster placement had turned into a permanent adoption. She thanked God every day for bringing Justen into their lives.

"Congratulations, Mama," Vivian said, approaching the bed and taking Tressa's hand.

"Congratulations to you, Godmama. I hope Justen wasn't too much trouble. He has the energy of several Jack Russell terriers."

"He was good practice," Vivian said, rubbing her protruding belly. "Having him at home with us made me even more eager to meet these two handsome fellows."

"Where's Alonso?" Roth asked, finally pulling his attention away from his boys.

"Yeah, I can't believe he let you and those boys out of his sight for one second." Tressa laughed.

Vivian shook her head. "Well, the godfather of your children is passing out cigars and telling anyone who will listen that he has another godson. Pray for him."

The room filled with laughter.

Vivian washed her hands and claimed Shiloh. It was the funniest thing ever watching her use her stomach as leverage. While Vivian entertained both boys, Roth pulled a chair to Tressa's bedside.

"How do you feel, Mama?"

"Like I've hit the lottery, over and over again."

Roth captured her hand and kissed the inside of her wrist. She loved when he did that.

"Woman, do you have any idea how happy you make me, how much I love you and our sons, our family?" he asked in a hushed tone, his eyes full of emotion.

"I do. You show me every single second of the day." She ran a hand over his stubble. "Man, do you have any idea how happy you make me, how much I love you and our sons, our family, our life together?"

"Of course I do, but will you keep telling me every single day?"

"I'll do one better. I'll keep telling you until I take my very last breath, because you make me feel, Roth Lexington. You make me feel like I'm soaring on love."

* * * * *

A PROPOSAL FOR THE OFFICER

CHRISTY JEFFRIES

To Brooklyn Bender, one of my best friends and a wealth of knowledge when it comes to Boston, *Top Gun*, Hockey, New Kids On The Block, and Type 1 diabetes. Thank you for answering my endless questions. You're never stingy when it comes to giving me feedback, constructive or otherwise. IAJS.

Chapter One

Leaning against a stack of cases of bottled water, Captain Molly Markham put a hand to her head as nausea overwhelmed her. Closing her eyes for a second, she debated whether or not she was at risk of passing out right there in the middle of Duncan's Market. She grabbed a liter of water off the shelf, unscrewed the cap and took a big swig. Her mouth was dry and suddenly her body felt weighted down.

Oh, no. It was happening again.

She'd sworn to the Bureau of Personnel reviewing her medical board that she could keep these episodes under control, but apparently they'd been right to doubt her.

Molly heaved herself off the tower of water and put one foot in front of the other, needing to get as far away from the curious glances of the shoppers who were sure to know her sister, Maxine, and would be only too eager to ask Maxine about her little sister's "incident" out in public.

She needed space and she needed to think. Maybe somewhere to lie down, too. Like her rental car. She grabbed another bottle and made it to the exit before she realized she'd left her purse back in the grocery basket. Damn. She also hadn't paid for the water.

When she did a one-eighty, her hip banged into a giant bag of ice. Or was it a bag of limes? A man dropped both as he reached out a hand to steady her.

That was gonna leave a bruise. The ice, not the guy's hand. His grip was actually gentle and balanced her. His black framed glasses made him look smart, serious. Maybe he was a doctor. Or a reporter.

He kind of had a Clark Kent vibe going for him. At least from the neck up. She took in his blue hooded sweatshirt and checkered canvas sneakers. Maybe *The Daily Planet* had sent him to do an undercover exposé of a nearby skate park.

"Are you okay?" He enunciated like a record player on a low speed. Or was it her hearing that was set to slow motion? It felt like someone had replaced her brain with hot, heavy sand. She licked her lips.

"Of course I'm okay. At least, I think I am." Molly lowered her own voice when she noticed the cashier staring in their direction. "By any chance, do you know how many carbs are in a fruit smoothie?"

His straight white teeth were visible beneath his smirk. "Probably a lot more than the ones in that peach muffin you gobbled down back by the juice bar thirty minutes ago."

"Oh, crap." It was good thing he was holding on to

her arm because trying to mentally calculate how much sugar she'd recently ingested made her want to sink to her knees. "The teenager behind the counter said they were organic."

"You mean the kid who also told you the baked goods on display were half price since they'd been sitting out since this morning and it was now late afternoon?"

Wait. How did this guy know what she'd talked about with the store employee? "Have you been following me?"

"No. I was sitting at that wrought iron table in the back of the store, trying to answer some work emails, but a bunch of clanging drew my attention to the display of soup cans at the end of an aisle. You were stocking up on the minestrone as though a blizzard had just been predicted." He tapped something on his watch and showed her the sunshine icon on the tiny display screen. "It hasn't, by the way. But then I saw you again when you were slouching against your shopping cart in the freezer section where you almost took out a display of ice-cream cones. Are you going to be sick or something?"

She didn't feel any less confused after that description of her sluggish attempts to make her way through the store. Or dizzy. "I don't think so."

"Come on," he said, and moved his hand to the small of her back. "There's a bench right outside and you can sit down."

"I need my purse," she said. *You also needed to use the restroom,* her bladder said.

"Where is it?" he asked.

The guy looked familiar, but his non-military-regulation hairstyle eliminated him as someone she'd served with. Molly had only been in Sugar Falls a few hours, yet her gut told her this man wasn't a local, either. Of course, she'd also been pretty convinced that anything with fruit in it was healthy so perhaps she shouldn't be so quick to listen to her instincts.

Who are you? she wanted to know. But she didn't exactly have time for formal introductions. Instead, she replied, "Back by the bottled water."

"Okay, stay here," he ordered as he sprinted away. Yeah, right. Molly wasn't about to stand around and wait. She weaved toward the parking lot, her only plan to get to the safe privacy of her rental car.

Her feet had barely hit the pavement when the Good Samaritan jogged up beside her, her very feminine tote bag swinging from his very masculine shoulder. "Should I call someone?"

"No," Molly said, her eyelids widening in frustration despite the fact that she wanted to close them and take a nap. "I don't want anyone to know."

"To know what?"

She clamped her teeth together, wishing she would've done so sooner to keep those telling words from slipping out.

"Never mind." She pulled the key fob out of her pocket. "The little white Toyota over there is mine."

"I seriously doubt you should be driving right now."

"I've got it," she ground out, despite the fact that she was practically leaning against him as he steered her toward the passenger side of her rental car. She collapsed down on the seat as soon as he got the door open, then she began digging in her purse.

Another wave of nausea tumbled through her as she unzipped a small black case. Ignoring the man's raised brows, she turned on the little machine, inserted a fresh test strip and pricked her finger. It took all of her focus to press the droplet of blood to the litmus paper. There was a series of beeps before the dinging alarm signaled that her glucose level was way too high. Stupid smoothie. And muffin. She should've known better. And she would have, if she hadn't been so starving after dropping her nephew off at baseball practice. She'd thought she'd been so smart, swinging by the market to pick up real groceries instead of grabbing a Snickers at the Little League snack bar while she waited.

It seemed to take hours for her to dial the correct dose on her insulin pen.

"What are you doing?" The panic in his voice probably matched the horror in his eyes. But Molly didn't have the energy to explain. She pulled up the hem of her shirt, not caring that she was exposing herself to the poor man. She could administer the shot in her arms or thighs, but the doctor said it would get into her system a lot quicker if she injected it into her stomach. She didn't even feel the sting of the needle and could only hope she'd landed it into the right spot before depressing the plunger.

"Lady, I really think we need to call an ambulance," he said, his once-calm voice now sounding about as shaky as her nerve endings felt.

"I'll be good as new in a second." She made a circle with her finger and her thumb in the universal signal for A-OK. "The insulin will help even everything out."

He kneeled on the pavement next to her, and she heard the hearty exhale of breath leaving his mouth. "Are you sure you're going to be all right?"

"I'm feeling better already." And it was true. She was. But Molly knew from the last time her blood sugar had spiked like this, it would take a little while to return to normal. She looked at the pulse jumping inside his neck and felt a wave of guilt wash over her. If this was how a complete stranger reacted to her hyperglycemia attack, how would her sister react? Or the rest of her family?

"Sorry for scaring you," she added, more resolved than ever to keep her recent diagnosis a secret. "I would've been fine on my own."

"You sure didn't look fine." His head slumped back against the open car door behind him, then he scrubbed a hand over his lower face. A handsome face actually. The trendy glasses made him look scholarly, but the square jawline made him look determined. Like he wasn't willing to leave her alone until he knew all the answers. "Does that happen often?"

Molly wished she knew. It wasn't like the time she got chicken pox, the itchy red scabs on her torso a constant reminder that she was sick. Curbing her sugar intake was tough enough, but remembering to stay on top of her glucose levels was even trickier since most of the time she felt perfectly fine. As a pilot, Molly had to be "combat ready" at all times. Sometimes she was on duty for twenty-four to forty-eight hours straight, which meant there was no way to ensure that she could eat on a certain schedule to maintain her insulin coverage. The military wasn't going risk both a multi-million-dollar plane and the flight crew because the pilot had hypoglycemia. Everything was still so unpredictable when it came to the disease she'd officially been diagnosed with over a month ago. According to the specialists, that unpredictability meant she could no longer do the only thing she loved.

She drew in a ragged breath and shrugged. "I'm still new to the wonderful world of diabetes."

"Wait. Why would you eat that much sugar if you're diabetic?" His expression looked the same as if he'd just asked, *Why in the world would you pull the pin out of that perfectly good grenade?*

"Because the guy behind the counter said it was healthy."

"And you take nutritional advice from a kid who isn't even old enough to shave?"

Kid! The realization made her scalp tingle and she felt her eyelids stretching wide open. She was officially the worst babysitter in the world.

"I need to get to the ballpark. Now."

"Lady, you're in no shape to be driving right now, let alone playing ball." Kaleb Chatterson adjusted his glasses while slipping the car key he still held into the front pocket of his hoodie. Normally, he had an army of assistants and interns he could've sent to the local grocery store to pick up the ingredients for his dad's margaritas. But he'd needed a break from his parents' nosy questions about his social life and his brothers' incessant teasing about the lack of one.

Coming to the aid of some strange woman in the middle of a medical crisis wasn't exactly what he'd anticipated when he'd volunteered for the errand.

"I'm not the one playing." She rolled her eyes, which were a deep shade of blue. "My nephew is. I'm supposed to pick him up from baseball practice at 1630."

Kaleb noted her use of military time and filed that nugget of information in the back of his mind. "How long does it usually take for you to recover from one of these, um, episodes?"

"Well, last time it took a couple of hours, but I got the insulin dose sooner this time so half that, maybe?"

Kaleb's stomach balled into a knot. He'd once had a crate of antibacterial hand sanitizer delivered to the office when several employees came down with a minor cold. He didn't do sickness or injuries or anything that might hint at the human body's susceptibility to disease. He most assuredly was *not* the person to go to in a medical crisis. And while it seemed as though the lady now had a decent handle on her situation, he would feel a lot more at ease if they had a second opinion. "Listen, my brother's fiancée is a doctor. Let me call her and she can drive over and check you out."

Or check *him* out. Luckily, his adrenaline was pumping his blood around so hard he wasn't likely to faint. Hopefully. He stayed squatted down, close to the ground. Just in case.

"No way. Especially not here where everyone in town would see me."

He eyed the barcode sticker on the rear window of her car, a sure sign that it was a rental. "Are you a local?"

"God, no. I'm just in town visiting my sister and her family. What about you?"

"I'm from Seattle. So if you're not from here, what does it matter if someone sees you?"

"Long story and I'm about to be late." She pulled up her blousy sleeve and looked at the sturdy chronograph watch. Her hand and forearm were equally tan, but a thin line of skin around her ring finger was strikingly white.

Telling himself that he wasn't one of his comic-book heroes and the lady beside him probably wouldn't like being considered a damsel in distress, Kaleb did what he always did when he was out of his league. He pulled out his phone, tapped on the voice to text feature and spoke into the speaker. "Angela, find out how to recover from low blood sugar."

"High blood sugar," the woman corrected him. Yeah, that made more sense considering how much she ate at once.

"Make that *high* blood sugar," he said into the phone, then nodded toward her lap. "Would you mind putting that thing away?"

"What, this?" She lifted up the object and Kaleb felt the color drain out of his face. "It's just a needle. You're not afraid of it, are you?"

"It looks like someone attached a syringe to Dr. Who's sonic screwdriver."

A blank look crossed her face. "What's a sonic screwdriver?"

"Sorry. Geek reference." An embarrassing flush normally would've brought his color back with a vengeance after that less-than-cool admission, but he was woozily watching her put the cap back on her insulin pen and zip it up in its case.

After several uncomfortable moments, the lady next to him broke the silence. "Who's Angela?"

"One of my assistants."

"Just one of them?"

He was saved from having to respond to her sarcastic question by the pinging of his phone. Several texts full of copied and pasted information flooded his screen.

"Hold on," Kaleb said as he read.

However, he was easily distracted by the woman beside him. Now that her color was returning, he could see that there was an edge to her girl-next-door appearance, an attitude that implied she wouldn't back down from a fight. She opened a bottle of water sitting in her center console and chugged it until the plastic concaved into itself. Then she used the back of her hand to wipe the dampness from her mouth. "Angela certainly is fast."

He nodded. That was why he paid her the second highest salary in his company. "Okay, so it says here that, depending on the levels, it can take one to several hours to feel better. She's also suggesting you drink more water and then eat something high in protein and complex carbs once your blood glucose levels return to a normal range."

"An hour? I can't very well sit out here in my car until I'm feeling better. Would you mind giving me a ride?"

"To the ER?" He felt his calf muscles clench, making him eager to stand up and run in the opposite direction. God, Kaleb hated hospitals more than he hated needles. Having multiple medical procedures during one's adolescence tended to do that to a person.

"No. Just to pick up my nephew."

"Can't you get someone else to pick him up?"

She looked at him as if he'd just asked her to hack into the CIA's router network. "His mom, my sister, left town this weekend on something called a 'babymoon' and put me in charge. I can't very well call her and say, 'Oops, sorry, I forgot to pick up your son because I was in a diabetic crisis.'"

"Actually, that's exactly what you could do. Maybe he can get a ride home with a friend?"

"Right. And then my sister would find out and wonder why I couldn't handle it myself."

Kaleb seriously doubted that this woman slouched on the seat next to him *could* handle it. His heart constricted and his head was heavy, which was why he had to keep it supported against the door behind him as he balanced beside her, their bodies only a few inches apart. He of all people knew what it was like to not want someone—especially an overly concerned family member—to think he was weak or needed help.

Still. He was shocked when she turned those pretty blue eyes on him and asked, "Can *you* give me a ride to the baseball field?"

His throat closed in on itself as if it were the plastic water bottle she'd just drained. He coughed to clear it. "But...you don't know me."

"Hi, I'm Molly."

Instinctively, because his mom had drilled good manners into him, he put his hand out and shook hers. "Kaleb."

"Good. Now we know each other."

"But you don't know if I'm a criminal," he argued.

"I know that you're the type to rush to aid a stranger, which means you have a hero complex."

"Ha," he snorted. His brothers would argue that he was the least heroic of all of them, or at least the most self-absorbed. "Maybe I have a villain complex and you're too weak to have figured it out yet."

"I am *not* weak." Her piercing look sent a chill down the back of his neck. He'd always associated the name Molly with a lovable cocker spaniel. But right this second, she looked more like a pissed-off Chihuahua. "Besides, a villain would've already robbed me or kidnapped me by now. And bad guys don't have trusty assistants named Angela."

"So you're the expert on bad guys?" Why was he arguing with her about this? *Just tell her you don't want to give her a ride.* Because he suddenly found himself actually wanting to take her anywhere she needed to go. She looked so delicate and fragile, yet he had a feeling there was a spine of steel under that petite frame. Plus, she was a mystery, a riddle, and he didn't like leaving things unsolved.

"If you'd met my ex, you'd quickly figure out that I'm definitely not an expert on jerks." He raised a brow at that little admission and she clamped her eyes shut. "God, forget I said that."

Too late. Kaleb never forgot anything.

"Sir," a cashier with salt-and-pepper dreadlocks called as she crossed the parking lot. "You forgot your ice and your limes."

"Oh, geez, don't let anyone see me like this." Molly slouched lower in the seat. Great, now she was a cowering Chihuahua. "They'll tell my sister."

Kaleb sighed and stood up. He jogged toward the cashier, trying to meet her halfway.

"Thanks, Donae," he said, reading the name tag on her apron. His father always said that people gave better service when you used their first name. Kaleb usually avoided the practice because it tended to invite familiarity when he was usually trying to keep the public from recognizing him. But he had a feeling he'd need all the allies he could get if he was going to survive the next ten days in this small town.

Kaleb took the dripping bag from Donae's hand and set it down on the asphalt. He reached into his back pocket and pulled out his wallet. "Listen, my friend isn't feeling well and she left her shopping cart in aisle eight. Would you mind ringing those things up and throwing in a liter of water and one of the prewrapped turkey sandwiches from the deli section?"

"No problem, Mr. Chatterson," she replied. Ugh, that was why he didn't do familiarity. It gave strangers the impression that they knew him, which was fine if they'd limit their long-winded conversations to his work life and not to which model or actress or pop singer he'd recently dated. Fortunately, Donae only gave him a wide smile and took the large bills he passed her. "And just so you know, your sister, Kylie, called the store a couple of minutes ago asking if you'd left yet. I told her you were on your way. You want me to call her back?"

His jaw went stiff and he fought off the urge to pinch the bridge of his nose. Just like that, one mention of his awaiting family cemented Kaleb's decision on whether he was going to give cute, determined Molly a ride to get her nephew. "Would you mind telling my sister something came up and I have to help out a friend?"

Okay, so "friend" was a generous description. In fact, Kaleb sincerely doubted his new acquaintance wouldn't have already blasted out of the parking lot without so much as a wave if he hadn't pocketed her car keys.

He hefted the ice into the bed of his dad's lifted, half-ton truck, knowing he'd have to stop somewhere and get another bag before returning to his sister's. Wiping a wet hand on his pant leg, he walked to Molly's car to check on her. She was dozing in the passenger seat and he wondered if he should wake her up. No. That was for concussions, not diabetes. At least he thought so. Hell, he was a software developer, not a doctor. And he certainly wasn't a damn taxi driver.

But a few minutes later, when the cashier pushed out a cart of bagged groceries, he told Donae to keep the change before loading them in the back of Molly's hatchback.

Kaleb was often reminded of the fact that he was the shortest of all the Chatterson brothers, yet he still had to slide the driver's seat back to accommodate his six-foot frame. He started the car and the stereo shot to life. If the booming bass of hip-hop wasn't loud enough to wake Molly up, the vibration of the cheap speakers through the vinyl seats would've done the trick.

"This is for when your levels stabilize." He tossed the wrapped sandwich on her lap and asked, "So how do I get to the baseball park from here?"

Chapter Two

"This bread has seeds in it," Molly said as she examined the turkey sandwich he'd given her. She was already dehydrated and couldn't afford to use the little saliva she could muster to swallow some tasteless looking cardboard.

"It's whole grain." Kaleb spoke slowly, as though he was explaining jet propulsion to a kindergartner. "It's one of those complex carbs you're supposed to eat once you drink enough fluid to flush out all the excess sugar from your system."

Her unsolicited rescuer was sure turning out to be quite the know-it-all.

"I'm well aware of what I'm supposed to be eating and drinking." As if to prove it, she took another long swig of the water he'd thoughtfully purchased after she'd already downed an entire bottle.

"Forgive me for doubting that when I overheard you asking some clueless teenager at the juice bar if the strawberry-banana smoothie was low in sugar."

"Well, I *will* be aware. As soon as I meet with the nutritionist at Shadowview." Molly actually had several appointments at the nearby military hospital, but she'd been putting them off. She could only handle one tailspin at a time.

"So you *are* in the military." It was more of a statement than a question.

Technically, she was. But she didn't know for how much longer. Ever since the flight surgeon wrote up a medical board determining that her recently diagnosed condition made her ineligible to fly, Molly had refused to think about where her career was headed. So instead, she changed the subject. "You can stop looking at the map on your phone. I know where we're going."

"But my GPS is saying it's quicker to take Snowflake Boulevard to Lake Street."

"Does your GPS also say that Lake Street is blocked off today because the high school drill team is practicing for next week's Sun Potato Parade?"

"Hmpf." His hand reluctantly dropped the fancy high-tech device into the center console, then loosely gripped it, as though he might need to grab it again at any second. "It probably would if there was a Sun Potato Parade app available to download."

"You can talk to my nephew about inventing one. He lives for dorky tech stuff like that." Molly saw Kaleb's hand clench tighter around his phone and she wondered what she could've said to annoy him. If she wasn't so exhausted, she might've asked him. She pointed to the next stop sign. "Make a left up here."

"Speaking of your nephew, won't he think there's something wrong if you show up with a stranger?"

"I'll tell him I had too much to drink." She felt the deceleration of the car before she realized he'd completely taken his foot off the gas pedal. She let her head roll to the side, which was a mistake since it only afforded her a full view of his handsome—and doubt-filled—face.

"You'd rather people think you were drunk than diabetic?" His incredulous tone hit her in the belly with a force. Or maybe she was still sore from where she'd given herself that shot. "Are you seriously that desperate to keep this from your family?"

"*Desperate* is a strong word," she said cautiously. In fact, it sounded a lot like *weak*. And she was neither. "I'm simply protecting them from worrying about me. And I didn't mean alcohol. His mom warned him not to have too much soda this weekend because it would give him a bellyache. So I was going to go that route."

He made a weird mumbling sound as he pulled into the parking lot. All the other kids must've already been picked up because poor Hunter was the only boy waiting by the bleachers. She curled her fingers into her palm, unable to release the guilt building inside her. Molly came from a big, busy family with at least one parent usually off on deployment. Getting forgotten at school or left behind at soccer practice was an all too familiar feeling and she hated that her condition was now affecting others.

She leaped out of the passenger door before Kaleb had even put the car in Park. Well, she didn't leap so much as stumble on shaky legs, feeling as if she'd just stepped onto solid ground after a ten-hour flight in a cramped cockpit.

"Sorry I'm so late, buddy," she said, wrapping her twelve-year-old nephew into a bear hug, made all the more awkward by the fact that he'd shot up a couple inches taller than her this past winter and was carrying a duffel bag in one hand and a batting helmet in the other. As well as by the fact that she'd just seen him less than two hours ago. "Have you been waiting all by yourself?"

"No problem, Aunt Molly. Practice has only been done a few minutes and Coach Russell is still here chalking the base lines for tomorrow's game." Hunter untangled himself from her overzealous greeting and opened the rear door to toss his gear into the back seat. "Hey! You didn't tell me Kaleb was coming with you!"

"Hunter, my man," Kaleb said casually as he pivoted in the driver's seat and did a complicated fist bump with her nephew.

"What?" Molly fumbled with the door handle. "You guys know each other?"

"Pfshhh," Hunter responded. "Anyone living in the twenty-first century knows Kaleb Chatterson."

"Oh, hell." She inspected her grocery store hero through squinted eyes. "You're a Chatterson?"

"That's another dollar for my swear jar, Aunt Molly."

"According to my birth certificate." Kaleb shrugged, then put the car into gear. "The DNA tests are still in question."

A throb started in her temples and Molly had to wonder if her visit to Sugar Falls could get any worse. She pulled her wallet out and tossed a ten dollar bill onto Hunter's lap. "Consider me paid up until Sunday."

* * *

"But you said you were from Seattle," Molly accused through gritted teeth as she latched her seat belt.

"I am." Kaleb was doing *her* a favor. Why was *he* the one being put on the defensive? "And would you mind telling me where I'm supposed to take you?"

"I'm staying at my sister's apartment. But I guess you knew that all along."

Whoa. This lady was coming at him with guns blazing. If that wasn't discomforting enough, a twelve-year-old kid had his seat belt stretched to the limits as he practically leaned between their two seats, not wanting to miss a minute of the action. "How in the world would I have known that? I didn't have a clue who you were until fifteen minutes ago."

In fact, it wasn't until Kaleb heard Hunter call her "Aunt Molly" that the puzzle began clicking together. The woman beside him must somehow be related to Maxine, who was best friends with his sister, Kylie. But he was still missing the pieces that explained why she was suddenly so annoyed with him.

"But you know me, right, Kaleb?" Hunter's voice cracked and it didn't take a rearview mirror for Kaleb to know the kid's eager freckled face was only inches behind his own. "Remember when we were at your sister's wedding last year and you promised me an internship at your company when I turned eighteen?"

Kaleb squeezed his eyes shut briefly. How could he forget? Of course, he would've called it a surrender more than a promise since, at the time, Hunter was the only person who'd been able to smuggle in a tablet—despite Kylie's ban of all electronic devices at the reception—and

Kaleb's Tokyo office was in the middle of negotiations to buy out a company that built virtual-reality headsets.

Yet, before anyone could comment on the circumstances surrounding the supposed internship, the kid's aunt interrupted. "If you're from Seattle, then what are you doing in Sugar Falls?"

As he turned onto Snowflake Boulevard, which could've just as easily been named Main Street, USA, he took in the grassy park in the center of downtown to assure himself that they were still in a free country. "The same thing you are. Visiting family."

She mumbled an expletive under her breath and he was pretty sure that, at this rate, Hunter was going to have enough money in his swear jar to get him through the first two years of college.

"Speaking of *family*." Kaleb emphasized the last word to remind her that children were present. "Does your sister still live above her shop?"

"Not anymore," Hunter answered for his aunt, who was silently fuming in the front seat. "We moved out to a bigger house when she and Cooper got married. But Aunt Molly is staying there while she's in town. She says it's because she doesn't want to be in our way, but Mom says it's because she doesn't want us knowing her business."

Molly gasped before turning in her seat to look at her nephew. "Your mom told you that?"

Hunter had his palms up. "Not in a bad way or nothin'… She said all the Markhams are like that."

"So where are we going?" Kaleb interrupted. If he wanted a front-row seat to watch family members bickering, he'd head back to his sister's house and watch his own brothers argue over who got to man the back-yard grill.

"To the apartment over the bakery." Molly sighed. Even an outsider like Kaleb knew that when some-one said *bakery* in this town, they actually meant the Sugar Falls Cookie Company. "It shouldn't be that far of a walk for you to get back to your car at Duncan's Market."

Not that far? It was at least a mile through town and both his phone and his watch—he never should've synced the two—currently sounded like winning slot machines with unanswered texts from his dad and his sister, probably wanting to know where the heck he was with their ice and limes.

"Why's your car at Duncan's?" Hunter asked. So far they'd avoided having to explain why he was driving them home, but if the kid was as observant as Kaleb had been at that age, it didn't take a computer genius to figure out Molly was hiding something.

"Because your aunt had a—"

"Wait." Molly pointed a finger his way. "Which Chatterson brother are you?"

"I'm Kaleb," he said slowly, second-guessing his earlier decision to go along with her pleas to not seek medical assistance.

"I caught the name." Her eyes were narrowed into slits. "I meant are you one of the baseball Chattersons or are you the one who plays video games for a living?"

Despite being on the cover of *Forbes* last month for their feature article on "World's Youngest Billionaires," Kaleb's siblings never let him forget that no matter how much money he made, he would always be the little brother. So when Molly said "video games" in that tone, she might as well have been asking if he was the one who set fire to small wildlife animals in his parents' basement. At least his back brace and teenage acne were long gone. Along with his self-respect apparently.

"Video games?" Hunter snorted. "Kaleb's, like, the most successful software developer in the world."

Oblivious to the tension in the front seat, the boy launched into a monologue about the company's top-selling games while Molly's eyes shot icy glares at Kaleb and her forefinger made a dramatic swipe against her throat. It took him a moment to figure out that she was referring to him staying silent about what had happened at the store, not his job profession. Or maybe she didn't want him to bring up either subject. All he knew was that he liked her soft pink lips a lot more when they weren't pursed together in a violent shushing gesture. Actually, he kind of liked them both ways.

He mouthed the words, "What's the big deal?"

But the minivan behind him honked to let him know the light had changed to green, and he didn't get a chance to lip-read Molly's response.

So she had diabetes. What was the big deal? Millions of people probably had the same diagnosis and didn't go into undercover stealth mode to keep it a secret. He needed to know why.

"Dude, all of your electronic devices are, like, going crazy." Hunter was apparently done with his rambling soliloquy about Perfect Game Industries, although it did give Kaleb's ego a boost to know that at least one person in the town of Sugar Falls—besides his mother—didn't think his company was a fallback career. "Are you gonna answer them?"

Kaleb glanced at the display. Speaking of his mother,

his family was certainly busting out the big guns if Lacey Chatterson was trying to track him down. Everyone knew he never avoided his mom's calls. If he didn't respond soon, he'd get a firsthand look at how this little ski resort town up in the mountains ran a full-scale search party.

"I'll call them back later," he said, slipping his cell phone into his front pocket. "Let's help your aunt take these groceries inside."

Falling completely off the grid and being the irresponsible Chatterson might be fun for a change.

Chapter Three

When Molly had initially been medically grounded, she'd still been living on base so the daily routine of military life made it easy to pretend that nothing would change. Just like the time she'd twisted her ankle after a postejection survival training exercise, she pulled office duty—pushing paperwork and keeping her personal life classified. There was no point in getting her family and squad mates all worried about something that would probably require a simple fix. She hadn't even told her fiancé about her diagnosis. Although, in her defense, she'd been about to when she walked into Trevor's condo with a bag of Chinese takeout from his favorite restaurant and found him eating pork dumplings from the ends of another woman's chopsticks.

Canceling vendors, returning wedding gifts and watching her savings account free-fall with all the forfeited deposits was only slightly more pleasant than undergoing a battery of doctor appointments and lab tests. In a last-ditch attempt to get away from it all, Molly had cashed in on Trevor's trip insurance and went solo on the honeymoon that never was. Unfortunately, besides a great suntan and a somewhat functional straw tote from a street market in Fiji, Molly's head wasn't any clearer than it had been two weeks ago.

As she looked around at her sister's apartment—which she'd been thinking of as her temporary duty station until she could figure out what she was going to do with her life—Molly felt as though she'd just overshot her landing and had to circle around and try it again. Exhausted, both emotionally and physically, she was halfway curled into a ball on the oversize white sofa in the living room, watching her nephew and Kaleb put away groceries she didn't remember selecting. What in the world was she going to do with all those cans of soup?

More important, what was she going to do with this guy who now knew her secret? She shuddered. Even thinking the word *secret* made her feel all dirty and cowardly, like she was hunkering down in some barren cave rather than Maxine's plush renovated apartment in the heart of quaint, touristy Sugar Falls.

Kaleb's face was so handsome the glasses almost looked fake. A few weeks ago, when she'd first experienced problems with dizziness, Molly had been looking at all the advertisement posters above the display cases at the ophthalmologist's office while she waited for her vision tests to come back. This guy resembled the sexy models in the pictures, trying to convince the middle-aged patients with cataracts and receding hairlines that they, too, would look like some gorgeous stud if only they invested in the right spectacles.

His brown hair was a bit too long and too messy. His jeans were a bit too new and too expensive, despite the fact that they certainly fit his slim hips well. And when he'd stripped off his hooded sweatshirt and she'd seen him in his shirt, Molly let out a breath she didn't know she'd been holding. His dark blue T-shirt appeared to be made for him, the fabric so soft and well-worn she could see the ridges of his lean muscles under it.

All in all, he didn't look like the owner of a multi-billion-dollar technology empire. Which was probably why she was so surprised to find out that he was related to her sister's best friend. Not that the rest of the Chattersons were much different than this one, with the exception of most of them being redheads. And they were only millionaires, as opposed to billionaires.

"Can we order some pizza from Patrelli's?" Hunter asked after digging around in the shopping bags and only coming up with food that would require a can opener to prepare.

She nodded and would've handed him her cell phone, but he'd already pulled out his own. "Get me a large meatball sub," she said as he started dialing.

"Actually," Kaleb interjected, "Molly is going to have the chicken Caesar salad. Dressing on the side."

Hunter gave his idol a thumbs-up before speaking to a person on the other end of the line. Apparently, being a favorite aunt had just been trumped by the guy who invented some stupid video game called "Blockcraft."

"But I wanted the meatball sub." Molly crossed her arms across her chest, her voice sounding whinier than she'd intended.

"And do you also want your nephew to have to call 9-1-1 when you go into another one of your blood sugar attacks?" One of Kaleb's brown eyebrows arched above his glasses.

Molly tried to arch her own brow in response to him, but only succeeded in looking like she had something stuck in her eye. Being tired was one thing, but she was beginning to feel completely useless.

"I'm gonna walk down the block to pick it up," Hunter said, pulling on a sweatshirt. "I sure like our new house, but sometimes I really miss living in the middle of town like this."

Kaleb handed the boy two twenty-dollar bills and her nephew was out the door before Molly could even protest. Or ask him not to leave her alone with the hunky tech guy who'd just saved her. Sort of.

"You didn't have to buy dinner, too. I have money," she said, looking around for her wallet. Actually, she didn't know how much longer her military salary would last and she probably shouldn't be wasting it on pizza—or dry salads, in this case.

"I think all of your cash went to the swear jar," Kaleb said, his hands loosely tucked into his front pockets. He was probably eager to get away from her. Not that she could blame him. She'd been trying to get away from herself for quite a few weeks, as well.

His watch rang again, or was it his phone? Nope, this time it was his cell. Picking it up from the counter, he said, "I really need to take this."

"Okay, but if it's your sister, don't tell her about... you know..."

"Why not?"

"Because then she'll tell *my* sister, remember?"

He rolled his eyes, then swiped his finger across the screen. "Hey, Kylie."

Molly dragged her tote bag onto her lap and pulled out her black case. She may as well check her glucose levels before Hunter returned. The distraction might also keep her from listening to Kaleb's smooth, deep voice.

As she pricked her finger and pressed out a droplet of blood, she heard him make several noncommittal sounds to whatever his sister was saying on the other end.

"Mmm-hmm." He walked around the coffee table to stand beside her, the waistband of his jeans right in her line of vision. Lately, in the guy department, Molly thought she'd been working on autopilot. However, a shot of electricity zipped through her, activating the dormant wiring circuits in her lower extremities.

"Uh-huh." He leaned over to see the digital reading on her compact machine. She tightened her lips, taking in a deep breath through her nose. Whoa. Did all billionaires smell this amazing?

"Is that good?" he whispered to her, his hand over the speaker and his eyes soft with concern. She had to force her own eyes away from his flat abdomen and toward the numbers on the screen in front of her.

She was almost back within normal range, yet still gave him an "okay" sign with her thumb and forefinger. His smile mirrored the relief she should have felt. Or would have felt if her heart hadn't started hammering at how close he was to her.

"No, Molly's fine." His voice snapped her brain out of whatever trance she'd just been in and she began waving her arms in front of her face, inadvertently hitting him in the hip and causing him to glare down at her.

"Don't say my name," she whispered.

"Too late," he mouthed.

"Here, let me talk to her." She reached for his phone, but her energy hadn't fully recovered and her criss-crossed legs got tangled when she tried to stand up. He sidestepped her and held his palm out, probably trying to cut her off because he thought he had the conversation under control.

"No, she wasn't too sloshed to drive," Kaleb told his sister indignantly.

Molly gave him a nod of encouragement. "Yeah, let's go with that."

"Oh, c'mon, Kylie. I'm not going to ask her if she's pregnant."

Hmm. Molly tilted her head to the side and tapped a couple of fingers against her lip. As far as red herrings went, it wasn't ideal. But she could work with it. Maxine knew about the breakup with Trevor and Molly hadn't exactly corrected her sister when she'd offered up the use of her apartment as a refuge for mending her broken heart. Pregnancy definitely would be a lot simpler to explain, at least for a few months while she bought herself more time.

"Because it's none of my business," Kaleb said into the phone. "And it's none of yours."

Molly's eyes widened in surprise. She couldn't believe that he was jumping to her defense, but she nodded her encouragement, anyway.

"Uh-huh." Kaleb pushed his hair off his forehead, then ran a hand through his dark brown curls, which fell in waves to his chin. "Fine. I'll be there in thirty minutes and we can talk about it then."

Molly collapsed backward, her head falling into a pile of down throw pillows. It would've been nice if he could've stalled a bit more. As it was, she would now have half that time to coach Kaleb on exactly what to say to throw his family off her trail. Or to figure out a way to prevent him from walking out of this apartment.

"No, you do not need to send Dad to come get me." Kaleb spoke into the phone, but he was staring straight at Molly. And his annoyed expression promised retribution for this farce she'd gotten them both into.

When he arrived at Kylie's house a while later, Kaleb surrendered the margarita fixings and tried to give his incredibly nosy family the look that usually sent his employees scurrying back to their cubicles. Or at least the look he intended to convey his authority and his unwillingness to discuss a matter. Unfortunately, his family didn't work for him and they certainly didn't respect any boundaries when it came to his personal life—or any facet of his life, really.

"Maybe you should've called one of her relatives," his mother suggested.

"Or brought her here so we could check her out ourselves," Kylie advised.

"You mean interrogate her in person?" Kaleb asked, and his sister rolled her eyes in response. "You guys, she was totally fine. It's probably some twenty-four-hour bug that's going around. In fact, I should probably quarantine myself in case I was exposed. Wouldn't want to get any of you sick."

"Nice try, Brainiac," Kylie replied. "As if Captain

Markham would be felled by some pesky flu. That woman is as tough as they come. Maxine told me that one time, when Molly was in flight school, she got her thumb stuck in a busted air shaft vent and almost ripped it clean off. Rather than tell her instructors or call for a medic, she used her good hand and a utility knife and cut off the strap of her bra to hold the digit in place. She would've cut into the fabric of her flight suit, but she didn't want to be out of uniform."

"Still," his mom said. "You probably shouldn't have left her alone if she's sick."

Kaleb had told himself that same thing during his walk back to the truck at Duncan's, during his wait at the checkout line at the market with a fresh—and unmelted—bag of ice and then throughout the entire drive here. "She was already feeling better when I left and she's not alone. She's with her nephew. And trust me, that kid is smart enough to call in for reinforcements even if his stubborn aunt isn't."

"So, you think Molly's stubborn?" His sister's eyes lit up and Kaleb knew from experience not to let her bait him.

"No, *you* said she was stubborn when she tried to fix her own thumb instead of getting help."

"I said she was tough, not stubborn."

"What's the difference?" Kaleb asked, then thought better of his question when he saw both his sister and his mom open their mouths to answer him. "Never mind. Listen, I'm gonna head over to Kane's house just in case I caught whatever bug Molly has. I'll call you guys in the morning."

Kaleb knew full well that what Molly had wasn't contagious, but if it got him out of the line of fire quicker, he'd say whatever he could to get a few hours' reprieve. And in his defense, he was doing it to protect her. To protect her secret. He wasn't avoiding his family because they drove him nuts. Truly.

Although, if his relatives even got the slightest suspicion that he, in any way, was attracted to an eligible woman, the teasing would never cease. Not that Molly was eligible. Or that Kaleb cared either way. Dating led to obligations and obligations led to commitment. The only commitment he had time for was his company.

On the drive to his brother's house—where he was staying alone since Kane had moved into town with his fiancée—Kaleb picked up his smartphone several times to call Molly and check on her, each time realizing he never got her phone number. He'd programmed his number into her cell and told her to call him in case anything came up. But she'd never offered to do the same.

Which was for the best. He had no business calling her, let alone fostering this bizarre sense of responsibility he now felt toward her. When he'd dealt with scoliosis, he'd hated people babying him, wondering if the brace he wore was uncomfortable, telling him he'd be able to play sports again soon enough. Kaleb couldn't imagine she'd respond any differently than he had as a surly teenager, determined to prove to the world that he was just as healthy and capable as everyone else in his athletic family.

But the silence of the truck cab felt unnatural, as did the feeling of not being on the phone with someone. So Kaleb used his voice command feature to call his assistant. He counted three rings, more than the usual two, before Angela answered.

"You're supposed to be on vacation," Angela said by way of greeting.

"I'm never on vacation."

"Does your old man know that?" his assistant asked. "Because Coach Chatterson gave me very specific instructions that nobody from the office was to bother you for the next ten days while you're with your family."

That was just like his father to go behind his back like that. And with one of his trusted employees, no less. "Does my dad pay your salary now?"

"No, but he promised to get me a baseball signed by your brother if I sent all the employees a memo instructing them not to call you."

"Sellout," Kaleb snorted.

"Can you blame me? Do you know how much authenticated memorabilia signed by the infamous Kane Chatterson goes for nowadays?"

"I didn't mean *you*. I meant my brother. He of all people should know not to interfere in my business."

"Aw, c'mon, Kaleb. You told your family that the only way you would take time off from *your* job was if they agreed to take time off *their* jobs. You can't blame them for wanting to get you back for scheduling this trip right during the middle of baseball season."

He grunted, but smiled to himself because he'd definitely outplayed his dad and brothers with that negotiation maneuver.

"Besides," Angela continued, "deep down, you know your family is looking out for your best interest."

"Story of my life," Kaleb said as he flicked on the turn signal. A few years ago, he would've been annoyed, but now the high-handed move was completely expected and Kaleb would've suspected something was wrong if his family *hadn't* tried to protect him in some way. Old habits were hard to break and all that. He didn't begrudge them their motivation, even when he grew exasperated with their tactics. "So, tell me how the testing of the avatar prototype went."

"It went great for the preliminary rounds. A couple of minor glitches to work out but our software team is on top of it."

"Have them meet with the graphic artists to go over—"

"They're already on it, Boss Man," Angela interrupted.

"What about the negotiations with the record label to let us use that song for the intro to 'Zombies vs. Alien Pirates'?"

"The legal department is drawing up the contracts this week."

He made a right turn onto the long dirt driveway leading to the house Kane had refurbished last year. Kaleb wasn't ready to call it a night quite yet, though. An unexplained restlessness simmered in his belly and he reached for his tablet on the passenger seat. He pulled up his electronic calendar on the screen as he steered the truck with one hand. "Where are we at with those new health care benefits for the administration staff?"

"They decided that they'd rather have a sushi chef in the cafeteria than affordable insurance, so HR is actively screening applicants at every Japanese restaurant in the greater Seattle area."

"Really?" Kaleb jerked his head up, stopping in front of the barn that had been converted into a garage.

"No, Kaleb. Not really. But I left a very good-looking

date and a warm cup of sake so I could step outside of Sensei Miso's and take your call."

Angela had been the first person Kaleb hired when he'd started Perfect Game Industries, which meant that she'd been with him since before he could legally drink alcohol and, therefore, felt free to give him her opinion—along with any other unsolicited advice she deemed suitable. Funny how in his quest to start a business that was completely independent of his family, he hired the one person who acted like his long-lost big sister all the time.

Which was probably why he sounded less like an authoritative boss and more like a petulant little brother when he replied, "You could've said as much when you answered the phone."

"Kaleb, you and I both know that my salary more than compensates me for these after-hours calls. But you're supposed to be on vacation. That means that all your vice presidents and department directors are getting a vacation from you micromanaging us."

"I've never micromanaged anyone in my life," Kaleb shot back, using his finger to scroll through his online notes to see if there was anything he'd missed regarding the marketing staff.

"Whatever you say, Boss Man." Angela's tone wasn't the least bit deferential.

"You don't know micromanagement until you've spent a day with the Chatterson family."

"If that's an invitation, I'm calling the company pilot right now and telling him to fuel up the Gulfstream."

"Perfect. Tell him that when he drops you off, he can take me back with him. Actually, bring that new admin assistant from accounting with you. I hear he's been angling for your job since he started. I bet he'll be glad to know that the position is finally opening up."

"You mean the one who wore the Bobby Chatterson retro jersey to the company roller-skating party last month? Yeah, I'm sure he wouldn't be above taking a bribe from your old man, either."

"Are you done with the sarcasm?" Kaleb asked. If he wanted to deal with people giving him a hard time, he'd drive back to Kylie's house. Or even to Molly's. How did he always inevitably surround himself with so many know-it-all women?

"You started it," Angela pointed out. "Seriously, though, Kaleb. You've hired the best of the best to work for you. The least you could do is trust us to handle things while you enjoy your vacation."

Kaleb would hardly call this trip to Sugar Falls a vacation. He'd much rather be at the office dealing with things himself, rather than delegating. But he'd made a promise to his parents to at least try.

Just like he'd made a promise to a petite, blue-eyed blonde that he'd keep her secret safe. He looked at the digital calendar on his smartwatch. Nine more days to go.

and the fact that she wouldn't have been able to order anything other than a starchy, cream-filled sugar bomb. She hadn't been back to Duncan's Market since Friday and Hunter had already exhausted the supply of leftover pizza for his past two breakfasts.

She was supposed to be the fun aunt. The aunt with no rules. The aunt who all the nieces and nephews begged to come chaperone their school dances or to take them and their friends on tours of Blackhawk helicopters. Or at least she would have been if she ever spent some quality time with any of them.

She'd like to think she'd been mostly fun this weekend, going hiking and kayaking and bike riding. But she'd also been feeding her growing twelve-year-old nephew a steady diet of canned soup, which was about the least exciting thing on the planet to eat.

"Finally!" Hunter all but shouted over the noise of the crowded restaurant. "Hey, Kaleb, there's a spot right here!"

Molly's shoulders froze, her coffee mug suspended halfway between the Formica counter and her clenched jaw. She should've gone to the Donut Stop and risked a maple-glazed-induced coma. Her pride forbade her from turning around to make eye contact with Kaleb, thereby encouraging him to accept Hunter's invitation to sit by them. But her curiosity told her pride to go pound sand.

That zapping electrical current shot through her body again. She shouldn't have looked.

He was still wearing those serious glasses, paired with jeans that were meant to look sloppy but probably cost more than her officer's mess dress uniform—which was the most expensive thing she owned. His green T-shirt displayed a replica of the blueprints for the *Millennium Falcon*, and Hunter immediately commented on their apparent shared love of *Star Wars* as Kaleb warily approached.

"Are you sure you don't mind me joining you guys?" Given the way his eyes were fixated on her face, he was directing the question toward her.

But Hunter answered before she could. "Heck, no. Hurry up before one of the tourists tries to snake this spot."

The waitress was possibly new, her gaze darting back and forth between the counter and the booths as though she didn't know who to help next. Her turquoise Cowgirl Up Café T-shirt seemed way too tight and didn't go with the long, flowing skirt. Molly remembered her high school job at a fish and chips place near Groton, Connecticut, when her parents had been stationed at the military base there. On her first day, she'd been tossed an oversize orange-and-blue striped polyester dress that smelled like battered grease and Atlantic cod and had the name "Dolores" stenciled on the front.

She felt this woman's pain. Thank God Molly had become a pilot, because she had sucked at every job she'd ever had before enlisting. Ugh! Did that mean that if she couldn't fly planes, she'd have to go back to waitressing? To being around all this delicious food and not being able to sample a single bite?

When Monica—at least that what the waitress's name tag read—finally made her way to them, she fumbled with her notepad and barely made eye contact before asking to take their order.

"You gotta get one of their cinnamon rolls, Aunt Molly," Hunter said. "They're world famous."

"As good as that sounds, I think I'm going to get the veggie omelet." She tried to ignore her nephew's gagging expression.

"Would you like hash browns or home fries with that?" Monica asked.

Even with Hunter sitting between them, and at least fifty other diners in the surrounding area, Molly could clearly hear Kaleb's swift intake of breath. She zeroed in on his disapproving scowl.

"What?" Molly asked.

"Potatoes are a starch, which basically converts into sugar as soon as it hits your digestive tract."

"They're also a vegetable. I'm sure a couple of bites would be fine."

"Look." Kaleb pointed to something on the menu before suggesting, "How about the sliced tomatoes?"

The waitress, who, up until that point, had looked as though she'd rather be anywhere that didn't require social interaction, lifted one of her eyebrows at Molly and gave her that look women give each other to silently ask, *Are you really going to let this guy talk to you like that?*

Each fiber of Molly's soul wanted to fight back and order every single potato product they served—which would've been quite a meal considering they were in the great state of Idaho. But she ignored the throbbing vein in her temple and only mildly defied him by forcing out the words, "I'll take the cottage cheese." And then in an effort to prove to this stranger that the controlling man sitting next to them wasn't the boss of her, she added, "And a side of bacon."

When Kaleb ordered the cinnamon roll French toast, Molly shot him the dirtiest look she could manage. It might've been juvenile, but it was either that or risk giving Hunter another IOU for his swear jar.

"I thought you guys were friends," her nephew said once Monica left to get Kaleb's orange juice.

"I don't know if I'd say we were—" Kaleb broke off when Molly drew a finger across her neck.

"Of course we're friends, Hunter." Molly held the tight smile as her nephew looked back and forth between them. She prayed her jaw didn't crack.

"Oh, I get it," the boy finally said. "My mom and Cooper used to argue like that before they got married."

"We're not arguing," Kaleb's mouth said, while his eyes added, *Nor are we getting married.*

Not that she needed him to spell it out. But clearly, Hunter did, because the twelve-year-old didn't look convinced.

"That's also what my mom and Cooper used to say." Hunter's knowing smirk was enough to make Molly sink down in her seat as she bit back an argumentative response.

Oddly enough, that wasn't the most awkward breakfast Kaleb had ever had. Even when he'd grabbed the check, only to have Molly tear the paper in two when she wrestled it out of his grip, he'd only been mildly annoyed. Too bad the business owners in Sugar Falls hadn't caught on to SmartPay; otherwise, he could've paid the bill with a simple tap on his watch.

In fact, the woman seemed to bring out his competitive spirit, a Chatterson trait that always seemed to intensify whenever he was in the same city as his antagonistic siblings. Plus, seeing her get all flustered and defensive every time she thought Kaleb might slip and say something was rather entertaining.

Most of the women he went out with were overly agreeable, always putting him—and his bank account—on a pedestal. Fortunately, the novelty of dating a billionaire wore off as soon as they realized Kaleb spent more time inside his company's headquarters than he did jet-setting around the world, making social appearances. So it was an interesting change of pace to be sharing a meal with an attractive female who wasn't trying to impress him or talk him into taking her shopping or to a swanky, new restaurant.

Actually, Kaleb got the impression that Molly couldn't wait for him to leave. They'd barely walked outside the café when Hunter invited him over to play video games. Kaleb was tempted to accept, if only to see Molly squirm some more.

"I thought we were going to head into Boise today to see that new superhero movie," Molly told her nephew.

"Superhero movie?" Kaleb asked. He knew exactly which one she was talking about because he'd been an adviser on set to Robert Downey, Jr., and had been invited to the premiere a few weeks ago. "Could you be a little more specific?"

"You know." Molly rolled her wrist in a circle. "The one where the guy wears that suit and he fights that bad guy who is trying to destroy that thing."

Hunter slapped a palm to his forehead. "He's called Iron Man." Then the kid looked at Kaleb. "You wanna come with us?"

"I wish I could." And he was surprised to realize that was the truth. He'd love to sit by Molly in a dark air-conditioned movie theater, sharing a hot bucket of buttery popcorn… Wait. Was she supposed to eat popcorn? He pulled out his phone to ask his voice-operated search engine, then saw the two sets of eyes eagerly awaiting his response to the original question. Although each set looked hopeful for opposite answers.

"Actually, I can't," he finally said, and Molly let out the breath she'd been holding. "I'm supposed to go with my family on some sort of ATV tour this afternoon."

Her look of relief suddenly turned to one of blanket envy. He recognized the expression from twenty minutes ago when she was staring at the maple syrup dripping off the cinnamon roll French toast he was eating, looking like she wanted to stab him with her fork so that she could lick his plate clean.

Just then, Hunter waved at a kid getting out of an SUV down the street. "That's Jake Marconi. Hold on a sec, I'm gonna go tell him something."

The boy left Kaleb standing there alone with his aunt.

"I'll give you ten dollars to switch with me this afternoon," Molly said under her breath, her nephew barely out of hearing distance.

"I'd gladly switch for free," Kaleb replied. "But my dad keeps accusing me of avoiding my family. Trust me. I'd much rather see the movie again than bounce along an overgrown trail, hanging on to some four-wheeled motorcycle for dear life."

Her face was incredulous. "Are you kidding? Who'd want to sit and watch a bunch of fake action on the screen when you could be out there living it?"

"Someone who doesn't want to spend the evening on his sister's sofa with a heating pad wedged under his back." Not that Kaleb was worried about a flare-up from his old surgery, but it was obvious that an adrenaline junkie like Molly—or at least like most pilots—wouldn't understand that some people preferred to get their excitement the virtual way.

"Hey, Kaleb." Hunter ran back to them, another boy

on his heels and a woman trying to keep up behind them. "This is my friend Jake. I told him you'd sign his copy of 'Alien Pirates: Martianbeard's Redemption.'"

"Sorry for imposing on you like this," Jake's mother said when she caught up to them. She pulled a plastic case out of her purse. "But my son heard you were in town and has been carrying this video game around in the hopes that we'd run into you and could get your autograph."

"Of course," he said as the mom handed him a Sharpie. He cleared his throat, mostly embarrassed that Molly was watching the entire encounter, but secretly hoping she was slightly impressed. Other women would be, but Molly was turning out to be unlike anyone else he'd ever met.

Mrs. Marconi, as if suddenly realizing someone else was standing there, held out her phone to Molly. "Would you mind taking a picture of us?"

"That's my aunt Molly," Hunter explained to everyone. "You might've seen her when she and Kaleb picked me up at baseball practice on Friday night. We were just having breakfast together."

Even to Kaleb's ears, the kid was laying it on a bit thick with the implications of how well they were acquainted. But he knew how twelve-year-old boys talked when they wanted to impress their friends. Unfortunately, Molly's face turned scarlet and she tried to hide it behind the phone as she held it up for a picture. She didn't even count to three or tell them to say cheese before quickly tapping the shutter and telling Hunter, "C'mon, bud. We better get going if we don't want to be late for that movie."

Kaleb didn't get a chance to say goodbye to her and

was left standing with Jake and his mom, who was possibly an even bigger video game fan than her son. If only his assistant could see him now. Take that, Angela. Some people might want his brothers' autograph on balls and team jerseys, but there were also people in this world who wanted his. Maybe he should call his director of marketing and look into producing more memorabilia.

Unfortunately, death by ATV would be preferable to all the personal questions Mrs. Marconi was soon launching his way. She wanted to know how long he'd be in town and how well he knew Maxine Cooper's sister. Kaleb tried to direct the conversation back to Jake and level eight of "Pirate Space Blasters." After about two minutes—which felt like two hours—he tapped on his watch and said he had an important conference call to get to.

Still driving his dad's truck, Kaleb slowly took the road to his sister's house. He didn't even notice that he hadn't activated his Bluetooth or punched in coordinates onto the navigation screen. He was too busy remembering the way Molly had looked at that syrup, wondering how his body would react if she looked at him the same way. So maybe the breakfast had been a bit awkward. But in a good way.

There definitely could've been worse ways to spend his morning.

When they got back from seeing the movie in Boise, Molly followed Hunter into Maxine and Cooper's house. They'd moved after they found out they were having a baby and would need something bigger than the two-bedroom apartment in town.

Her sister looked even more pregnant than she had on Friday morning when she and Cooper had left town. Hunter didn't seem to mind his mother's increasing belly as she held the boy in a firm hug and told him how much they'd missed him.

Cooper agreed, and when he wrapped his arms around his stepson, he practically lifted the twelve-year-old off his feet. Molly hung back, shifting from her left foot to her right. The Markham family hadn't been big in the demonstrative affection department and Molly never seemed to know what to do when she saw parents openly displaying their love for their kids. Sure, she was technically related to them, but she and Maxine weren't the kind of sisters who got blubbery and emotional whenever they saw each other. As children, they'd been physically close by default. It was difficult not to be when six kids shared two rooms. But all that togetherness only made the Markham siblings anxious to spring out on their own as soon as they hit adulthood.

Being military brats, it wasn't like they'd had a childhood home to go back to, so their visits were few and far between and the distance became more and more natural. Not that Molly was complaining. There were plenty of things she wasn't ready to discuss with her family just yet, anyway.

"Did you guys have fun?" Maxine asked.

"So much fun," Hunter replied. "I got to see Kaleb Chatterson a bunch and we went kayaking and biking and saw a movie and everything. It was a blast."

"Kaleb Chatterson, huh?" her sister asked Hunter, but Molly knew the question was really directed at her. Luckily, Hunter launched into a dialogue about some video game something or other and Molly took the opportunity to excuse herself and go to the restroom.

She'd been careful about monitoring her blood sugar more often while she'd been babysitting her nephew, administering her doses of insulin prior to every meal. At the theater, she'd calculated the amount of carbs in her popcorn, but then mindlessly shoved a handful of M&Ms in her mouth when Hunter had passed her the box during the movie.

Molly had been mentally kicking herself for the mistake the whole drive here and had even been pushing her rented four-cylinder Toyota to mach speeds to make it back to Sugar Falls just in case she had another episode. She heard the machine beep and let out a sigh of relief at the number. It was a little high, but she was still within the normal range. Knowing that she'd be eating soon, she gave herself another dose.

When she stepped out of the restroom, the scent of garlic and whatever else her brother-in-law was cooking reached her. The kitchen was huge and opened up to a sprawling living room. Cooper somehow managed to look incredibly manly while he bustled around with mixing bowls and pans as Maxine pulled out one of the counter stools next to hers and waved Molly over.

"How was the babymoon?" Molly quickly asked her sister, hoping that if she could keep them talking, she could avoid answering questions about herself. At least, it had worked well enough when Hunter occupied Kaleb with plenty of inquiries throughout breakfast. Mmm. Breakfast. Her stomach rumbled. That had been quite a few hours ago and the popcorn she'd inhaled at the movies wasn't holding her over. She was starving.

"I said, how long is your leave?" Maxine asked, and Molly realized she'd totally tuned her sister out.

The truth was Molly didn't know how long she was staying. Her commanding officer had told her to take some time off and to think about things before making any big decisions about her career. Assuming the Bureau of Personnel told her she would still have one, which was doubtful. "Oh. Maybe a couple of weeks? You know how the military is when it comes to that sort of thing."

"In that case, I'm glad Cooper is making all your favorite foods for dinner tonight. Baked macaroni and cheese, sweet potato casserole, garlic bread and coffee cake with brown sugar crumble."

Uh-oh. Carbs, carbs and more carbs. Molly couldn't eat any of that. At least, she didn't think she could. Did sweet potato casserole count as a vegetable?

"Were you planning to serve any salad with that?" Molly asked, then immediately regretted it when her sister squinted at her suspiciously.

"Not unless your diet has done a complete one-eighty from the last time I've seen you, Moll Doll."

Actually, Molly's entire life had just done a complete one-eighty, along with a few barrel rolls, a pitchback and quite possibly an upcoming defensive spiral. But she wasn't about to admit that. "Nah, I think I just ate too much popcorn and my stomach has been a little sensitive lately."

She caught her sister giving a pointed look to Cooper.

"I saw that!" Molly said.

"Saw what?"

"That face you made right now at your husband. What's that supposed to mean?"

"It's just that my stomach was sensitive a few months ago," Maxine said, then gave her an encouraging smile. "Back when I was in my first trimester."

Molly gasped. "I'm not pregnant."

"Don't get mad at me for asking. All I know is that you and Trevor called off the wedding and you never said why, and now you're on some sort of extended leave, and I just figured…" Maxine let her voice trail off.

"I'm pretty sure I wouldn't have called off my wedding if I was expecting a child."

"Some people do." Maxine shrugged her shoulders. "So then, why did you guys break up?"

The question threw Molly for a loop. This wasn't the kind of thing her family normally talked about. In fact, when Beau, Maxine's first husband, died in a car crash ten years ago, Molly had no idea that her sister's marriage had been on the rocks until she overheard Kylie and their other friend, Mia, whispering in the restroom at the funeral home.

Molly looked at Cooper, who had his back to them and was chopping lettuce, presumably for an unplanned salad. No doubt, he was attentively listening to their discussion—he was a cop, after all. Fortunately, though, he was polite enough to pretend otherwise.

There were other things she wasn't ready to divulge, but her breakup was the least of her worries. "He was cheating on me."

"With someone else?"

Molly glanced at her brother-in-law, who was holding himself perfectly still. She hoped he was better than his wife when it came to interrogations. "Of course with someone else. That's usually how cheating works."

"Sorry. You're right. Did you confront him?"

"I didn't really have to. He was there when I walked in and…they were…in the middle of…um, a very romantic meal."

"How do you know it was romantic?"

"Because they were feeding each other directly from Chinese takeout containers."

"But didn't he try to explain or anything?"

"They also weren't wearing any clothes at the time." Molly shrugged. "What was there to explain?"

Cooper made a choking sound, but instead of being shocked into minding her own business, Maxine only studied her.

"What?"

"You don't sound very heartbroken."

Crap. Her sister would never buy the excuse that Molly was in Sugar Falls recovering from a failed relationship if she couldn't squeeze out some sort of emotion. But the truth was, she'd hardly given Trevor that much thought lately. In fact, she initially went on her non-honeymoon thinking she would sort some things out and mourn the breakup. However, all she ended up mourning was her formerly healthy, active, career-filled life. Having only gotten her formal diagnosis a few days before she'd caught Trevor, the broken engagement was just a temporary diversion from facing everything else going on in her life. By the end of the vacation, she'd wound up feeling more like she'd just dodged a bullet.

"You know me." Molly lifted her hands up in a careless gesture. "I like to keep my head down and focus on the mission."

"Is the mission to distract yourself with a new guy?" Maxine smirked, then shifted toward the front of her seat when Molly tilted her head to the side. "I know it's none of my business but the word on the street is that you and Kaleb Chatterson were looking pretty chummy on Friday afternoon in Duncan's parking lot."

Molly felt hollow. Her mouth moved, but no words came out.

"Small town," Maxine explained. "And Elaine Marconi said she ran into you guys at the Cowgirl Up Café this morning, which only confirmed all the gossip."

This was it. Molly could come clean and tell her sister about the diabetes and how Kaleb had helped her when she'd needed some insulin the other day and that everything was fine and under control. That's what a normal, courageous person would do. And Molly had always considered herself extremely courageous, if only relatively normal.

Which was why she was surprised when the only explanation she gave was a nervous chuckle.

"I knew it!" Maxine pointed an accusing finger at her. "You and Kaleb Chatterson are a thing. I can't wait to tell Kylie that it's true. Frankly, as far as a rebound relationship goes, you could do a lot worse."

Molly made a noncommittal sound through her tense lips. Cooper had abandoned the lettuce on the cutting board and had his hands linked behind his neck—either to use his forearms to cover his ears or to brace for impact.

"I mean, it *is* only a rebound thing, right?" Maxine asked.

Molly's stomach felt like the empty hull of a bombed-out cargo plane, but she chalked it up to hunger. If this was what it took to get her family off her back, then who was she to throw them off her misguided course?

Chapter Five

Kaleb was sprawled out on his sister's sectional, stretching out his back and trying to overcome the lingering soreness from that jarring ATV ride this afternoon. His cell phone vibrated in his pocket and he had to wait until his twin nieces created a suitable distraction in their high chairs so that he could pull the thing out and check it without getting another lecture from his dad about today's technology-dependent society.

He didn't recognize the number on his screen, but when he opened the message, he couldn't help the smile that floated to his face. It could only be from one person.

We have a Code Sister in effect. I repeat. A Code Sister.

He typed back a response. What in the world is a Code Sister?

A few dots appeared on his screen, only to vanish just as quickly. Damn. What had Molly been about to say? Did Maxine find out about her diabetes? He typed another question mark and pressed Send. His toes twitched inside his sneakers and his palms itched. He didn't take his eyes off the screen as he sat up straighter. The only time Kaleb got frustrated with technology was when the person on the other end took too long to respond.

But Kylie's loud exclamation of "Oh my gosh!" drew his attention away. "Maxine just texted me and asked if I knew you were dating her sister, Molly."

Kaleb blinked three times. "Dating?"

"Which one is Molly?" Bobby Chatterson, Sr. asked nobody in particular. "Was she at the wedding?"

Kaleb didn't even hear the answer because his pulse was pounding too loudly in his ears. Was this what Molly had meant by a Code Sister? That both of their sisters thought they were dating? *Each other?*

His phone vibrated again as Molly's response appeared. Pretty please just go along with it. I'll owe you.

Something tugged at the corners of his mouth. He doubted Captain Markham used the phrase *pretty please* very often.

"Is it true?" Kylie finally asked him.

"Is what true?"

"Don't try to use the stall tactics on me." Kylie walked over to the couch, one hand firmly planted on her hip, the other waving her electronic tattletale device at his face. "My husband's a psychologist, so I know all those mind tricks."

"If by *dating*, you mean *hanging out*—" Kaleb hated the fact that he'd just used air quotes "—then yes, Molly Markham and I have spent some time together."

That wasn't exactly a lie. He was pretending to be on vacation, anyway, what difference did a pretend girlfriend make at this point? Wait. Was their fake relationship at the girlfriend/boyfriend stage? Molly really should've clarified that. Kaleb desperately avoided those types of conversations with women in his real life. He didn't do commitments, and he certainly didn't discuss them. Usually, when a woman he was dating starting dropping hints about getting more serious, he had Angela email them on his behalf. So then how did one bring that up with a lady who wasn't even programmed into his contact list? He quickly remedied that by typing in her name under the information screen.

"Is it serious?" his mom asked. Lacey Chatterson's soft eyes grew round and hopeful, her fingers clasped together in front of her in a semiprayerful state.

"Mom!" Kaleb rolled his eyes. "We met for the first time on Friday."

"That doesn't mean anything," his dad said, bringing a bowl of chips to the coffee table. Great, his family was now cornering him on the living room sofa. "Kylie and Drew only knew each other for all of five hours before *they* got married."

"Dad!" His sister followed with a bowl of salsa. Man, they were really settling in for this interrogation. "Drew and I had special circumstances."

It was no secret that his baby sister and her straitlaced husband had gotten drunk in Reno and accidentally ended up at a wedding chapel. But Kaleb didn't believe in accidents. He liked having a plan and sticking to it. Unfortunately, with his family hovering around him, he couldn't exactly text Molly back and ask her what the damn plan was.

Kaleb's company had developed some of the best role-playing games on the market, but those usually involved alternate universes with alien pirates and zombie dragons. Normally, he was good at games as long as he knew the rules. Unfortunately, someone had suddenly thrown him into the role of boyfriend—and unlike the online versions he'd created, this one might actually affect real lives.

"I'm sending Maxine a text inviting her family for dinner on Wednesday," Kylie said as she typed furiously on her phone.

"Wait." Kaleb held up his palm. "I think everyone is getting way too ahead of themselves here."

"Too late." His sister grinned and held up her display screen. "Maxine already accepted."

"Don't you think that's going to be awkward?" Kaleb had been looking down at his own phone so long he had to push his glasses back into place.

"Trust me." Kylie reached out and squeezed his left shoulder. "It's much better to get all this relationship stuff out in the open."

"Listen to your sister, son." His dad squeezed his other shoulder. "She of all people knows what she's talking about."

"Dad!" Kylie gripped the left one tighter, thereby pulling him away from their father. Bobby Chatterson yanked back.

"This is what I mean by awkward." Kaleb dislodged himself from their not-so-reassuring grips and stood up. "Our family always gets so competitive and loud and chaotic and you guys are going to end up scaring her away."

His sister's inspecting scan moved from his messy

hair down to his feet and back up again. "The only thing that's going to scare Molly away is that outfit."

"What's wrong with my clothes?" Kaleb asked, holding out the hem of his T-shirt so he could see what design was on it. He loved his collection of quirky T-shirts.

"Nothing, if you're a fifteen-year-old boy," Kylie replied.

"No fifteen-year-old boy of mine would wear sneakers that cost as much as those." His dad pointed to Kaleb's custom-made designer shoes. "Are those supposed to be suede?"

"Perhaps you have something a little more impressive?" his mom asked. "What do you normally wear to meetings?"

"I normally wear this to meetings." Kaleb crossed his arms in front of his chest. "I don't exactly have a suit-and-tie kind of job."

Actually, he did have a couple of well-tailored suits back at his penthouse. In Seattle. Where he wasn't on vacation. Yet, even if he had access to all the best clothes in the world, he still wouldn't wear them. It was one thing to pretend to be dating a woman he'd barely met. It was another to pretend to be something he wasn't.

Which brought him back to why he didn't do relationships in the first place. People, especially the pretty female variety, always wanted to believe that he was some sort of superstar—some sort of megapowerful billionaire who was in the market for a trophy wife. In reality, all he wanted was a simple life where he could be left alone to concentrate on his work. Unfortunately, the women who tended to throw themselves at him weren't interested in the boring, geeky version of Kaleb Chatterson. In the end, they ended up wasting their time when they found out he wasn't going to change.

His phone finally vibrated again.

"Is that her?" His sister jumped up from the couch, trying to read the display. He put his hand on her forehead, holding her at a distance the way he'd done when they were kids and she'd wanted one of his collector's edition action figures for her Barbie Dreamhouse.

He had to read the screen quickly because Kylie's kicking range had apparently gotten longer since she was seven years old. It also seemed as though all the splits and cheerleading jumps from her college years had perfected her toe points.

Don't worry about dinner happening on Wednesday. I'll try and tell my sister everything by then.

He'd barely gotten the phone safely tucked into his pocket when he wrapped Kylie into a fierce bear hug. She pinched his ribs before finally hugging him back.

"We're only nosy because we care about you," she mumbled into his shoulder.

"That explains the nosy part, but not the embarrassing part," Kaleb replied, patting her on the head.

"Embarrassing? I promise to be on my best behavior." Kylie stepped out of his arms, her right hand raised as if she were swearing an oath. "But I can't speak for Dad or the rest of our siblings."

Kaleb groaned. While he'd dated his fair share of women, he'd never brought a girlfriend home—pretend or otherwise. If teasing was an Olympic sport, his brothers would win the gold medals, with Kylie tying their old man for the silver. Hopefully, Molly would come clean and tell her sister the truth by then. It would be way less painful for everyone. Or at least for him.

Did you tell her yet?

Kaleb's text was in Molly's in-box when she woke up on Tuesday morning. The digital clock on her screen was still set to military time and she tried not to deliver bad news to anyone if the word *oh* was part of the hour. Then she realized he must've been talking about last night. She hoped he wasn't as mortified about hearing the lie as she had been telling it. Although, really, it wasn't so much a lie as a diversionary tactic. It was unfortunate that Kaleb was caught in the crosshairs, but he was the one who'd put his reputation in harm's way. Twice, she might add.

I tried to, Molly wrote back. Then added, Couldn't find the right time.

It was the truth. If Maxine would've asked her about her job again, Molly would've probably said something. Or if her sister had made a comment about her not eating all her favorite foods—and, oh, man, had that been a challenge when she'd shoved mouthful after mouthful of salad into her mouth and then claimed to be too full for more than a small bite of anything else—she might have mentioned it. But their family didn't get all up in each other's business like that. They certainly didn't talk about personal things. In fact, that whole conversation about Trevor cheating on her was more than enough failure to share in one night.

Molly would like to think that it was a matter of respecting boundaries. So if Maxine wasn't going to pry, then Molly didn't want to burden her with any unnecessary knowledge.

But maybe the Chatterson family wasn't like that.

Her phone chimed again and she looked at the image Kaleb had just sent her. It was a cartoon elephant up in a tree, balancing its huge, cowering body on a tiny branch with a tiny mouse below.

She replied with a picture of what looked to be a honeycomb.

What is that?

Beeswax, she typed. Then added, So that you can mind your own.

She pulled the soft, expensive sheets over her head. At least she had her sister's apartment to herself today. She could spend the day researching healthy meal options and forming a plan to tell her sister the truth.

A motorcycle engine revved outside her window.

Or she could do one of those ATV tour things that Kaleb had mentioned yesterday. She'd been beyond jealous when he'd brought it up. While it wasn't a plane, with a powerful motor, some off-course trails and the wind in her hair, it could be the next best thing. Molly did her clearest thinking when she was piloting something.

She sat up in bed and placed a call. But the company who did the tours had a group from the senior center scheduled for that morning and Molly didn't want to get stuck going the speed recommended by the AARP. In fact, she didn't want to go with anyone at all. Not even a guide. She assured the man who answered the phone at Russell Sports that she knew what she was doing and only required the rental. It would also be cheaper that way.

Surveying Maxine's cupboards, she found a questionable-looking granola bar and pulled a couple of bottles of water from the fridge. She threw those and her insulin kit into a canvas cinch sack she could sling onto her back during the ride. Then she questioned whether she should pack something else. She didn't want to go to Duncan's and risk running into another gossiping biddy. However, she also didn't want to get stuck out on some wilderness trail with only one healthy snack.

In the end, Molly stopped off at Domino's Deli in town and grabbed a turkey sub on a whole-wheat roll and a bag of pretzels, which looked like the least caloric option on the potato chip rack. What else did she need? It was more food than she would've taken on a twenty-four-hour combat training exercise. Even Kaleb would've been proud of her foresight.

Nope. She refused to think about him and what he would think. Today was for her. Molly would deal with her sister and Kaleb and everyone else tonight.

Unfortunately, by the time she'd made it back to the apartment that evening, she was covered in mud and so jacked up on adrenaline the only thing she wanted to confront was a hot shower and the last half of *Pearl Harbor* on the movie channel.

On Wednesday morning, Molly awoke to another text from Kaleb.

We're grilling chicken tonight, but I don't know what the sides will be. I'll let you know as soon as I can, but make sure you check your levels before you get here. Maybe bring a snack just in case.

Molly almost threw the phone across the room. She didn't know what annoyed her more. The fact that he was bossing her about food choices again or his assumption that she still hadn't talked to Maxine.

It didn't help her mood that the sweet vanilla scent of the cookies baking downstairs had permeated the apartment. And she couldn't have any. Probably ever again. Ugh. She needed coffee.

She sat up in bed and checked her blood levels, giving herself a morning dose of the longer lasting insulin. Then she weaved her way to the kitchen in nothing but her dingy gray Air Force Academy T-shirt and a loose pair of running shorts she had to roll up at the waist to stay on her hips. Turning on the coffeemaker, she caught her reflection in the microwave glass and yanked on her rubber band to adjust her sloppy ponytail from the side of her head to more of a forty-five-degree angle.

Molly had just set a fresh K-Cup to brew when a knock sounded at the door. She figured it had to be Maxine taking a break from the shop downstairs and sighed. They might as well get this talk over with.

When she swung open the door, Molly wasn't braced for the shock of seeing Kaleb on the small landing, holding a brown bag from Duncan's Market.

Molly looked past him, down the stairs toward the bakery below. He followed her gaze and—without her asking the question on the tip of her sleepy tongue—he said, "Yes, your sister is down there, and yes, she saw me come up."

Her caffeine-deprived brain was still a little fuzzy, so

she scratched at her head, then froze, realizing how her hair must look. She crossed her arms, then uncrossed them to tug the hem of her shorts down so it wouldn't look like she wasn't wearing anything below, before crossing her arms again. "What are you doing here?"

"Now, now. Is that any way to greet the man you're dating?"

Her reflexes shot to life and she whispered, "Get in here," before snatching the front of his T-shirt and yanking him inside.

The problem came when she didn't sidestep quickly enough and the solid muscular wall of Kaleb's chest crashed into her, forcing him to wrap an arm around her to steady them both. The cotton of his shirt was soft and worn under her fingers, and when she took a steadying breath, she inhaled the lemon and cedar scent of his soap.

He wiggled his eyebrows and said, "This greeting's more like it."

"Huh?" His hand slid lower until it cupped the rounding curve just below her waistband and her palms instinctively moved up over his pecs toward his wide shoulders.

"Definitely more like the kind of reception I would expect from my girlfriend."

Girlfriend? He had a girlfriend? His heavily lidded eyes were staring intently at her lips and it suddenly dawned on Molly that he meant her. She banged her big toe into the hardwood floor as she hopped backward.

"Don't worry." She held her palms up. "I'm going to tell Maxine this morning so we don't have to do that whole dating charade thing tonight."

"Too late," he said, then strode past her and set the bag on a kitchen counter.

"What do you mean, too late?" She tried to get her breathing under control as he pulled groceries out. "And what are you doing?"

He held up a carton of eggs. "I'm fixing you breakfast. What does it look like I'm doing?"

That didn't explain anything at all. But she certainly wasn't going to turn down a free meal. "Did I miss something?"

"Yeah. You missed your opportunity to tell your sister the truth."

"Dinner isn't until six." She looked at the clock on the microwave. "I have all day to tell her."

He propped up an electronic tablet on some sort of holder and began tapping the screen. "Not anymore, you..." He was so intent on whatever he was doing he didn't finish his sentence.

Molly waved a hand in front of his face. His only response was to sigh and look up at her.

"What's going on?" she asked.

"I had my assistant, Angela, send me a video on how to make an omelet and the Wi-Fi at Duncan's was spotty this morning so I need to watch it again to make sure I bought all the right ingredients."

"Kaleb!" Molly had to restrain herself from banging her head against the cabinet in frustration. "I meant what is going with us?"

"Sorry, I thought we had the kind of fake relationship where we don't explain things to each other."

She closed her eyes and counted to five. When she opened them, he had his hands on his hips, one brow raised as if he needed to ensure her full attention. "I guess I deserve that. But I said I was going to talk to Maxine and come clean. I would've texted you the all clear afterward."

"And I said it was too late."

"But you didn't say why."

"Because I had to spend the entire day yesterday trapped on a white-water raft with all of my family, answering questions about you. Questions I didn't necessarily know the answers to, but had to make stuff up as I went along so that I could keep your secret safe."

"I'm really sorry about that." She tried to make an apologetic face. "But at least you got to go white-water rafting."

"Molly," he growled, then pinched the bridge of his nose. "Aren't you paying attention?"

She nodded, then slowly shook her head. "But I'm trying to."

"My family now thinks we're dating. On Monday night I simply didn't correct them. But yesterday I actively engaged in, well, I hate to use the word *deception*, but it's the only thing that fits."

"Oh."

"Then, this morning, my mom told me that my eyes lit up whenever I talked about you and that she was so glad I'd finally met someone I was interested in because she worries about me working too much."

A tingling of warmth started in her toes and spread up to her torso. "Your eyes lit up when you talked about me?"

His neck turned a charming shade of pink as the muscles near his jaw line pulled tighter. "No, it was probably only the river water. I had my contacts in. Anyway, my

point is that my family now thinks there's something between us and I've never lied to them before."

"But we're not dating."

"We are now. This—" he gestured to the groceries on
the counter "—is a breakfast date. I'm told that women
think it's very romantic when men cook for them."

"But you didn't ask me."

"Did you ask me when you told Maxine we were
dating?"

"I didn't tell her! She assumed."

"However, you didn't correct her."

"You didn't correct your family, either."

"Which is why I'm not going to make liars out of
us." He smiled in triumph, as if he'd just masterminded
some great escape.

"I don't get it. Are we or are we not pretending we're
dating?"

"We're not pretending anything. We don't have to.
You're not in town long, I'm not in town long. We'll go
on a few dates—in a strictly platonic sense—and then,
when we leave Sugar Falls, we say goodbye."

"We do?"

"Yes." He began cracking eggs into a bowl. "You
hate long-distance relationships."

"I also hate being told what to do. Even by someone
who is strictly platonic."

"Well, too bad." He unlocked his phone and pulled
up her text messages. "You said it yourself. You owe
me."

She took a gulp of coffee, but without the half-and-
half to cool it down, it burned her tongue. "I know
what I said."

His tablet, phone and smartwatch all chimed simultaneously. "I forgot I have a video chat in half an hour."

"You're going to take a conference call over here?" She smirked, her eyes narrowing. Kaleb acted like he was the one doing her the favor, but she bet the real reason he came over here was to get some work done without his family bothering him. "While we're on a date, Cupcake?"

"Cupcake?"

"Isn't that what we call each other?"

"No. We call each other by our names. Because we're grown-ups."

"Well, I'm going to go take a shower, Cupcake. Let me know when my omelet's ready."

Chapter Six

That evening, Kaleb stared at his reflection in the bathroom mirror at his sister's house. Molly and her family would be here in less than an hour and Kylie's words about his taste in clothing were coming back to haunt him. Not that he was trying to impress anyone, but when Molly had answered the door this morning in her T-shirt and short shorts, Kaleb had been tempted to kiss her right there on the spot. Then she'd pulled him toward her and it was all he could do to remind himself that this whole dating plan they'd come up with wasn't supposed to be serious.

Speaking of which, their official first date this morning hadn't gone exactly according to plan. Well, the omelet part did at least. He'd no more than plated the vegetable-filled eggs when Molly'd come out of the bathroom wearing athletic leggings and a sweatshirt so loose the oversize neck draped to the side, leaving a tan shoulder bare. Well, bare except for the pink bikini strap tied behind her damp, wavy ponytail.

She smelled like the coconut-mango smoothies he used to get when he was a kid vacationing in Hawaii for real with his family, as opposed to the forced kind they now endured as adults. Kaleb had been tempted to draw her in closer to see if her skin tasted as good as it smelled. Instead, he'd doused the flames of attraction by handing her a plate and a stack of papers he'd printed out that morning.

"I thought you could look over these while I'm on my conference chat," he'd said. She rolled her eyes as he set up his laptop on one end of the table, and at some point between his conference call with his lawyers in the Tokyo office over the Japanese production rights to his latest game and his brainstorming session with his writing staff about the possibility of giving one of his video characters their own cartoon show, Molly had taken off.

He'd been wearing his headset and pacing back and forth in the small living room when she'd given him a discreet wave, pointed toward the stairs and made a gesture with her two fingers indicating she was going downstairs. He'd assumed she was going to hang out with her sister, but after an hour, he'd discovered she'd left him a note on the back of the diabetic menu plan Angela had emailed him this morning.

Thanks for the "date." And for bringing up white-water rafting. I'm going to spend the day on the river. M.

In the past, when a woman he was dating was annoyed that he wasn't paying her enough attention, she pouted or started a fight. However, Molly hadn't looked the least bit annoyed. Actually, when she'd left, she'd looked pretty carefree and a little relieved. Just to be sure, he'd sent her a text apologizing for being occupied with his business calls, and she'd replied with a thumbs-up emoji. Clearly, neither one of them were expecting candlelight and roses out of this relationship.

So then why was he standing here in his sister's bathroom suddenly concerned with his appearance? It wasn't like he was back in high school, wearing pimple cream and his back brace under a *Battlestar Galactica* T-shirt?

The doorbell sounded over the barking of his brother Bobby Junior's six-month-old goldendoodle and his five nieces and nephews. Or was it seven now? Did Kylie's brother-in-law's kids count as honorary Chattersons? Kaleb braced his hands against the counter and reminded himself that no matter how good Molly might look out there, they were only dating—in a strictly platonic sense—for eight more days.

Besides, she was probably more worried about whether he'd slip and bring up her diabetes than whether he was wearing some fancy collared shirt.

What was he so worried about, anyway? Kaleb was a global leader in a multi-billion-dollar industry. Surely, he could handle one crazy family dinner.

He ran a hand through his hair, then made his way toward the living room, dodging a Nerf football, shaking off a puppy sniffing his pant leg as if it was about to mark its territory and stepping over his twin nieces working on something called "tummy time." Through the cluster of men standing in the corner discussing the best bull pens in the major leagues, he caught a view of the open kitchen where Molly was thanking his father for the plastic cup the older man just handed her. Knowing that whatever frozen concoction his dad was serving was most likely on her discarded list of high sugar foods to avoid, he sprang into action.

"Hey, you," Kaleb said when he put an arm around Molly's shoulder, somewhat out of breath after the obstacle course of kids and pets he'd had to wade through to get to her. His approach must've lacked the finesse he'd intended because her body jerked back just enough to slosh the fruity liquid around in her cup.

She frowned in response.

"Oh, great. Strawberry daiquiris. My favorite," he exclaimed, prying the beverage from her hand and taking a huge gulp before whispering in her ear, "You're not supposed to drink stuff like this."

"And you're supposed to be my fake date, not my endocrinologist," she whispered back.

"Not fake," he mumbled, then took another sip. "Platonic."

"So, Molly," Kylie interrupted them, her eyes sharp and focused as though she was ready to pounce on the merest hint of tension between them. "I know you've already met Kaleb, the black sheep of our family. But let me introduce you to the rest of the Chatterson clan."

And so it began. Kaleb would try to make things go as smoothly as possible, but when it came to his loud, opinionated family, he knew better than to make any promises he couldn't keep.

"Maxine ran through your family tree on the car ride over here, so I think I've got all the adults' names," Molly said to Kaleb as they stood on the deck overlooking the lake, her initial jitters of meeting everyone tamped down now that she knew the only nerve-racking part would be to get through the rest of the evening without blowing their cover. "But I can't remember which kids go with which parents."

Most of the men were gathered around the grill, which had been moved to the grassy area below. Maxine was sitting with her swollen ankles propped up on another seat, the ladies clustered nearby drinking their strawberry daiquiris while Hunter and the rest of the kids played some sort of made-up game that resembled Wiffle ball. Or badminton. Or a combination of both. Molly wondered if they were even following a set of rules.

"So the twin girls in that playpen thing belong to Kylie and her husband, Drew." Kaleb used his beer bottle to point. "Those three redheads chasing after the dog who just stole the pink ball belong to my brother Bobby Junior. His wife is off at some health spa this week, which is fine because she hates our family vacations and isn't afraid to let everyone know."

"How could anyone hate this?" Molly asked. It was true; so far everyone had been so nice and some of the stories they'd told about Kaleb were not only hilarious, they also took the attention off her. They were nothing like her family. Sure, they teased each other mercilessly, but each sibling gave as good as they got. Nobody was spared and no secret was safe. The Chattersons were open and warm and playful and, within thirty minutes, made Molly feel more relaxed and at ease than she'd been during the past few weeks.

"Are you kidding? It's a circus, but with more prodding of the caged animals and a few extra clowns who aren't very funny."

"I think you secretly love it," she said, then laughed when he rolled his eyes. "You've only looked at your smartwatch five times and haven't called your assistant once. Clearly, you're not that bored."

"Not bored? I'm on high alert. I can't let my guard down for a second around these jokesters. You know what these big families are like."

"Actually," she said, then cleared her throat when a hint of emotion welled up in her chest, "I don't. I mean, there's a lot of us, but we're not exactly the type of family that vacations together."

"Um, aren't you vacationing with your sister right now?" Kaleb asked.

Molly schooled her expression so that she didn't appear too uneasy. "This isn't exactly a vacation."

"What do you mean?"

"It's more of a temporary medical leave. I don't know when I'll be going back to work." She refused to make eye contact with him, not wanting to see the concern she knew would be reflected there. But because she'd already admitted as much, she added, "If I return to work at all."

"I'm guessing you're not going to tell your sister about that, either?"

"Eventually. Maybe." So much for that short-lived feeling of relaxation. When he kept looking at her, she felt the need to explain. "People always assumed that because we're sisters we're born confidantes. I mean, don't get me wrong. It isn't like we fight or dislike each other. But growing up in the Markham household, there was a pretty high value placed on privacy. Especially when you were number five out of six. By the time I came along, everyone had already been forced to share rooms, toys and even their ice-cream bowls. Anyway, nobody wanted to have to share their dreams or their innermost feelings, either. At least, not with their kid sister. On the rare occasions when we did have family dinners, silence was certainly golden. My siblings definitely aren't as informative and entertaining as yours. You're very lucky, Kaleb."

He studied her in the fading sunlight and she rocked back on her sandaled heels. Was he going to kiss her? Did she want him to? Desire curled around her tummy. A part of her had craved his lips on hers since the first time she saw him. But she certainly didn't want him making a move only because he felt sorry for her.

To get his attention—and hers—off a possible very public display of affection, she went back to their original conversation. "And those two boys, the other set of twins, who do they belong to?"

"Those little rascals aren't technically Chattersons. But they might as well be. And between me and you, they might be my favorite kids ever. Their parents are Carmen and Luke. Luke is Drew's twin brother."

"That makes three sets? Wow!"

"Yep. Moving on, the overweight basset hound belongs to Kane and Julia. And my brother Kevin over there—" he pointed to the guy wearing a ball cap and sunglasses, nursing a hangover on a lounge chair "—he can't even take care of a houseplant, let alone another living thing."

"Hey, Molly," one of the twin boys yelled up to them. "You ready for another drink? Uncle Kevin pays us five dollars every time we bring him a beer."

Before she could politely decline, Kaleb announced to the entire family below, "She's had enough."

Molly felt her face turn as red as the melted liquid in her red plastic cup.

"You don't have to make me sound like a lush who needs to be cut off." Then, to prove to his family that Kaleb wasn't calling the shots, she said, "I'll have one more, but I only have two dollars."

"You're on," the boy said, hustling over to the bar before his stepmom, who was still on duty and dressed in her police uniform, slapped a hand to her forehead and followed behind.

"I really don't think that's a good idea," Kaleb said, close on Molly's heels as she descended the steps. "There's a ton of sugar in those things and you don't want to…you know…with everyone watching."

"I also don't want to stand out or have your family think that there's something wrong with me," she replied through a tight smile. "I won't actually drink it."

He maneuvered himself in front of her path and quickly turned to face her, forcing her to stop one step above him. Their eyes were on the same level. "How about a Diet Coke instead?"

"How about I act like a normal houseguest and take an extra dose of insulin later?" She tried to step around him, but his hands reached out to grasp her hips and another one of those currents of electricity shot through her. Yet she didn't know if this was from desire or anger.

"Hey, look," the other twin called out. "Uncle Kaleb is gonna kiss her!"

If she hadn't already been blushing to the roots of her hair, she certainly was now. "You weren't going to kiss me, were you?"

"I didn't intend to, but now that everyone is watching us, it'll look weird if I don't. Unless you don't want me to…"

"Kiss her, Uncle Kaleb!" a little redhead girl yelled.

Molly's eyes widened, hoping he'd give her some sort of direction on how to handle this situation. When Kaleb placed a chaste kiss on her forehead, Kevin led all the kids in a round of disappointing boos.

"That was the best you could do?" Molly whispered before Carmen handed her the strawberry daiquiri and waved away the two dollars. She took a slug of the drink, hoping to cool her cheeks down, then quickly handed it over to Kaleb when the sugary contents hit her throat. Whew. She was going to pay for that later.

"I assure you, I could do a lot better," Kaleb said quietly, his thumb making slow circles along her hip.

Looking at the heat in his eyes, Molly didn't doubt for a second that if they didn't have a captive audience, the man would more than prove himself right.

The following morning, Kaleb told himself that he was only going to the Cowgirl Up Café for breakfast because he'd been craving some biscuits and gravy and he wanted to escape Bobby Junior's three noisy kids, who had overflowed from Kylie's lakefront house and were now intruding on his solitary stay at Kane's place. Not because he was hoping to see Molly in town. And definitely not because he was still looking for the opportunity to get her alone and make good on his promise of a more thorough kiss.

He parked the truck on Snowflake Boulevard and as he passed two horses—he did a double take to see that the animals were real and not just some sort of small-town stage prop—tied to a post outside the restaurant, the aroma of bacon and coffee almost made him forget the teasing his brothers had put him through after Molly had left last night. Almost.

When he pulled open the saloon-style front door of the café, his relief at seeing her sitting in a back booth upholstered with cow print was short-lived. Because sitting across the table from her was Kylie and Mia, a friend of his sister's and Maxine's from college.

There was a row of empty seats at the counter, but there was no way Kaleb could get away without acknowledging his sister, her friend and the woman he was supposedly dating. He dropped his laptop bag on one of the chairs at the counter, claiming his space in a way to announce to everyone that he had no intention of joining the women. He'd go say hello quickly, then come back over here to go through several financial reports and send out a few emails before his father started calling around looking for him.

"Ladies," he said by way of greeting, right before he spotted the half-eaten cinnamon roll in front of Molly. "What's going on?"

Really, he was asking Molly about her food choices, but thankfully Kylie thought the world revolved around her and assumed he was speaking to all of them.

"We're planning a baby shower for Maxine," Kylie said. "You remember my friend Mia, right?"

"Of course." Kaleb reached across to shake the petite brunette's hand. "Nice to see you again."

His sister and Mia went on to tell him about when they were having the party, but his eyes were drawn back to the pastry Molly had no doubt been eating before he'd arrived. Their talk of baby bottles and finger foods and stork decorations distracted him from what he really wanted to do, which was scope out Molly for any evidence of symptoms that might suggest she was about to have another one of her episodes.

However, Molly's expression was suspiciously riveted on whatever the other women were saying and she'd barely acknowledged his presence. She was so busted.

"Well, it sounds like you guys have things under control, so if you'll excuse me—" Kaleb nodded toward his laptop bag on the counter stool "—I'm going to have a quick bite before Dad calls me with whatever plans are on today's Chatterson family agenda."

"It's Jet Skiing," Kylie said. "Drew and Kane were pulling the Sea-Doos out of the boat shed when I left, and if they find out you're over here on that stupid computer again while they're taking orders from Dad, you're going to be put in charge of filling up all the water balloons for the Aqua Battle this afternoon."

"Nobody likes a rat, Kylie." Kaleb winked at his sister before turning to Molly. "Since you're not going to eat this, I'll finish it for you."

He snatched the cinnamon roll from the table just as she was reaching for the plate. The heat of her glare penetrated his back as he returned to his seat, but he didn't care. She would be thanking him later. He opened up his computer as an older waitress with hair much bigger and more peach colored than nature had intended leaned a spandex-covered hip against the counter. He recognized Freckles, the owner of the restaurant, from his last visit to town.

"It's been two years since you had one of my famous cinnamon rolls, Kaleb Chatterson," she said as she pulled a pencil from behind an earlobe lined with studded earrings. "You know I'd give you your own. You don't have to go around stealing them from my pretty customers. Even if you *are* dating her."

Kaleb risked a peek at the woman in question, praying she didn't hear what the sassy waitress had just announced. But the older woman snorted. "Small-town rumor mills been around long before you fancy computer kids ever invented that social media nonsense."

"Technically, Freckles," Kaleb defended himself, "I had one when I was in here on Monday."

"No, you had the cinnamon roll French toast. Two different things." Freckles used the pencil to gesture toward Monica, who'd waited on them a few days ago. "Darlin, even on my days off, I know what people are eating in my own restaurant. And more important, I know who they're eating it with."

The woman's wink revealed a smudge of green eye shadow that didn't match the fuchsia lipstick on her smirking grin. Kaleb didn't mind the good-natured teasing, especially since it kept her from noticing the way Molly had just downed two glasses of ice water and was beating a fast retreat to the restrooms.

"Well, today, I'll be having the biscuits and gravy and I'll be eating it alone," Kaleb said, not bothering to look at the menu.

When Freckles turned toward the kitchen, Kaleb waited a full forty-five seconds before following Molly to the back of the restaurant. Thankfully, the bathrooms were down the hall and none of the diners could see him as he waited outside. After a few minutes, or maybe only one—who was counting—he knocked on the door to the ladies' room. There was no answer so he jiggled the handle. It was unlocked, and he knew that if it was anything like the men's, there was only one separate stall inside.

He weighed his choices briefly before a vision of Molly, pale and nearly passed out as she had been inside Duncan's Market that day they'd first met, replayed in his mind.

He opened the door and was only slightly relieved that he hadn't walked in on another woman. He recognized her green sneakers under the stall. "Molly, is that you?"

She gasped. "Who else would it be?"

"Are you okay?"

"Kaleb, do you know this is a ladies' room?"

"If I didn't before, the hot-pink cowboy hat wallpaper would've given it away."

The sound of a plastic lid being snapped shut, followed by a zipper came from inside the stall before she finally emerged, shoving her little black case into her tote bag. "What are you doing in here?"

He nodded toward the straw purse. "What was your number?"

"My number is *supposed* to be that I don't have a stupid number. Two months ago, nobody cared about my levels. I didn't even know I *had* levels. Yet, now I'm living in this completely foreign land with a whole new language I never knew existed and every few hours, a drop of blood on a little test strip is supposed to tell me what kind of day I'm having."

"But you're not alone. People are going through exact same thing you are and—"

"Where, Kaleb?" Molly cut him off. "Where are these people who are going through this? Because they aren't here in the ladies' room with me. And they certainly aren't in my squadron, which is where I belong. I know that other people have this same disease. I even know that they have support groups. But right now, I'm still grieving my former life—the life that I probably will never get to go back to—and I don't need anyone else scrutinizing my every move and constantly reminding me of what I've lost."

His throat constricted and he wanted to argue that she hadn't lost everything. He'd downloaded several books on diabetes to his iPad and was convinced that she could manage it if given the right support tools. However, he also knew that she needed to grieve in her own way and come to these conclusions on her own. At least, that's what some of the experts said.

However, he couldn't stand by and let her hide her head in the sand on the deserted island she'd created for herself. "You're right that I'm not going through this, and I can't begin to imagine how I would react if I was. But you can't get mad at me for caring about you."

"I don't *need* you to care about me." She sighed but her lips weren't pressed into the rigid line of annoyance she usually made whenever he told her something she didn't want to hear. He hated seeing her defeated and had a feeling that she would respond better to being pestered than to being pitied.

"Well, too bad. I care about all the women I rescue from grocery stores." The barest hint of a smile quirked her lips. "Now, do you want to tell me what your level was or do I need to need to wrestle that glucose meter away from you and read it for myself?"

"Wrestle?" A spark suddenly flashed in her eyes and he knew the anger route had been the way to go. "I may not be as big and muscular as you, Kaleb Chatterson, but I've been trained in hand-to-hand combat and there's no way I'd go down without a fight."

"Is that a challenge?" he asked, taking a step closer to her.

Her eyes narrowed, her nostrils flared ever so slightly and he knew she was thinking of what would happen if both of their bodies came into that type of physical proximity. Because that was the exact thing he was thinking.

He moved closer.

"One fifty-eight," she said in a rush. "A little high, but I got my insulin quickly enough, so I'm fine."

He let out a deep breath toward the ceiling. "Good thing you didn't eat that entire cinnamon roll."

"You mean before you stole it from me?" She put her hands on her hips.

Yep, putting her on the defensive was the best way to get her to respond. The problem was, with the slight hitch in her breathing and the way she was looking at him, his body was beginning to respond, as well.

And he did still owe her a kiss. In fact, her pouting lips looked soft and full and pink and even more inviting than they had last night.

He told himself not to do it. But when he took another step toward her, her chin lifted.

He told himself that this would be a mistake. But when he cupped her cheek, her eyelids lowered.

He told himself that after he had one taste, there would be no going back. But when he grazed his lips against hers, she sighed.

He didn't tell himself anything after that.

Chapter Seven

Kaleb's mouth was warm and welcoming and so very persuasive. One minute, Molly'd been in the bathroom stall, angry at herself for being weak and eating the wrong foods, feeling overwhelmed and like a failure. The next minute, Kaleb was there letting her know that her body was still very much alive.

Molly lifted up onto her tiptoes to wrap her arms fully around his neck, pulling his chest against hers. She didn't know if he'd deepened the kiss or if she did, but their tongues were stroking, exploring and staking claim. He'd been right last night. He definitely could deliver a better kiss.

Still, Molly wanted more. His arousal pressed against her lower belly and she needed to feel that throbbing hardness somewhere else. She hooked a leg around the back of his thigh, tilting her hips upward. Kaleb groaned before sliding his hands under the legs of her running shorts, cupping her bottom in his palms and lifting her up against the wall. She wrapped her calves around his waist, moaning into his mouth as he pressed himself between her open thighs.

She heard an automated whirring sound each time his hips rocked inside of hers, but dismissed it as one of his annoying smart devices. If Kaleb was too focused to worry about his electronics or his company, then who was she to distract him from his mission?

And, oh, what a mission it was. As his lips trailed down her neck, her breathing became labored and she arched her head back, giving him better access while sucking in more air. She slid her fingers through his dark hair, pulling his mouth back to hers right as a cool rush of air came from the doorway.

The open doorway.

"I know it's a small town, but we *do* have hotels here in Sugar Falls," Freckles said before letting out a quiet—thankfully—giggle and slapping her thigh. In Molly's scramble to put her feet down, her knee moved under the sensor of the paper towel machine, and all three sets of eyes followed the trail from the roll inside to the pile folded upon itself on the floor. Freckles giggled again before pulling the door closed behind her.

Left alone with their embarrassment, Molly's choices were to face Kaleb or look at her reflection in the mirror above the sink. She chose the less judgmental of the two options and watched him use the hem of his T-shirt to clean the fog off his glasses. A little bubble of satisfaction floated inside her at the realization that she'd been partially responsible for making him get that steamy. But that bubble was soon skewered through by a sharp needle of returning desire when she saw the tight muscles of his abdomen revealed.

"Here." She tore off the thirty dangling feet of paper towel and held the upper part out to him. His eyes were even bluer without the thick, trendy black frames and she wished she was in a cockpit with an ejection seat so that she could better escape this situation.

"Sorry about that," Kaleb said as he replaced his glasses and bent to retrieve the rest of the towel to stuff into the giant cowboy-boot-shaped garbage can.

"Sorry that you kissed me or sorry that we got busted like that?" Molly asked.

"Actually, I was sorry that we accidentally set off that machine and wasted all that paper. I'm not the least bit sorry that I kissed you. And it certainly doesn't bother me that we got caught."

Of course it wouldn't bother him. It played right into his big dating plan, making everything seem more realistic. Molly tugged on the edges of her running shorts, ensuring they were back in place. But that was a mistake since it drew his gaze to her thighs, causing her muscles underneath to clench as a shudder made its way to her center. If Kaleb kept looking at her like that, they would end up finishing what they started right here in the ladies' room of the Cowgirl Up.

"Kylie and Mia are probably wondering what's taking me so long," she said, then gasped. "Wait, did they see you come in here?"

"I hope not, but to be honest, I was worried that you were getting sick and needed me, and wasn't really paying attention to them."

"Well, we can't very well go back out there together," Molly said. "One of us should stay here."

"You go on ahead. I need a little more time to, uh, get myself under control."

As she retrieved her tote bag from where she must've dropped it on the floor, a flush of warmth rushed up her neck. As she rushed toward the door, the buzz of the paper towel machine was activated again and the sound mocked her all the way out into the hallway.

Mia had already left by the time Molly made it back to the table and Kylie was paying the check. "Are you feeling okay?" Kylie looked up from the credit card receipt she'd been signing, concern evident on her face.

"Fine." Molly forced a smile, not trusting herself to say more to the sister of the man who'd almost taken her against the wall of a public restroom.

"Have you seen Kaleb? I hope he didn't slip out without saying goodbye." The woman didn't look suspicious, but Molly wasn't going to risk further questioning by admitting anything.

"I heard him talking to his assistant on the phone in the men's room."

"Doesn't it drive you crazy that he's always in work mode and can never just relax and let someone else run things for a change? I can't even imagine what he must be like on dates."

"I, uh, we're not really…" They weren't really what? Dating? At least, not seriously. What could Molly say without making it sound like she didn't mind being ignored by a guy who was supposed to be interested in her? "We're not exactly on a date right now. And his business is pretty important."

"His business is successful, not important. The world doesn't need another video game. If that guy thinks he's too busy to… There you are, Brainiac," Kylie said to

Kaleb as he approached the table. "Dad thinks we need to rent a couple more Jet Skis and he's looking for you because they need someone else to drive them over to our house from the rental place."

Jet Skis? Seriously? Why did the Chattersons get to do all the fun, high-speed activities?

"I might take a pass on the lake today, sis." Kaleb's hand on the back of Molly's waist startled her initially, then she realized they were supposed to be together. Or at least making people believe they were together. "I think I'm going to hang out with Molly this afternoon."

"That's sweet," Kylie said, zeroing in on her brother. Uh-oh, someone wasn't fooled. "What do you guys plan to do?"

"Oh, you know. Maybe just relax." Kaleb's fingers were drawing soothing circles along Molly's lower back. "Take things easy."

The gears in her brain finally clicked into place and Molly realized what Kaleb was doing. He was playing nurse again. And it was rather insulting. But before Molly could announce to him and everyone else in the restaurant that she didn't need looking after, Kylie pointed her finger at him.

"I know what you're up to, Kaleb," she said, and Molly's stomach sank under the deep breath she'd just sucked in. "You're trying to avoid your family so you can hide out at Molly's and get a bunch of work done."

Oh, was that all? Molly slowly let out the air she'd been holding in. That wasn't exactly a secret, but she'd probably set him up for that accusation when she'd told his sister he'd been taking work calls in the bathroom. However, he deserved it after following her into the ladies' room thinking she needed to be rescued. She remembered the video chat that morning at her apartment after he'd fixed her breakfast and how that'd turned into a slew of emails and conference calls. Sure, Kaleb was legitimately overbearing in his self-appointed nursing role. She'd almost leaped up from the booth and lunged after that half-eaten cinnamon roll he'd confiscated from her earlier. But she also knew that taking care of her gave him the opportunity to take care of his own agenda.

When she was a kid, her parents used to make her oldest brother, Tommy, babysit them. He'd use money from his job at the car wash to buy a couple of frozen pizzas for dinner and a huge tub of licorice. Then he'd let all of them watch his prized VHS copy of *Top Gun* so that he could go out on the back porch with his girl-friend without his younger siblings bugging him.

"No, I'm not," Kaleb snorted, pulling her up against his side. "Molly would rather keep things low-key today. That's all."

Oh, no, that was *not* all. Kaleb was now using her as a pawn in his family avoidance game and she wasn't about to become a part of it. Especially if it meant sitting around the apartment listening to him make phone calls while she was bored out of her mind.

"Actually—" she placed a hand on his bicep and smiled sweetly at Kylie "—I would much rather go Jet Skiing with you guys."

Kaleb watched Molly peel off her cotton sundress and squeeze the top half of her bikini-clad body into a life vest. After their kiss in the ladies' room an hour ago, he hadn't trusted himself to ride in the same car with her to the lake. Instead, he stayed behind to finish his biscuits and gravy and listen to Freckles making jokes about his breakfast not being the only thing that was cooling down.

And now that he was here signing for the Jet Ski rentals, he certainly didn't intend to ride on the same watercraft with Molly. Unfortunately, since Kylie had dropped her off, it was either ride with her or ride with Bobby Junior and his six-year-old son, Bobby Three. So Kaleb sat on the Sea-Doo listening to the dock manager explain how to use the throttle while a group of college-age boys gassing up a pontoon boat ogled Molly's tan legs.

She reached up to secure her ponytail, flashing him a glimpse of her taut belly button, and Kaleb missed whatever it was the manager said about the lack of brakes. Gripping the handlebars too tightly, he accidentally revved the engine when she put her hands on his shoulders to climb on behind him.

"You ready?" he asked. She gave him a thumbs-up and they were shoved away from the dock. He tried not to notice her knees straddling his hips as he motored along slowly, following his older brother to the white buoys marking the end of the no-wake zone. This was supposed to be a family day, but after the way he'd kissed her up against the bathroom wall this morning, all he could think about was the different possible ways for her legs to end up wrapped around him.

When they hit the open part of the lake, Kaleb's thumb gunned the throttle and the sudden launch forward made Molly grab onto his waist. She shrieked and laughed and begged him to go faster. He tried to oblige, keeping a safe distance away from other boats and skiers, but after only a few minutes, she called out over his shoulder asking him to stop.

"What's wrong?" he asked after shutting down the engine.

"Nothing," she replied as she stood up, rocking the watercraft. "I want a turn to drive."

"Are you sure you're okay?"

"Kaleb, I fly million-dollar planes at mach speeds up in the air. I think I can steer a little Jet Ski at sixty miles per hour."

"I wasn't doubting that you *could* do it. Only whether you *should* do it. Did you check your blood sugar back at the dock?"

"No, but I did when I went home to change. I don't have to check it every five minutes, Dr. Chatterson." She reached over his head and grabbed onto the steering bars.

"What are you doing?" he asked from his forced crouching position.

"Switching spots with you."

"Shouldn't we pull over first?" he asked, looking at the shoreline.

"Kaleb, we're in the middle of a lake. This is as pulled over as we're going to get. Hold us steady." They rocked to the left briefly before she swung her right leg around in front of him. She brought it down on the other side and stood there straddling the seat, her rear end only a few inches from his face. "You're going to need to scoot back so I have room to sit down."

"I don't want you to sit down. I'm kind of enjoying the view from here."

She made a squeaking sound before wedging her butt against the front of his board shorts and wiggling herself backward.

"Are you trying to kill me?" he asked, finally

relinquishing control of the handlebars so that he could grab onto her hips and hold her still.

"Did you guys break down?" Bobby Junior called out as he lapped back toward them. The last thing Kaleb needed was for his brother to see him in this aroused state and then go back and tell the others. He'd never hear the end of it.

"No, we're good now," Molly yelled back before the engine roared to life. Kaleb barely had time to grab onto the seat strap in front of her before the Jet Ski lurched out of the water.

Water spray was hitting his prescription sunglasses and her hair was whipping against his face by the time she reached the top speed. God, he hoped this was the top speed because if she went any faster he'd fly off the back. She dove behind boats and jumped their wakes, spun in doughnuts and leaned into fast turns. Normally, he'd be recording notes so that he could recreate this experience in some sort of immersive video game. But for once in his life, he didn't want to miss out on the actual experience.

Kaleb decided that no virtual-reality screen or head-set could mimic this very real fear of imminent death. Nor could it replicate the rush of adrenaline racing through his heart. And the slippery feel of their bodies as they slid back and forth on the wet seat, their most intimate parts colliding against each other? Forget it. Nothing would ever beat the real thing.

By the time they pulled up to the shoreline near Kylie's house, Kaleb's biceps were sore from holding on for dear life. And surprisingly, his cheeks were aching from grinning so much.

"Are you still back there?" she said, casting a saucy smile over her shoulder.

"Were you trying to make me fall off?" he asked as she turned off the engine and they coasted the rest of the way in. He took off his sunglasses and let them hang from the strap around his neck.

"Trust me. If I wanted to throw you, you wouldn't have lasted five seconds."

"Is that a fact?" he asked, gripping the plastic handle attached to the seat behind him and stretching his back. He waited for her to turn around and smile at him again, and when she did, he braced his foot on the right edge, grabbed her by the waist and tipped them over.

She was laughing when they came up from the cool water. He dove toward her and she splashed a spray of water toward his face and kicked away from him. His brothers might be world-class baseball players, but swimming was the sport he excelled at. It only took him a couple of strokes to catch her by the foot and pull her toward him.

"No fair," she said between giggles. "You're taller than me and can reach the bottom."

"So you forfeit?" he asked, drawing her closer.

"Never!"

She squirmed and wiggled against him until he had his arms locked around her. She stilled and her hands reached up to settle on either side of his face. A drop of water traveled from her temple to the corner of her lip, and as Kaleb leaned down to catch it with his own mouth, a little voice from the shore called out, "Are you gonna kiss her again, Uncle Kaleb?"

"You bet I am," Kaleb yelled back before planting a not-so-platonic kiss on her. It wasn't as long or as intense as the one they'd shared earlier today—not by a long shot—but there were children watching. And apparently everyone else in his family, he realized as one of his brothers let out a whistle.

"Hey, loverboy," Kane called out. "The Sea-Doo is floating away."

Both of them had to swim after the wayward watercraft, and by the time they pushed the thing back to shore, Molly's face was no longer as pink as her bikini bottoms. He didn't want to acknowledge that the sweetness of the latest kiss hinted at something real starting to form between them, but that didn't stop Kaleb from holding her hand as they walked up to the outdoor chairs and collapsed side by side.

Molly had never enjoyed being around another family as much as she enjoyed spending time on the lake with the Chattersons. She'd been lucky enough to be assigned to the same squadron since her graduation from the Air Force Academy, and while she had a bond with those guys, this was smaller. More intimate. Kaleb's family was fun and down to earth and didn't take themselves too seriously. And boy, could they put away the food and drinks.

She'd been careful to stay away from all the chips and snacks that Mrs. Chatterson was constantly fetching from the house. And every time Mr. Chatterson—who insisted on being called Coach—whipped up another blender full of frozen cocktails, Molly would politely refuse and grab another bottle of water.

As the sun began dipping below the mountains, Molly realized that playing on those Jet Skis all day had really tired her out. She yawned as they hauled towels and water toys to the deck upstairs. Actually, she was beyond exhausted. Her arms felt weak and her legs were sluggish.

When did she check her levels last? As the women crowded into the kitchen to give Drew tips on how to grill the carne asada for tacos, Molly excused herself to go to the restroom. She had to ask Kylie where her purse was since Kaleb's sister had brought their belongings back to the house after dropping them off at the dock earlier.

By the time she got the bathroom door closed, her forehead was damp with sweat. She sat on the closed lid of the toilet, her hands slightly shaky as she pricked her finger. Molly knew the number was going to be low before the digital screen came to life. Sixty-eight. She twisted the cap off one of the glucose gel tubes her doctor told her to carry in her black case. The heavily sweetened lemon flavor made her lips pucker as she sucked it down quickly.

Looking at the tube, Molly decided that the advertised "pleasant taste" was a load of bull. Fortunately, the rapid absorption promise was legitimate because she was already feeling better. She used the facilities, then washed her hands, holding her mouth under the faucet afterward so she could greedily gulp down more water.

When she stood up, her hands were braced on either side of the sink, her complexion slowly returning to normal in the mirror's reflection. She thought she'd been so good by not eating any junk food today. Apparently, by avoiding everything, she'd gone too far in the opposite direction.

"Ugh," she groaned at herself, stopping just short of banging her fist on the marble countertop. There was no winning with this stupid disease. The military had trained her to adapt and overcome any snafu. She was smart, she was capable of anything her instructors and commanding officers had thrown at her and she'd always been healthy and physically active, taking decent care of her body. She'd thought she'd done everything right. So why couldn't she get this damn thing under control?

Maybe because she hadn't felt like her old self since she'd gotten the diagnosis. And if she wasn't herself, then who was she? Molly inspected the person in the mirror. The one with tired eyes and sunken cheeks and fingertips that looked like pincushions. More important, if she didn't get control over things soon, what would she become?

A knock sounded at the door. Molly drew in a ragged breath and squared her shoulders before turning the knob, bracing herself to confront Kaleb on the other side. Instead, she saw Julia, Kane's fiancée.

"Is everything okay in here?" the woman, who also happened to be a Navy surgeon, asked. Molly prayed for serenity, but decided she was too cursed to be spared another interrogation.

"Never better." Molly pushed her exhausted cheek muscles into a grimacing smile. But then she followed the doctor's eyes to where the little black case lay open on the counter, the glucose meter and insulin pen all but jumping up and waving hello.

She might not officially be a Chatterson yet, but clearly Julia had been hanging around them long enough to disregard the idea of personal boundaries because she pushed past Molly and asked, "Why don't you wear a medical alert bracelet?"

Molly sighed and shut the door, hoping nobody outside the hallway powder room could hear them. "I was just diagnosed and I'm not big on jewelry so I haven't found one that I'm ready to commit to yet."

"Does Kaleb know?" Julia asked, and Molly nodded. "It certainly explains why he's always stealing your drinks or offering you Diet Cokes. Does your commanding officer know?"

"Unfortunately." A look passed between the women and Molly didn't have to explain to the military doctor that type 1 diabetes was a whole different breed from its more manageable type 2 relative, and that her need for insulin was an instant disqualification for keeping a pilot's license. "I'm supposed to be seeing a few doctors over at Shadowview and get their reports before I can appeal a medical discharge."

"How're you holding up?" The question seemed simple enough, but Molly felt her tough resolve slipping. Nobody had ever asked her that. The doctors pushed information and statistics and instructions at her. Her commanding officer asked her to keep him in the loop. She hadn't told her squadron yet because she didn't need their pity, nor did she want to be a reminder to them that even the best pilots could have their careers cut short like this. Kaleb, who was the only noncivilian that knew, seemed more concerned with trying to fix her than trying to understand her.

"I was just trying to figure that out." Molly sniffed, blinking back the tears.

"From what I understand, it can be a very lonely and confusing road." Julia put a gentle hand on Molly's shoulder.

The light touch stirred up something inside her. All

the emotions and the burdens and the worries twisted into a tornado inside her chest, swirling around and lifting into a funnel of words spilling out of her mouth.

"Every day for the past month, I'm constantly doubting myself, questioning myself, pricking myself to check to see that I haven't eaten too much or not enough. It's like taking a test I haven't studied for and no matter what the stupid number is on the screen, it's still a failing grade because it's a constant reminder that I'm going to have to live like this for the rest of my life. From here on out, I will always be a prisoner to this disease and I hate it. I resent the power these numbers have over me. It's so much easier to just avoid testing altogether and tell myself that I'm still the same person, that my body hasn't betrayed me. So I guess I'm not holding up very well at all. I've lost a piece of myself, and no matter what I do, I'll never get it back. I can never go back to what I was."

Unlike the rest of the medical professionals she'd talked to—which hadn't been all that many—Julia just nodded, a calm understanding in her eyes. And then she did the most surprising thing of all and drew Molly into a tight hug. A sob spilled out of her throat, and the next thing she knew she was crying in a stranger's arms. Yet, it felt so good to be able to just talk and have someone listen without giving advice or speaking in platitudes or trying to make things better.

When every last tear had been wrung from her, Molly stepped back and looked at her splotchy red face in the mirror. "I hate being weak."

Julia grabbed a washcloth from the cabinet below and ran it under the cool stream of the faucet. She wrung it out before handing it to Molly. "You are not weak. You might have weak moments, or even weak days. But if you keep trying and fighting, you will always come back stronger. In fact, you're about to find out exactly how strong you can be."

Another knock sounded at the door and Molly looked around the tiny half bathroom. "I don't think we can fit anyone else in here."

Julia smiled and cracked the door open. Molly heard Kaleb's hushed voice on the other side, and instead of being annoyed that he was checking up on her again, she melted. When Julia told him to wait in the hall and turned back to ask her how she wanted to proceed, Molly leaned a hip against the counter in relief. Finally, someone was letting her be in control.

"I should probably go home. But I don't want to cause…"

Another knock, but this time, Kaleb didn't wait for a reply before opening the door and letting himself in. So much for being in control.

"Did you tell her?" he asked Molly, jerking his chin in Julia's direction.

"Lower your voice, Kaleb," Julia said, trying to reach around him and squeeze the door shut. "Sorry, all the Chattersons can be a little loud and overbearing. But they mean well."

"Are you seriously comparing me to the rest of them, Julia?" Kaleb squished past his soon-to-be sister-in-law to stand closer to Molly. He put the back of his hand against her still-splotchy cheek, as if the only thing wrong with her was a slight fever. "You hardly ate anything this afternoon and your blood sugar got too low, didn't it? I had a feeling that was going to happen."

Because he was now standing between them, Molly

had to make eye contact with Julia in the mirror. "Do all of them also have a tendency to act like they know what's best for everyone else?"

"For everyone but themselves sometimes," Julia said, then gave Kaleb a slight shove when he opened his mouth to respond. "Molly was just about to tell me how *she* wanted to proceed."

"I was saying that I should ho home, but I don't want to cause a big scene." Molly twisted her lower lip between her teeth before continuing. "I, uh, haven't told Maxine or anyone else in my family yet, so..."

"Don't worry." Julia winked. "Unlike the rest of the Chattersons, I know how to keep my mouth closed. And if anyone suspects anything and asks, I can claim physician/patient confidentiality."

Except Julia hadn't acted like a doctor. She'd acted like a friend. And if she thought it odd that Molly would emotionally unload upon a complete stranger in a bathroom about things she didn't feel comfortable sharing with her own sister, the kind woman didn't mention it.

"*I* can keep my mouth closed," Kaleb muttered under his breath.

"Do you feel up to driving?" Julia asked her.

"I'll drive her home," Kaleb said, causing Julia to roll her eyes.

"Molly, what do *you* want?" she asked.

Nobody was more surprised than her when she said, "I'd prefer Kaleb take me."

Chapter Eight

For the second time that week, Kaleb found himself shoved behind the steering wheel of Molly's cramped rental car, driving her to the apartment in downtown Sugar Falls. Julia, thankfully, had promised to come up with an excuse for their sudden departure while they slipped out the French doors of Kylie and Drew's master bedroom.

He had a million questions to ask, but he kept silent, letting Bruno Mars's soulful melody on the hip-hop station do the talking for both of them. The streetlights came on as they turned off Snowflake Boulevard, and when he pulled into the parking spot behind the bakery, Kaleb finally asked, "Are you hungry?"

"A little," Molly admitted.

"I'll come up and make you some dinner." He tried to make it sound more like an offer, but the truth was that there was no possible way he was going to leave her alone. Julia hadn't told him what they'd talked about, and while Kane's fiancée assured him that Molly was fine—physically—she'd also suggested that it wouldn't be a bad idea for Kaleb to stay the night with her. Okay, so maybe Julia hadn't come right out and made that suggestion, but he would've if he were the doctor in this situation. It was definitely implied that Molly shouldn't be alone until her levels were stabilized.

"I really miss the days of just ordering a pizza. I'm going to need to make that appointment with the dietitian because my diet is starting to get pretty limited," she said halfheartedly, not quite convincing Kaleb that she was back to her feisty self.

He was just happy that she wasn't sending him on his way. When they got inside the apartment, she yawned, then said, "Make yourself at home. I'm going to go rinse off."

Kaleb was left in the kitchen, debating whether he had enough time to download another cooking lesson on his smartphone before she got out of the shower. Then he decided that he probably shouldn't be thinking of her in the shower. He rummaged around in the fridge and found some sliced turkey and a block of Havarti... but no bread. He sliced it all up, then cut up an apple and grabbed a handful of grapes, putting it all on one platter. He inspected his culinary masterpiece. Nobody was going to offer him a contract for his own show on a cooking channel, but it'd do.

When Molly came back to the kitchen, she was wearing a short white robe, her tan legs still damp from the hot steam. "That was fast," Kaleb said.

She helped herself to some turkey and grapes as she propped her elbows on the counter. "I was too tired to wash my hair." She ate slowly while he stared at the sun-dried curls piled on top of her head in a messy ponytail.

Kaleb's lips turned down in worry. She really did look exhausted. He stacked a piece of cheese onto a slice of apple and popped it into his mouth. They were both hungry and ate in silence for a few minutes.

He found a couple of bottles of unsweetened tea in the fridge and handed one to her. "Just for the record, I like your hair like that."

"If you think this looks good, just wait until morning." Molly extended her hands a few inches away from her head. "When I wake up, it'll be out to here."

Kaleb swallowed down his last bite. If he wasn't so tired himself, he would've asked if she was suggesting he spend the night. But neither one of them were in the mood for teasing and he didn't want to give her the opportunity to argue. Instead, he simply said, "I can't wait to see it."

"Pfshh." Molly ate more turkey and he was relieved to see that over half the plate was now gone. "That's easy for you to say. Even after a day in the lake, Kaleb Chatterson, you still look perfect. Not a single, smooth brown strand out of place."

He held himself perfectly motionless as she reached out and ran her fingers over his head. But if Molly kept touching him like this, he wouldn't be able to stay still.

"Come on," he said, grabbing her hand.

"Where are we going?" she asked, although it had to be pretty obvious that he was leading her to the master bath.

"I'll wash your hair for you," he said, his voice much gruffer than he'd intended.

"How?" Her eyes suddenly seemed less tired in the

bright light of the white tiled bathroom. In fact, they almost looked determined.

"I'm sure I can think of a way." He studied the sink, then the bathtub, weighing the options. "Wait here. I'm going to go grab a cup from the kitchen."

When he returned, Molly was standing in the same spot where he'd left her. Either she was too weak to protest, or she really wanted clean hair. Grabbing a stack of folded towels, he dropped them on the tile floor by the claw-foot tub.

"Sit on these and lean back against the bath," he instructed.

Molly eyed him doubtfully, then plopped down, her tan, bare legs extending out of the center opening of white robe. Desire raced through him.

Kaleb turned on the faucet, letting the water heat up as he looked around the bathroom for some shampoo. Coming back to the tub with the bottle he found inside the glass-enclosed shower stall, he slowly sank to his knees as Molly's gaze never left him.

It took a lot of trust for someone like her, someone who liked being independent and in control, to allow another person to perform such a personal task for them. Kaleb needed to prove that he was worthy of the responsibility.

Pulling a hand towel off the nearby rack, he draped the terrycloth over the curved edged of the tub, then lifted the tendrils of hair off her neck as he guided her head back.

When he paused for a second to study the elastic band holding up her ponytail, Molly said, "Let me get it."

Her voice was low, sounding as if it came from the deepest part of her throat, and Kaleb's heart stopped as she reached up, causing the V-neck opening of the robe to gape open and revealing the silhouette of the top of one breast.

When her hair cascaded around her face, his pulse shot back to life, beating at a more frantic pace. Molly closed her eyes as he used the plastic cup to slowly poor warm water over her scalp, smoothing back strands with the palm of his hand.

Molly moaned, her relaxed shoulder pressing into Kaleb's chest as he leaned over her. Even though his fingers were trembling, he carefully massaged the shampoo against her scalp, trying to focus on evenly distributing the suds instead of watching her chest rise and fall with the long, drawn out breaths she was taking.

Kaleb didn't know how much more of this intimacy he could experience without taking things to the next level. He began rinsing out the soap, but it was a longer process to get all the lathered suds out of her curls. When he finally shut off the spout and grabbed another towel to wrap around her wet hair, Molly opened her eyes, her lids heavy, her pupils dilated.

Her voice was still throaty as she said, "Suddenly, I'm not so tired anymore."

Kaleb stood up, then held out his hand to help her rise to her feet. The towel tumbled off her head just as she looked at their reflections in the mirror. Molly ran a hand over the tangled, wet curls.

Molly turned to him and Kaleb held his breath.

Before he could say a word, she unknotted her robe and let it fall to the floor.

His heart slammed against his chest and his lungs weren't capable of expelling all the oxygen trapped inside. She'd been in a bikini all day and his brain had pushed itself to its limits imagining what was underneath. Yet, even his imagination and the tiny peeks he'd stolen earlier when her robe had loosened couldn't do her body justice. She was perfect. Her small breasts were high and proud with tight pink nipples centered like regal crowns. Her waist was tiny, which made the curve of her hips that much more round. Her legs were lean, but strong and toned. And if he looked at the spot where they joined, he would be a goner. "You're beautiful."

She blushed at his compliment before turning around and reaching inside the shower to turn on the spray. When the water heated up, she stepped in and left the glass door wide open before looking back at him and saying, "I don't know if there are any shirts here that might fit you, so unless you want to get yours all wet…"

She didn't finish her sentence, nor she didn't have to. He heard a seam rip as he yanked the cotton T-shirt over his head. And then, because it seemed like the only fair thing to do, he untied his board shorts and let them fall to the floor. He set his glasses on the edge of the sink, giving silent thanks that he wasn't farsighted, before stepping into the steamy shower with her.

Her eyes were closed as the hot water sprayed against her scalp, steam misting over their bare skin. Kaleb wrapped an arm around her waist, pulling her away from underneath the shower nozzle, then picked up the bottle of conditioner and squirted some in his palm. She put her hands on his chest, making slow wet circles against his pecs.

He massaged the cream into her hair, and as his fingers slowly worked through the tangles, she dipped her head back and moaned. He didn't trust his voice enough to say anything but her name. "Molly."

"Hmm?" she asked.

"I need to rinse you off."

Their bodies slid against each other as they changed places once again and the water sluiced through her hair, causing silky rivers to trail over her nipples and past her flat stomach. He had to bite back a groan before he managed to say, "Okay, it's rinsed."

She opened her eyes and he recognized the playful, yet determined look from when she'd wanted to drive the Jet Ski. "Now it's my turn."

She reached for the bottle of bath gel. His chest rose and fell as she took her time sliding her soapy hands across the planes of his body. Except unlike her, he watched as she washed him, not wanting to miss a second of this erotic experience. When she lifted her hands to his shoulders, she looked in his eyes and smiled. "You're beautiful, too, Kaleb."

This time, he didn't hold back the groan before bringing his mouth down to claim hers. His rigid length pressed against her stomach and their lips and hands slipped against each other as they both tried to gain traction. "Molly, you better tell me to stop or I'm going to take you right here in this shower."

"Hold that thought," she said before opening up the glass door. She stepped out without grabbing a towel and walked over to the sink. He stared at her dripping wet body as she bent to retrieve something from the cabinet underneath. When he saw the box in her hand, he didn't even bother to turn off the water before stepping out and striding across the tile floor to her. She barely had the foil packet opened when he lifted her up and set her on the counter. He stepped between her knees, and, as she rolled the condom on him, he prayed he didn't lose himself right then.

She raised her lips to his and he entered her at the same time. She gasped and he held himself still, letting them both acclimate to the feel of each other. But when she gasped and rocked her hips forward, he took the invitation. He hooked his forearms under her knees, each stroke bringing him deeper and closer to her.

He could tell by the little panting sounds coming from her throat that she was on the edge and he pulled his face back, just enough to watch her as he delivered one more fulfilling thrust.

Molly was curled up against Kaleb's side on the queen-size bed, the sheets still damp because, apparently, they didn't like wasting time with towels. He'd carried her here after their rushed coupling on the bathroom counter. He hadn't said anything about what had just happened between them and, while Molly had never slept with a man she wasn't in a relationship with, she also wasn't the kind of woman who mistook physical attraction for love.

And what had happened between her and Kaleb was pure physical attraction. Okay, so maybe the hair washing thing had been a bit intense, but only because of their mutual desire. It had been building all week and things had come to a head when they'd kissed this morning in the café. Sure, some of her raw emotions might've affected her better judgment and caused things to happen sooner than she was used to, but she'd been dealing with so many setbacks in her life lately, she needed to prove to herself that she was still a woman, capable of feeling something other than disappointment and doubt. She could still experience pleasure.

When she'd dropped her robe in front of Kaleb, she felt a rush of power and confidence that she hadn't experienced in so long. All thoughts of physical inadequacy and failure floated away and she was back in control of her body.

"Thank you," she said to him, doubting that he would ever comprehend how grateful she was in that very moment.

The muscles of his abdomen flexed as he gave off a short chuckle. "I think I should be the one thanking *you*. I've never felt so clean and yet so dirty at the same time."

She lifted her head to face him. "Just so you know, I don't always invite the men I'm platonically dating into the shower with me."

"I don't think there was anything platonic about what we just did." He smiled and she traced a finger along his bare chest. Maybe not. But that didn't mean that Molly could afford to go falling for someone when she had no idea what her future held. Not that she was falling for anyone. This was pure sex. It had to be. She had enough to deal with; she didn't need to further complicate things by adding a relationship to the mix. He cupped her chin and lifted her face up to meet his gaze. "What's wrong?"

The guy was ridiculously good at reading her emotions. So she might as well be honest with him. "I'm enjoying spending time with you, Kaleb. Even when you deprive me anything worth eating."

The corners of his lips turned down and his jaw grew hard. "But...?"

"I know that you have your own life waiting for you when you leave here." She put her finger on his lips when he started to speak. "And I'm still trying to figure out what I'm going to do with mine."

"So you don't want to make any promises while you're going through an adjustment phase?" he said around her finger.

"Ha! It's a bit more than just an adjustment phase, Kaleb." She didn't want to touch on the making promises part of his statement. Did he *want* her to make a promise? She had no business even wondering. "My career, my health, my goals, all of that is up in the air. There's so much I don't know."

"Then why don't you start looking for those answers?" he asked.

She flopped back onto the pillow. Of course it was just that simple for him. He had an army of assistants and attorneys and experts on speed dial, ready to advise him so he could solve everyone's problems. "That's what I'm trying to do. In my own way and on my own terms."

He shifted on the bed so that he was leaning over her. He gently tugged on the sheet and then lightly drew his thumb over her exposed nipple. "For someone who likes to go so fast all the time, it sure seems to me like you're taking your sweet time."

She hooked a leg around his waist and rolled him onto his back. When she rose above him, she asked, "You want to see how slow I can go?"

He smiled and slid his hands up her legs, settling them on her hips. After that, they didn't talk about speed or anything else.

"Are you doing it for her sister, who you obviously have the hots for?" Before he could deny it, Kylie began singing, "Kaleb and Molly sitting in a tree. *K-I-S*—"

"Oh, grow up," Kaleb said before disconnecting the call.

"Who aren't you doing what for?" Molly asked as she came into the kitchen, wearing a skimpy tank top and little pajama shorts. Even dressed and after three rounds of lovemaking last night, Kaleb was still aroused by her.

"My sister just volunteered us to drive into Boise and pick up gifts for Maxine's baby shower. And I use the term *volunteer* loosely."

"Together?"

"Is that a problem?" After all the togetherness they'd shared in and out of bed last night, Kaleb didn't see how it could be. But then again, he also hadn't been the one to deliver that lets-just-enjoy-spending-time-with-each-other speech last night. It wasn't that he was in the market for anything serious or long-term, either, but it was definitely a blow to his male pride to think that there was a woman out there that wouldn't consider him a good catch.

"I guess not." She sniffed at the vegetables sautéing in the pan. "But I'll have to stop at the military hospital on the way down the mountain to do some blood work and I know how you feel about needles."

He settled his hand along the back of her neck and leaned in close. "I'm going to need the promise of some sort of reward to get my mind off all the needles and baby shower talk I'm going to have to endure today."

"Maybe if you're a good boy at the doctor's, I'll get you a lollipop," she said as she pressed a kiss along his lower lip. Before he could tell her all the other things he'd rather taste, she added, "And I won't tell the rest of your family on you when you use your work laptop in the waiting room."

"Please don't remind me about my annoying relatives when I'm trying to seduce you."

"You could better seduce me by throwing out those vegetables and adding some ham and cheese to my omelet." She gave him a playful smack on his rear before heading down the hall to get dressed.

"It's a frittata," he called out.

An hour later, Kaleb didn't know how he'd gone from being a private chef to a chauffeur, but he drew the line at folding himself into Molly's tiny car for the entire ride to Boise. After eating breakfast, they drove back to the lake to get the truck. Despite Molly's insistence that she knew where they were going, he typed the address for the military hospital into the navigation system, then synced the playlist from his smartphone with the truck's radio.

"Are you ever not playing with a gadget?" she asked, tapping her fingers on the armrest.

"They're not gadgets. They're complex computerized systems that make our lives simpler."

"Kaleb, you just spent an extra twenty minutes programming a bunch of stuff we don't need for a drive that only takes half that amount of time."

He pointed to the estimated time readout on the digital map. "It actually takes thirty minutes to get to Shadowview."

"Not if I was driving, it wouldn't," she muttered.

He thought back to her trying to set a speed record on the Jet Ski yesterday. "Well, some of us would prefer to arrive at our destinations without all the blood centrifuging down to our feet because of sustained G-force acceleration."

"While it's a top-of-the-line truck—" she patted the leather dashboard "—I doubt even I could get us up to a whole G in this."

"But with all those turns going down the mountain, that's a lot of changes in velocity, which can add to the G-force."

Molly laughed. "Now I see why Kylie calls you Brainiac."

"You're only now seeing that?" he asked. He put the vehicle in gear and tried to pretend that she wasn't blatantly studying him as they drove out of the parking lot.

"Not that I'm saying I'm smarter than any of them—except maybe Kevin—but I had a lot more time to study."

"Why's that?"

"Because they were always busy with their after-school sports and I...well... I wasn't."

"You seem pretty athletic to me," Molly suggested. He lifted a brow at her, and when her cheeks turned crimson he knew she was also thinking of how he'd carried her from the bathroom counter to the bed last night. She cleared her throat and continued. "Were you just not that into sports growing up?"

"No, I was," he admitted. "But I was diagnosed with scoliosis when I was ten and wasn't allowed to play most of them, unless they were noncontact and approved by my physical therapist. I was decent at swimming, but each time I had a surgery, it would set me back."

"That must've been tough considering most of your family members are professional athletes."

"I don't mind so much now that I'm an adult, but

back when I was a kid it bugged the hell out of me. Everyone got to be on the field while I was on the sidelines watching. I think it would've been easier if I'd been diagnosed later on, after I'd already been able to prove to people that I was just as good as my brothers. But now, none of us will ever know if I could've had a different career."

"Hmm." Molly propped her chin on her fist as she looked out the window. "If it were me, I think I'd rather not know. People say it's better to have loved and lost than to have never loved at all. But I call bull on that. It sucks to get a shot at something others can only dream about, experience a feeling that's better than you ever could've imagined, know in your heart that it's what you were made to do—and then have it ripped away from you."

"So if you could go back in time ten years ago, you never would've joined the Air Force? You wouldn't have become a pilot?"

"I just don't know." Her voice was soft. "I can't see myself as being anything but that."

"I bet you'd go back and do it all over again," he said. "You're too stubborn to do anything else."

"Well, the question is totally irrelevant unless your company is currently developing the latest software for time travel," she replied, a spark of attitude pushing the sadness out of her tone.

"How do you know we're not?" he asked as he steered the truck into the Shadowview parking lot. Just seeing that big, red cross on the sign already had his heart hammering. Telling himself that he wasn't the patient did little to help.

"You're not the only one who researches stuff, Kaleb.

I looked up Perfect Game Industries and found out that if it doesn't involve crafting alternate dimensions, or shooting aliens, zombies or pirates, you can't be bothered."

Whoa. That didn't exactly sound like a compliment. He waited for her to wink or chuckle or do something that would indicate that she was teasing him. Instead, she grabbed her tote bag and opened the passenger side door.

He followed her across the asphalt and toward the large automatic glass entrance. "By the way, do you know where we're going?"

"What? You don't already have the building blueprint downloaded on your phone?" she asked, this time with a cheeky grin.

Instead of figuring out where they needed to go, he watched her as she examined the information signs with arrows pointing out the directions. Maybe he was on edge because he hated hospitals, but something about her dismissive comment about his company wasn't sitting well with him.

"Looks like the lab is this way," she said, then tugged on his hand when he stood there planted in place. He allowed her to lead the way, keeping his fingers linked with hers as they followed a maze of hallways toward the bowels of the building.

They got to a set of double doors, and when they entered the large waiting room on the other side, the smell of antiseptic and blood made Kaleb's nostrils twitch. She signed in at the desk and when she joined him on a cold plastic bench, she whispered, "You look a little pale."

"I'm fine," he sniffed, before shifting in his seat.

"The receptionist said it's just some routine blood work and won't take long. There's a lounge area across the hall and you can wait for me over there."

"I'm fine," he said again, before curling and flexing each individual finger.

"You're making me anxious with the way you're squirming in your seat and jiggling your leg like that."

He let out a snort. He wasn't that bad. "I think it'd be more supportive if I stayed."

She patted his knee. "I wasn't asking."

"Okay." He stood up. "But text me if they move you to a different room or if you get some bad news or if anything goes wrong. Sometimes, they can't find the vein and they end up poking you over and over—"

"Kaleb," she squawked, then frantically motioned her head toward a little girl who was watching them with bulging eyes as she clung to her father's arm.

"I'll just be down the hall, then." He didn't fully exhale until he was out of the waiting room. Putting his hands in his pockets, he walked to an area that said Rehabilitation Lounge.

When he went inside, the first thing he noticed was a big-screen television set with level eight of "Rookies" playing on the screen, and a wave of pride washed through him. He wished Molly was here so he could point out that his company produced sports-related video games, as well. They were even exclusively contracted with all the major franchised teams.

A young man with a bandage wrapped around his head was dressed in Green Bay Packers pajamas and sitting on a sofa, a black wireless controller in his hand as he positioned his offensive line. His opponent was the woman wearing a robe and sitting in a wheelchair, both of her legs missing below the knees.

"Hey, man," a guy sitting behind a bank of computers said to Kaleb. "Nice shirt. I had the same one when I was in junior high."

Kaleb looked down at the silk-screened image of the Pac-Man character and the sting from Kylie's earlier comment about him dressing like a fifteen-year-old boy festered.

"Don't pay any attention to him," the woman said as she blocked a virtual field goal. "He's just mad that we got here before he did and he can't watch *The Price Is Right* in HD."

"Whatever." The man stood up from behind the computer and Kaleb saw the cast that started at the guy's wrist and went up and over his shoulder. "All there is to do around this place is sit in front of a screen. It's as if they *want* to rot our brains and make us lazy. All this supposed technology out there and none of it is helping me get back to the front lines any quicker."

He passed by Kaleb, taking one last look at the T-shirt before shaking his bald head.

"You ready to go?" Molly asked from the doorway as the guy with the cast walked out.

Kaleb had never been more ready. Unfortunately, that was the exact second that Hunter and Maxine's husband, Cooper, walked in the door.

Chapter Ten

"What are you guys doing here?" her nephew asked.

Molly saw her brother-in-law's eyes zero in on the stretchy blue bandage wrapped around her elbow and she knew the former-MP-turned-police-chief was dying to hear her answer. Her brain spun trying to come up with a plausible explanation. Was it flu shot season? Best to stick to something vague. "Just some routine stuff."

"Captain Markham!" A corpsman chose that precise moment to come into the room holding out a sheet of paper. "You forgot the printout we downloaded off your glucose meter. We already sent the data electronically to the endocrinology department."

She pried her fingernails out of her palm to take the offered paper.

"What's a glucose meter?" Hunter asked. "Is that

one of those new virtual-reality headsets for the Play-Stations?"

"Speaking of virtual reality," Kaleb said a bit too loudly as he put his arm around the boy's shoulder. "I had an idea for a new game and you're just the person I needed to brainstorm with."

Molly was left standing there with Cooper as Kaleb lead the boy to the hallway and distracted him with talk of high-tech gadgets. Her brother-in-law studied her without making a sound, as though he had a target lock on her and was deciding how and when to launch the missile.

Instead, she launched her own counterattack. "So what are *you* guys doing at Shadowview today?"

"Drew asked me to speak at one of his PTSD support groups," Cooper responded. "Hunter was out of school today and likes to come hang out in this lounge and play video games with the patients who are recovering from their surgeries."

"How fun. I mean, for Hunter. I'm sure your group isn't, um…" She glanced at the clock above the doorway. "Well, Kaleb and I better get to the store before it closes."

"It's not even noon," Cooper said, unwilling to back down. "You want to tell me what's going on, Molly?"

"Not really." She wiped a trickle of sweat off the back of her neck. Someone needed to work on the air-conditioning in here.

"You don't have to," he said, shrugging his shoulders. "Just keep in mind that I was in the Marine Corps once and the only time I ever got an indefinite leave of absence was when I was being medically discharged."

She squeezed her eyes shut and rubbed her temples.

"Nothing's official. That's why I haven't said anything to my sister yet. But I will."

"In that case, I'm not going to ask you for details because I don't want to keep anything from my wife. A word of advice, though," he said before using his chin to gesture toward his stepson. "You should probably tell Maxine before Hunter figures out that he doesn't actually want to include a glucose meter on his Christmas wish list."

Molly exhaled. "Right. I'll definitely tell her before Christmas."

Cooper just shook his head. That was still seven months away.

Whatever Kaleb had discussed with Hunter was sufficiently exciting enough to make the kid forget about why his aunt was at the hospital in the first place. She promised him a trip to Noodie's Ice Cream Shoppe later in the week and they made their goodbyes. Kaleb waited until they were in the parking lot before he brought it up.

"So did you swear Cooper to secrecy?"

"Not really. He purposely didn't ask me anything. But he clearly knows that something is up and that whatever is going on could result in a medical discharge."

"Molly." Kaleb let out a ragged breath. "You're going to need to tell her."

She swallowed down a lump of guilt. "I know. I'm going to."

"When?"

"Maybe when I know something more definite," she said as he held open the truck door for her. When he narrowed his eyes, she added, "Fine. I'll tell her after the baby shower this weekend. I don't want to make her big day all about me."

He nodded and she climbed into the cab, settling herself deep into the expensive leather seat. As he walked around to the driver's side, she let out a sigh of relief at dodging another bullet, as well as getting one annoying errand crossed off her list of things to do.

Kaleb started the engine, and as he navigated out the lot, it was obvious to see the tension finally easing out of his body. She'd noticed how fidgety and nervous he'd been earlier and regretted making him come with her. When he pulled onto the highway, Molly apologized. "I would never have expected you to go inside if I'd known how uncomfortable you would be."

"I don't know why hospitals bother me so much. You'd think that after all my surgeries, it'd be like a second home."

"How many surgeries did you have?"

"Three."

"That sounds pretty intense." She'd noticed the scar down his back when he'd taken off his life jacket out at the lake. Molly had been curious, but hadn't asked him about it at the time because she didn't particularly enjoy discussing her own medical history. She knew Kaleb wouldn't be any different. Besides, after hearing the way the Chatterson brothers all teased each other, she'd figured it would only be a matter of time before one of them regaled them all with some story involving teenage boy shenanigans. Yet, interestingly enough, nobody mentioned it. And that family mentioned *everything*.

Then, when she'd seen it last night in the shower, there'd been steam and soap bubbles and too many other body parts that required her attention. Yet, now he'd openly brought it up, so she cleared her throat and asked, "Does your back still bother you?"

He chuckled, then said, "Only when I'm being whipped around on the back of a Sea-Doo."

Shame burned her cheeks. "Why didn't you tell me?"

"Probably because of the same reason you don't go around telling people you're diabetic. I don't want people thinking that I'm limited."

"Hmm," she murmured. No, their situations weren't exactly alike, but something about Kaleb's experience resonated with her and suddenly she didn't feel like the only person who'd ever had to give up their dreams. Maybe that's why she'd connected with him initially. Either that or the way he'd filled out his jeans. Looking at the expensive denim covering his muscular thighs, she wondered if it was a lot easier to move on from what you'd lost when your fallback career involved becoming a billionaire.

Her cell phone rang and Molly was surprised to see her mother's name on the screen.

"Are you going to answer that?" Kaleb asked as he exited the freeway.

"I should. But don't say anything in the background. I don't want her asking me any questions about who I'm with."

"Am I another one of your secrets?" Kaleb's forehead creased above the frames of his glasses.

Instead of reminding him that he hadn't been all that excited when his own family had tracked him down to Maxine's apartment the evening they'd met, Molly answered the phone. "Hi, Mom."

"I'm just calling for a status update," her mother replied. Every month or so, their parents would take turns calling all their offspring to make sure everyone was safe and accounted for—like a mama duck counting her ducklings as they crossed a bridge before using her bill to nudge them off into the water to swim on their own. These were usually short conversations. After all, they had half a dozen of them to make at a time.

"I'm in Sugar Falls visiting Maxine," Molly said. Then, before her mom could ask for more details, she added, "Well, technically, I'm about to walk into a department store in Boise to buy her a baby shower present."

"Oh, that's right. I mailed her a gift card last week and could've signed your name to it like I usually do," her mom said, making Molly feel about as responsible as a five-year-old. "What are you getting her?"

"I have no idea," Molly replied, feeling about as clueless as a five-year-old, as well. She looked at Kaleb, hoping he knew what they were supposed to be picking up. But he was stoically facing the road, staying as silent as she'd asked him to. "What does she need?"

"Probably nothing. This is her second kid. Back in my day, we had a baby shower for the firstborn and then you were on your own with all the others and had to make do with whatever hand-me-downs lasted long enough."

Considering the fact that Colonel Cynthia Markham had six children and Molly was number five, a sympathy pang shot through Molly's heart. Being so close to the caboose on the secondhand train was its own challenge and she decided to get her upcoming niece or nephew the biggest, most special gift of all.

"Anyway, have fun with your sister and give me a call when you get assigned to your next duty station," her mom said in her no-nonsense tone, then disconnected abruptly without saying goodbye. It was one of the Markham family habits that Trevor's socialite mother complained about back when they were planning rehearsal dinners and seating charts. No point in using an excess of words.

"Roger that," Molly said to nobody. She tossed the cell phone back in her purse, telling herself it was a relief that her mother hadn't asked her for more details. The weird thing was that her relief felt surprisingly similar to the seed of disappointment sitting in the bottom of her stomach.

A steady beep echoed inside the cab of the truck and Molly realized that the digital map on the dash had turned into a backup camera. Her eyes squinted in confusion and she asked, "Are you seriously using the parking assist feature?"

Kaleb didn't bother to check his rearview mirror before reversing into a spot with no other cars nearby. "Why wouldn't I? It works and the manufacturer clearly installed it for a reason."

"They install it so that people like you will pay extra for a feature that you don't need."

"People like me," he repeated, his voice soft. "Right."

He exited the truck and didn't say another word as they walked inside together. It wasn't the silence that bothered Molly as much as the fact that she wasn't accustomed to Kaleb being off his smart devices and still not bombarding her with a million questions. Something wasn't right. While this shopping trip didn't fall under a routine mission for her, it wouldn't serve any purpose to have her wingman pissed off at her. "Did I insult you or something back there?"

"Nope." Instead of looking at her, he pulled out his cell phone and tapped on an app that gave the layout of the store. "The baby section is toward the back."

"Do you know what we're supposed to get her?"

"Kylie sent me a list of things to buy. But I think we're supposed to pick out our own gifts."

Right. As Maxine's sister, of course she should pick out something special. Her mother's words about signing her name to a gift card ricocheted in her head. Surely, she could decide on something as simple as a baby shower gift. It was a baby. All it could do was eat, sleep and poop.

Yet when they walked into the baby department, the sheer volume of choices overwhelmed her. How was she supposed to narrow all of this down to just one item? They passed something called a BOB jogging stroller and Molly paused. Maxine was an avid runner, so maybe something like this would work. Then she spotted the price tag and had to do a double take to make sure the thing didn't come with a four-cylinder engine and a kidney off the black market.

"Maybe we should focus on the stuff on the list first," Molly suggested.

"Right." Kaleb blew out a long puff of air. "What in the hell is a onesie?"

"Beats me. With all the kids in your family, I thought you'd be an expert at this stuff."

"Your family is bigger than mine and you don't seem to know either," he pointed out.

"Touché."

"Well, they come in a pack," he said, staring blankly at the electronic notepad on his phone. He tapped his watch and spoke into it like some secret agent. "Angela, send me a picture of a package of onesies."

"Did you seriously just tell your assistant to figure out what one of the things was on your list?"

He studied her for a moment before speaking at his wrist again. "Also, send me a picture of a diaper genie, a boppy pillow, a swaddle sack—"

Molly reached out and wrapped her hand around the face of his watch. "Why don't we just find someone who works here and ask them?"

"Because I trust Angela."

"Doesn't she have more important things to do than research baby gear?"

"Don't we all?" He dropped a light kiss on Molly's mouth and she was reminded of how they'd spent their time last night.

He pulled her closer and her heart quickened. "Good point."

Something vibrated against the side of her waist and it took Molly a second to realize that his cell phone was still in his hand. He lifted it up to see the pictures, swiping through at least twenty of them as Molly looked on.

"How much stuff does an eight-pound human being need?" he asked, echoing her earlier thought.

She pursed her lips. "This coming from a guy who is using two electronic smart devices simultaneously?"

"The voice-to-text feature works quicker on the watch, but the images come up clearer on the phone," he defended.

"You know what else comes up clearer? Asking someone who actually works here." Molly walked toward the end of the aisle looking for anyone wearing the store uniform of a red shirt and khaki pants.

After crossing over into the toy department, Molly finally honed in on a young woman restocking the board games. "Excuse me, could you help us find some stuff in the baby section?"

"Sure." The lady stood up and clipped a walkie-talkie onto her back pocket. "What are you looking for?"

"Something called a bopsie and, um, hold on. We have a list over here." She waved the clerk toward where she'd left Kaleb, who stood rooted in the center of the aisle, his eyes bouncing from his cell phone to the display racks, then back to his cell phone. Molly called out, "I brought reinforcements."

Kaleb quickly relinquished his phone over to the store employee, which was saying something since the only time she'd seen him without his phone was in the shower last night. Heat stole up Molly cheeks and she pretended to be very interested in a natural flow baby bottle that supposedly reduced colic.

"It's for a gift," he clarified.

The woman eyed Molly's flat stomach before saying, "I'm guessing you two don't have kids of your own yet?"

"Not together," Kaleb said swiftly. His eyes widened as he quickly amended, "Or separately."

Molly found herself wondering if she should've been offended by his initial instinct to clarify that they weren't a couple—or at least a couple who might produce offspring. Kaleb's tone suggested that their having babies together was ludicrous. Perhaps it was.

Instead of allowing herself to dwell on it, Molly followed Kaleb and the store clerk as the woman pointed out where all the items on their list were located. Unfortunately, that only solved the first part of the shopping conundrum because now they needed to narrow things down by colors and patterns.

After the employee left, Kaleb turned to Molly and asked, "Do you know if the baby is a boy or a girl?"

Molly racked her brain for the answer. How could she not know the sex of her expected niece or nephew? As much as it'd stung to hear the kid say it out loud, Hunter had been correct when he'd announced that the Markhams weren't the type of family who got bogged down in each other's personal business. But surely, something as momentous as a new baby would've been discussed. At her blank expression, Kaleb said, "I'll text Kylie and ask."

"Wait!" A light bulb went off in Molly's brain. "I just remembered. They're waiting to find out the gender."

She exhaled hard enough to blow a curl out of her face, relieved she was only forgetful, not completely oblivious to what was going on in her sister's life. Granted, Hunter had been the one to clue her in on that little detail when he'd stayed with her last weekend, but still. She eventually would've asked.

Needing to prove that she really did care about her family, Molly decidedly chose a pack of onesies with a neutral pattern. Once they'd selected everything off Kylie's list, Kaleb leaned against the red shopping cart and asked, "So what are *you* going to get her?"

Right. She still needed to come up with a gift. Something she could sign her name to. Something…sisterly. Her analytical mind told her that nursery furniture would be the most functional. Unfortunately, it was also the most expensive. Molly kept scanning the shelves.

"What about a crib mattress?" she asked Kaleb. It was half the cost of everything else she'd seen in the nursery section, but could still be considered a big-ticket item.

He shrugged his shoulders and Molly held her breath, wishing he'd text his assistant and ask for Angela's opinion. No such luck. Ugh. She could fly multi-million-dollar jets while firing short-range missiles with deadly accuracy. Decisiveness and confidence used to come a lot easier to her. Okay, she needed to regroup. If she were having a baby, what would she want?

Her own parents, both career military officers, rarely stretched their budget for brand-new shoes, let alone bedroom furnishings. Molly recalled her first big-girl bed, which looked perfectly fine when it was covered with Maxine's faded pink butterfly quilt. But underneath it'd had a big yellow circular stain on the mattress from when her oldest brother, Tommy, had been the first owner. She gave an involuntary shudder. Yep, that decided it. Her niece or nephew was getting their very own mattress and would be the first one to pee on it.

Molly reached for one of the plastic wrapped rectangles lined up on the metal ledge above her head, then cursed her five-foot-four-inch frame.

"Show me which one you want and I'll grab it," he said, stepping in front of her. Oh, sure. Now he was being helpful, after she'd had to do the decision making.

"Oh. Uh, that one. I guess." She pointed to the mid-priced mattress and stood back as he easily slid the thing off the shelf and set it on the floor in front of her, balancing it between his long, smooth fingers. His hands were well-shaped and all she could think about was the way they'd brought her body to life last night. And again this morning. Molly's knees gave another slight wobble and she commanded her brain not to bug out on her.

She tilted her head to the side. To her, the mattress looked a bit thin, although Molly had slept on much worse on the last aircraft carrier she'd been aboard. "Do you think this is a good enough brand?"

"How am I supposed to know?"

"You know they have a baby registry, right?"

Molly jumped at the sound of Freckles's voice behind her. The waitress from the Cowgirl Up Café was standing alongside another woman who looked very familiar, although Molly couldn't quite place her.

"Can we borrow that list?" Kaleb asked Freckles's conservative counterpart, who was wearing a pantsuit with tasteful jewelry and a hairstyle so stiff and formal not a single strand of the bob would dare to fall out of place.

The older woman passed over some printed pages and told them, "But I already called dibs on getting Maxine the jogging stroller."

Molly leaned into Kaleb's arm to read the list, but Freckles and her friend were openly staring at them and smiling in a weird, expectant way. Whether they were trying to confirm that Molly and Kaleb were actually dating or whether they were just curious about what she planned to buy her sister, Molly squirmed under their blatant scrutiny.

"Look." She pointed at the list. "Here's something in the electronics department. Let's go take a look at that."

Molly had no idea what the item was, but at least it allowed them to make a quick escape to a different part of the store. Kaleb easily tossed the mattress that she hadn't decided on onto the top of the shopping cart and made their goodbyes.

It was then that Molly realized her mistake. The baby monitor had been easy enough to find, but Kaleb had to talk to every store employee and his assistant, Angela, before settling on a newer, more expensive model that would link to a special app on the user's phone.

Then the young man who worked in the video game department recognized Kaleb and asked for a photo. It was another hour before they were finally pushing two full shopping carts into the parking lot.

This was supposed to have been a quick and easy errand. But she was finding out that nothing about Kaleb Chatterson was easy at all.

Chapter Eleven

After arguing with Molly for a solid ten minutes about physics and mechanical engineering, Kaleb went back inside to buy a coil of rope so that all their purchases wouldn't fly out the back of the truck.

"I still think all of this is overkill," Molly told him when he secured the last knot.

"I like being prepared."

"You probably were an excellent Boy Scout."

"I would have been if…" He trailed off at the memory.

"If what?"

"I wasn't allowed to go to the scouting camp like my brothers. I spent a whole summer in a traction bed once reading the handbook, though, and learning how to pitch a tent, start a fire and tie ropes. I never got around to doing the first two, but I'd used up a couple of spools of dental floss practicing the more complicated knots. Anyway, I quit going to the den meetings because I didn't see the point in hanging out with a bunch of kids learning how to do things I could research and learn about at home."

"I'm surprised your parents just let you quit."

"I think they were initially overwhelmed with having a kid who wasn't perfect. I don't mean that they didn't love me," he rushed to say when he saw her horrified expression. "In fact, they probably loved me too much because they treated me with kid gloves. Even my brothers took a hiatus from picking on me. But don't worry, they bounced back after my first surgery when the doctor told them that I actually needed to exercise in order to get better. Of course, I still wasn't allowed to do the contact sports, but my dad found a swim coach and I had daily strengthening workouts. By the end of middle school, I could easily outdistance any of my hot-shot baseball-playing brothers in the pool."

She smiled at him before getting into the passenger seat. "Being a kid sister, I'm pretty impressed that you were able to beat them at something."

He walked around to his side of the truck and climbed in. "Ha. Apparently, you've never raced against a Chatterson. They're horrible at losing. Kane and Kevin started going to practice with me during their off-season so they could challenge me to a rematch."

"Yeah, I caught a glimpse of your family's competitiveness when they were playing badminton at the barbecue on Wednesday." Molly smiled as he started the engine. "Yesterday, Kylie was still sporting that bruise from that shuttlecock Bobby Junior served during the last match."

"Trust me, they've really mellowed out since we were teenagers."

"So did they ever beat you at swimming?"

"Kevin did once, but only because he reached over into my lane and grabbed hold of the waistband of my Speedo."

"That's horrible," Molly said, but the words were muffled by her giggles.

"You have no idea. The girls' water polo team was meeting for tryouts and were all on deck and watching."

Molly's nose was practically touching her knees, she was bent over laughing so hard. When she'd wiped the tears from her upturned cheeks, she asked, "Did he get in trouble?"

"Yeah, he got grounded for two weeks. One week for cheating and one week for embarrassing me. Although, he had an out-of-state baseball tournament during the second half of his punishment and I decided that justice wasn't exactly being fulfilled."

"You mean you took matters into your own hands?"

Kaleb shrugged his shoulders. "I might've hacked into his computer account and printed out some of his correspondence to a certain high school junior who he had this huge crush on."

"Were the emails pretty scandalous?"

"Unfortunately, no. They'd mostly been sharing pictures of cute kittens and discussing civics homework. But it taught him that I would always be one step ahead of him when it came to technology. Anyway, I'm starving. How're your levels? Should we go grab a bite to eat?"

Kaleb silently cursed himself when the smile suddenly left her face. He hated that he'd gone and ruined their playful banter with that reminder, but someone had to look out for her health. Molly hadn't had a meal since she'd only managed to swallow down a few bites of the well-done frittata he'd made. Not that he could blame her. The online video didn't say anything about baking times being converted for the high altitude.

Without replying, she pulled the black case out of her purse and pricked herself. He put the truck in gear to avoid staring at her, knowing how it felt to be the subject of strict medical scrutiny. Yet he couldn't stop himself from holding his breath until she told him the number.

"Kane told me about a restaurant near this shopping center. It's called the Bacon Palace. Does that sound good?"

"It does, but—" she looked out the back window "—I don't think we should leave all this stuff in the bed of the truck. Someone could steal it."

"Right." Personally, Kaleb didn't see what anyone would want with a bunch of random baby gear, but he'd hate to have to go back to the store and find all those items again. He pulled into another parking spot and tapped on his cell phone screen.

"What are you doing now?"

"I'm searching for nearby drive-through restaurants."

"Or you could just lift your head and look at the big signs on the side of the road. We passed at least several of them on the way here."

"Yeah, but I have this app that shows the menu and the guest ratings so we don't waste our time going to somewhere that isn't good."

"Kaleb, it's fast food. I think you're going to need to lower your billionaire expectations for at least one meal."

Billionaire expectations? What was that supposed to mean? First, his sister made fun of his cheap shirts and now Molly was making fun of his financial situation. Someone needed to pick a lane. "Do I come across as some sort of snob to you?"

"Not a snob exactly. But sometimes you can get a little controlling about how you want things done. Don't you ever just live in the moment? Do something without a plan or a map or a phone call to your assistant?"

"Fine," he said, rolling his stiff shoulders backward in an effort to loosen them. "Let's just fly by the seats of our pants and go to the first place we see."

"This is killing you, isn't it?" Molly smiled at him as he pulled out of the parking lot. The dare in her eyes was the only thing that kept his fingers away from the navigation screen.

"Nope. I'm great. Call out a restaurant as soon as you see it."

"There's a place called Burger X-Press," she suggested.

"I don't trust businesses that can't spell out their full name."

"Across the street is Big Smokey's Pit House."

"It looks closed," he said, ignoring the fact that the lights were on, a cloud of barbecue smoke was billowing from the roof and the parking lot was packed.

"Krispy Kreme." She pointed to the giant doughnut-shaped entrance sign. "That counts as a drive-through."

"You wish," he said.

She nodded at a take-out building shaped to look like a giant taco. "How about Señor Shaddy's Taco Shack?"

"That shack looks like one of those places where people used to drop off their pictures to get developed."

They continued another block before she asked, "Fantastic Falafels? Or do you have something against alliteration?"

"I'm good with that." He made a casual shrug and flipped on the turn signal. What he didn't say was that before she'd shamed him into closing out his phone app, this restaurant was the first one to pop up and he'd already seen its four-and-a-half-star rating.

There was also an outdoor take-out window and picnic tables with orange-striped umbrellas, so they could still keep an eye on the truck in the parking lot as they ate. He bit his tongue when she ordered the falafel platter with a regular pita, instead of the whole-wheat option. And she didn't make fun of him when he asked the virtual assistant feature on his watch how to pronounce *gyro*.

It was almost rush hour and she asked if she could drive the truck back to Sugar Falls because it had been a while since she'd been behind an engine with more than four cylinders. But the memory of Molly racing around on the Jet Ski still had Kaleb's muscles clenching, so he told her she could be in charge of the radio instead.

They were halfway up the mountain when he lowered the volume and asked if they could listen to something with a little less bass. "It makes me feel like I'm at a dance club in Vegas."

"Do you go to a lot of dance clubs?" she asked.

"Never."

"Why am I not surprised?" Molly's smile was teasing, but all day long he'd had a weird feeling that he was the butt of some sort of joke nobody was telling him about. Maybe it was all the teasing he'd been taking from his siblings recently. Or maybe it was that soldier's comment about his juvenile shirt at the rec lounge at Shadowview. Or maybe it was the fact that he'd never slept with a woman and then spent the entire day with her afterward. All he knew was that he hadn't been this insecure since high school.

He pulled into his sister's driveway and the first thing he noticed was the lack of cars parked in front, although the lights were on inside. His chest expanded and he let out a relieved breath. Hopefully, most of his family would be gone and they'd be able to drop off the baby presents and escape another evening filled with smart-aleck Chattersons.

No such luck, he realized when he swung open the front door and saw the chaos bouncing around the great room. One of Kylie's twin daughters was lying in her playpen chewing on the corner of a Dr. Seuss book, the other was sliding halfway out of her swing. Aiden and Caden Gregson were in the kitchen, stirring something in a big pot over a lit stove while a boy Kaleb had never seen before sat on the counter beside them giving them instructions. Two of Bobby Junior's kids were jumping on the huge sectional sofa, which was suspiciously missing all of its cushions.

A major-league baseball game played on the big-screen TV, the volume turned way up, but there was no other sign that another adult was present. Kaleb grabbed his cell phone, prepared to call 9-1-1.

"What's going on, guys?" Molly hollered over the noise.

"We're making chili goulash," the nine-year-old twins in the kitchen called out in unison.

"We're practicing gymnastics." One of the redheaded

girls used the arm of the couch to do a backflip onto the wooden floor.

The baby in the playpen blew a slobbery raspberry.

Molly jogged over to rescue the other baby, whose diapered rear end was now dangling out of the swing.

"Who's supposed to be in charge?" Kaleb finally asked, now that it seemed like everyone was accounted for.

"Uncle Kevin is," the extra boy sitting on the counter said. Was his family suddenly multiplying and nobody had told him?

"I'm down here." His brother waved from underneath the poorly constructed blanket fort on the living room floor. "Trying to watch the game in peace."

"Kaleb," Molly said as she looked around, holding a baby on her hip. "I think one of the kids is missing."

Kaleb did a quick headcount as Kevin climbed out from his hiding spot. "Who's missing?"

His brother pointed around the room as he called, "One, two, three, four, five, six, seven. Nope, everyone's here."

"Um, Kevin." Kaleb nodded toward the dark-haired boy. "That's not Bobby Three."

"I'm Choogie Nguyen." The kid waved a box of macaroni at him before dumping it into the pot on the stove. "I live next door."

"Okay, back to my original question." Kaleb turned toward his brother, who was now sitting on the cushionless sofa muttering something at the umpire on the TV. "Who is supposed to be in charge?"

Kevin glanced around the room, then shrugged. "I am."

That couldn't be right. Nobody would put Kevin in

charge of a load of laundry, let alone seven children. Aiden—or was it Caden?—stepped off his chair in front of the stove.

"Well, our parents went out for a date night so Aunt Kylie told them to drop us off over here. Then she and Gramma Lacey had to go to the party-supply store because Grampa Coach bought bridal shower decorations instead of baby shower decorations. One of Uncle Drew's patients called him with an emergency, so he had to leave. And Uncle Bobby is in the back bedroom talking to his wife on the phone." The kid glanced at the two girls doing cartwheels way too close to the coffee table and lowered his voice to a whisper. "Aunt Kylie said she thinks they're gonna get a *D-I-V-O-R-S-E*, but we're not allowed to say that word in front of his kids."

Molly carried the baby she was holding over to the playpen and set her down inside before taking away her twin sister's chewed book. God bless the woman for not running out the front door.

"So where's Dad and Bobby Three?" Kaleb asked his brother as he began tossing cushions back onto the sofa. It wasn't his fault that Kevin wasn't quick enough to dodge the one flung at his face.

"Oomf." Kevin hurled it back at him. "Dad took him to pick up some ice cream. You want me to call them and tell them to bring extra for you and your girlfriend?"

Kaleb felt a flush spread up his neck at his brother's purposeful use of the term. But Molly hadn't heard him or else was doing a really good job of pretending she hadn't.

"No. We're just dropping off the stuff for the baby shower." He walked over to Molly and whispered, "Do you mind if we hang out for a few minutes until a responsible adult comes back? I'm afraid someone might call child services on us if we leave them alone with Kevin."

She chuckled and it caused the warmth to spread from his neck to the rest of his body. "I don't have anywhere else I need to be."

"Is it true that you're Uncle Kaleb's girlfriend?" Caden, or possibly Aiden, tugged on Molly's hand.

Now her cheeks were the ones turning crimson. "Um…"

She looked at him with pleading eyes but before Kaleb could answer, Kevin muttered, "Not if she's smart, she's not."

"But you have to be smart to be a combat pilot, right?" Caden asked.

"Well, I did have to go to college and I like to think I'm pretty smart." Molly smiled through her confusion.

"Are you as smart as Uncle Kaleb? Aunt Kylie calls him a Brainiac," the other twin said as he walked over.

"Why does she call him a Brainiac?" Choogie, the neighbor kid, asked as he joined them in the living room.

"Because Uncle Kaleb is a computer genius and a gazillionaire and invented 'Blockcraft.'"

"I'm not allowed to play video games," Choogie announced. "Both of my moms say that junk will rot my brain."

And the ball of insecurity in Kaleb's stomach grew, making him blurt out, "Actually, there are no scientific studies that back that up."

He knew that not everybody was sold on the successful educational game he'd developed as a counterpart to the more recreational Alien Pirates series. But this was twice in the same day that someone had referred to his creations as mind-rotting junk. Of course, maybe his brain *was* rotting if he was standing here defending his life's work to a nine-year-old.

"So then if you're smart—" Caden continued his conversation with Molly "—does that mean that you're *not* Uncle Kaleb's girlfriend?"

"It's, um, complicated," Molly said before brightening up.

"Do you have another boyfriend?" Aiden asked. "Uncle Bobby told Gramma that his marriage was complicated and Aunt Kylie said that's because his wife has another boyfriend and wants a *D-I-V*—"

"No," Molly interjected quickly when she saw one of Bobby Junior's daughters somersaulting toward her. "I don't have another boyfriend."

"Have you ever had one before?" Choogie asked.

"Wow." Molly's smile was frozen as she widened her eyes at Kaleb. "Your family sure asks a lot of questions."

Technically, the neighbor kid wasn't part of his family, but Kaleb was curious about the answer himself so he just lifted his eyebrow at her. *Well?*

She let out a long breath. "I used to have a boyfriend, but we broke up."

"When?"

"Why?"

Molly gulped, but Kaleb was enjoying this too much. "Because he liked Chinese food and I didn't."

Seven sets of eyes—including Kevin's—gawked at Molly. It would've been eight, but one of the babies had fallen asleep. What did somebody's meal preferences have to do with anything?

"Do *you* like Chinese food, Uncle Kaleb?" one of the boys asked.

"Sometimes." Kaleb decided it was time to bail Molly out. "But it doesn't matter because Molly and I are just friends."

"Friends don't kiss," Aiden argued. "And we all saw you guys kiss right there in the middle of the lake. Even Coach Grampa saw it and said—"

Molly sniffed at the air. "Is something burning?"

"The chili goulash!" one of the boys hollered as he ran to the kitchen and turned off the stove.

Thankfully, Kaleb's mom and sister walked in the door at that exact moment. He tugged on Molly's hand. "Okay, so we were just dropping off the presents for the baby shower. Now that some responsible adults are here, I'm going to take Molly home."

"Don't you guys want to stay for dinner?" Lacy Chatterson asked.

"We already ate."

"Are you staying at your girrrrrrrlfriennnnnnnd's house tonight?" Kevin asked, and their mom smacked him on the back of his head. "Gah, Ma! I'm missing a doubleheader today because Kaleb demanded we take our family vacation right in the middle of the season. The least I can do is give him some grief for not spending any time with us."

"All you kids ever do is give each other grief…" his mom started, and Kaleb pulled Molly toward the door.

They were just about to the truck when his sister came out onto the front porch and yelled, "We have a big day tomorrow, Molly. Make sure my brother lets you get a good night's rest!"

Chapter Twelve

Molly was still trying to process everything as they drove back to her apartment. As they passed Duncan's Market, she finally said, "So I guess your whole family now knows that we're sleeping together."

Kaleb sighed. "Yeah, sorry for all the questions and wisecracks back there. My family isn't used to me bringing a woman around."

"You mean you've never brought a girlfriend home to meet them?"

"Can't you see why?" he asked.

"I think your family is fun."

"They're a blast. To everyone who didn't have to grow up with them or constantly have them up in their personal business."

"Well, I grew up with a family who kept to themselves

all the time. You should be glad they're nosy. It means they care about you."

"Maxine seems to care about you," Kaleb replied, bringing stirring up Molly's guilt again.

"I know she does. But it's different between us. We love each other, but your siblings are more vocal about it. More affectionate. They don't hesitate to actually *show* their love."

Kaleb snorted. "How? By annoying me?"

"That's part of what makes them so enjoyable," Molly wiggled her eyebrows. "But, seriously. Haven't your girlfriends wanted to meet them?"

"I try to go out with the women who are only interested in where I'm taking them and whether or not there will be a red carpet there."

Molly puzzled over his response for a few moments. "So you don't like women with substance? Or you purposely only date shallow women so you don't have to do serious relationships?"

"Asks the woman who broke up with a guy because he liked Chinese food."

She shifted in her seat so that she could look out the window. "What I didn't say was that our breakup had more to do with *who* I caught him eating Chinese food with. I'll give you a hint. It wasn't me."

"Ouch. How long ago was that?"

"A few days after I was first diagnosed." She used her finger to draw a zigzagging pattern along the leather of the armrest.

The car noticeably slowed down and she guessed that Kaleb had taken his foot off the gas pedal. He did that every time he felt compelled to better understand something. "You mean he cheated on you when you found out that you had diabetes?"

"No, he didn't know about my condition. Still doesn't. I showed up at his house to tell him because I figured he deserved to know that I was no longer the same woman he planned to marry. And that's when I caught him with his fortune cookie already unwrapped."

She heard the gurgle of him swallowing back his laughter and he resumed driving. But after a few seconds, she knew his silence was too good to last. "Okay, so back up. You were going to get married?"

Molly already had one strike against her with all the complications that came along with the whole diabetes diagnosis. It was humiliating to admit that she'd also been stupid enough not to know that her fiancé had been cheating on her, as well. "Do we really have to talk about this right now?"

"Let me guess, this is also something you're keeping from your sister?"

"Actually, Maxine knows about Trevor. My whole family does, since we'd already sent out the wedding invitations before I called it off. In fact, that's why my sister thinks I'm in town. To take a break and mend my broken heart."

"So this was all pretty recent?" he asked. "Does that make me the rebound guy?"

"No!" she exclaimed. "There wasn't anything to rebound from. To be honest, I'd been having reservations about going through with the marriage, anyway. I don't think I ever really loved him. Otherwise, I would've been more upset about the other woman. He was also a pilot, assigned to another squadron, so our relationship was easy and he never demanded anything from me.

My parents' marriage is the same way so I've never really known anything different. But now that I've been spending time with Maxine and Cooper and all the head over heels in love couples in *your* family—with the exception of Bobby Junior, I guess—it's become clearer that marrying Trevor would've been a huge mistake."

He pulled into the parking spot near her rental car in the alley. He didn't make a move to get out of the truck, but he'd never been the type before to wait for an invitation. Was he suddenly changing his mind about spending time with her? Her chest sunk with disappointment.

When he didn't say anything, she tried to joke, "Now if I could get the rest of my life clearer, then maybe I'd be back in business."

Finally, he reached his hand across the center console and picked up her hand, bringing it to his mouth for a soft kiss. "Just for the record, I wouldn't mind if this was a rebound thing, but I'm glad it's not."

Thankfully, he didn't ask what "this" was between them. Because Molly had no idea. All she knew was that she wasn't quite ready for it to be over.

"So are we just going to sit down here all night or are you going to come upstairs and make sure I get a good night's rest?" she asked.

He smiled before turning her wrist over and planting another tender kiss there, as well. And then nobody got any rest after that.

Molly tugged the top of her strapless sundress back into place as she looked around at the other women clustered into friendly groups, drinking prosecco sangrias and discussing their own pregnancies and labors. So far, nobody had been able to beat Cessy Walker's—Molly *knew* she'd recognized the woman with Freckles at the store yesterday—story about her water breaking at a Barry Manilow concert and her refusal to leave until after the singer's encore performance of "It's a Miracle."

Baby showers must be quite the social event in Sugar Falls because the back room of Patrelli's Italian restaurant was at full capacity and all the ladies were wearing their best pastels and floral prints. Molly had borrowed a dress from Maxine, but the ill-fitting clothes were not only a reminder of the fact that she didn't own a suitable wardrobe for a ladies' luncheon, but that her recent weight loss was most noticeable in her chest.

Kylie clinked a spoon to her glass of fruit-filled sangria. As the room quieted, Molly desperately wished she could have just one sip. More for the sugar buzz than the alcohol content. Instead, she stuck to her unsweetened iced tea.

"Okay, everyone. We're going to start our first game," Kaleb's sister announced.

Molly would've pumped her fist if it she could do so without letting her dress slip. She might not be able to drink the fancy cocktails or discuss childbirth or even contribute to the latest Sugar Falls gossip, but finally there was something she *could* participate in. She thrived on healthy competition and didn't care whether it was a combat mission or a game of gin rummy back in the barracks. She liked to win. And it had been so long since she'd won something.

Kylie passed out papers as she explained the rules of the game. "When I call time after five minutes, everyone drop your pens. The person who knows the most about Maxine wins."

Molly's face went slack as the blood rushed to her

feet. Couldn't they compete at something she'd actually be good at?

"It's not fair if you and Mia and Maxine's sister play because you guys know her the best," one of the ladies called out. Molly recognized her as the owner of the gas station and the mother of the boy who'd asked Kaleb for his signature outside the Cowgirl Up Café. The woman didn't even know Molly's name—only that she was Maxine's kid sister. But she was right, on at least part of her complaint. Kylie and Mia were Maxine's best friends and could easily win this game. Molly doubted she could even get half the answers right.

"Of course the three of us aren't playing," Mia said as she handed out pens. "We're the ones who came up with the questions."

They were? When had they done that? Molly recalled their meeting at the Cowgirl Up a few days ago. They'd briefly discussed what they intended to play, but when exactly had they... Oh. Her cheeks heated. They must've come up with the list when she'd been in the ladies' room making out with Kaleb.

As the guests began writing, Molly maneuvered herself to where Kylie and Mia were huddled. Hopefully, they had the answer sheet with them and Molly could sneak a quick peak. How sad was that? She had to rely on a cheesy baby shower game to gain a little insight into her big sister.

Better to just paste a neutral expression on her face and make herself less conspicuous. Oh, look. The gift table could use some rearranging. Molly walked over and sorted the packages in order of size, bringing the small items toward the front of the table.

"Sixty more seconds," Mia announced.

Freckles waved her sheet over her head. "I've already finished and you might as well give me the prize."

Several women groaned, because of course the waitress from the local café knew everything about everyone.

Molly held herself still while Maxine read off the answers. "Biggest craving is salt-and-vinegar potato chips."

Well, that was no surprise. Anyone with eyes and standing in the same room as her sister would've guessed that.

"Circumference of my stomach is currently forty-two inches."

Yeah, Molly would've gotten that, too, because the turboshaft in the first jet she'd flown was that exact same size.

"Does 'Tears of a Clown' count as a favorite lullaby?"

Duh. Growing up, their CD player at home always had a stack of Maxine's favorite Motown discs on it. And Hunter always sang Smokey Robinson songs as he got ready for bed.

"Foot size?" Maxine continued. "I'm still wearing my size eight shoes, but they're getting tighter."

In addition to the sundress, Molly had had to borrow a pair of wedge sandals from her sister for this party, so she would've gotten that answer, as well.

And everyone correctly wrote down that Maxine had met Cooper through her son, Hunter, because of a pen pal program at school. Hmm, maybe Molly knew more about her sister than she'd thought.

Her heart resumed its normal pace and she eased herself closer to Mia and Kylie's side, suddenly feeling less like an outsider. When lunch was served, she skipped Patrelli's famous garlic knots in the buffet line, instead loading up on the antipasto salad. Afterward, she volunteered to cut and serve the red-velvet cake so that nobody would notice that she was the only person in the room who wasn't enjoying a slice. Although she did lick some of the cream cheese frosting off her finger when she was done passing out the plates.

"So what about you?" Elaine Marconi asked Molly when she finally resumed her seat at the head of the U-shaped table by her sister. "Are you planning to have kids, too?"

The spotlight was suddenly thrust onto Molly's flaming cheeks and she turned to Maxine, looking for some sort of signal on how she should handle such a personal question. Unfortunately, her sister was distracted by something Mrs. Chatterson was saying to her.

Molly knew this was a small town, but why did people think it was appropriate to ask others about their procreation plans? Or, in her case, a lack of them. Molly took a big gulp of her iced tea. "Not any time soon."

"No, of course not *now*," Elaine replied. "You and Kaleb should take some time to get to know each other first, but maybe after your wedding."

Her eyelids popped open. What wedding? They weren't even dating. Well, they sort of were, but it was only temporary. And just for appearances. It certainly would never get to the point where they would ever need to discuss the possibility of babies.

"Not everyone wants to have kids." Julia, Kaleb's soon-to-be sister-in-law, came to her rescue. "I know Kane and I have our hands full taking care of our dog."

"That's a shame," Cessy Walker said to Julia. Molly

moved to the edge of her seat, getting ready to defend her new ally. Then the woman added, "Your and Kane's babies would be a lot cuter and smarter than that dog of yours who keeps lifting his leg on my Lexus tire every time you walk him downtown."

"Sounds like a pretty intelligent dog to me," Maxine whispered to Molly, who fought the urge to giggle because she wasn't yet convinced that this conversation didn't have the potential to take a judgmental turn. Some women had a tendency to think every other female should follow their example. It was one of the reasons Molly had loved being in a male-dominated profession. Yet, before Molly could prepare her plan of defense, someone else jumped in.

"Our son is smart and beautiful," one of Choogie Nguyen's moms said. "And he doesn't have either of our DNA."

Carmen Gregson lifted her glass of sangria. "Cheers to that. I couldn't love the twins more if they'd come from my own body."

"I never had kids," Freckles said as she helped herself to the rest of Cessy Walker's cake. "And to be honest, I don't regret my decision."

Molly had not been prepared for this. It wasn't so much that any of the women were explicitly protecting her. But they were being open and honest with their feelings and their situations and nobody was trying to pretend to be anything they weren't. Well, except for Elaine Marconi, who kept her judgmental chin firmly in the air.

"So who's ready for another game?" Mia asked, and Molly settled back into her seat as her cohost explained the rules for the blindfolded diaper races. The rest of the shower passed in a flurry of laughter and friendly competition and oohing and ahhing over presents of hand-knitted blankets and tiny, delicate outfits.

When Molly won the bingo game for having five gifts in a row on her card, she traded prizes with Freckles, who'd earlier been awarded a gift certificate to a free kayaking lesson from Russell Sports.

"Are you sure you don't mind switchin'?" the waitress asked as everyone helped clean up all the discarded bows and wrapping paper.

"I'm positive." Molly put up a hand to assure her. "I won't be in town long enough to use up a month of free yoga classes at Mia's studio."

"I wish you could stay that long," Maxine said beside her, catching Molly off guard with a one-armed hug around her waist.

"You do?" Molly searched her sister's face.

"Of course I do. I love you, Moll Doll."

The childhood nickname sent a funny flutter through her tummy and she couldn't stop herself for leaning into Maxine's side.

"Hold it right there," Kylie said before using the camera on her phone to snap a photo.

"Make sure you send me a copy of that," Maxine said to her friend before turning to Molly. "I can't remember the last time we took a picture together."

It wasn't accusatory, but since her sister had lived in the same city for the past twelve years, Molly knew that it was her own career and her countless relocations that had kept them apart for so long. Everyone smiled at their sentimental display of sisterhood bonding but the guilt weighing on Molly's shoulders made her feel like a fraud.

At least it did until her nephew and brother-in-law walked into the room and Hunter announced, "Hey, Aunt Molly, we played golf with Kaleb today and I told him about this awesome idea I had for his next video game. He's going to bring you over to our house for dinner tonight so we can talk about it."

Chapter Thirteen

Kaleb's lower spine had barely made it through the eighteenth hole when he finally asked Hunter—who thought the sport of golf was slow and boring and only perked up when he got to race Kevin in the golf carts—to drive him back to the pro-shop for a package of ibuprofen and an Icy Hot patch while everyone stayed behind for a postgame putting match. Before Cooper and the rest of the Chatterson men met up with them for a round of beers and Reuben sandwiches, Molly's nephew had proposed a decently thought-out plan for the development of a new concept game.

The twelve-year-old invited him over to dinner at Maxine's so they could talk to Molly about the plan. Since he'd spent the past two nights at her apartment, Kaleb didn't want the woman thinking this was becoming a habit. In fact, when he'd kissed her goodbye this morning before she'd left to help set up for the baby shower, he no longer felt like they were role-playing.

When he headed back to Seattle in a couple of days, they were going to have to break up—or at least make the pretense of breaking up. He didn't know what to call it anymore. Whatever was going on between them still wasn't real, but they'd definitely crossed that platonic line and now the only awkward part of their relationship was the fact that it no longer felt awkward.

So he'd purposely not made plans to meet her directly after the baby shower, knowing that spending less time together was the key to getting their lives back to normal. But when the babysitter Kylie had hired called Drew and Bobby Junior to tell them that two, possibly three, kids appeared to have poison ivy, Kaleb sent Molly a text asking if she wanted to ride together to Maxine and Cooper's.

"So what's this big plan Hunter wants to tell me about?" Molly asked when she opened the apartment door. She was wearing snug white jeans and a light blue sweater and looked so much more comfortable than she had in the sundress she'd had on this morning when she'd left.

"It's actually not that big of deal, but he made me promise to wait until we got over there to tell you about it."

"Since when does Kaleb Chatterson wait for anything?"

"Since I saw you in those jeans," he said, sliding in close to her and putting his hands along her rib cage before giving her a kiss hello. She was wearing that mango coconut lotion again, and as his thumb brushed against the underside of her breast, she gave a soft moan. "Maybe we can be a little late."

"You know that if we're not there by six, Hunter is going to blow up both of our phones with text messages demanding to know what's taking so long. So if I have to wait to hear about this big plan, then you can wait until after we come home to finish this."

Home. He'd never trusted a woman's motives enough to let her into his inner circle, let alone live with one. Yet, the amount of time he spent with Molly felt so natural to him, so right, he didn't want to stay with anyone else. The word *home* should've scared him but instead of dwelling on it, he pushed for a more playful tone. "People are going to talk if they know you keep begging me to spend the night."

"Begging?" She grabbed her tote bag and he stepped aside as she locked the door. "I heard all about the poison ivy so don't pretend that you weren't hoping to catch another reprieve from your family over here. Besides, people are already talking."

"I'm not *only* over here for a reprieve, you know." He followed her down the stairs.

"You proved that in my bedroom last night. And the night before that," she said saucily over her shoulder. But before his ego could grow too much, she added, "It just so happens to be a bonus that since you don't have any employees here to boss around, you can also get your CEO fix by constantly micromanaging my levels and monitoring what I'm eating."

He grabbed her hand, forcing her to stop and turn around. "Do you really think I'm trying to micromanage you? Like you're some kind of project for me?"

She tilted the corners of her lips into a smirk, but it

didn't quite reach her eyes. "Well, I know it's not for my Wi-Fi since you always bring that ridiculous portable satellite thing over with you. Luckily, I don't have insecurities about the type of internet availability I can provide my guests."

Kaleb cupped her cheek. "What you lack in Wi-Fi capabilities, you more than make up for with the way your mouth does that thing—"

His watch let out a shrill ding. He yanked his hand back and silenced the ringer, but not before she had to tug on her earlobe and rotate her jaw. "Talk about overkill. Does that stupid device even serve a purpose? I mean, other than to make me go deaf?"

"Sorry," he said, then laughed when he saw the text message pop up on the screen. "But you were right about Hunter looking for us if we didn't show up on time."

He opened the passenger door for her and waited until he pulled onto Snowflake Boulevard before asking her if her hearing had returned.

"What?" she said playfully, then smiled.

"So you mentioned something earlier about people already talking about me spending the nights. What are they saying?"

"Actually, it was only one person who brought it up, but she did it in front of everyone at the baby shower and in this really uncomfortable context. But don't worry. The conversation ended up going in a different direction and I was saved from responding."

"You know that you didn't exactly answer my question, right?"

"You're doing that micromanaging thing again." She wagged a finger at him.

"And you're doing that thing where you avoid giving details so you can pretend everything is fine."

She grunted and let her head fall against the back of the seat. "She asked me if we were planning to have children."

"Together?" His stomach did a somersault and he had to command his foot to return to the accelerator. That had been his same response to the employee at the department store yesterday. Why did the idea of having children with Molly keep popping up in his mind?

"Actually, she asked if I wanted to have them, then implied that you and I had plenty of time to figure that out."

"*Do* you want kids? I mean, in general. Not necessarily with me."

She shrugged. "I don't know. I mean, I always assumed I'd have them someday, but now I don't even know if I can. Anyway, it's not something I need to figure out right this second."

"But you know you're going to have to think about your future eventually." Kaleb was only pointing that out because he wanted her to be receptive to Hunter's idea. And because he wanted her to think it was brilliant. That *he* was brilliant. He couldn't explain this sudden urge to prove that he was more than just the technology dependent overgrown kid people had accused him of being lately.

Her response was to roll her head in his direction and give him a pointed look. Not that he could blame her.

They didn't speak the rest of the way, but when they pulled into the driveway, Molly asked, "Who's car is that?"

"Maxine, don't you think it's a little weird that your former mother-in-law comes over to family dinners with your new husband?" Molly whispered to her sister in the kitchen as they heated up the leftover food from Patrelli's. Cessy Walker, the woman in question, was in the living room overseeing the men's assembly of a bassinet.

"Not any more weird than inviting her to both my wedding and my baby shower," Maxine replied. "I know it's a bit unorthodox, but after Beau died when Hunter was two, we were the only family Cessy had left. Plus, Cooper won't admit it, but he secretly gets a real kick out of her."

Molly shook her head in doubt. "One of the blessings of calling off my wedding with Trevor was the knowledge that I'd never have to go to another luncheon with his mom again. Yes, she was actually stuck-up enough to call them 'luncheons.'"

Maxine nodded her head in Kaleb's direction. "Looks like that's not the only blessing to come out of your breakup."

Yeah, except it was tough to get too optimistic about another relationship that would be ending in a few days. Of course, since she couldn't correct her sister's—and everyone else in town's—assumption she changed the subject. "Do you know what this top secret plan of Hunter's is?"

"No clue," Maxine admitted. "He used to tell me everything but he's getting to that age. You know how it goes."

"How would I know how that goes?" Molly asked. "I don't have kids of my own, remember? Your friend Elaine was such a dear to bring that subject up in front of everyone today."

"Whoa." Maxine held up her pot holder–covered

hand. "First of all, I meant because you became the same way when you were Hunter's age. Second of all, Elaine is not my friend."

Before Molly could ask Maxine to expand on her initial statement, Cessy pulled out one of the counter stools and joined them. "Max, I told you I was sorry for inviting her. I was at the clerk's office in city hall talking to Mae Johnston about the shower cake we ordered from that fancy bakery in Boise. How was I supposed to know that Elaine was in line to get a permit for the remodel of the Gas N' Mart?"

"It's not your fault." Maxine squeezed the woman's shoulder. "Mia accidentally mentioned it at her yoga class last week, as well. Besides, it's a small town and Hunter is friends with her son."

"At least she brought a nice gift." Cessy poured herself another glass of wine, then extended the bottle.

"No, thanks." Molly took a big gulp of her water. "So did you like all your presents?"

"Oh, my gosh!" Maxine squealed. "I meant to tell you, that crib mattress you got me was so perfect. I got rid of Hunter's when he was a toddler because I didn't think I'd ever have another kid. When I found out I was pregnant, one of the ladies who works at the cookie shop gave me her daughter's old one. It was in great condition, but when we got it home, the mattress had all these yellow stains and it reminded me of that hand-me-down bed we got from Tommy."

Molly pointed at her sister. "That was my exact same thought when I saw them in the store."

Maxine laughed, then said, "Remember when he would babysit us, then put a cheap frozen pizza in the oven and force us watch that Tom Cruise movie so we'd leave him and his girlfriend alone while they made out on the back porch? We should've told her about his bedwetting problem. That would've put an end to his romantic endeavors."

"I loved those pizzas!" Molly put her hand to her heart.

"Too bad I can only provide you with the good stuff from Patrelli's tonight." Maxine opened the oven and the scent of garlic and pepperoni was like a punch in the gut since Molly knew she would have to limit herself to just one slice. "But we can ask the guys to find *Top Gun* on Netflix."

"I wish I would've had a sister," Cessy said. "You two are so lucky to have each other."

Were they? Molly had never thought about what it would be like to be an only child. Sure, there were times growing up when she probably wished that she could have something new or have more of her parents' attention, but she'd never resented her brothers and sister. She'd also never appreciated them, either. They were just there. She had no other basis for comparison until she'd met the Chattersons and caught a glimpse of what she'd been missing.

Suddenly, it felt like the most important thing in the world was to connect with her sister. To make up for lost time.

"Is dinner ready yet?" Hunter asked, a crumpled set of instructions in his hand. "We need to take a break from bassinet building."

"But I've almost figured out what we're supposed to do with the rocker base," Kaleb called out from behind the screen of his phone where he was probably watching a how-to video.

As Molly and Cessy carried the food to the wooden farmhouse table in the dining room, Cooper gently massaged Maxine's lower back and told her she should sit down and put her feet up. How sweet was it that her sister had found a man who was so caring and always concerned for her well-being.

"Do you want me to grab your meter for you before we eat?" Kaleb whispered from behind her shoulder. Huh. For some reason, it didn't sound as sweet and caring when Kaleb did it. It sounded bossy.

"I already did." When his eyebrow didn't go down, she sighed. "It's at eighty-eight."

"You're perfect," he said, then kissed her cheek. "And that's a pretty good number, too."

Maybe it was all the baby talk and childhood memories and lovey-dovey affection between all the couples in this town, but Kaleb's compliment made her glow. Or maybe her brain was still baffled by how he never needed to look at the miniature chart she carried around with her as a cheat sheet of what her levels were supposed to be.

"Aunt Molly, come sit on this side of the table by Gram," Hunter said, holding out a chair. "I want to be next to Kaleb when we tell you so we can both see your excitement."

Great. She got to be the center of attention when all she'd wanted to do today was hide out. Expectation crackled in the air. This better be something good. Otherwise, she couldn't promise that her reaction wouldn't disappoint them.

Everyone began passing food and Molly told herself that she could have just a couple of garlic knots. She'd been so good with all those stupid salads lately. When the last platter had been set down, Hunter used his fork and knife to drumroll the table.

"So your nephew came up—" Kaleb started.

"No, let me tell her," Hunter interrupted. "So, I was asking Kaleb about what games his company was working on next, and he said that when you guys were at Shadowview the other day, he thought about creating some training simulators for wounded soldiers who might feel like they're missing out on the action."

"What were you doing at Shadowview, Molly?" Maxine paused midbite. Everyone turned to stare, and the feeling made her want to jump out of her chair and run out of the house. Or sob out a confession. It would've been a good time to come clean if Cessy wasn't sitting beside her, absorbing every word quicker than she was absorbing the pinot noir. Plus, the use of the term *wounded soldiers* ruffled the hairs on the back of her neck. She didn't know where this was going, but she certainly wasn't wounded.

"Just some routine tests and stuff," Molly answered before shoving a bite of sausage and mushroom pizza into her mouth.

"Anyway, we were talking about how cool it would be to make flight simulators that make people feel like they're sitting in a cockpit. Or even a tank. We could do tanks, too, right, Kaleb? Hey, what about submarines? That would be so sweet!"

"Sure," Kaleb replied, his fingers steepled under his chin and his eyes dialed in on Molly as if her opinion was the most important thing in the room. The problem was, she didn't know what her opinion was.

"Uh-huh," Molly said since everyone was clearly waiting for a response. "And this would relate to me how?"

"Kaleb would hire you on as a consultant to help him design everything for the jet ones." Hunter's grin grew wide, but Molly's rib cage seemed to narrow. "Like a real job. He'd pay you and everything. Do you know how much money software developers make at his company?"

Kaleb's face suddenly swiveled to look at Hunter and she would've laughed at the surprise on his face if she wasn't trying to process what exactly was happening. "How do you know how much my employees make?"

"But, sweetie." Maxine brushed her hand over Hunter's hair, preventing him from incriminating himself. "Aunt Molly already has a job. When you're in the military, you can't just take off for a better paying gig."

Cooper didn't say a word, but his look spoke volumes. Molly fired back at her brother-in-law's silent chastisement with a sharp but subtle nod toward Cessy. She really didn't want to have this conversation right now with so many witnesses.

While Molly couldn't deny her curiosity at the idea, any potential excitement stirring to life in her belly was easily doused by the threat of Maxine learning the truth. She was already dreading the time when she would have to make a decision about her career, Molly didn't want to think about her limited choices in front of an audience. And she especially didn't want to think about the fact that her nephew and her nonboyfriend had gone ahead and mapped out her future—over a round of golf, no less—without even bothering to consult her.

Chapter Fourteen

Kaleb took one look at Molly's expression and sat up straight in his dining room chair, realizing that he had to reassure her that he wasn't blowing her cover.

"You wouldn't need to leave your job. Unless, you know, you wanted to." Kaleb was quick to hedge his bets. "With all of our technology, we could do a lot of the work via emails and video conferences and what not. In fact, you wouldn't necessarily need to be there in person. A lot of it would be, uh, advisory."

"Well, I think that's a fabulous idea, you two." Cessy clapped twice, making a row of gold bracelets jingle along her wrist. "What can I do to help?"

"Um, what do you mean?" Kaleb looked across the table. Who was this woman again? Maxine's mother-in-law? Or former mother-in-law? He wished he hadn't been so quick to throw out his life preserver to Molly because he had a sudden premonition that *he* was the one who would need to be saved after this dinner.

"What about interior decorating? I could do that," Cessy suggested. "I mean, obviously you're going to need someone to pick out the leather for the cockpit chair or design where all those blinking lights go inside the submarine. Do they have beds in tanks? Because we could do some darling coverlets that incorporate a camouflage theme. Ooh, we could probably come up with some very neutral color schemes to appeal to people who aren't into all that military stuff."

"Why would someone not into military stuff want to drive a tank?" Maxine asked.

"It wouldn't be a life-size tank," Kaleb clarified. "Just a simulator of one. Really, we only came up with the idea this afternoon. It's not actually in the works. Yet."

"But he'll do it," Hunter assured everyone at the table, including Kaleb, who still had more than his share of doubts. "I watched that interview on *60 Minutes* when you told Lesley Stahl that once you visualize an idea, you always see it through to completion."

Kaleb shrugged. "Yeah, but my visualization process is pretty in-depth and—"

"I already drew up some designs." Hunter stood up. "I'll go grab them so we can get the ball rolling."

Molly rubbed at her temples before sneaking a sip of wine from Cessy's glass. Kaleb should probably ask her to step outside so they could—

"Ohhhh," Maxine moaned as she grabbed her stomach and her husband sent his chair flying backward.

"Are you okay?" Molly asked her sister.

Cooper's face grew pale. "I think it's time."

* * *

Kaleb had never been more thankful to have a woman go into labor than he was at that second. Maxine and Cooper left for the hospital while Cessy and Hunter quickly packed up a bag of everything they thought she would need and followed in a separate car.

Molly volunteered the two of them to clean up the dishes and put the food away. Because she had already been on edge before, Kaleb didn't say a word until the kitchen was spotless.

When there was nothing left to do but start the dishwasher, he asked, "Do you want me to drive you to the hospital?"

"I don't know," Molly replied. "I probably should wait to hear something from Cooper. What if it's a false alarm or something?"

"Should we stay here?"

"I don't know," Molly repeated. Kaleb's muscles twitched, anxious to do something. To make some sort of decision.

"I'll tell you what. Why don't we head down there? If they send her home, then we come back. But sitting around and waiting is going to make us nuts."

"Us? Or you?"

He rolled his eyes. "Us, because I'll eventually get so stir-crazy that I'll get on your nerves."

"Fine." She grabbed her purse and they locked up the house. When they climbed inside the truck, she added, "You don't have to drive me all the way down there, though. Just drop me off at the apartment and I can take my own car."

He tried to ignore the uncertainty settling on his

chest. He hated being unsure of something even more than he hated waiting. "You don't want me to take you?"

"I've seen how you get in hospitals."

"Well, I've seen how you get behind the wheel. I think we'll all be safer if I drive."

"If you think I'm such a bad driver, why would you create some sympathy pilot consultation job for me?"

Aha! He *knew* she was annoyed by that. But he didn't understand why until she'd implied that he'd only done it out of pity. "Actually, Hunter was the one who suggested that you'd be good at it."

"So you're not really offering me the job?"

"Is there a way for me to answer this question without you being pissed off at me?"

"Probably not." It was too dark inside the cab of the truck to see her face so he couldn't tell if she was joking. "Is this really something you're planning or was it just something you went along with to appease my nephew? Like that summer internship you promised him?"

"When it comes to my company, I don't appease anyone."

"Hmm." She shifted in her seat. Kaleb sensed her studying him and he wondered if her ex had made her mistrustful of all men. "So this is seriously something you're considering doing?"

"I've wanted to get into a project bigger than video games for a while now, but I hadn't been able to figure out what. My roommate from college is designing robotic lasers that can perform complicated surgeries, and one of our classmates invented photovoltaic software for solar panels. Other people in my industry are coming up with self-driving cars and technology that nobody had even dreamed about five years ago. And I sell computer-animated worlds where people can craft things with blocks, or pretend they're a sports MVP, or force aliens and pirates and zombies to fight for control over the galaxy. When we were at Shadowview, that bald guy made a point about how the video games they were playing weren't doing anything to benefit them or benefit the world."

"Really? Because I watched those other patients playing your games and you brought them joy," Molly argued.

"I used to think that, too. Yet, lately I'm wondering if that's enough."

"Kaleb, sometimes people need an escape from the real world and you've been able to provide that. That man in the cast was working on his own demons and you can't take it personally. You can't solve everybody's problems."

Yet, that's what Kaleb did. He invented, he developed, he solved. His family, and even Molly, had made enough pointed comments over the week to make him question whether he was really the corporate genius and a successful entrepreneur he thought he'd become. So Kaleb didn't admit that the soldier wasn't the only one who'd brought his attention to some deep-seated inadequacy he hadn't known existed.

"He also dissed my T-shirt," he complained.

Molly laughed. "For the record, I like the way you dress. Could you imagine how unapproachable you'd be if you wore fancy suits?"

"What do you mean unapproachable?" he asked, hating that he was fishing for affirmation.

"You're this billionaire, hotshot, computer whiz. Kids want to be you when they grow up. Do you know how many people would kill for your intelligence or for even a quarter of your fortune? And if that's not unfair enough, you're always the most handsome man in the room."

"Will you tell Kane that I'm the most handsome man in the room and tell Kylie that you like my character shirts?"

"No way. Watching your family tease you also makes you more approachable. So don't worry." She reached across the center console and squeezed his leg. "In a couple of days you can go back to your old life and be as powerful and superior as you like."

Right. So then why did that sound like a punishment?

Chapter Fifteen

Sunday was the day of the Sun Potato Parade and Festival, not to be confused with the Ski Potato Parade and Festival, which took place in the winter. Kaleb woke up in Molly's bed that morning knowing that tomorrow would be their last day together. He studied her sleeping form curled against his side. Her tan skin soft and warm, her blond curls tangled and sexy.

Last night, just before they turned onto the highway to go into Boise, Cooper had sent Molly a text saying it wasn't actual labor, only something called Braxton-Hicks contractions, and they were sending Maxine home.

So Kaleb had turned around and driven them back to the apartment. He knew Molly was emotionally drained so it hadn't surprised him when she'd fallen asleep before they returned. What had surprised him was that she'd dozed off with her smartphone in her hand, the screen still lit up with results from her internet search of "pregnancy and type 1 diabetes."

He'd never thought about having kids, but it broke his heart to think that she might want children and wouldn't be able to have one of her own. When he parked in the alley behind the cookie shop, he let Molly sleep in the seat beside him as he used his own phone to do some research. He was relieved to find out that while it could be risky, it was still possible.

Then he'd tried to be romantic and lifted her out of the passenger side of the truck to carry her up the stairs to the apartment. But she woke up and drowsily commanded him to put her down before he hurt his back.

They'd made love only once last night, and even though they'd used protection, Kaleb couldn't stop thinking about the possibility of having a child with her. Kids had never really been on his radar before. There were just so many other things he'd envisioned doing with his life first. But if he was going to have a son or daughter, he would want them to have a mother as strong and as courageous as Molly. As he held her close and drifted off to sleep, the idea of fatherhood didn't seem quite so far-fetched.

Waking up, all the baby thoughts began to permeate his mind again, just like the sun pushing itself through closed wooden shutters. He tried to shut them out. To tell himself that by this time next year, he'd be a distant memory for her and she'd be the punch line of an embarrassing story his brothers told about him. *Hey, you guys remember that time Kaleb fell for the sexy combat pilot and she shot him down?*

He knew she'd said that she wasn't looking for a

relationship because she had her future to figure out. Kaleb hadn't been looking for one, either. He'd never had to. Back in high school and college, he'd learned early on that the only girls who were interested in him cared more about his family's money and his famous last name. And those weren't the type of girls hanging out in the video game lounge at the student center or in the computer store, where Kaleb tended to spend most of his time. When he'd started Perfect Game Industries after his junior year, he was so busy launching his company, there wasn't any spare time to eat, let alone date.

The more successful he became, the more people wanted something from him, the more he was invited to attend lavish social events. He hated going, but he knew that he was the face of his corporation, and as much as he wanted to, he couldn't hide behind his laptop all the time. Then, the more social events he attended, the more women threw themselves at him.

But no matter how much money he made, Kaleb remained the same person. The same shy, geek who would rather go to the office than go to parties. Which only cemented the fact that women who wouldn't normally give a guy like him the time of day, were only doing so because of the perks that came with dating a famous billionaire.

If he needed a date to walk the red carpet of a premiere or to be his plus one whenever he was the guest of honor at some convention, there was always one willing to escort him. Usually, they were equally willing to stay the night with him afterward if he was in the mood. Most were comfortable with the arrangement, but every once in a while, he'd date a woman who expected something more and he'd have to ask Angela to send a bouquet and his apologies. He'd never understood those expectations.

Until now.

Kaleb had formed some sort of attachment to Molly this past week and he wasn't quite ready to move on. A few days ago, it would've been easy to tell himself that after he returned to work and fully immersed himself back into the business, his feelings toward her would eventually cool. But what if they didn't?

Molly was unlike any of the women he'd dated in the past. She wasn't impressed with his company or his money or what he could do for her. In fact, he got the feeling that she would probably like him more if he was just an average guy with average resources. Perhaps he was simply suffering from a case of wanting what he couldn't have.

And right this second, there was no denying that he wanted her.

Currently, she was sleeping soundly with her knee hitched across his thighs and he couldn't bring himself to untangle his body from hers long enough to use the restroom. How in the world was he going to go back to Seattle without her?

He could try to return to work, waiting and biding his time until she finally figured out what she needed. However, he'd had enough waiting in hospital rooms and traction beds and back braces while his teenage years had passed him by. Clearly, she was holding out hope of returning to the military but he'd done plenty of research lately and the writing was on the wall. Molly had a doctor's appointment tomorrow and he was pretty sure that they were going to confirm her medical discharge. So it seemed clear to him that the best path for her was to come and work for his company as a consultant.

Kaleb stared up at the ceiling, plotting the best way to get her to come to that decision on her own. When they'd told her about the flight simulator idea last night, Molly hadn't seemed as excited about the prospect as he would've hoped. But he had a feeling that was because she was more concerned with the fact that they'd brought it up in front of Maxine and she was worried that he'd let something slip.

They hadn't discussed salary, but only because he doubted Molly was the type to be persuaded by the almighty dollar. After all, she chose to be a military pilot rather than a commercial one, which made it pretty clear where her priorities were. Maybe he should appeal to her sense of adventure?

Kaleb was used to giving orders and she'd been trained to follow them—as long as they came from a commanding officer and not from him. He was also used to solving problems and she needed a solution. He'd found the perfect one. All he needed to do today was convince her that his plan was in her best interests.

Being careful not to wake her, he gently raised his forearm up and reached over her sleeping head as he typed out a text message on his watch.

Snowflake Boulevard was closed to traffic and the last Miss Sun Potato contestant's float had just passed Molly and Kaleb. The volunteer mounted rescue patrol—which was actually only four people on horses—carried the final banner that would close out the parade.

Two months ago, if someone had told Molly that she'd be standing on the sidewalk of a small town wearing a Styrofoam potato on her head and waving a minia-ture version of the Idaho flag at the local high school marching band, she would've doubled over in laughter. Yet, here she was on a sunny Sunday afternoon, Kaleb standing behind her with his arms wrapped around her waist, and her sister's family beside them.

It was a little too relaxed, a little too simple, a little too everything. And by tomorrow evening, it would all be over. Molly leaned against him, but resisted the urge to intertwine her fingers with his, to hold on to him a little longer.

She would be going to the doctor in the morning, and although she'd once held out hope, there was no longer a doubt in her mind that the news wouldn't be what she wanted to hear. Molly had no idea when Kaleb was planning to leave town, but his company jet was supposed to be picking him up tomorrow. As far as Mondays went, the upcoming one was promising to be pretty brutal.

Reminding herself that it wasn't like the world was going to crash down around her, she pasted a smile on her face and set out to have a perfect last day together. They walked along the vendor booths set up in the town square park and Molly was surprised by how many people said hello to them. More shocking was the fact that she actually knew at least half of their names. She wasn't convinced that small-town life was for her, but with all the uncertainties she was experiencing lately, there was definitely something comforting about the familiarity and the slower pace.

"You want a snow cone, Aunt Molly?" Hunter asked her.

"No way, buddy." She tugged on the bill of his baseball cap. "That's pure sugar."

"What about a funnel cake?" he asked. Molly spotted an older man with a toothpick hanging out of his mouth, carrying a plate of some sort of fried dough buried underneath a pile of canned cherry compote and whipped cream.

"I'll just have a bite of whatever you get," she told her nephew.

Kaleb, who was walking with his arm draped over her shoulders, used his hip to slightly bump her. "Check you out, making all the healthy choices."

"And I didn't even need you to boss me about it." She wrapped her hand around his waist. "I told you that I would eventually figure it out for myself."

But instead of returning her playful smile, he gave her an odd look. After a few more steps, he tried to steer her toward a booth with an enormous fabric sign that read Sugar Stitchers.

"Are you in the market for a new quilt?" she asked him with a sideways glance.

"Maybe. Do you know there's a whole niche of software programs for designing quilting patterns?"

"That's fascinating. And here, I thought you were trying to avoid running into all your brothers who are lined up over by the dunk tank."

"That, too." He kept his attention locked on to the sunflower pattern of a displayed blanket. "Are they taking bets yet?"

"I can't tell from here. But it looks like the mayor is coming down from the perch over the water and Kevin is taking his spot."

"In that case, things might actually get interesting."

Kaleb immediately switched directions and yelled over the crowd, "I get first pitch!"

As much as Molly wanted to watch the competition, her tote bag vibrated and she reached inside to pull out her phone. Looking at the screen, she gulped. "This is my commanding officer. I better take this."

Kaleb's face was completely expressionless. "Do you want me to stay with you?"

She tried to chuckle, but her mouth had already gone dry. "I'm sure I can handle a phone call by myself. Go play with your brothers, and if you dunk one of them, I'll buy you a corn dog."

"Hopefully, you'll have something to celebrate, too," he said with a smile before walking off.

That was an odd thing to say, Molly thought before she swiped her finger across the screen. "Hello, Sir."

"Markham," his gravelly voice barked out. "How's your leave going?"

"I'm currently at a potato festival in Idaho, so I'm not sure if that's a good thing or a bad thing, Sir."

"What have the doctors at Shadowview said?"

Nothing. Because she'd been putting off her appointment until tomorrow. She bit her lip before giving a mostly true answer. "We're waiting for some test results."

"I know the Bureau of Personnel isn't likely to give you your wings back, but I've got some good news. Someone must have pulled some strings for you because I just got a call from the Joint Staff Surgeon over at the Pentagon and they're willing to give you a desk assignment if you'll agree to serving as an adviser on a special training program they're coming up with."

Pulled some strings for you? His words sent off an alarm bell. "What kind of special training program?"

"I've never heard of it because it's still in the beginning stages. Something about flight simulators," he said, and Molly's blood went cold. "Anyway, they'll let you retain your rank and your pay scale. So unless the doctors tell you otherwise, it's either this new gig or a medical retirement."

"Thank you for calling, Sir." Her jaw was clenched so tightly it was a wonder she could say that much. "I'll let you know what I decide to do."

She disconnected and saw a haze of red as she stormed over to the dunk tank. Looking for Kaleb in the crowd, she narrowed her eyes when she spotted him sitting on the perch over the tank, laughing at something a soaking wet Bobby Junior said to him.

"Hey, Molly." Kevin, who was also drenched, handed her a baseball. "You want to give it a shot?"

"Whoa," Kaleb yelled from over the tank. "I thought the rules were Chattersons only. No bringing in a ringer."

Oh, she'd show him ringer. She squeezed the sewed seams on the ball until she thought it might burst as she yelled, "I just had a very interesting call with my commanding officer."

Kaleb's smirk fell. "Why don't I climb out of here and we can talk about it in private?"

"In private? Apparently, that's how you like to operate, isn't it, Kaleb? Behind the scenes? Like the wizard hiding in back of the curtain?" Molly didn't notice that the crowd had doubled in size or that the only sound now came from the Dixieland band in the gazebo on the other side of the park. "Well, then, let's just get it all out in the open."

"I've been waiting over a week for you to get things out in the open, Molly." He sent her a warning look, but it didn't faze her. She was beyond furious and she didn't care who knew.

"So all week you've been planning on creating some fake duty assignment for me out of pity? Poor Molly has diabetes and can't take care of herself. Have you been leading me on this whole time?"

"You have diabetes?" Maxine whispered, but Molly was too fired up to worry about her sister's reaction to the unexpected announcement of her diagnosis. This was between her and Kaleb. She'd deal with the fallout later.

"I never lied to you, Molly," Kaleb argued. "I told you that Hunter and I came up with that idea yesterday. You didn't seem to object, so I put out some feelers after that."

"Some feelers? You were able to call the Pentagon and send this down the chain of command on a Sunday morning!"

"I know some people who know some people. And I promised them a free prototype and a lowball bid."

"And what about me? What do I get out of this?"

"You get the chance to fly again, Molly!" He fired back.

Feeling an arm slip around her waist, she looked at Maxine, who was standing beside her—tall and pregnant and released from the hospital less than twenty-four hours ago, ready to do battle on her sister's behalf. Molly squared her shoulders, her sister silently giving her the strength to fight.

the day; however, all he'd done was screw things up. When he finally broke the surface and came up for air, he looked around for Molly, but she was gone.

Half the crowd was still there, though, including his three brothers and his dad, who was shoving fistfuls of popcorn into his mouth. Kevin reached his hand into the striped box but their father yanked it away.

"Go get your own," Bobby Senior said, then looked at Kaleb. "You gonna sit in the dunk tank all day or are you going to drag your dumb keister out of there and find the long-lost sense you were supposedly born with?"

Kaleb took plenty of teasing from his family, but it was rare when anyone accused him of not being smart. Yet, even he had to admit that he'd just pulled one of the most stupid moves ever.

It took a couple of tries to heave himself from the water because each time he would reach for the perch to haul himself up, one of his brothers would push the target-shaped lever, causing him to fall back in. He shot them all a ha-ha smile when he finally climbed over the Plexi-glas side and plopped onto the grass outside the tank.

The early-evening mountain breeze had picked up and sent a shiver coursing through him, wiping away his short-lived triumph. "It's freezing out here."

Kane, Kevin and Bobby Junior were still damp from their own forays into the tank—one of their dunkings courtesy of Kaleb—so they gave him no sympathy. At least his old man was able to muster up some pity. "Come on, son. Let's get you warmed up. Then we can talk about this mess you got yourself into."

Kaleb didn't exactly want to talk about anything with anyone except Molly. "Do you know where she went?"

"I know where she *didn't* go." His dad firmly patted him on the back, propelling him across the midway. "To get you a towel."

The breeze picked up, reminding Kaleb that it might be best to dry off before he went looking for her. Molly wasn't the type of woman who would care about his appearance, but if he was going to go begging for forgiveness, he didn't want to resemble a drowned rat. The three hundred-dollar bills he pulled from his waterlogged wallet were still dripping when he exchanged them for a homemade quilt at the Sugar Stitchers booth.

The cookie shop was only a few blocks from the park, so he turned to head there first. Until his dad put a beefy hand on Kaleb's shoulder.

"Hold up, kiddo. Let her cool off a little." Bobby Chatterson hadn't called him "kiddo" since his final spine fusion surgery. That meant his dad thought the situation was pretty serious. "Let's grab a seat. It wouldn't kill you to learn a little patience."

As much as he wanted to race after Molly, perhaps now wasn't the time to rush into things if he didn't have a strategy in place. And Coach Chatterson prided himself on being a master strategist. Kaleb had his doubts, but settled in next to his father, anyway. "You know, the last time I sat next to you in a park with a blanket wrapped around me, I was twelve and had just been released from the hospital before Kane's Little League tournament."

"Huh." His dad nodded. "I remember your mom insisted that you stay home with her but you called old Mrs. Kenmore across the street and asked her to babysit you so that your mother wouldn't miss the playoff game. Then you snuck into the back of the car and covered up with that old fleece throw. You really pissed your momma off with that stunt."

"But it worked. The babysitter never even knew I was gone because I'd built that humanoid robot, stuffed it under my covers and programmed it to switch positions every thirty minutes. And I got to stay and watch the game with everyone else."

"Stay and watch the game?" His dad gave him an incredulous look. "Kaleb, you only lasted through the second inning because those metal bleachers were hell on your spine after that surgery. I had to drive you home while you laid there all stiff like a mummy in the back seat. It added a whole month onto your physical therapy regime. I sold that stupid robot to the scrap yard and poor Mrs. Kenmore refused to ever babysit any of you again after that."

"I'm pretty sure she refused after Kevin turned the hose on her the same day her daughter gave her a home permanent."

"My point, son—" Bobby Chatterson waited until he had Kaleb's full attention "—is that even the best-laid plans can result in consequences. And I have a feeling that this stunt you pulled on Molly today wasn't well laid at all."

"It wasn't a stunt, Dad. I was actually trying to help her."

"By getting her commanding officer to order her to come and work for you? Trust me, ladies don't like it when you interfere with their careers."

Oh, please. His dad was the biggest interferer of all the Chattersons.

"That's not exactly the way it went down." Kaleb looked at all the people still lingering in the town square and partaking of the festivities. Not that it mattered who overheard them at this point. Most of them had already

CHRISTY JEFFRIES

heard Molly inadvertently announce her secret to the world. "A few weeks ago, she found out she had type 1 diabetes, which is an immediate disqualification for having a pilot's license."

"That diabetes is nasty stuff. My doctor told me I had the same thing. Put me on some pills and now I'm good as new."

Kaleb stared at his father's heavier frame. Like three of his sons, Bobby Chatterson had also been a professional baseball pitcher, but he'd stopped running the bases—or running anywhere—after he became a coach. "Actually, Dad, you have type 2, which is a lot different than type 1. Molly can't regulate it with a pill or with diet alone. She has to carry around insulin and constantly check her blood sugar levels because she's always at risk for an attack."

His dad frowned. "Kane's right. You really are a know-it-all."

"Do you want to hear this or not?"

"Carry on."

"The type 1 diagnosis also automatically makes her ineligible for service because she's not fit for duty."

"But she's perfectly fit!" his dad argued, and Kaleb thought, *You have no idea.*

"Right. But it's still a military regulation that she be 'operational ready' at all times, whatever that means. As a combat pilot, it's common for them to go on training missions for twenty-four to forty-eight hours straight. And with her body requiring constant monitoring, along with needing food and insulin doses on a certain schedule, they can't take that risk. So her flight surgeon wrote up a medical board, which is this big file documenting her condition and the lab findings. She can fight it on an appeal, but basically it's a losing battle. Right now, she's in a holding pattern until she goes before the Bureau of Personnel and they determine how much of her base pay she'll be awarded for a medical discharge."

"Damn shame," his father muttered, and Kaleb had to agree.

"I know how much she loves being a pilot and how much the Air Force means to her. Plus, I'd been toying with the idea of designing some flight simulators—" okay, so really, he'd only been toying with the idea for twenty-four hours, but his dad didn't need to know that "—and thought she'd make a perfect consultant. I called up someone I knew in the Pentagon who owed me a favor—"

"Hold up. You have contacts in the Pentagon who owe you favors?" his dad asked in a hushed voice, then waved his hand. "Never mind. We'll talk about that later."

"Anyway, I think you and the rest of the town know about her commanding officer calling her and the job assignment and all the rest. But really, Dad, it's a foolproof solution to her problem."

"Except you're forgetting one little thing."

"What's that?"

"Molly Markham is no fool."

Kaleb threw his head back. "Nobody knows that better than me, Dad."

"Really? Because I'm having a hard time believing that. You're an independent guy, right? You pride yourself on the fact that you never followed in my or your brothers' footsteps and played ball."

"Uh, because I couldn't, Dad. Remember my back

surgeries? Remember your and mom's rule about no contact sports?"

"Meh. Since when did we ever enforce any rules at our house? Sure, we would've been scared to death to let you play, but you could've gotten us to back down. Just like you did when you hid in the car and talked us into letting you watch Kane's game. You never pushed because you weren't passionate about sports. You preferred computers and gaming and that was what you were good at. So you built your career the way you wanted it."

"What do you mean you would've backed down? Are you saying that all this time I could've played baseball if I'd wanted to?"

"Son, if you could leave your company today and become the starting pitcher for a major league team, would you do it?"

"Depends on which team," Kaleb murmured, knowing there was no way he'd play for the one his old man coached.

His dad cupped his ear. "What's that?"

"I guess not," Kaleb admitted.

"See, you chose your own path and it was the right one for you. Now, here's what you're going to do. Give Molly some time to cool down. Then you go talk to her. Tell her what a dumbass you were and how you'll never meddle in her life again."

"How do you know that'll work?"

"Because that's what I did when I made the same mistake with your mom. And we're going on thirty-five years next month."

"I think I'm afraid to ask for details on how you interfered in Mom's life."

"Oh, she had it in her head that she wanted to be an interior decorator. She was even in this special school for it and everything. But then I got her knocked up with Bobby Junior."

"Yeah, but that could've happened to any… Oh, geez, Dad, you did it on purpose?"

"No, not on purpose," his father snapped. "But I did spill the beans to your grandad and he told us in no uncertain terms that there wouldn't be a long engagement. Besides, she went back and got her degree and I've given her plenty of houses to decorate over the years. My point is that I apologized, even though I wasn't really all that sorry."

"So you think Molly will forgive me?"

"Does she love you?"

He thought about her speech the morning after they'd first slept together. She was clear that she wasn't looking for anything serious because she needed to figure her life out. Kaleb had merely been trying to hurry the process along. It didn't occur to him that she might not share his feelings because until this morning, he didn't even know what his own feelings were. "We've only known each other for a little over a week."

"Do you love her?"

"I don't know," Kaleb said, then sneezed. His head pounded.

"Well, this isn't something you can ask your assistant or the Pentagon about. Only you can solve that one. I know you're used to getting instant answers, but relationships take time."

Kaleb's only response was to sneeze again.

"C'mon. Let's get you home. Your mother's going to kill me if I let you catch pneumonia."

As they walked to his dad's truck, Kaleb asked, "How long do you think it'll take?"

"To know whether or not you love her?" His father draped an arm over his shoulder. "Kiddo, if you don't already know, you will by tomorrow morning. You've never been able to wait for nothin'."

Molly's heart leaped when a knock sounded on the apartment door late that evening. She grabbed a paper towel from the kitchen and used it to scrub the tears off her face before she unlocked the dead bolt.

But it wasn't Kaleb on the other side.

"Do you mind if I come in?" Maxine asked.

"It's your apartment," Molly said, standing aside.

"Do you want to talk about it?"

"Not really."

Her sister waddled over to the sofa and collapsed on the cushions. "Then I'll just wait here until you do."

And because stubbornness ran in the Markham blood, Molly sighed and took the armchair across from her. "I'm sorry I didn't tell you what was going on sooner. But I was dealing with a lot of new feelings and uncertainties."

"When you took off from the festival, I wanted to run after you. I would've been here sooner if I had. But we've never been the kind of sisters who tell each other everything and I decided that I should try to get as much information as I could before I offer to give you any advice."

"So you stayed and talked to Kaleb?" Molly asked.

"No. I went over to the police station and Cooper let me use his laptop. I researched type 1 diabetes."

"Why does everyone do that?"

"Didn't you?"

"No. I was too busy looking up every other possible disease it could have been. I was hoping for a misdiagnosis."

"One of the online articles I read was that it can feel like a very lonely condition."

"Well, I'm used to being alone."

"You don't have to be," Maxine said, pushing a strand of hair behind Molly's ear. "Why didn't you tell me?"

"I was going to. But I wanted to do it in my own way."

"In front of the whole town at the Sun Potato Festival?"

Molly dipped her head in shame. "No. But I was so mad at Kaleb, it just came flying out of my mouth before I could stop it. I'm sorry you had to find out that way."

"Well, at least I finally found out," Maxine leaned her head back and let out a sigh. "I had a feeling something was up, but I didn't know what to do or how to help."

"That's why I didn't say anything because I didn't want you worrying about me."

"I'm your big sister. Even when we're not together, I still worry about you."

"I'm sorry for keeping it a secret." Molly's heart expanded and she squeezed her sister's hand. "I've always taken care of myself, done things on my own. Then when I came to Sugar Falls, I was forced to confront the fact that I was no longer in control of everything. But now that you know—along with everyone else in this small town—I already feel like a huge weight's been lifted off of me."

"I'm glad you're here, Moll Doll. I want you to know that I'm here for you, too. Whatever you need emotionally, medically, heck, even nutritionally. I already make gluten free cookies at the shop. I'm sure I can come up with some sugar free ones, too."

Molly held up her hand. "See? Now that you know, you're babying me. I don't want people treating me like I'm going to fall apart if I eat a baked good. I'm going to mess up and get my levels wrong and make mistakes. It's now obvious that I'm going to need some support, but I also have to figure things out on my own."

"Fine. I'll try not to be supportive without going into overprotective mode and smothering you with my concern."

"Good. Because I've gotten more than enough of that from Kaleb. He always thinks he knows what's best."

"It's obvious that he cares about you."

"I don't really want to talk about him," Molly murmured. She'd already said too much in front of too many people and her emotional well was running dry.

"Okay." Her sister paused before switching tactics. "So what's going to happen to your career?"

"I really don't want to talk about that, either."

"Then what do you want to talk about?"

"I don't want to talk. I just want to go to sleep."

"That's another thing I read when I was researching. That sometimes you'll get tired for no reason at all. Have you been sleeping okay?"

The truth was, with Kaleb spending the past three nights, neither one of them had gotten much sleep at all. Instead of replying, she yawned.

"Fine, then we'll go to bed," Maxine said. "We can talk about everything in the morning."

But when Molly stood up to walk down the hall, her sister followed. "Don't you need to get home?"

"Nope. I told Cooper I was going to stay with you tonight."

"You really don't have to do that."

"I know."

"When it comes to being overprotective, you might actually be worse than Kaleb," Molly said as she began to arrange pillows on the bed.

"So then you *do* want to talk about him?"

She shot Maxine an annoyed look, but really, she was glad her sister was here. For the first time in her life, she didn't want to be alone. They didn't say another word, and in the morning, Molly was surprised to see her sister sound asleep on top of the covers.

"What are you still doing here?" she asked when Maxine finally opened her eyes.

"Sleeping. It's not like it's the first time we've had to share a bed."

Molly rolled her eyes. "But it's the first time you were almost nine months pregnant and snored the whole night."

"I don't snore."

"How sweet that your husband lets you believe that."

Maxine swacked her with a pillow. "So what are you going to do about Kaleb?"

"There's nothing to do. He's going back to Seattle today and I don't know where I'm going. Or what I'm going to do when I get there."

"Have you thought about taking his job offer?"

"Of course I have! It would probably be the next best thing to flying. But I can't stand the fact that he came up with it as a way to micromanage my life."

"Do you think you're being a little stubborn?" It took a couple of tries for Maxine to heft herself up into a sitting position. "What does it matter whose idea it was? If it's a good one, you should jump all over it."

"But what if I actually had to work with him? I don't think I could handle that."

"Because you love him?"

Molly squeezed her eyes shut. "Maybe."

"Then it's worth a shot."

"You don't understand. This whole dating thing? It wasn't even real." Heck, if she was going to open up with her sister, she might as well tell her everything. "It was all for show to keep people from finding out about my condition."

"People or me?"

She wished she could wipe the injured look from her sister's face. "Mostly people. Because they would end up telling you. I needed time."

"So you guys weren't really involved romantically?"

"We were, but…it's complex."

"Then try to simplify it."

"We were supposed to only be going on platonic dates."

"What in the world is a platonic date?"

"Like enough of a date to make it look like he wasn't lying to his family outright, but not so serious that we would develop actual feelings for each other."

"It's nice that someone in the relationship didn't want to lie to their siblings," Maxine mumbled.

"It wasn't a lie. I said last night that I was just waiting to tell you. Even Cooper knew that."

"Wait, my husband found out about this but didn't tell me?"

"Not exactly." Molly cringed. How had she let the web spin so far out of control? "Remember how he and Hunter ran into us at Shadowview after I was getting some blood work done? Well, he kind of guessed that something was up, but didn't want to be responsible with knowing the details. I promised him that I would tell you after my appointment today. He said that if I didn't, he would."

"Did Hunter know about it, too?"

"No. At least, I'm pretty sure he didn't. Although sometimes it surprises me what that kid can find out."

"Okay, so back to the platonic dating," Maxine said. "How platonic are we talking about?"

Molly's cheeks burned. "Uh, pretty unplatonic."

"Did you guys…" Maxine swirled her fingers in a circle.

Molly hesitated. She was finally opening up and she wanted to continue sharing, but she was unsure of how much she should say. "Let's just say that things progressed way past the kissing stage and emotions got involved. At least, they did for me."

"But not for him?"

"Who can tell? He thinks about things down to the last detail. Everything is a game or a strategy for him. It's like being stuck in a perpetual chess match and I've only been given the rules for checkers."

"How did he benefit from this so-called game?"

"I don't know. He got to avoid his family, I guess."

"Oh, come on." Maxine flung her palm out. "Nobody buys that excuse. You've met the Chattersons. Who in their right mind would avoid that hilarious mess? They're dysfunctionally perfect. And no matter how much he says otherwise, the man adores them. I've been friends with Kylie for over ten years and Kaleb's never missed a family vacation. Four summers ago, he threw his parents a humongous thirtieth anniversary bash on some buddy's island off the coast of Bora-Bora. Those guys all act like they can't stand each other, but really, they thrive off each other. So since we can rule that out, why else would he insist on platonically dating you?"

Molly shrugged. "I guess he did it to keep my secret."

"Then you're just as big of a game player as him."

"How am I playing games?" she huffed.

"You said it yourself. You were trying to keep your diabetes a secret. From you own sister, no less," Maxine attempted a look of chastisement. "But what did Kaleb gain from this arrangement?"

"He got to boss me around?" Molly asked.

Maxine made a loud buzzer sound. "Try again."

All Molly could do was shrug.

"I've seen the way he looks at you," her sister continued. "And a man doesn't call in a favor to the Pentagon and create brand new flight simulator technology for a woman unless he cares about her."

"But Kaleb said he's not the serious relationship type."

"Would you be if you thought most of the women throwing themselves at you were only interested in your money and your famous name?"

"I guess not. But surely he knows that I don't care about any of that stuff."

"Of course he does." Maxine shot her a smug grin. "That's why he's doing everything in his power not to let you go."

Chapter Seventeen

Kaleb had tossed and turned on his sister's sofa all night. He finally fell asleep at five o'clock and woke up to the smell of frozen waffles burning in the toaster. The battery on his smartwatch had died, so he sat up and turned to Kylie, who was fanning at the smoke in the kitchen.

"What time is it?" he asked.

"It's time you go find Molly and apologize for being such a dumbass yesterday."

"You know, I'm not exactly a fan of these new nick-names everyone's giving me. Whatever happened to Brainiac?" Kaleb, who'd slept in a pair of sweatpants he'd borrowed from his brother-in-law, pulled on a T-shirt.

"When you start acting like you have a brain, then maybe we'll start using it again." She poured coffee into a travel mug and held it out to him.

"Your waffles are burning again."

"Damn," she said as he headed to the restroom.

Ten minutes later, he was in the truck, scrolling through the recent destinations list until he found the address for Shadowview. Molly's appointment was for eight o'clock and it was now thirty minutes after that. Okay, so maybe he didn't need the GPS to tell him how to get there when he'd driven to the same place only a couple of days ago. But he was hoping to find a shorter route.

First his watch battery died and he'd slept through his alarm, and now this digital map on his dashboard was reminding him that there was only one road going in or out of Sugar Falls. Molly's past comments mocking his dependence on technology were coming back to haunt him.

Luckily, rush hour traffic through downtown was minimal and he quickly breezed through the city's four major stoplights. Unfortunately, he got stuck behind a tractor trailer slowly meandering down the highway, hauling one of the parade floats from yesterday. He eased across the yellow stripes, only to swerve back into place when he saw a lumbering RV steaming up the opposing lane, a line of cars trailing behind.

Molly probably would've gunned the engine and gone for it, but Kaleb wasn't that desperate. Yet. He used the radio controls embedded into the steering wheel to shuffle through his playlist, and when he couldn't find a song he liked, he switched off the radio. He hooked his Bluetooth headset onto his ear, then realized there was nobody he wanted to talk to but her. His watch, which was plugged into the charger in the center console, was finally at 20 percent so he switched it on to see if he'd missed a text from her.

He'd only been looking down for a second when one of the lengths of tinsel streamers from the float in front of him ripped off and landed on his windshield. He yanked the steering wheel to the right, applying the brake. However, he didn't see the object in the road until it was too late. The bounce jarred him as he thumped over it, then there was a loud bang before the rear of the vehicle began to shimmy.

Rolling down the window, he stuck his head out to watch for oncoming traffic as he hugged the shoulder of the road. Thankfully, there was a turnout ahead and he eased the truck off the highway.

Kaleb jumped out, yanking the streamer off his windshield and tossing it inside the cab before walking around to the back. A scrap of torn metal was completely embedded in the right rear tire. He lifted his head to the sky wondering if the universe was trying to send him some sort of signal.

Getting back in the truck, he pulled up his location on the GPS. His initial instinct was to call Angela and ask her to route a roadside assistance company to him. But he knew that all the money in the world wouldn't guarantee the response time he needed way out here on the mountain.

He'd already forced himself to wait more than twelve hours to go after Molly. Yet, now that he was finally so close, his patience was being tested again. But this time, he would take his time and he would do things himself—without the help of technology or assistants. Like his father had told him last night, when he wanted something badly enough, he didn't give up. Kaleb needed to prove it to himself before he could prove it to her.

The white paper liner crackled and ripped as Molly climbed down from the exam table in the endocrinologist's office. The specialist had just walked out of the room and Molly held the once-dreaded forms in her hand. A copy of her medical board. Nothing had changed.

She'd already met with the registered dietitian down the hall for an assessment and had discussed setting up a meal plan, but even following the most stringent of diets wouldn't affect the final recommendation. She would never get to fly again. Molly could try to appeal, but realistically, there was no chance it would be overturned as long as she required insulin. The process would take months and meant she'd be assigned as a "random tasker," riding a desk or shuffling files or whatever job the Air Force could find for her while she waited for them to ultimately reject her anyway.

She was done fighting. She was done pretending that she could keep doing what she'd always done. Yet, she wasn't angry or sad or grieving. In fact, Molly was surprisingly calm. Or, at least, way more calm than she'd expected. The decision had been taken out of her hands and she would be a good airman and follow orders.

It was time to move on.

She got dressed and threw the forms in her tote bag. The sun warmed her face the second she stepped into the parking lot. She had her whole future in front of her and suddenly it didn't look so dark. Sure, she had no idea what she would do or how she would do it. But she also didn't feel so alone anymore.

Maxine had wanted to come to the appointment with her, but Molly didn't want anyone influencing her decision. While it was a relief that everything was now out in the open, she wasn't totally willing to give up her independence. Knowing that she had her sister's full support in whatever she decided was reassuring enough.

Steering onto the highway, Molly determined that the first order of business for her new civilian life would be to get rid of the rental car and invest in something more permanent. And definitely more fast. If she couldn't be inside a jet, she would need to get her speed from somewhere else.

Her second order of business would be to find a job. Even if it was only temporary. Maxine had offered to put her to work at the bakery, but while she'd grown attached to the cute little shops and the people of Sugar Falls, Molly was holding out for a position that would utilize her aeronautical engineering degree. Besides, working with cookies all day might not be the best place for her, given that she was still learning the maneuvers of her daily nutritional minefield.

There were plenty of civilian contractors who designed military-grade planes. Maybe she should interview with one of those firms. For the first time in over a month, Molly finally saw that the world was full of possibilities. If nothing else, she could thank Kaleb for coming up with the idea of staying in the same field.

She looked up in the sky, wondering if he'd already hopped aboard his corporate jet, eagerly returning to his own life. She'd checked her cell phone several times this morning, hoping he'd call or even send her a text to tell her goodbye. But after the very public fight they'd had yesterday, she couldn't really blame him for wanting nothing else to do with her. If what Maxine had said about him not wanting to let her go was true, the determined man would've reached out by now.

Okay, enough of that. She zeroed in on the pavement and yellow dotted lines ahead of her. Her third order of business would be to forget about Kaleb and the amazing week they'd spent together.

Unfortunately, that would've been way easier to do if she hadn't spotted his dad's truck pulled over alongside the highway, the back axis sitting at an odd angle. Molly slowed down as she approached, then waited until an SUV passed before flipping a U-turn and pulling up behind him.

He was sitting cross-legged on the asphalt beside the tire he'd just pulled off, black smudges on his fingers and a confused expression on his face.

"Car problems?" she asked as she slammed her door shut and walked toward him.

He startled at her approach, but he was so focused on his task he didn't stand up. "I hit something in the road and popped my tire. I'm trying to change it."

"Have you ever changed one by yourself?" She squatted down next to him.

"No. But as you can see, I'm more than halfway there."

"How long have you been here?"

"About an hour or so."

"And nobody stopped to help you?"

"Plenty of people did. But I waved them on."

She slipped her phone out of her pocket and saw a full signal of bars. So he clearly wasn't out of cell service. "Why didn't you just call someone?"

"Because I can do it myself."

"Where's your tablet?" she asked, scanning the area around him. "Surely you watched a how-to video…"

"Nope. I'm determined to do it on my own."

She nodded, then stood up and put her hands in her back pockets. "Then you might want to go grab that lug nut that rolled under that hedge over there."

He muttered an expletive before rising and stomping toward the bushes. "I probably would've solved that problem. Eventually."

"Yeah, I hear that attitude is going around lately." Molly picked up the spare and lined the rim up with the lug bolts. "Unless you want to be out here for another hour, pass me the wrench."

"Listen. I'm sorry for making you think that I didn't believe you could handle things on your own." He passed the lug nuts to her one at a time.

She sighed. "How could you when I didn't even believe in myself?"

"But you were right about me being a micromanager. I saw a problem and I wanted to fix it."

"You thought I was a problem that needed fixing?"

"No. I'm getting this all wrong. Let me try and explain." He adjusted his glasses, leaving a smear of grease on his nose. "When I was in ninth grade, I was recovering from my second back surgery. We were driving home from my doctor's appointment and swung by the batting cages to pick up my brothers. At an intersection, this minivan in front of us broke down and was blocking the lane. All of my brothers jumped out to help push the car to safety, but my mom reached over and grabbed ahold of my seat belt buckle, not letting me unclasp it so that I could get out and help, too. The woman in the other car was crying and thanking my brothers and came over to the window to tell my mother that her sons were heroes. I never got to be a hero. Then, when I saw you in the grocery store that day, it was finally my chance."

Molly used the crank to lower the jack and slide it out. She stood up and wiped her hands on her jeans. "So now we're even. You saved me back in Duncan's Market and now I'm the one saving you on the side of the road."

"That's the thing, though, Molly." He hefted the old tire into the back of the truck. "I initially thought I was rescuing you, but it turned out that you saved me in more ways than you could imagine."

Her heart spun like a propeller and her head began to buzz. "What do you mean?"

Kaleb turned to her. "I was so absorbed in my company, in my life back in Seattle, in all my electronic gadgets. But then you bumped into me and suddenly I had something else to focus on. Something that was real, that wasn't just a game or a way to improve profits. For the first time in a long time, I felt needed. I felt necessary."

Her throat tightened. She'd never been anyone's focus. All her life, she'd been flying under the radar, trying not to draw any attention to herself. How did she respond to this?

"I'm pretty sure that you were the one who bumped into me," she murmured, not knowing what else to say.

"And I'm pretty sure that even small-town grocery stores have video surveillance."

"Well, if anyone could get their hands on it, you could."

He winced. "Listen, I'm sorry about calling the Pentagon and all that overhanded business with your commanding officer. It was totally out of line. And I promise I'll never get involved in your life like that again."

The propeller feeling stopped and she gulped. The finality of his statement sounded more like a threat than a promise because it was coupled with the fact that he was leaving today. Of course he would never get involved in her life again because he had no future plans to ever be in it.

"So…" She handed him the wrench. "Were you on your way to Boise or did you arrange for your corporate jet to meet you at a local airfield?"

His eyes did a double blink behind his glasses. "No, I was on my way to Shadowview but my watch battery died and my alarm didn't go off. I guess I missed your doctor's appointment?"

"Wait. You were driving to see *me*? At the hospital?"

"That's where you were, right?"

"Yes. But what I mean is, why?"

"To apologize. And, you know, to provide some moral support when you got the lab reports."

"But you just said you weren't going to interfere in my life again?"

"I meant like a boss."

"Is there a different way for how you do things?"

"Not really. But if we're going to be together, you might have to indulge me sometimes."

"Be together? Like as a couple?"

"Look, I know you said that you weren't ready for a relationship and needed some time to figure your life out. I have no problem with that and am more than happy to wait."

She put her hands on her hips. "Kaleb Chatterson,

have you ever had to wait for anything in your entire life?"

He looked to the side as if he was doing some quick calculations. "Not really. But I've waited twenty-eight years for you already, so I figure what's a couple more weeks?"

"A couple more weeks? You're pretty confident of yourself."

"Nah. I'm just confidant that you'll come to the right conclusion," he said, putting his hands on her waist and drawing her closer. "Eventually."

She wiped the grease off his nose. "And what conclusion is that?"

"That I love you." His lips brushed across hers and she lost her breath. "That I need you." His second kiss lasted a split second longer and she became light-headed. "That I can build you your very own flight simulator."

She wrapped her arms around his neck, joy ricocheting inside her. "Maybe I don't need a few weeks, after all."

"Was it the flight simulator that convinced you?" Kaleb nuzzled her neck.

"That was part of it." She smiled.

"What was the other?"

"The promise of another family vacation with all the Chattersons?"

He groaned and squeezed her tighter.

She giggled. "Okay, I give up. The other part is that I love you, too, Kaleb."

"Yeah?" He tapped the screen on his watch. "Say it again so I can record it."

She brought his hand back down to her waist. "I

love you. I didn't realize it until last night when my sister came to check on me and I was so disappointed it wasn't you."

"I was going to run after you, but my dad told me I should let you cool off. And he was worried I'd get pneumonia and my mom would blame him."

She cringed. "Sorry for sending you into the dunk tank."

"You have a pretty good arm, but I deserved it. I never should have interfered with your life like that. You trusted me with something huge and I tried to use it to my advantage."

"I never should have made you keep my condition a secret in the first place. When the military placed me on leave, I had never been so lost and so afraid. I thought my condition was bigger than me, and as much as I needed to control it, I couldn't. I'd always been able to do things on my own and then, in a matter of weeks, I felt all alone. But then I came to Sugar Falls and it's quite impossible to ever feel alone here. Like seriously. Nobody would leave me alone. And I needed that. I needed you to show me that it was okay to allow myself to be vulnerable, to let someone else look after me. I needed my sister and Kylie and Julia and all the other ladies in town to show me that it was okay to share, to be myself. I'm not saying that I'm glad I have diabetes or that things are going to be easy from here on out. But now that everything is out in the open, I'm finally seeing how strong I can be."

"Just know that you don't always have to be strong." He pulled her closer. "I'll love you whether you're having a bad day or a good one."

She stood on her tiptoes, pressed her lips to his and showed him just how great of a day she planned to have.

"Well, what do you think?" Kaleb asked, a proud grin stretching across his face.

"When you said you were going to make a flight simulator, I thought you meant like one of those faux cockpits you sit in at the arcade. I didn't think you meant an actual, full-scale model of an FA-18 Hornet."

The replica jet sat on some sort of raised mechanism that housed all the components for a moving simulator. A huge movie screen lined the wall in front.

"Well, this is a one-of-a-kind prototype. The final models will be a third of this size because they'll be cheaper to ship and won't take up as much room in the VA rehab hospitals."

"Still, how were you able to make this look so realistic?"

Kaleb cleared his throat. "You know my contact at the Pentagon? Well, he talked to the people over at Mc-Donnell Douglas and they sold me the prefabricated pieces—at double the government cost, I might add. Plus, I had to get top secret clearance and sign these papers promising I'd never sell it to our enemies."

"This is amazing. Looks like you didn't need to hire me as a consultant, after all." Molly had been traveling with Kaleb to various air and space museums around the country—the pilot of the corporate jet always letting her ride up front with him when she wanted—so they could do research while she waited for her discharge paperwork to come in. She would've thought that being around all the planes might depress her, but it ended up motivating her to go back to school and get her graduate degree in aeronautical design. She'd moved into Kaleb's apartment two months ago and registered for classes at the University of Washington.

"Oh, don't worry. You're going to earn your paycheck. I need you to climb inside and tell me if the motion part is realistic. But I'm forewarning you, we have a lot of bugs to work out still."

He followed her as she scrambled up the steel caged steps to the cockpit. She used the outside crank to open the dome-shaped canopy. She was about to climb inside when he said, "Wait!"

He pulled off a piece of tan paper taped to the side of the aircraft to reveal the stenciled letters.

CAPT MOLLY MARKHAM

Her hand flew to her mouth. "You mean it's mine? You built me my own jet?"

He shrugged as if all he'd done was given her a gift card to the Cowgirl Up Café. "I didn't want you to miss out on your old life."

"Kaleb, you are the most incredible man I've ever met."

"Keep that in mind when you see the next part."

"What next part?" she asked, and he motioned to another rectangle of tan paper after her name.

She peeled it back to see a hyphen and an additional name. It took her a second to put it together and when she did she gasped.

CAPT MOLLY MARKHAM-CHATTERSON

"Does this mean…" she started to say as she turned to look at him. Tears filled her eyes when she realized he was down on one knee, holding open a jewelry box with a… "Um, is that a smartwatch?"

Kaleb looked down.

"Hold on," he said as he tapped on the screen. When it lit up, a picture of a diamond solitaire blinked back at her.

Molly tilted her head to the side. "Are you proposing to me with a digital ring?"

"The real one is hidden inside your flight suit," he said, reaching for the zipper at her neck. "If you agree to marry me, I'll help you find it."

Molly's heart spun into a nosedive and all she could do was tearfully nod yes, then happily, actively, help him search.

* * * * *

MILLS & BOON
True Love
Romance from the Heart

Celebrate true love with tender stories of heartfelt romance, from the rush of falling in love to the joy a new baby can bring, and a focus on the emotional heart of a relationship.

MILLS & BOON
MODERN
Power and Passion

Prepare to be swept off your feet by sophisticated, sexy and seductive heroes, in some of the world's most glamourous and romantic locations, where power and passion collide.

Julia James

PREGNANCY SCANDAL

Jennie Lucas

SHEIKH'S ROYAL BRIDE

Kim Lawrence

A WEDDING of the ITALIAN'S DEMAND

Sharon Kendrick

The **SHEIKH'S SECRET BABY**

Eight Modern stories published every month, find them a

millsandboon.co.uk/Modern

MILLS & BOON

THE HEART OF ROMANCE

A ROMANCE FOR EVERY READER

MODERN

Prepare to be swept off your feet by sophisticated, sexy and seductive heroes, in some of the world's most glamourous and roma... locations, where power and passion collide.

HISTORICAL

Escape with historical heroes from time gone by. Whether your passi... for wicked Regency Rakes, muscled Vikings or rugged Highlanders, the romance of the past.

MEDICAL

Set your pulse racing with dedicated, delectable doctors in the high-... sure world of medicine, where emotions run high and passion, comf... love are the best medicine.

True Love

Celebrate true love with tender stories of heartfelt romance, from th... rush of falling in love to the joy a new baby can bring, and a focus ... emotional heart of a relationship.

Desire

Indulge in secrets and scandal, intense drama and plenty of sizzling action with powerful and passionate heroes who have it all: wealth, s... good looks…everything but the right woman.

HEROES

Experience all the excitement of a gripping thriller, with an intense ... mance at its heart. Resourceful, true-to-life women and strong, fearl... face danger and desire - a killer combination!

To see which titles are coming soon, please visit

millsandboon.co.uk/nextmonth